UNTIL I DIE

DEIDRA DUNCAN

CONTENT WARNING

If you would like to read this book spoiler-free, please stop reading now. This work contains explicit sexual content, scenes with gore and violence, and references to the sexual assault of a POV character. Non-consensual sex and forced labor camps are referred to, and the degradation of certain classes of humans is a core theme of *Until I Die*. There are descriptions of unlawful executions, bodily branding, torture, suicidal ideation and the death of minor characters. Please consider your wellness before reading.

PART ONE

I

CASUALTY VALUE

> ...we shall pay any price, bear any burden... to assure the survival and the success of liberty.
>
> —JOHN F. KENNEDY, INAUGURAL ADDRESS

It shouldn't have ended like this.

But in some respects, was there any other way for it to end?

As I latched Theo's office door behind me, curiosity sparked at the tableau I faced, at the look on his face, and I just knew.

This was the beginning of my very slow end.

Our Prime Delegate, Nia Williams, sat beside Theo behind the desk. "Good evening, Sophia," she said, her dark eyes gleaming with some hidden emotion. Something like interest or maybe even intrigue. I hadn't laid eyes on her in months. As the leader of the Defiance, she traveled frequently. Short black hair stylishly trimmed, outfit pristine, she was a queen mingling with us peasants. No one had clothes that clean anymore.

Her full lips split into a welcoming smile as I hesitated near the threshold. I should have known she was inside Theo's office given the security detail outside the door, should have prepared to be intimidated.

And yet...

My questioning gaze landed on Theo. He motioned me to sit. "An opportunity has arisen."

Right to it, then.

"Okay..." What sort of opportunity could possibly involve me, a lowly medic with a proven track record for recklessness in the field?

"A Hunter has come forward offering information." Theo shifted in his seat. "We need a contact to meet with him on a regular basis."

My pulse stuttered, then pounded as I fell into the chair he indicated. "You want *me* for that?"

Theo dropped his gaze to the crudely soldered nameplate on his desk. *Gen. Theodore Harrison.* His office at our improvised headquarters was cramped, lined with empty glass display cases—a remnant of the museum gallery it had been before the Fracture. A dusty crystal chandelier hung from the ceiling and shed fractured light across every surface, including the shiny dark skin of his bald head.

Unlike Theo, Williams held my gaze. "The man had explicit criteria. Not many people fit the description."

A hysterical laugh burst from my mouth. Inappropriate, yes, but nothing else would suffice. When it subsided, I managed to say, "What exactly did he ask for?"

Theo rapped twice on his beat-up oak desk, *still* not looking at me. "He wants someone discreet. Someone who won't be noticed when they disappear at odd times. Someone I trust implicitly."

I pursed my lips. The trust part significantly narrowed the pool of applicants. Theo did not trust easily.

"And he only wants a female," Williams added.

Ah. The catch. There had to be one, yet the breath whooshed out of me, anyway. "Did he say why?" I asked, even though I knew the answer.

Why else would a Hunter want a woman? They weren't exactly known for their subtlety.

The expression on Williams's face could only be described as pitying, and I hated her for it, but I wanted her to admit what they were asking of me.

Out loud.

Deep in my stomach, something began to ice over. Began to ache.

"Come on, Miss Reeves," she said. "Isn't it obvious? He's offering information, and he asked for a woman in exchange."

Theo finally met my eyes. Studying the familiar lines of his square face, I tried to peer behind his expressionless mask. He merely shrugged. "He *said* he wants a contact, but given how the NAO...feels about women, we assume there will be certain expectations—"

The ache in my abdomen turned to lead at the unspoken words ringing through the silence.

He wants a plaything.

The Hunters—or the National Security Force, as they called themselves—served as specialized armed forces for the New American Order, answering to Richard Haynes, the Commander of the Unified States of America, who had little love for opposition.

Dissenters were exterminated. All hail the Commander.

The NAO detested many things—equality and foreigners among them—but their stance on gender was the crown jewel of their platform. It started as an ode to family values, an homage to tradition, but as years passed, the rhetoric changed. Loyalists began to view wives as property. Women became objects to use. The rise of the independent woman was the beginning of our downfall, they said. Our rights were stripped away one by one, and women were made into servants, mothers, vessels for pleasure, property for trade.

If I were the currency for this Hunter's information, I'd be at his mercy, expected to be compliant. Enthusiastic.

I wanted to ask why.

Why would they ask this of me? Why was it even an option?

But I knew the answer to these questions, too.

While the NAO luxuriated in the resources of the Unified States, the Defiance struggled to find advantages against them. With a censored media and barely any electricity, news and resources were scarce. Information on the NAO was worth a great deal, even if they had to blur the lines of morality to get it.

Did they really want me to volunteer my body in exchange for information? What other things had they offered him? What else was he getting for his defection? And why would a Hunter want *me* when he had entire brothels full of slaves for his pleasure?

And if he really wanted it, could I do it?

Ugh.

Tekqua's bright, friendly face leapt to my mind, her smile I missed so much.

"Just a quick patrol today. I should be back before lunch."

My best friend had been gone for two months, and with more intel, maybe we could find her. Maybe *I* could find her. My body was a small price to pay for that.

Ignoring the bile in my throat, I hardened. "I'll do it."

Williams smiled, but Theo's eyes widened. "Why don't you sleep on it, Sophia? Give it some thought."

"I'll do it," I said again.

He frowned. "We can still ask—"

Williams laid a hand on his arm. "She said yes."

Theo stiffened. "But—"

"He's offering intel we can't afford to turn down," Williams said, tone sharpening. "The Defiance is floundering. We don't get opportunities like this."

My gaze fell to my hands, and I picked at my cuticles until red welled.

Williams continued, "We've got spotty communication and dwindling supplies. You *know* this, General. We're at a stalemate, and Miss Reeves has agreed to help."

Theo expelled a quick breath. "He may be playing games. Messing with our heads."

And they wanted to whore me out despite that risk. An invisible fist squeezed my insides.

So *this* was rock bottom.

Theo had chastised me on more than one occasion for throwing myself into dangerous situations without regard to my safety. He used to protect me from that instinct. Now he was letting Williams exploit it.

Had they truly grown so desperate?

I thought of the bodies heaped over each other on the execution block, the bare rations that comprised our meals of late, the dwindling hope in our soldiers' eyes.

Of course they'd grown this desperate.

The NAO had only to wait us out. Without help, the Defiance would go extinct soon.

"We've already talked about this," Williams said. "I'll leave you to give her the details. Remember what we discussed."

Theo nodded, and the Prime Delegate departed, leaving faint traces of citrus-scented air behind her. The door clicked closed.

Theo's dark eyes met mine. "I advised against this."

"You *advised* against it? How hard did you fight for me, Theo?"

His eye twitched, but he said nothing.

Theo had withdrawn me from the front line and forced me into the medic unit months ago, an effort to protect me from the escalating violence. He probably would have sent me to Canada if he thought I'd go, but I wanted to keep close to my people.

Now, few of those people remained to care where I was.

One by one, I'd lost them to the battlefields.

The isolation seemed to have depleted my casualty value, and Theo knew it. Who would care if I died? It made me a perfect candidate for a man in want of a woman who wouldn't be noticed if she disappeared—likely why Williams requested me.

"Am I allowed to know who this traitor is?"

He clasped his hands, elbows resting on his desk, and braced his forehead on his thumbs.

"Theo, come on. You can't keep this from me. Do I know who he is?"

After one slow exhale, he said, "It's Lucas Scott."

Lucas...Scott?

Not *the* Lucas Scott.

Lucas Scott, the Blood Colonel. The cutthroat. The man who could erase dozens of human lives in seconds.

No.

My heart clenched, and air stalled in my lungs. Memories flashed of his scalpel...the slaughter. My throat grew dry. "A Blood Colonel? You're giving me to a Blood Colonel?"

Silence.

"And not just any Blood Colonel. *Lucas Scott.*"

"I know," Theo said.

"This is a trap. There's no way this is real."

"You don't know that." His voice cracked.

Acid churned in my stomach with the knowledge that it didn't matter. They'd send me even under threat of murder or rape. That was the extent of their desperation. My hands curled into fists, fingernails digging into my palms. "What's in it for him? It can't be about wanting a woman. Why would he turn?"

"He said they hurt his sister. I've tried to verify his story, but I can't find her." He hesitated. "He didn't even ask for immunity when we win. All he asked for was a female contact. Take everything he says with a large grain of salt."

If he said anything at all. What was to stop him from giving me nothing and taking everything? What safeguards did I have?

None. I had none. And it didn't matter.

I was worth sacrificing.

Focus on your breaths.

In. Out.

The panic washed over my mind like it always did, in flares and flashes of the horrors that haunted the past three years of my life.

They lower Princeton to a cot, and Dr. Grayson lifts his bloody shirt to reveal a bullet hole through his abdomen. "It might be okay if it didn't hit anything," Dr. Grayson says, prodding gently around the wound. He checks for an exit wound, and there it is, straight through Princeton's back, lower than his kidney should be.

A seed of hope sprouts in my heart, and I grasp for Princeton's hand. He squeezes back, warm and strong.

"What can I do?" I ask, ignoring all his squad members hovering around us.

"See if Adam has any of his moonshine left."

I force out a laugh.

Dr. Grayson cleans and dresses the wound, but we have no surgical capabilities. We operate on prayer alone. Russian roulette, military style.

Time passes.

His hand grows hot.

His teeth chatter.

"What do you think happens when we die?" he asks.

"We meet Jesus," Tekqua says, certain. "And our Father in Heaven."

I press my lips together. It's a prettier answer than the one I could supply—we simply cease to exist.

"Even if we've killed people?" Princeton asks.

Tekqua's voice gentles. "Have you prayed for forgiveness?"

"I don't pray."

"I'll pray for you, then."

And she does. Her palm presses over his heart, and she pleads to a god I've never trusted to watch over him, to take him peacefully when his time comes. Her words morph until she's praying for all of us, begging God to end the war and help our enemies see the error of their ways.

I lay there, bitter, imagining the supporters of the NAO doing the same —wishing we would recognize our wrongness and fall into the fold. Tekqua thanks God for His mercy and grace while I recount all the things —all the people—that have been taken from me.

When she finishes, a single tear falls from Princeton's closed eyes, trailing over his temple. The sight is a jagged shard of glass, cutting. Shoving down the burn in my throat, I grip his hand. The rapid tattoo of his pulse beats against my fingers like a drum.

His body relaxes into sleep. I exchange a worried glance with Tekqua, but no words exist to encompass the sheer degree of fear that overtakes me.

He isn't getting better. We both know it.

Eventually, I drift off.

When I wake, Princeton's hand in mine is finally cooler. His fever has broken! I rise to my elbow to smile down at him, but his eyes are shut.

His eyes are...shut. His chest isn't moving.

"Princeton?" I shake his shoulder, ignoring the frigid temperature of his skin.

Tekqua wakes. She blinks at me, confused.

"No!" I shout, shaking him harder. "Princeton!"

"Sophia!" Theo's voice broke through the memory, and suddenly, I was back in his office, curled over my lap, breathing into my knees. His hand rubbed circles between my shoulder blades, familiar. He'd walked me through these attacks before. "Think of the forest," he said as my breathing slowed. "Tall trees. Warm rain."

I nodded, doing my best to imprint my forest over the memory of Princeton. He'd been shot on patrol just a few months ago. The last of my original squad to die.

Unless Tekqua...

No! She wasn't dead.

"Sorry. I was just thinking about Princeton."

Theo's mouth set in a grim line. "At least with this Blood Colonel's information, you could help us end this. You could stop losing people you love."

My eyes narrowed, and I wanted to hurt him. "There are none left to lose."

The stricken flash of sorrow on his face lent me a strange vindication. He took a quick breath. "I didn't want you to do this. He's a Hunter. He could hurt you. He could be a double agent and screw us over. But Williams is right. We're running out of time, and there's no help in sight. We can fight until we all kill each other, or we can take drastic steps to stop it."

Happy to be the drastic step you take, I wanted to say.

But I didn't. What difference would it make?

Trapped in this war-torn portion of the Ohio River Valley, I had nowhere else to go. The Defiance was all I knew, all that mattered. The NAO had stolen everything from me, including my country, and most likely, my best friend. If there was an opportunity to find out vital information about Tekqua, I had to take it.

I should have escaped to Canada when we still had fuel, but back then I was naive enough to believe the good guys would win. I stayed because it was the *right thing to do*. Nia Williams convinced me we could win the fight for equality. I laid my name to rest on the Defiance registry willingly. I gambled my life on an unwinnable game.

And now?

Leaving was suicide.

Hunters hid in the dark like predators, waiting to pounce. My only chance at safety was staying with the Defiance. Maybe I was in the lion's den, but I was with Theo, and that had counted for something. Until now.

He returned to his chair, slumped. Grief had weathered him. The stress of commanding this failing rebellion had etched lines into his face. As my late father's best friend, Theo had always been part of my life. Before all this, he'd still had that soldier stiffness—he'd been a ranking officer in the Special Forces—but he used to smile as I'd run and clutch onto his legs.

"Throw me again, Uncle Theo!"

He'd toss me high in the air.

A different world. A lifetime ago.

Shoving down the pang of nostalgia, I straightened, exhaling a measured breath. My heartbeat slowed and my skin turned clammy. "When do I meet him?"

"Thursday night. Seven o'clock." He made me memorize an address on Evanston Avenue.

Binding information. Irrevocable.

A permanent handcuff to my new jailer.

The Blood Colonel would have priceless information. He could warn us of devastating attacks. Navigate us through enemy territory. Help us steal their supplies. He could save lives instead of take them.

If he was telling the truth.

I glared at the floor, and two thoughts struck me.

First, the stark and surprising awareness that I didn't *want* to die. There had been times, moments, when I'd thought death preferable. I'd longed for the comfort it could provide, the end of the suffering.

The second thought was a hot wire slicing through my mind.

You deserve this.

"Thursday at seven?" I asked, my voice lifeless.

Theo nodded. "This wasn't an order." His eyebrows drew together, pleading. "I thought you'd say no. I—"

"Well, I didn't. It's too late to go back now." I left the room before he could say anything else, hurrying down the main stairs, cursing all the circumstances that had brought me to this point.

The NAO and its power-hungry Commander.

The declaration of war against our peaceful allies.

The civil war that destroyed us.

It had been three years since the NAO ratified the New Constitution.

We the People of the Unified States, in Order to restore our greatness, secure our borders, and uphold the rights given to us by God, establish this Constitution to ensure freedom, prosperity, and law and order for all true American citizens.

The worst part?

We did nothing. We willingly stepped into a cage and realized too late that a fire had been lit beneath it. Each small move on their part was a match added to the flame. We let a censored media calm our worries while we slowly burned alive.

Because autocracies do not happen overnight.

They start slow. Prettily. With words like *unity* and *patriotism*.

They grow with bribes and manipulation.

They bud in the death of free speech, where saying the wrong thing can earn you an execution.

They thrive when fear outweighs morality.

Then they disseminate, and nothing short of civil war will stop it.

Except we were losing that war, and I wasn't sure that a damn thing I did could help. This was the end. My certain death at Lucas Scott's hands would be in vain, and all I could think was...

It shouldn't have ended like this.

2

THE FRACTURE

> The National Stability Force shall oversee all corrective measures to enforce compliance and re-education of nonconformists, including compulsory labor and supervised custodial interaction with military personnel.
>
> — ENFORCEMENT MEASURES AGAINST INSURRECTIONISTS, N.A.O.C. 6 § 3218

It shouldn't have started the way it did either. As I stepped out of Theo's office, the events that had brought me to this moment played through my mind like a horror show through a child's viewfinder.

Richard Haynes had been president for six months when I first heard about the controversial New American Order. Their ideals centered on this idea of uniformity. True Americans, they said, fit a certain mold. They looked a certain way. Held certain values. In a televised speech, the New American Order was lauded by President

Haynes as a much-needed organization to bring the US back to its grand origins—one people, one religion, secure borders.

And I *laughed*. Because hadn't we done this before, a century ago? This was 1930s Germany all over again. No way would people fall for this. My father, on the other hand, was a political journalist, and their rhetoric appalled him.

We demand the union of all Americans.

Only true Americans should be citizens.

All non-American immigration must be prevented.

It wasn't long before the NAO disseminated throughout the administration. American citizens of *questionable descent* were imprisoned and expatriated. Women were systematically removed from employment for the *betterment of the nuclear family*. Our overextended government was dismantled, and the people thought, *Good. It's gotten too big anyway.*

We were all idiots.

Now, walking away from Theo's office was like floating in a dream. My gaze drifted over the familiar surroundings of headquarters, suddenly colorless as I balked at what I'd agreed to. The museum we'd covertly transformed into our home base was a winding building. Rooms led into more rooms with seemingly no end. Half stairs would fade into oddly shaped alcoves with glass display cabinets, now empty except for the ever-present layer of dust. Sporadic ornamental fireplaces and dried-up fountains decorated several rooms that had been converted into sleeping quarters or training facilities.

On the ground floor, three French doors led to stone terraces, though the windows had been shuttered by metal. The back patio opened out onto extravagant sloping gardens, decorative ponds, and a gazebo with a single bench inside, all overgrown and rundown with time. Far behind that, a creek was crisscrossed by quaint wooden bridges.

An ode to what once was.

Tragic beauty.

In the current state of cruelty and unrest, the artistry seemed wasted.

Violence had darkened our lives even in the days when the gardens had still been manicured and neat, so much that by this point, I hardly thought twice about it.

I was thinking now.

I didn't want to do this.

I didn't want to be a plaything for a Hunter.

Hunters enjoyed violence the way normal humans basked in sunlight—it was an expected boon to life on earth. When President Haynes was found guilty of violating the Fourteenth Amendment two years into his term, I rejoiced. Surely this meant people would finally see the ruthlessness inherent in his administration.

But the next day, the judges were doused in gasoline and set on fire. Members of the NAO murdered them—unofficially, of course— and their loyalists celebrated.

His dissenters went quiet. Fear seeped into our bloodstream, an icy poison.

"It is a tragedy," President Haynes said in a statement following the event. *"Sad. Very sad. My thoughts are with the families of Judges Hannity, Armstrong, and Strauss. Even though I disagreed with their decisions, no one should face violence for doing their job. I have always said our legal system needs reform. These are the things that happen when you let illegal criminals into your country, when you forget the importance of loyalty and family, when you allow women and dissenters to serve in positions of power. We must restore law and order to make this country safe for all true Americans."*

The subsequent spree of brutality against judges and representatives who disagreed with the party went ignored and unchecked.

No one saved us from the violence.

Just like no one would save me from it now.

I passed a doorway to one of the downstairs common rooms, and Devon's voice called out, "What did the general want?"

For two seconds, I considered ignoring him. Did I have the mental capacity to pretend everything was fine?

Instead, I entered the room and flopped onto the couch next to him. "Nothing important. Checking on me. You know how he is."

Adam sat nearby, strumming his guitar, but he stopped, curious eyes meeting mine. Born with a level of trustworthiness that shouldn't be allowed, Adam was often privy to information most didn't have. Would he find out about this? Did he already know?

"Heard the Prime Delegate is here," he said, referring to Williams.

"Yeah," I replied. "Something happened with the Hunters, I guess. Theo wouldn't talk."

Adam raised a brow. "No surprises there. Hunters gonna hunt."

Oh, the truth of that.

Toward the end of his term, when presidential elections drew closer and we had the slimmest chance of ousting him, Haynes enacted martial law and instituted the National Stability Act—a sweeping set of legal doctrines that dismantled the presidency and created an autocracy under a white flag boasting the symbol of the NAO, the Brotherhood Cross. With it, he also created a brand new branch of the military.

The National Stability Force.

The NSF was sold to the American people as a body to protect us. Really, it was the militarized police force of the NAO, intent on eradicating dissidents. We started calling them *Hunters* the moment we realized they were authorized to shoot citizens dead in the streets. A protest near the Capitol turned into a bloodbath when Hunters gunned down hundreds of Americans merely for disagreeing with the NAO.

The verdant grass of the National Mall ran crimson, ornamented with the bodies of innocent men and women, people who only wanted to exercise their right to peaceful protest.

The Capitol Hill Massacre had been proof that the NSF didn't exist to protect the people. It existed to protect the party.

A Hunter has come forward offering information.

Another roll of my stomach brought the acrid taste of bile, which I had to swallow down. Why had I agreed to be his contact?

I forced Tekqua's face to the forefront of my mind. Insider information would likely be the only way I'd ever gain knowledge of what happened to her. If she'd really been captured, maybe I could find her —even if I had to succumb to *compulsory labor* or *custodial interactions* to do it.

More than that, maybe I could help end it all.

Because the worst part was that the NAO had achieved their goal —we *were* living in a New America, one in which the government had been weaponized against those who didn't fit the mold. They'd infiltrated our schools and hospitals, determining what our children would learn and who our doctors would treat. They censored our internet, allowing us access only to NAO-approved sources. To *end the war on deliberate political mendacity*, they allowed a single national news outlet—Unified News—and controlled all the information disseminated.

The mass exodus that followed the Capitol Hill Massacre was the nidus of war. With our airports controlled by the NAO, Americans became refugees as they drove, biked, or even ran across the militarized borders to safer territories. These dissidents were called rebels and charged with treason. Border patrol was ordered to gun them down on sight. Suddenly, the NAO wanted everyone kept inside as opposed to kicking everyone out.

Our neighbor to the north opened its arms, appalled by the new regime. President Haynes deemed this an act of aggression and claimed Canada was harboring enemies of the state.

He declared war, sending troops to the borders to attack the peaceful nation north of us.

The Security Restoration Campaign.

With the presidential office suspended, Haynes named himself the Commander. He ratified a novel constitution for the NAO and called his new nation the Unified States of America.

He tore our country in half, and the people who didn't agree, the dissidents, those still brave enough to fight back... Well, we did the only thing we could.

We sank our nation into the sea of civil war.

It would be years before anyone called it the Fracture, but whoever coined it hit the nail on its bloody, jagged head. It divided the entire world into slivers.

The UN, dismantled.

NATO, destroyed.

The WTO, demolished.

No one ever believed it could happen. There were too many fail-safes, too many protections. We overestimated the strength of those defenses against a power-hungry man in want of a kingdom to rule. A man with a loyal following of zealots. A man who'd convinced them all their greatest enemy was within.

He tore us apart from the inside.

Even now, I wondered where we'd gone wrong. How had it come to this? How were we losing?

I gazed at the haggard remains of our rebellion—off-duty soldiers, clustered around janky tables, conversing on threadbare loveseats and sofas. Devon fiddled with the threads on the cushion between us, bringing my attention back to him. He was thin, almost delicate, with devious and fine-spun features. Adam, on the other hand, was a teddy bear. He had a quick, easy smile and warm eyes.

Cursed with watching everyone I loved die, I'd pushed these friends so far I couldn't truly call them friends anymore, but both of them were good men. Great men. Men worth dying for, surely.

Maybe what I'd just agreed to with the Blood Colonel would save their lives.

I seized a faded magazine from the coffee table to avoid Adam's stare. "I can't believe they used to care about this bullshit." I glared at a comparison of two women wearing the same dress—an entire page dedicated to who looked better.

What a fucking joke.

"These are the things you worry about when you have nothing to worry about," Devon said.

"Well." I threw the magazine back onto the table. "Both of those women are probably dead now. Wonder who wears *that* better."

Adam snorted and returned to his guitar. "I found some chocolate on a raid the other day, Soph. You take my KP duty and I'll give it to you."

"No deal," I said. "Last time you stole me chocolate, it was chalky and terrible."

He faux-gasped. "The things I had to do to get that chocolate!"

I forced a laugh. We'd all done terrible things for scraps of information or supplies. Our resistance was built on theft. Even our soldiers were stolen from the NAO—Americans who refused to bow.

In the early days of the war, the NAO's military was focused on the Security Restoration Campaign in Canada. During that time, renegade bands of the US forces turned against the new government and joined the rebellion, forcing the Commander to divide his military. He called troops inland to fight the rebels, strengthening the NSF into a true hunting force. In a speech made over our only remaining television network, Commander Haynes called the rebel forces *weaponized defiance*, and the phrase took fire.

Defiance.

Soldiers like Adam flocked to us to fight. To *defy*.

After the attacks on our peaceful neighbor, worldwide panic set in. Within days, Europe sent troops to bolster Canada's tiny military and neutralized our overseas bases. In a week, cyber-attacks and EMPs took down our internet and power.

World war erupted, everything destabilized, and for a scary few weeks, I was certain it would all end in a nuclear holocaust.

But that never happened.

Instead, information disappeared, trade was disrupted, and the civil war became our entire lives. We lost access to medicines. To gas. To food.

Including chocolate—my favorite.

I'd done many things for chocolate, but never anything like what I suspected Lucas Scott would want from me. At once, I succumbed to thoughts of those things—being choked, bent over in humiliation, forced to beg for it until he gave me the information I needed.

It's your turn to suffer, I thought. *You deserve this.*

I had three days to prepare and no idea how to do it. Maybe I should try to make myself as ugly as possible. Would it anger him to receive an unattractive, unkempt woman? Would he punish me for it?

Probably, since he was a Hunter specifically requesting a woman.

Maybe he'd expect me to be flirty and accommodating, like an escort. Did I know how to do that? I'd been sleeping with only one person for the last year, and Jayden was only a fuck buddy, someone to relieve the stress. I didn't *flirt* with him.

Well, if Lucas Scott was expecting skill, then fuck him. He'd be disappointed and could request someone else.

Still, cold shivers of dread chased themselves down my spine and goosebumps rose across my body. I didn't want to die. I wasn't ready.

I couldn't do it, could I?

I waffled back and forth between duty and desire, pitting selfishness against self-sacrifice.

An off-key twang of Adam's guitar jolted me from my thoughts when the front door of headquarters banged open, spilling chaos into the house. I locked eyes with him before we both raced downstairs at the noise, shouts preceding carnage as bleeding bodies were dragged inside.

Adam and Devon scurried to help while the rest of the medic team flooded in. Springing into action, I helped transport the injured soldiers to the hospital wing. It filled quickly. *Too* quickly. So many bodies and too few ways to help. I pressed both hands against the blood spurting from a crossbow injury to a man's chest, trying to stop the bleeding with pressure and prayer. He gasped for oxygen. The bolt rose and fell with each breath.

"Look at me," I said.

His chest heaved.

I glanced at his dog tags. "Aiden, look at me!"

His brown eyes met mine.

"You're going to be okay. Alright?"

We both knew he wouldn't.

"Just do it!" he hissed between breaths.

No.

I didn't want to.

If I ripped the bolt from his chest, his time spent in agony would shorten with his life. We had no resources to save him from an injury like this. No surgeries. No blood. Nothing. This was the way of things.

But choosing to take his life instead of letting it end naturally...

"Do it!" he demanded.

Obeying his wishes, my shaking hands closed around the shaft, and I yanked it from his chest. Two more gasps, and his muscles relaxed as he bled out into his chest cavity. His eyes went glassy, and he was gone.

I sat back, staring at his slack face. Handsome. Young.

What did it say about me as a human that it had grown easier to watch them die?

A hand squeezed my shoulder in passing. I didn't bother to check who it belonged to. The compassionate touch was familiar. Dr. Grayson had been our lead physician since the beginning. He always offered comfort when one of us lost a patient, even when he was rushing to save one himself. His partner—and my friend—Zara Akbari did the same.

Hours flew by in minutes, and when I finally looked up from my last patient, now stabilized, Dr. Grayson and Dr. Akbari sat beside each other, heads in their hands. A pang pierced my chest as I made my way to them. It had become a common sight, the two of them mourning those we couldn't save. My mentors, losing hope.

"What's the final count?" I asked Zara.

"Twenty-seven soldiers," she whispered, exhaustion and grief spilling from her hunched posture. She was the most beautiful woman I'd ever seen, but the sorrow had broken her face into fragments—splotched cheeks, creased brow, sad little diamonds that dripped from her eyes and sparkled in the light.

"What happened?" I asked her.

Before she could answer, a survivor with burns across her face and arms spoke up from her bed. "We were sent to attack what we thought was a Hunter center of operations, but it was a decoy. We were the only ones who escaped. Left fifty behind."

Zara and I exchanged pained glances.

"This world is like the devil's playground," she whispered. "Death lives in every shadow."

I'd joined the war effort with the belief that I was doing the right thing, that good would always triumph. But that was sheer naivety. Good and evil didn't exist. There was only strength and weakness, and the NAO retained the might of what used to be the United States. We were just a rebel band of do-gooders fighting the most powerful empire of all time.

We needed intel. *Good* intel. Not the stuff that would send soldiers uselessly into the line of fire, but information that would save thousands.

A small sacrifice on my part could turn the tides of this war. People died today to fight the NAO. To consider backing out of my deal with the Blood Colonel was unforgivably selfish.

So I wouldn't.

3
WAR WHORE

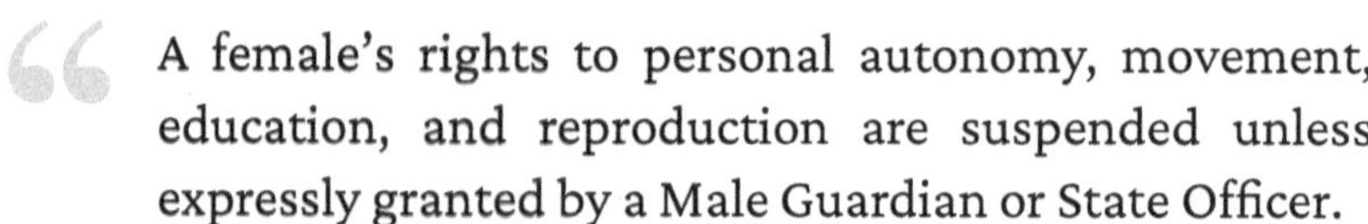

A female's rights to personal autonomy, movement, education, and reproduction are suspended unless expressly granted by a Male Guardian or State Officer.

— FEMALE CITIZENSHIP RECLASSIFICATION ACT,

N.A.O.C. 42 § 3308

I sit hand-in-hand with my mother in the backseat of a car while Theo drives across the Appalachians to the river valley on the other side. The lights are strange—foggy and twinkling like starlight— but I stare at my mother's face. Parts are blurry, almost as if I can't quite see them, can't remember what they look like even as I stare and stare and stare.

Eventually, Theo leaves the highway and takes a long, dusty road that leads to a church. I stagger into the cool spring air to stare at the unassuming building, trying to ignore the prickling sensation along my skin.

My relationship with religion is complicated. Raised Catholic, I should cross myself like Mom, but I haven't put much faith in higher powers of late. As I stare at the large cross erected before the Protestant establishment, I wonder what sort of god would allow the current circumstances.

Other cars have crammed into the spaces around us. From within the building, shouts and rumbles bleed through the open doors, leaking between the nascent grass blades and delicate spring blossoms that surround me.

It's so pretty.

Stay here, *part of me whispers.*

It already knows what's about to happen.

It's better out here, *it says.*

But Theo leads us to the entrance, and the three of us follow, trusting and docile.

In the sanctuary, hundreds of people yell and snipe.

Theo scans the crowd and meets the eyes of a Black woman standing near the pulpit. "There she is."

We follow him down the aisle toward her.

"Williams," Theo says as the woman nods to us. She's tall, with large, pretty eyes and hair cut short, curls swept to one side. She greets Theo with a handshake, allowing him to kiss her cheek.

"Williams, this is Chris and Diana, and their daughter Sophia. Everyone, this is Nia Williams. My contact."

He goes on to explain that Nia Williams used to be a representative in California, but I'm no longer listening. I've heard it all before—she's the ringleader of the NAO's biggest critics, been working on a counter movement.

No, I don't listen.

This time, I study our Prime Delegate's face. There's something trustworthy about it. Perhaps her large eyes or her wide smile.

Looks can deceive, *I think, wishing I'd known better than to trust that face.*

"We're calling ourselves the Defiance," she says, white teeth gleaming. "Max Aota has several dozen regiments headed our way."

"Who's Max Aota?" I ask.

"He was a colonel in the US Army," Williams says. "Now he's a Defiant. Why don't y'all take a seat and we'll get started soon."

My parents usher me to one of the front pews, and before long, Williams steps forward.

"Thanks for coming," she calls to the crowd. "You all know why you're here—or at least have some idea. Our country is at war."

Murmurs from the crowd greet those words.

"I'm sure you've all seen the tragedies. Some of us have lost family, friends. Our leaders have failed us at every level. Commander Haynes's extreme nationalism, intolerance, and blatant disrespect for our established laws have turned the free world into an autocracy."

Louder murmurs and sounds of agreement.

"This here is Lieutenant Colonel Theodore Harrison, US Special Forces. He's been gathering intel for weeks, and what we know is this: Hunters have dispersed throughout the country. Their sole purpose is to extinguish those defiant to the party, to quell our rebellion. Haynes's army is advancing into Canada. He wants that territory for his own. He's grasping for too much. His military is mighty, but it's split. He cannot handle a war on so many fronts."

Gasps and cheers.

"We are facing dangerous times. You are all likely here for different reasons. Either you oppose the radical takeover of our country, or you're seeking asylum as an at-risk citizen, or maybe you had nowhere else to go. No matter the reason, we have a fight ahead of us, and we need your help."

The mumblings turn angry.

"I've been working with a group of dissidents since the NAO first formed. We've established safe houses and a headquarters west of Louisville. We are organizing, and we need people like you to join this fight. This is not the first place I've been, and it won't be the last. The Defiance will recruit across the country to end the oppression of the NAO."

"You're—you're talking about full-scale war," says a man in the front row. "Not just riots, but—"

Theo steps forward. "War. Yes. We've fought this kind of tyranny and hate before. This country was born from the fight for freedom, and now, we will fight again. The Defiance has commandeered weapons and equipment from the NAO's military. Commander Haynes has lost a large portion of his army to us." He looks around the crowd, his voice strong and sure. "We will not lay down and allow this to happen. We will fight for our freedom. We will fight for our country! We will fight for what's right!"

As the crowd goes wild, I lean into Mom. "What will we do?"

"We'll sign our names and go with Theo," my mother answers. "We'll fight."

My gaze trails to the surrounding crowd, and the light around each face grows dreamy.

Don't do this, *a voice whispers.*

It will be impossible, *it says.*

Wake up, *it screams.*

Consciousness ripped me from the dream.

In my chest, my heart pounded against thick, icy blood as I fought to pull myself away from that familiar panic. My subconscious mind often revisited the memory of that church, wishing I'd made another decision. Back then, death wasn't something I thought about regularly. Now, it stared me in the face with matte black eyes and a rictus of a smile. I was haunted by it, wondering when it would come for me.

Perhaps it was time.

Lucas Scott would be my reaper.

Still embroiled in the dream, I battled a profound urge to cry. When I signed my name that day, I didn't want this war to be my new reality. Nia Williams asked me to lay down my history, my future, my desires, my ideas of the life I had wanted, and follow her into a lost cause.

I think I'd known even then our chances were slim. The Unified States possessed the most expensive and heavily armed military in existence. Who could win against that, even if it was divided? A ragtag army against a world superpower?

Maybe I was just cynical. I'd never been an optimist.

Still, when it was my turn to sign my name, I laid it on the page, girly loops and scrawls to seal my fate. Standing in that church, uncertain and afraid, I signed away my life.

Sophia Elena Reeves.

Of course the dream would surface the day I had to meet Lucas Scott. I forced down a sickening roll of my stomach as I left headquarters for the meeting house on Evanston Avenue.

Theo gave no words of encouragement before I slipped away. He tried to smile, but it emerged as a grimace. If the Blood Colonel wanted to kill me on the spot, I would have no self-defense. Theo knew this, but we'd both learned long ago it was better not to say goodbye. There were simply too many to say, with too little time to spare.

My feet dragged as the sun sank low into the late March sky. The chill in the air prickled my skin, but it was nothing compared to the fierce pang of longing that stabbed through me as I reminded myself why I was doing this—for Tekqua. I'd lost many people, but she was the most recent, and perhaps the most painful. When she was captured on patrol a couple months ago, she'd taken with her all the interest I had in outlasting this war. If she hadn't survived, then I didn't deserve to. She'd been more dedicated. Stronger. A soldier to her core.

So what did it matter if I died today?

I marched toward my inevitable demise in a neighborhood that should've had people walking their dogs, children playing in the street. Instead, the lifeless shells of houses served as a reminder of how things used to be. When I arrived, I studied the home. The porch spoke of happier times, with a swing and a couple chairs by the door.

Large windows across the front warmed the entire facade. Diaphanous white curtains veiled the interior.

I crept up the stairs, counting as I went. The warped boards of the porch creaked with each step. A brass knocker hung on the crimson door, the shape of a lion, but I didn't use it. The entry had been left open, cracked wide enough to fit my body through. I stood at the threshold—*deep breath*—then slipped inside.

A combined entryway and living room greeted me. Two blue couches bracketed a coffee table with a burning candle in the middle. A wide doorway led to a dining room on one side and the kitchen beyond it.

The space was empty.

So... where was he?

A smooth, deep voice cut through the darkness. "Are you the war whore?"

Nearly choking on my gasp, I spun to face him. He stood in the doorway of a shadowed bedroom on my left, leaning a shoulder on the jamb. The dim light obscured his features. Dark wavy hair softened a sly, angled face, one brow lifted as he gazed at me.

My insides contracted at the sight of him, and every inch of my skin turned clammy as the realization occurred that he was *young*. So much younger than he looked on TV. He couldn't be but a handful of years older than me, and yet a deadly air of danger and ruthlessness practically dripped from his pores. Long, thin fingers curled around his biceps the same way I imagined they twined around throats. Scars across his skin demonstrated his familiarity with violence, his will to survive. Mouth turned down into a frown, expression wintry and closed, Lucas Scott radiated don't-fuck-with-me vibes in a steady, petrifying rhythm.

The TV screen didn't do him justice. This man wasn't human. The cold, almost robotic calculation on his face proved it. He was nothing but a killer.

Terror snaked its way through me, razor sharp. My heart sped, and instinct compelled me to search his body for easily accessible weapons.

He had none.

No holsters, no knives. But I wasn't safe. He needed no weapon to take my life. He was a weapon in the form of a man.

I forced my suddenly dry mouth to open. "I'm not a whore."

Seriously? Why was *that* the thing that came out of my mouth?

His attention slipped down my body before returning to my eyes.

Ew.

Did he just check me out? Perusing the goods, or something? What a monster.

"They sold you to me for information," he said. "Would you prefer the term *slave?*"

Oh, fuck you, Lucas Scott.

Hackles raised, I put a bone-chilling level of frost into my voice. "My name's Sophia. That's the term I'd prefer."

A vicious emotion I couldn't identify flickered in his eyes, there and gone again, and my body stiffened. Whoa. The danger pouring from him ratcheted upward. I fought the urge to back away.

The door was still open beside me. Could I outrun him?

I took in his long legs with a grimace.

Probably not.

"Pleased to meet you, *Sophia.*" He said my name as if it were a joke, his lip lifting in a sneer. "Before we agree to this, let's discuss this arrangement."

"O-okay." I wasn't aware I still had a choice, but now that he presented it that way, I wondered...could I say no?

"We'll meet every Thursday at seven."

I nodded.

"Everything said here will be reported directly to Theodore Harrison. No one else. Understood?"

Well, duh. Who else would I report to? "Yeah, got it."

His eyes turned calculating. "From this point forward, you are *my* messenger, which means this takes priority over everything else. Unless you're serious, I won't give you anything."

I pinched the fabric of my pants to keep my hands from shaking. "What do you want in exchange?"

His voice went feral—dark and violent and terrifying. "I'd like to escort the NAO straight to hell."

My eyebrows rose. Okay, then. "And what do you want from me?" I whispered, almost afraid to hear the answer.

"Compliance."

My skin went cold. *Compliance* could encompass so many things. In this transactional exchange, I wanted to understand exactly what payment he'd exact. Lucas Scott, however, didn't appear to want to elaborate further. I would comply with his wishes, or he'd...what?

Return me to my people?

Force my agreement?

Kill me?

"So you agree?" he asked.

It took every ounce of strength I possessed to dip my head in a nod.

"I'll have your word, please?"

Please?

What...was...that?

Was Lucas Scott a *polite* killer? A fucking psychopath?

I placed a hand over my heart, more an attempt to guard it from hidden weapons than to show my dedication. "You have my word." I tried not to give myself a moment to second-guess, but he said nothing, so I filled the quiet. "I'll do as you ask, as long as you don't interfere with any efforts to bring the NAO down. Whatever you want, it's yours."

He stared at me without blinking, the long silence making me squirm, making my heart pound, making my thoughts go wild. Had I said something wrong?

It went on so long, I had to glance away. My attention fell on the lit candle, the only light in the room.

"Do you know who I am?" he asked after a while.

"Other than a murderer?" The candle's flame burned into my vision, and I could have kicked myself. Why did my mouth always shoot off before my mind could consider the words?

"Yeah," he said, unfazed. "Other than that."

It hurt to do it, but I forced myself to look at him. "Lucas Scott. Killer extraordinaire."

"Cute." His smile raised the tiny hairs on the back of my neck. "You've never taken a human life?"

"Anyone I killed deserved it."

His brow lifted. "You sure? What made them so unworthy of life?"

"They were Hunters."

"And that warrants a death sentence? Without due process? Sounds familiar."

I frowned at him, bristling. "I didn't come here to argue the morals of the war with you."

"No, but your being here proves your side has just as few morals as mine."

"*Excuse me*?" I gripped my hips. Was this asshole mocking me?

His gaze dropped to my hands, and his smile widened. "Does Theodore Harrison whore out all his women? Or are you just special?"

"I am *not* a whore!"

He let out a scornful snort. "The truth getting under your skin a little, *Sophia*?"

Why did he say my name like that? Like it was an insult. Or a lie. Glaring, I snapped my mouth shut.

Because I hated that he was right. I hated that I'd been the one chosen. I hated that I was broken enough to do it.

He dug into the psychological wound with rough, dirty fingers. "A whore for my intel. That was the deal, right? One who wouldn't need her legs pried open like the rest of you Defiants."

Wow, there it was. The truth of what this was. I'd suspected, of course, but having him say it was just...

His embittered laughter slithered around me. "And the hypocrite was only too happy to oblige."

Fear strangled me, debilitated me. Sweat bloomed on my palms and beneath my arms. My heartbeat pounded in my throat and temples.

Why had I agreed to this? Why had Theo *let* me agree to this? Did he care about me at all?

But it didn't matter. Because I was here, and I was doing this. No turning back now.

Resigned, I took a deep breath and dove headfirst into my fate. "You won't have to pry."

He stiffened. "A *proud* whore. How charming."

Fuck off.

I strode toward the bedroom, trying to slink past him and throw myself on the bed, to show him I wasn't afraid even though I was mind-numbingly terrified. As I reached the doorway, however, he grabbed my arm, holding me in place. I expected him to be cold, like his icy heart might affect his core temperature, but his hand was hot on my skin, burning an invisible brand there.

Gross, gross, gross.

Let me go!

His voice lowered. "Ah, ah. As charming as you are, I'm not interested. Something Harrison would have known if he'd bothered to ask."

I froze and stared at his face, marred by faint tracings of the war. He had dark circles beneath his eyes, and the beginnings of a permanent line between his eyebrows. Silvery scars crisscrossed his forehead and one cheek. His body was long and lean and sharp. No indecision darkened his eyes, no trace of regret or shame, and the cold fury in them—or maybe the darkness—hid their color.

"Not...interested?" I whispered.

"Go to the kitchen. I'll bring you what he wants." He dropped my arm and turned away, heading back into the bedroom.

I stood unmoving for a few more seconds, but relief got the better of me and I fled through the house, then collapsed into a seat at the kitchen table. The woodgrain captured my entire attention while my world tipped sideways. What did he mean he wasn't interested? Not interested for now, or not interested at all? And if he wasn't interested in *that*, then what did he want in exchange for his information? I had nothing else to give him.

Harrison would have known if he'd bothered to ask.

Why hadn't Theo clarified the terms of this agreement?

Reappearing after a couple of minutes, Scott flopped a folder onto the table and dragged a chair close to me—close enough to touch. Every time his arm brushed mine, my heartbeat stuttered, and my skin set on fire. Why was he so warm?

Or was I just cold?

Was I going into shock?

"One condition of this arrangement is that you know the intel I give them." He slid the folder between us and flipped it open. A delicate gold band glittered on his left pinky. "The information will be in your head alone."

"Why?"

"Because it keeps the power dynamic in my favor, and it makes you incredibly valuable. If only you know the information, then you're indispensable. I want a contact they won't kill for knowing too much, and I don't want a paper trail."

"And you want a woman."

He flashed me a quick glance. "I do."

But why?

I'm not interested.

Harrison would have known if he'd bothered to ask.

Resisting the temptation to dive into that, I instead asked, "Why would you care if they kill me?"

"I plan to give a lot of information, and I don't want to adapt to a new contact every time they feel the previous one has learned too much. The more people know about this, the more dangerous it is. I don't particularly want to die in the way the NAO reserves for traitors."

The monthly executions flashed through my mind. Treason was punishable by death. *How* a traitor achieved that death, however...

I gazed at his profile, frowning. "What makes you think I'd care how you die? I could turn you in today, and it would save a lot of people's lives."

"Would it?" Curiosity sparkled in his cold eyes. "We have more than enough soldiers to offset my absence."

"You—you kill more than any of the others."

His jaw flexed. "I'm good at my job."

He *was* good at it. Too good at it. Terrifyingly good at it.

Icicles crystallized my bones at the memory of his cold-blooded executions, freezing to the point of pain. He could kill me in seconds.

His voice softened. "I'll be good at this, too. If you'll cooperate."

We studied each other, and I pushed away the instinct to flee. I was in no danger from him.

For now.

It wouldn't always be true. He wanted something—some as-yet-unnamed condition of this arrangement. His cold was threaded with an intricate anger he tried to hide. It flaunted itself with twitches of his eyes and clenches of his jaw. Lucas Scott held himself like a restrained animal, ready to attack. What, exactly, was restraining him? When would he strike?

"What do you really want from me?" I whispered once again.

His jaw clenched. "I already told you."

"But... Why are you doing this?"

"They hurt my sister."

"It's just... Why would they do that?" She must have done something wrong. As far as I knew, the NAO didn't harm their women for fun, though corporal punishment was widely utilized. "You're a colonel in the NSF. Wouldn't she have protections?"

His fist clenched on the table, and spots of color appeared on his cheeks. "That's not important."

But I wanted to understand. *Needed* to understand. "It's important to me."

"I don't give a fuck what's important to you." It came out sharp, cutting straight through my composure. My fear returned full measure. "Do you want this information, or not?"

"O-of course I do."

He paused, engaging in some agonizing, intrusive perusal of my eyes. His face gave nothing away. He sat straight, tall, harsh emotions vibrating beneath his skin. "I assume they chose you because you're trustworthy. I'm banking on their judgment. Probably makes me stupid."

"Stupidity is likely the least of your faults."

Oh my god. *Shut up, Sophia!*

His eyes flashed, and some of his anger finally spilled out. "Christ, you have a smart mouth, don't you?"

"I—"

"Shut it or I'll find something else for it to do."

Blood drained from my head as a wave of nausea rolled through me. It would be one thing to dissociate and allow a killer to fuck me, but to suck him off... To actively participate...

My tone went leaden. "I thought you weren't interested."

He stared at me, unimpressed. "I'm not. I wanted to know whether you believed me. And you clearly didn't since you're about to faint right now."

Was he...testing me?

"That's a good instinct, at least," he said, eyeing me with a tiny iota of approval. "Never believe someone just because they're saying something you want to hear. But if this is going to work, I'll need you to trust what I say is true."

I swallowed and nodded even though nothing in the world would ever make me trust him.

"Also, *think* before you speak," he continued. "Especially when you're talking to someone who wouldn't hesitate to kill you. Play the player, not the game. It will save your life."

Life advice from a Blood Colonel? No thanks.

With that, his attention fell to the open folder between us. He withdrew two sheets of paper and showed them to me—marked city plans. He launched into details about an upcoming attack.

Afterward, I eyed the papers, swallowing. "I don't know if I believe you."

He sighed. "Only one way to find out."

Right. By leading my people into potential slaughter. Why would he give us this for free? He *had* to want something in return.

"How exactly did you manage to get in contact with Harrison?" I asked. Theo would have killed him on sight.

The corner of Lucas's mouth lifted. "Ask him."

Theo would never tell me, so I abandoned that line of questioning. But how else could I delve into Lucas's motives? If he made our victory easy, wouldn't it put his life at risk? Unless he was lying...

"If we don't identify our source," I said, "you could be killed during these raids."

"I'm pretty good at not dying."

The truth of that statement was absolute. The Blood Colonels weren't just lethal. They were survivalists. There was a reason that amongst thousands of Hunters, only a few dozen had risen to his rank.

I touched my forehead, a headache burgeoning. "This makes no sense."

He sighed again, put-upon and impatient. "I thought they'd send someone smart."

I side-eyed him, finally quelling the impulse to spout off something rude.

"I am Lucas Scott," he said. "High-ranking strategist and executioner of a violent, authoritarian regime. I approached the Defiance of my own free will, offering intelligence. Surely you don't think I'd do that assuming I'd survive?"

What?

He was a Hunter! The NAO specifically created his branch of the military to eradicate the Defiance. Why would he help us knowing he'd probably die doing it? What was I missing?

"*Why?*" I asked again.

When he replied, his voice was clipped, each word honed and pointed. "They hurt my sister."

"They hurt a lot of people."

"Not the person I care about."

Ten seconds passed while I merely stared, speechless. He would topple their entire regime for a slight to his sister?

No. No way. No fucking way.

But I didn't care enough to pursue it further. Or maybe I was too scared. I left after memorizing everything he told me, eager to get away. When I returned home, Theo's relief at seeing me alive was palpable. He gave me a careful embrace before I spilled the information I learned. Theo didn't pry into whether any extracurricular activities had occurred, bless him. How would I explain the utter enigma?

Mountains and mountains of regret and turmoil piled atop my shoulders. What exactly had I gotten myself into? I'd walked into that house and met the devil himself, a man with pinpoint objectives and unclear motives.

That night, I settled into my pillow, haunted by the words of Lucas Scott.

Not the person I care about.

Not *people*, but *person*. As if nothing else deserved his time or energy. They hurt his sister, and he decided to dissolve them from the inside. It was a seemingly impossible task, and yet, by the livid certainty in his demeanor, I had no doubt he possessed the ability.

Still, did no one else matter to him? He would be responsible for countless deaths, for the demise of his own people, all for an offense against his sister.

What would he do if she died?

I trembled and curled into myself, shutting my eyes against the possibilities... Because if a man like Lucas Scott—bloodthirsty and coldhearted—lost everything, if he cared about nothing and no one, what was to stop him from destroying the world?

4

COLD-BLOODED KILLER

In the days after I met Lucas Scott, Devon detected my disquiet. "What's *wrong*?" he asked at least five times.

"I just miss Tekqua," I finally responded, and he didn't ask again after that.

Adam, however, continued to eye me with interest. "Something bothering you, Soph?"

I smiled in that sarcastic way that always got him laughing. "Just the usual death and destruction."

He grinned. "Come to the meetup tonight."

Oh, jeez.

Adam's whole schtick revolved around camaraderie. Playing the class clown lured in friends like lemmings to a cliff, despite that he was also a formidable soldier. Without fail, he believed that togetherness and acceptance were what made us different from the NAO, and he fostered those ideals through fellowship.

What's the point of dying if you don't like the people you're doing it for? he'd say.

I used to love his weekly meetups, but it'd been many months since I'd attended. It was fun, once upon a time. When fun still existed.

"Eh. Thanks, Adam, but I'd rather not." I slipped away before he could pursue it further.

I headed back toward the sleeping wing, planning to hide in my room, but froze as my gaze caught the light reflected on the metal sheet covering the window. Already surrounded by thick, forested land, the museum we called headquarters had natural protections. With the metal shrouding each window and the underground corridors we used to come and go, the building had every appearance of abandonment. If the Hunters knew where we were, they certainly never hinted at it.

These metal sheets, though...

I stepped closer, my finger trailing over the rivets.

After leaving that dusty church behind, my parents and I arrive at headquarters to a flurry of activity. Theo is whisked away on official business as soon as we enter the building, and a woman named Tekqua escorts us to our quarters. She has dark skin and darker hair pulled into two Dutch braids. Her lashes are long and natural, and her smile sets me instantly at ease. After she shows us to our room, she promptly returns to her work riveting metal sheets to the windows.

Once my parents are settled, I seek her out.

"Hey!" she says when she notices my interest.

"Can I help?" I ask, pointing at the pile of metal sheets.

"Sure, girl! Get that drill there."

She points at a power tool that doesn't want to fit in my hand. I hold it at an awkward angle, and she chuckles at my difficulty. "They're made for man hands."

I nod to the others working on the windows. "Where did the metal come from?"

"We stole them from Lowe's."

I fake a gasp. "Stolen, you say? I am scandalized."

Her laugh is hearty. "Come on. I'll show you how to do it."

With the first few, I'm slow and clumsy, but I swiftly get the hang of it. I help her close off multiple windows before we move to the museum café, where the glass panes rise from floor to ceiling, at least twenty feet high. Several others brainstorm a solution for these while the two of us chat.

She's the easiest person I've ever talked to.

"I wound up here by luck," she says. "After the Capitol Hill Massacre, I wasn't sure where to go, but I'd heard some whispers that people were gathering nearby, and here I am."

"How long have you been here?" I ask.

"Few weeks. We went on a few raids trying to get supplies, but the Hunters are everywhere. It's like they can't wait to claim their first kill."

I shudder.

"Yeah," she says, clocking that reaction. "Unified News says they have it well in hand, but—"

"What a bunch of liars," I say.

"I know." She picks up a rivet. "We'll have more intel once we get organized. Now that General Harrison's here, things will start moving. I heard they're planning an assembly tonight."

I almost chuckle at Theo's new title. "I guess we'll learn more tonight then."

She grins. "I can't wait..."

I returned to myself with a start, my finger still brushing one of the rivets, now rusty with the passage of time. A sharp ache lanced through my chest, but I shrugged off the tears that wanted to spill. Instead, I fled to my room to hide.

Once I was safely ensconced inside, I pressed my fist to my mouth to keep from screaming in frustration at my fraying emotions. Every nerve was stretched so tight that they threatened to snap entirely. What was I even doing with my life, agreeing to be Lucas

Scott's contact? Was my sanity worth this? Could one spy really change the course of this war? Could I truly save Tekqua?

The longing for her friendly face ripped through my thoughts. I *had* to save her, but where to look? Where to start?

According to the deceptive propaganda, the NAO's army continued to advance into Canada for the Security Restoration Campaign, and their godforsaken NSF had the domestic conflicts well in hand. In reality, most of the West was still embroiled in hostilities. Some parts of the country existed in normalcy, yes, but the Hunters hadn't made as much headway against the Defiance as they touted.

Their true deception, however, was how they dealt with prisoners.

The *Articles of the Defiance*—our constitution of sorts—stipulated humane and fair treatment of our POWs. The NAO held itself to no such standards. They claimed that captured Defiants were *reassimilated*, but in actuality, the NAO labeled them traitors to the Commander. Unable to deport those they no longer considered citizens, the NAO had built camps to detain us. The Stability bloc had been a migrant detention facility, but they filled it instead with *traitors* sent to starve and work off their crimes like cattle. They labored in arms warehouses, building weapons and ammunition for the NAO's war efforts. Worse, the younger women were imprisoned in the House of the Rising Sun, a genteel honorific for the correctional houses the NAO declared would reinstate a traditional family values system.

Slave brothels, Theo called them.

I hated the idea of it, but I assumed Tekqua had been sent to the House. She was in a brothel. I was certain of it.

The idea made me sick. Escapees from both the House and the Stability bloc seemed to have transformed into wraiths—starved, unsmiling, their mental health in tatters—and I didn't want that for Tekqua. But prisoners unfit for either of these places were put to death, and the thought of her death was like fingers of ice gripping my throat.

Still, I knew what she would have chosen.

Death before slavery.

I had to get her back.

If Lucas's information was to be believed, the Hunters planned to raid one of our larger safe houses—an apartment building off Yorktown Avenue packed full of refugees awaiting transport to Canada. The Hunters' primary goal was neutralization of the opposition, but they also kept us from smuggling people out of the country. If the Hunters infiltrated that building, the people inside would face terrible fates.

Theo's best squads spent days relocating the families inside that building and setting traps for the Hunters. On the night of the raid, I was called for field medic duty along with a handful of others, including my shift-mate, Liliana.

She and I weren't the best of friends, but we served all our medic shifts together. She was a quiet, competent woman with black hair she always pinned in a topknot. It was enviable, really, how easily her hair submitted to her orders. Mine had no such inclinations. It wanted to be wild and free, much like the Defiance.

With our medic bags slung over our shoulders and our red cross bands tied tight around our arms, we set out under a blanket of stars for the building Lucas Scott claimed would be overrun by Hunters in just a few hours. Fuel had been practically nonexistent for the past couple of years, so we traveled on electric ATVs over time-roughened streets to the square that had once housed trendy shops and upscale restaurants.

Inside the apartments, soldiers lay in wait. A sniper lurked in the building across the street—not that he had many rounds to shoot. In the beginning, gunfire had been the soundtrack of our lives, but as time wore on and materials grew scarce, so did ammunition.

Then came the Comprehensive National Firearms Regulation

Directive. It was established last year, when countrywide civil protests against the NAO had grown especially violent and deadly. The NAO peddled the *radical* idea that escalating gun violence was a threat to national security and domestic tranquility. They instituted a moratorium on the possession, distribution, and use of firearms and explosives.

The Gunlock Law, they called it.

"Effective immediately," Brandon Sikes from Unified News had read on air, *"the right to possess, carry, transport or discharge firearms or other explosive weaponry is hereby limited to active-duty personnel of the Unified States Armed Forces. Unauthorized possession or use of firearms shall be considered an act of domestic terrorism and constitute a capital felony offense, subject to life imprisonment or death."*

Clips had followed of calm citizens handing over their weapons with smiles. Tranquil neighborhoods with children playing scrolled over the screen. The golden sunlight streaming overhead bestowed a sense of peace.

If only...

What really happened in the weeks following that edict was not peaceful. The right to bear arms wasn't a catchphrase or a passing fancy to the people of the US. It was a governing principle. A staple with which they were raised. A fundamental right.

Revoking it did not go well for Haynes.

Hunters marched into private homes on raids, and civilians revolted. Guns were pried from cold, dead hands as the citizens clung to one of the founding tenets of our country. It all made obtaining weapons infinitely harder, and for the Defiance, killing became a contact sport. We still made our own bullets and bombs, we pillaged NAO supplies when we could, but we'd learned to rely on blades and crossbows, and our soldiers tonight were as prepared as they could be.

We set up our medical space in the abandoned kitchen of a nearby restaurant. The metal tables would serve as beds, and I cleared the delivery door of obstacles. Once ready, all four of us spied through the small windows toward the apartment building, though we could see nothing in the moonless dark.

"I wonder where they got the information for this," said Michael, one of our oldest medics. He'd been an ICU nurse before the war, and a damned good one, if you asked him.

"Me too," said Shari, who fell into the medic game due to a desire to help and a lack of skill at anything else. "This is a large-scale operation they've got here."

I kept my mouth shut tight, afraid they'd see through any lies I tried to tell.

Liliana set her hand on the glass, her gaze heavy. "I always hate this part."

I did too. The waiting before a mission ate away at my sanity. Once I was in the thick of it, I was too busy for anxiety, but standing there knowing that people were about to die and nothing I did could stop it grated on my soul. Sometimes, I felt my humanity had whittled to nothing, but at times like this, I remembered I still possessed a heart.

The four of us settled into a tense silence broken several minutes later by a shout in the distance. The air grew taut.

Two gunshots cracked like bones breaking. Boots pounded on concrete. Outside the relative safety of our makeshift medical space, shouts and the clangs of metal shredded our nerves. We tried to see through the dark, but the chaos was faceless. The succinct voices disappeared as the fight vanished inside the apartment building. From there, we winced at the occasional gunshot and muffled yell.

Glass shattered. A shrill scream. A sickening thud.

"Christ," Michael muttered. "Hope that wasn't ours."

After belabored minutes, the first soldier burst into our medical unit through the swinging delivery door. A deep gash in his leg spat blood all over the floor.

"Over here!" Shari helped him onto the metal table. I tied a tourniquet around his thigh before he had a second to cry out. With a quick snip of the scissors, his pant leg was gone. I surveyed the injury in his mid-thigh, now only trickling blood.

Combat gauze was a scarcity, but this wound required it. I ripped open a packet and stuffed it into the gash, ignoring the agonized scream he restrained with sheer willpower. Liliana gave him a leather to bite. Breathing hard, he fell back onto the table when I finished.

The door slammed open, and two more soldiers stumbled inside. As the gap swung shut, a sharp, "Fall back!" echoed through the night.

Which side was retreating?

One soldier had the arm of another around her neck. I took the other arm, and we helped him to a second table.

The man's body convulsed with shivers.

"Where's he injured?" I asked, patting his body.

"There!" The soldier pointed to the man's chest.

I lifted his shirt to find a bullet hole. Fourth intercostal space. Mid-chest. Nodding, I slid his shirt back down.

"Make him comfortable," I told her.

He wouldn't make it.

Again, the door opened and more soldiers poured through, some with serious injuries and others with none at all.

"They're running," one told us. "Weren't expecting us. We slaughtered 'em."

Yeah. They kind of slaughtered us, too, I thought as Shari and I worked on pulling shrapnel from the neck of his comrade-in-arms.

The door swung again. "Help!" a soldier yelled. "He needs a medic!"

I left my patient in the care of Shari and joined Liliana to follow the soldier into the night. We ran toward the apartment building. My gaze darted left and right, searching for movement.

"Don't worry. They're all gone," the soldier said.

Sure. Trust but verify.

Near the back of the building, where an alleyway formed a

divider between the apartment complex and a strip of stores, one of our soldiers lay writhing on the concrete, the entire left side of his body macerated.

"It was a grenade," his friend said, choking over the words. "Please help him."

I squared my shoulders. "Right. Help me get him up."

Liliana rushed to the man's side, as did his friend. The soldier groaned, the guttural, exhausted sound of a man too tired for agony.

A sharp pop echoed through the alley. The man went limp, a new hole in his head.

I spun and froze at the sight before me. Four Hunters stood at the mouth of the alley.

My heart leapt straight into my throat, suffocating me.

Liliana and the soldier dropped the dead man. While she backed away, he went for his weapons.

"Come peacefully and we'll let you live," said one Hunter, his face a pale smudge in the dark.

No.

Death before slavery.

I would die before I succumbed to what they called *living*.

The Hunters drew closer, and my switchblade slid easily from its permanent resting place in my bra. My heartbeat expanded to my throat, my stomach, my fingertips, but I was ready, and I wouldn't hesitate. Killing had long ago become an act of survival, and with the Brotherhood Cross stitched into their combat clothes, I found it difficult to find reasons they should live.

"Ah, a medic," another said, eyeing my red cross armband. "We could use you. Come with us, and we'll find a nice House for you."

The others snickered. Beside me, the soldier who'd dragged me to this alley to die spat at their feet.

"No?" the Hunter said. "Alright, then."

They advanced, and my soldier threw himself in front of me. The fight exploded in a flurry of arms and legs. He was a good fighter. His knife buried in the throat of a Hunter, and he spun for another. I leapt at a third with my switchblade, but he dodged to the left. In my periphery, Liliana had joined the fight with her own blade.

I swiped my blade and missed. The Hunter grabbed my wrist and whipped a blow to my chin. Stars danced in my eyes as he threw me to the ground.

Pain lanced through my elbow and throbbed in my jaw. My knife clattered away. A foot landed a hard kick in my stomach, knocking the air from my lungs.

My chest spasmed, and I lay helpless, wheezing, as my soldier snapped the neck of another Hunter, then choked when a Bowie knife sliced deep into his abdomen. He clutched the wound and dropped to his knees.

In the dark, his blood was blacker than the night, and by the sheer amount of it, I knew they'd nicked something vital. He fell onto his stomach and didn't get back up.

I tried to stand, but the Hunter's boot pressed into my spine, and I was pinned to the ground like an insect. Still, I reached for my blade, lying a yard away.

I needed that weapon.

With it, I had options—continue fighting, bury it in my own stomach, jam it in the eye of this bastard on top of me. Without it, this was over.

I'd be theirs.

Liliana gasped, and I twisted enough to see her fall, a knife jutting from her side.

Despite everything, my heart clenched. "Liliana," I wheezed through staccato breaths. "Hold on."

But for what? Why should she hold on? We were both fucked.

Reaching again for my blade, I sensed a stiffening of the soldier above me. He turned toward the mouth of the alley.

"Colonel," said one of his comrades. "Found some before they could escape."

Any hope left in me withered at that one word.

Colonel.

If a colonel had arrived, then I had no chance. The best I could hope for was death.

My hand fell to the pavement. The blade was too far. This was over.

Trapped as I was, I could hardly make out the dark figure as he approached with even steps, silent as a panther. He was dressed the same as the rest of the Hunters—in a black combat uniform—but he wore no helmet, and the telltale scarlet insignia of a Blood Colonel shone bright on his shoulder, even in the darkness.

Lucas Scott peered down at me, expressionless, and my body went boneless. It hadn't occurred to me that he might actually show at a mission he'd purposely sabotaged. A long moment passed in which we stared at each other, him utterly dispassionate, and me speculating whether he'd let them kill or imprison me. It wasn't like I was important to him, and he'd maintain his cover by leaving my fate in his soldiers' hands. With a simple missive, he'd have a replacement Defiance contact and would be rid of me for good.

Fuck.

He was going to let them have me, wasn't he?

As I reached this conclusion, anger stirred like hot coals in my chest. My gaze turned lethal, and I hoped he could see the hatred within it. *Fine. Let them kill me, you bastard.*

He sighed out a testy breath, almost as if this whole situation was a mere nuisance, some unfortunate clerical task that had been dropped into his lap.

The next moments happened in a blur. He moved like a snake, whipping a throwing knife through the air toward the man holding me down.

The other Hunter gasped when Lucas Scott's blade disappeared into his abdomen and scored a straight line from left to right. He fell, crying out, trying to hold his organs inside his body.

On my back, the man's foot loosened. He choked and sank to his knees, ripping the knife from his throat.

A mistake.

Blood poured in a waterfall down his neck. The light fled his eyes, and he toppled to the side.

I blinked at the carnage all around me, then at Lucas Scott, who wiped the blood from his knife as one would scrape a paintbrush to remove the excess paint—impassive and calm.

A gasp drew my attention to Liliana, still alive. I crawled to her, pain biting into my injured elbow all the way to my shoulder. The weapon in her side was buried deep, right into her liver. If I left it there, the bleed would be slower. I could get her to headquarters...

"You're going to be okay," I said to her, my words wobbly. My shaking hand grasped hers. A weak grip squeezed back.

Behind me, Lucas Scott swiped something from the ground. His throwing knife, I saw, as he cleaned that too, then holstered it.

"So—Soph—" Liliana rasped, and even in the dark, her pallor was apparent.

The dark presence behind me prowled closer. He stood only inches away. "Get up," he said, low and sharp.

I ignored him. My grip on Liliana's hand tightened while hers diminished.

His razor voice cut through the darkness. *"Get up."*

"I'm—I'm not leaving her." My breath hitched when Liliana's mouth tilted up at one corner. The air around me grew tense with the anger simmering from the man at my back, but I refused to let go.

Muttering a curse, Lucas Scott bent, and in one swift move, he unsheathed the blade from Liliana's body. I cried out a protest, but it was too late. Blood poured from the wound—far too much of it.

"How could—how could you do that?" I took Liliana's face in my hands. "You're going to be okay. I'll get you back—"

I was jerked upright by my arm, and I hissed at the zing through my elbow. "Stop!"

He spun me to face him. "Don't be an idiot. You're a medic. You know a fatal wound when you see one. I just did her a favor."

He was right. I *knew* he was right, but my conscience hadn't quite accepted the idea of brutal mercy. After all these years, I still couldn't bear the thought of euthanasia. Perhaps I clung to hope like a child grips a favored toy—no matter how battered or mutilated, they still sought comfort in its presence.

Liliana would have died regardless of my help, but I was searching for a miracle, like a moron, and that realization infuriated me. "You—you—"

"Why are you here?" he hissed, dragging me deeper into the alley, deeper into the dark. "Are you not a vitally important resource for the Defiance now? Why do they have you on the streets like a common foot soldier? You're clearly not experienced in combat."

Despite everything, heat suffused my cheeks, and the flush of blood only made my face throb harder. *Experience and competency don't always go hand in hand*, I wanted to tell him. I'd had enough *experience* to last me a lifetime. "I'm a field medic," I said. "We're assigned on a rotating basis."

He swore, but then his body went rigid as he shot a cutting look toward the mouth of the alley. Only then did I become aware of the sound.

Footsteps.

The previous flush of blood in my cheeks drained away. "Who is it?" I whispered.

He yanked me, his hand a manacle around my upper arm as I struggled to keep up with his near-silent steps. A metal staircase connected to a second-story doorway, with a rainbow stack of crates beneath it. He manhandled me into the tiny space between the crates and a dumpster, and my back hit the brick wall.

His palm covered my mouth, and he stepped close. Too close. So close that my hands rose instinctively to push him away. Except I didn't.

I paused.

My gaze lifted to his face, twisted in fury. A warning flickered in his eyes.

Don't make a sound.

He… He was protecting me.

My hands dropped back to my sides. I tried to even my breath, but my body was inexplicably starving for oxygen, and I sucked in air through my nose like I'd never get to do it again.

He should have smelled of gunpowder and blood. Of metal and sweat. Instead, Lucas Scott's scent reminded me of incense—something heady and warm and so out of place that my heart rate slowed from the intrusive confusion.

Incense?

Several sets of boots trotted down the alley, jolting me back to myself. My body was compressed so tightly against Lucas's that anyone passing by wouldn't see me at a glance.

"Look at this, Powell," a voice bounced against the bricks.

"Christ," said another. "Blood bath. I'll get the cleanup team. Fucking Defiants."

"Yeah, you go on," the first man said, a little closer now. "Alley looks clear now. Colonel said to make sure the building's empty."

The solid thunk of a foot kicking in a door made me jump, and Lucas's hand pressed tighter against my mouth, his chest harder against my own. After a few more seconds, the parade of boots entered the building and the heavy door slammed shut.

The alleyway plunged into silence.

Lucas's hand freed my mouth by degrees, almost as if he thought I might scream the moment I had the chance. No way. I might have been a terrible combat soldier, but I wasn't stupid.

Lucas Scott was a cold-blooded killer. His attacks weren't survivable. In his wake, he left no prisoners. But he was also the only thing standing between me and capture. He'd committed fratricidal treason by eliminating his own men to keep me safe. I'd have to dwell on the *whys* of that some other time because in that moment, I recognized him for what he was: my deliverer.

I would not scream. If he could get me out of this alley alive, I'd do anything he asked. Awaiting instruction, I gazed into his eyes, obscured by the darkness except for a tiny glimmer that proved he was indeed human.

"Run," he said. "Take Yorktown north. Run and don't stop."

I nodded, frantic. He withdrew, and I pushed off the brick wall. Later, everything would hurt—my arm, my face, my soul—but right then, the adrenaline held it all at bay. It gave me the energy, the drive, to escape.

Eager to put his instructions to use, I almost didn't hear the deceptive softness of his voice as he spoke my name.

The look on his face gave me pause. It was familiar somehow, that awful mix of rage, desperation and despondency. It reminded me of how withdrawn I'd been of late, how cold this life had become.

"This doesn't happen again," he said. "Tell them to do better. The agreement was *one* contact. If they waste you, they lose me. That is non-negotiable."

Six interminable heartbeats passed.

If they waste you, they lose me.

Why? What value was I to him? If I died, and a new contact was sent, his secret would still be contained.

But I didn't question it. If Lucas Scott wanted to value my life, who was I to argue?

"*Run,*" he said once more.

So I ran.

5

HEARTLESS

 The day you stop feeling remorse over taking life is the day you no longer have a heart.

— CHRISTOPHER REEVES, THE FATHER OF SOPHIA
REEVES

Tires shriek as the Humvees skid to a stop. Hunters pour from their innards, dressed in black fatigues, like a swarm of spiders.

"You!" one shouts. "Stop!"

Fear takes me in a vise grip. My thoughts scatter like the broken shards of an icicle as it crashes to the ground. We'd only been escorting these people to a safer area! We weren't doing anything wrong.

"Take the kids!" yells my squad mate, Rodrigo.

"You, there!" the Hunter says again. "On your knees!"

Tekqua and I usher the children toward another squad mate, Daniela.

"Go!" Tekqua hisses to her.

Nodding, Daniela lifts the smallest child and takes off at a run, urging the kids and their mothers to follow.

"Get behind us," a sergeant commands as his combat squad forms a barricade in front of us.

"What do we do?" I whisper.

"If we run, they'll chase," Rodrigo says.

"If we don't run, we're theirs," I reply. My hand brushes the gun holstered at my hip, the cold metal as foreign and unpleasant as the hate in those Hunters' eyes.

Their leader bears down on us, face hidden by his combat helmet. "On your knees, I said!"

My heartbeat clogs my throat.

"On my mark, you run," says our sergeant. "Zigzag through the neighborhood. Force them to split up."

"Lower your weapons and get on your knees!" the Hunter shouts.

A shot blasts through the sky.

I choke on a startled gasp. Was that a gun? Was it ours or theirs? Is anyone dead?

My ears ring.

"Now!" Sergeant yells. "Run!"

Tekqua grabs my wrist and yanks. I trip in my effort to keep up. The others fan out, but Tekqua and I stay together.

More gunshots pop behind me. Beside my head, a burst of disturbed air has me ducking. "Shit! Did you see that?" Just a few inches to the left...

"Come on," Tekqua says, dragging me into the neighborhood.

The large front yards in this older area of town—now abandoned to the war—bloom with stately oaks and budding poplars, fantastic for hiding. Parked cars and hedges provide cover as we dart for safety.

Footsteps pound behind us, and a smattering of gunfire rents the once placid air.

Six houses down, Tekqua's hand curls around the handle of an SUV. It speaks to the previous wealth of this area that the owner hadn't bothered to lock it. The door wedges open, providing us cover so I can catch my breath.

Shouts of Go right! *and* Behind you! *play a harmony to the gunfire.*

Firearm in hand, Tekqua creeps into the SUV's backseat, her gaze on a pair of Hunters jogging our way. She raises her pistol.

If it had been me, I would have missed.

Tekqua's bullet lodges in one man's neck. The Hunter's partner bellows, his head whipping toward us. Arm raised, his bullets dart toward us like lightning. The windows of the SUV shatter, little bits of Plexiglass pelting me and catching in my hair.

Tekqua scrambles out of the car and grabs my elbow.

"Come on! Keep your gun up."

I yank it from its holster, trying to recall how to hold it, how to fire, but my brain can't remember—probably since the breath in my lungs is composed singularly of fear instead of oxygen.

I follow Tekqua like a lifeline.

Ducking low, we dart through grass and flowerbeds, weaving between trees and picket fences.

"Get out here!" the Hunter behind us screams.

Endless streams of bullets chink against the metal of cars or burrow into wood as we run. How many guns does he have? He has to run out of ammo eventually. We've been set upon by a predator, and this guy isn't stopping until we're dead.

"What do we do?" I whisper as we pause behind a dried-up cement fountain.

She looks up the street. It curves to the south. "We have to lose him."

"I don't think we can outrun him."

We edge our way to the next driveway and duck behind a diesel truck. A bullet ricochets off its roof.

Tekqua peeks around the truck bed.

"There she is!" the man calls, and she pulls back quickly.

"Fuck! There's two of them now."

I sneak to the other end of the truck and inch my way toward the front bumper. A Hunter stands alone beside a tree, catcalling Tekqua.

With a thunderous boom, a hole tears through the Hunter's chest from behind. He slumps to the ground, wheezing and clutching at the wound.

Who the hell did that?

A thump draws my attention back to Tekqua.

She's pinned to the truck by another Hunter, a gun pressed to her temple.

"You dare kill my man, bitch?"

All thoughts flee my brain, and I react on instinct alone. I stand from my crouched position, raising my pistol.

Click. Click. Boom.

The Hunter sinks to the ground, lifeless.

And something wrenches hard inside my chest.

I just killed a man. I've never killed anyone before.

Shaking, Tekqua stares down at the dead man. "Holy shit."

Two of our men run past. "Come on!" one shouts. "They're backing off now. We've got to get out of here."

Tekqua takes my hand once more, and we sprint the half mile to the safe house. She drags me to the downstairs bathroom, where I collapse onto the edge of the tub.

She leans over the sink. "Shit just got real."

I stare ahead, seeing only that man's profile in my mind's eye. "I killed him."

"You saved my life."

I glare at my hands. Murderer's hands.

Tekqua bends over to take a deep breath, dropping her forehead to the sink's edge. "We're soldiers now."

Yeah. Soldiers on the front line, afraid and unprepared, hoping those taking aim at us would miss.

We allow ourselves five minutes of panic time before rejoining the others to help organize the families. Mahmoud's group has already arrived with their charges, and they're dividing up rooms in this large house. Rodrigo is last to arrive, speckles of blood marring his face like some morbid Jackson Pollock painting.

"We lost three men," is all he says before disappearing into the bathroom.

A woman from one of the houses we'd vacated rushes forward, a frantic gleam in her eye. "Jeremy? Did Jeremy make it back?"

One of the combat soldiers takes her aside.

In seconds, her wail fills the home.

It's like the fine edge of glass, that howl—so sharp I don't realize I'm bleeding until much, much later. Her agony oozes into my soul and haunts my thoughts. I'm not even sure how I make it back to headquarters, but somehow, I'm sitting on my bed, Dad perched beside me.

I won't look at him.

I can't look at him.

I killed someone.

"How was your first mission?" he asks.

I shrug. "How was yours?"

"Successful," he says. Nothing further.

I stay quiet for a time, contemplating that.

He strokes my hair. "Is there anything you'd like to talk about?"

"No," I say.

"Alright. Then just listen."

I shift on the bed so I can see his face.

"Sometimes we reach a point in our lives where we're faced with a choice between two terrible options. Neither choice is good. Today, you chose between taking a life or letting a life be taken. When you make a choice like that, it changes you, Sophia."

I say nothing. Tears swell in my throat.

"Remorse is a symptom of a healthy mind," he says.

"It feels awful," I choke out, unable to hold back the sobs.

"Yes, but it's proof that you understand your decisions are not just black or white. There is subtext and nuance in every choice we make. When you decided to kill that man, you saved an innocent life."

"Or maybe he could have gone on to solve world hunger." My tears soak the pillow beneath me, but he continues to stroke my hair, the same way he had when I was still little, and my tears spilled over innocuous things like bad grades or mean girls.

"Exactly," he says. "It's healthy to have remorse. It keeps you human. The day you stop feeling remorse over taking life is the day you no longer have a heart."

I woke from the dream gently, indulging in the deep hum of my father's voice.

The memory of his words, however, was what stuck in my thoughts like a piece of gristle between my teeth.

The pitiless indifference in Lucas Scott's countenance as he killed his own men stole over my senses. I'd suffered such guilt over killing someone to save Tekqua's life, but Lucas had been remorseless. Apathetic. Their lives mattered so little to him, he couldn't even be bothered to crease his brow.

The memory made me shiver, and I curled into myself, refusing to open my eyes. He'd killed, yes, but he'd also saved me, and I wasn't sure how to feel about it or what it meant. Still, I'd have to meet him again and again, fully aware of what he was.

Because if my father was to be believed, Lucas's detachment proved he wasn't just cold-blooded.

He was heartless.

6

NOT DEAD

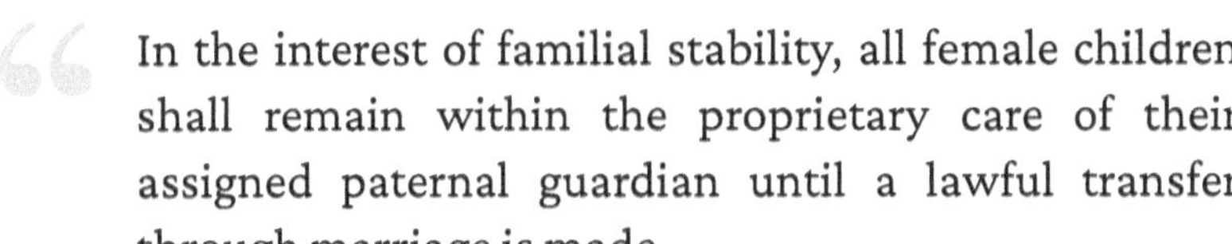

In the interest of familial stability, all female children shall remain within the proprietary care of their assigned paternal guardian until a lawful transfer through marriage is made.

— OWNERSHIP OF FEMALE OFFSPRING, N.A.O.C.

42 § 8539

After Theo debriefed me regarding my near capture at the Yorktown safe house the next morning, we stewed in a prolonged silence in his office. I picked at my cuticles while he stared frozen at his clasped hands on his desk, gripping so tight his knuckles had blanched.

"Do you think he meant it?" I asked after a time. "You know, *if they waste you, they lose me.*"

Theo's dark eyes lifted. "I have no reason to believe he's lying."

I swallowed. "Right. I guess it just doesn't make sense."

"Do you feel as if I'm *wasting* you, Sophia?" he asked, his voice a mixture of military hardness and perverse curiosity.

You can't waste something that's useless, I almost replied.

"Your father wouldn't have wanted this for you," he said, quieter now, like the words hurt him to say.

My mind cast back to last fall when I sat in this very chair, having a very different conversation with Theo.

"It's...your father," Theo says, his expression anguished, his words hesitant.

Pain lances through my chest, sharp as a blade of diamond. The rest of my body goes numb.

Bang!

My chair hits the floor as I stand. "He promised he'd come back," I say.

"I know, Sophia—"

"HE PROMISED HE'D COME BACK!"

Theo's eyes grow suspiciously bright.

"You're wrong," I say and attack his desk, swiping up that abused sheet of paper lying before him, the one he'd been looking at when he hinted my father is dead.

He doesn't stop me, so I blink down at the words, confused why I can't read them, why everything is blurry.

Tears fall on the paper.

I sink down, down, down. My knees hit the floor first, then my hands, and then I crumple to my side, clutching the paper I can't read through my tears, the letter that apparently confirms my father's death.

"It's a mistake," I whisper. "This isn't real. You're lying."

Theo rises from his chair to crouch beside me. "I'm going to bring your mother back, okay? As soon as I can."

I try to focus on his blurry face, but instead I'm seeing my father's smiling one, feeling his tight hugs. "Mom? She's still alive?"

He swallows. "Yes, she's alive and well."

"H-how did he die?"

"I don't know."

Is that true? Would he lie to spare my sanity? Would I be able to handle it if my father was tortured to death?

I roll onto my back, and the fractured chandelier light dances in my vision, rainbows sparking in the crystals.

My heart is mutilated. Am I even human anymore?

"What can I do?" Theo asks.

Nothing. He can do nothing.

I wish I'd never met Theodore Harrison.

When I don't speak, he continues, "I'm taking you out of the field, Sophia."

Too numb to respond, I blink at the chandelier.

"Your squad will be dissolved, with the remaining members moved to another. I promised your father I'd keep you safe, and you're too reckless for fieldwork. I will not let him down."

"What will you do with me instead?"

He pauses to lower himself to the floor beside me. "You wanted to go to med school, didn't you?"

I almost laugh at the absurdity of that, my silly desires from the life before. I've killed more people than I will ever save.

"We can train you in the hospital wing. You can be a medic."

I say nothing.

His voice gentles. "You can save lives instead of..."

"No," I said to Theo now, shaking myself of the memory. "You're not wasting me."

He scrutinized me, his mouth tight with displeasure. "I wish you hadn't agreed to this assignment."

"Williams clearly wanted me to do it."

"Williams is desperate."

I shrugged. "Aren't we all?"

Somehow, his posture grew more rigid. "There are some things that should not be sacrificed."

I smiled. Or I thought I smiled. Maybe I frowned. Or laughed. "Like me?"

A silence stretched before he said, "Yes."

"I am no one," I said. "And you know that, or you wouldn't have even considered asking me."

"She didn't give me a choice," he said, and I detected the faintest hint of defeat wafting from his very essence. He was so different now from what he'd been at the beginning. His impassioned words back then had given me hope.

"The Defiance is in its infancy," he'd said, pacing the stage of the museum's amphitheater, hundreds of eyes locked on him. "But that doesn't make us weak. We were not born to kneel. You are here today, which means you remember a time when unity did not mean uniformity, when diversity did not divide us. The time has come to dissolve ties to the NAO and the hate they represent, because we still hold these truths to be self-evident, that all men are created equal. You are entitled to life, liberty, and the pursuit of happiness. You are standing when it would be easier to fall, fighting when it would be safer to stay silent. You are our future. You will fight and sacrifice for what is right, what is just, what is *yours*."

My life had been nothing but fight and sacrifice since the moment those words left his mouth. He'd been so passionate, and I believed him when he said this was a fight worth dying for. But watching people die for a cause was easy. Keeping them alive to fight for it was harder. Theo's zeal had faded long ago, sacrificed to the gods of war alongside his optimism, his morals, and me.

Finally, the silence between us reached a breaking point.

"Can I go?" I asked. He dipped his chin, and I excused myself in a hurry.

That night, sleep played hide-and-seek with me. As soon as my mind drifted, my subconscious would throw out the image of Lucas Scott, swathed in Hunter black so dark he was like a void of nothing, his catlike steps carrying him closer to me in that gritty alleyway. Half of me bathed in terror at that image. The other half sighed in relief.

I tossed to my other side, punching my pillow in hopes of comfort, trying not to think of the shrinking amount of time before I saw him again.

He'd killed people for me.

What was I supposed to do with that? How much risk had he undertaken, leaving his own soldiers dead in the street? What if he was caught, and I showed up at the Evanston house on Thursday only to find it empty?

I flopped onto my back and threw my arms over my face.

I didn't want to return to his house, despite that he'd saved my life. The idea of facing him now, knowing the last time he saw me I was fleeing into the night at his command, made my body break into a cold sweat. I was alive thanks only to the mercy of a heartless killer. Pondering why made my head hurt, and I writhed in the misery of curiosity and sleeplessness.

They hurt my sister.

Why was it so difficult for me to believe his motivation? If I had a sister, wouldn't I be angry she'd been hurt? But would I betray the Defiance for a slight against her? Would I abandon my entire belief system for it?

No, there had to be another reason, and I would likely never learn it.

Finally, I drifted to sleep.

As Thursday drew closer, dread sank dirty claws into me. I assumed he'd lead us to the slaughter, and I'd never have to see him again, but instead, he'd saved hundreds of lives.

Including mine.

It should have made me happy, but it left no recourse to refuse my assignment, knowing the potential advantage he'd provide. What if he helped me find Tekqua? No justification existed to renege on our agreement, and I became a twisted, muddled wreck as Thursday arrived.

What did he want from us? From me? Why wouldn't he just tell me?

Was it worse to *wonder* when he'd cash in, or for it to actually happen?

Hands shaking, I walked the mile to his meeting point, glancing over my shoulder every minute to find nothing but budding maple trees on abandoned neighborhood streets. When I reached the cement stairs to the front porch, I dragged my feet. The door wasn't open, so I knocked.

No answer.

I turned the knob.

Locked.

Um…

Uncertain what to do, I tried the knob again. Funny enough, *still* locked.

Maybe I'd been right about his getting caught. Maybe the NAO had uncovered his duplicity and put him to death. Perhaps I'd never have to see him again. I stared at the locked door, calculating how long I needed to wait before I could consider him a no-show.

Was it utter villainy to hope another person was dead?

As I dithered, an icy presence slinked over my consciousness and hovered at my back. Fear wrapped around me like hands sliding over my waist, pulling me backward, leaning down to whisper in my ear.

"Do you routinely wait at locked doors out in the open where anyone could see you?"

I froze at his voice, as smooth and dark as it had been the night he'd saved me.

"I don't make a habit of it, no," I said through thickened vocal cords and the desire to vomit.

"So this display of idiocy is special for me then?"

I scowled at the door. My gaze dropped to the brass knob as his long-fingered hand entered my field of vision to insert the key into the lock. With a twist of his wrist, the door swung open. Teeth gritted, I stepped into the dark interior.

Once the door was shut, I spun to face him. He crossed the room to the coffee table and lit the single candle with a lighter he'd left lying beside it. "You have the reflexes of a sloth," he said, all testy like this fact profoundly annoyed him. "You didn't even hear me."

I crossed my arms. "In my defense, you make no noise when you walk. I think you might be a ghost."

He rolled his eyes. "You don't flaunt yourself out in the open, looking like you do, waiting for someone to grab you."

My attention snapped to his face. "Looking like I do?"

"You're an attractive woman in the tightest pants I've ever seen. Do you have any idea what they'd do if they caught you?"

I glanced at my leggings and loose T-shirt—not remotely risqué—and tried to drive away the memory of Daniela's death that wanted to break the surface. "I have a fair idea."

He threw the lighter onto the table. "Wear a fucking hoodie."

If my glare could scorch the earth, it would have. *"Excuse me?"*

"You can't be this stupid."

Uh, this motherfucker said that to my face?

"Wow, look at that glare," he said with a humorless smirk. "Did I hurt your precious feelings?"

"Shut up—"

"You have to know how Hunters are by now. If you're picked up, you'll be raped before they bring you in. Possibly by multiple men. Does that sound appealing to you? Then they'll bring you to me to determine what to do with you. Do you think you could realistically pretend we've never met? And if you don't somehow give us both away as spies, then I'll have to decide whether you're imprisoned or you die. So tell me, Sophia. Is your current outfit worth it?"

My glare deepened. *"You're* the one who sentences the prisoners?"

"Yes."

This man had decided Tekqua's fate. Barbed claws in my stomach sliced deep as the overwhelming urge to ask him rose. I swallowed the words before they fell from my mouth. He wouldn't remember her—one face in hundreds he'd sent to a cruel fate without any sort of trial or due process. But I *would* ask him. Eventually. One way or another, I'd uncover what happened to her.

"You're a bastard."

His face was all stone and fury. "Wear. A. Fucking. Hoodie."

"What the hell is a hoodie going to do?" I yelled.

"Oh, I don't know. Hide your breasts and face and long, curly hair?"

My voice dropped low, turned deadly. "I shouldn't have to hide that I'm a woman."

Some of the tension eased from his limbs. "No. You shouldn't. But you have to protect yourself in this world where your gender makes you unsafe. Do you even have a weapon on you?"

Of course I did. I lived in this violent place the same as he did. No one went outside without a weapon. I extracted the small switchblade from my bra and showed it to him.

He stared at it blank-faced, then squeezed the bridge of his nose. After one slow breath, like he'd never come across a more senseless creature than me, he murmured, "How are you not dead?"

Good question.

He wouldn't like the answer.

I'd survived merely by the grace of luck. My impulsiveness and clumsiness had landed me in dangerous situations, but I'd always been in exactly the right spot, protected by the right people.

One day, my luck would run out.

I replaced the blade while he stared above my head, a faraway look in his eyes, and his distraction finally allowed me to study their color.

So many colors. Brown at the center, blue at the outer, flecks of green and amber in between. They'd technically be termed hazel, but a flicker of irritation burned at the ocean of hues there.

Evil wasn't supposed to be pretty.

Those faceted eyes locked on mine. "You have no survival instincts. You don't know how to fight. You can barely keep quiet when you're hiding from a group of men intent on killing you.

What skills do you have? Why would they send me someone like you?"

I sucked in a fortifying breath. "They sent someone expendable. You know, just in case."

His face drained of color. "Expendable?"

Yeah, probably shouldn't have admitted that to him.

Hi, I'm the reject they didn't care to lose. Want to trust me with your secrets?

He scratched his neck. "It didn't occur to me to ask for someone competent. They were supposed to send a soldier."

"I *was* a soldier. They made me stop." I scrutinized the floor. "For obvious reasons."

I thought of the scant questions I was asked before they allowed me into the Defiance army three years ago.

"Name?"

"Sophia Elena Reeves."

"Age?"

"Twenty-one."

"Do you have any military or combat experience?"

"No."

"Do you have any trade skills?"

"Er... No."

"Have you handled weapons before? Are you familiar with firearms?"

"Still no."

"Do you have any medical illnesses?"

"No."

"Are you pregnant?"

"Definitely no."

And that was it. That night, I was a Defiance soldier with a gun and everything.

"So they...what?" Lucas demanded. "Sent you here to die?"

I rocked on my feet, unwilling to look him in the eye. "I don't know. Maybe." Time wobbled around me while those words settled into all the cracks between us, somehow both lightning fast and interminable. He didn't speak, so I finally filled the silence. "What do you want to do? Do you want someone else?"

At first, he didn't answer, but then his voice floated toward me, softer and closer than it had been before. "Is your name really Sophia?"

My gaze lifted to his, and I sensed a thread of disquiet that hadn't been there before, despite that his expression remained unyielding. I pulled my dog tags from underneath my shirt to show him.

REEVES
SOPHIA E.
290 98 1240
A POS
CATHOLIC

"My friends call me Soph." A moment stuttered past. "But you can't call me that."

His stare lasered in on my name debossed into the metal, but the edge of his mouth lifted an infinitesimal degree. "Are you saying we aren't friends?"

Was that...a joke?

"Come on." He jerked his head toward the kitchen, and I followed. I sat at the table while he took the seat opposite. We faced each other, almost like a poorly lit interrogation room. The fading daylight from the large kitchen window cast a lavender pall over us. Shadows crept from the corners, stretching fingers toward us, wanting.

"So, does Harrison believe me now?" Lucas asked.

"I think he was pleasantly surprised." As was I, not that it mattered.

"It isn't always going to be easy. It was Bennie's plan, so it was poorly organized. He's better at battle than stealth."

My ears perked. "Benjamin Cook? One of the other Blood Colonels?"

He snorted. "No one calls him Benjamin. And no one calls us Blood Colonels."

"They do where I come from."

He gave me a flat stare. "Well, *Benjamin* is not one for details. He has good ideas, but I've been editing his plans since I started."

I reflected on what Theo had said when Lucas joined the NSF ranks.

"Wherever he came from, he appears to be a talented strategist."

"He appears to be a serial killer," I mutter into my stew, to which Theo chuckles darkly.

"There's no pattern I can trace, no strategy I can pin down," he says. "They're gaining the upper hand, and they know it. It's like fighting someone who knows the moves you're going to make even before you do."

"Sounds like we need a secret weapon."

"I know," he says. "I'm looking for it."

Who'd have thought the secret weapon would be the man himself?

"I was conveniently unavailable to help him with this," Lucas said, guiding me back to the conversation.

"Hmm. How sad."

Those pretty eyes brightened, penetrating. Now that we were back to business, the cold wrath cloaked him like it had last week. Ice crystals could have sparkled on the planes of his face, and I wouldn't have been surprised.

"I have information about General Wyatt."

A flutter rose in my stomach. General Dean Wyatt was the chief of staff of the US Army. He commanded all their forces, including the Hunters.

"He'll be visiting in a month," Lucas said.

"How long?"

Lucas ran a hand through his dark hair, tugging a bit. "Not sure. He doesn't tell anyone his plans. Makes it harder to track him."

"Right. Anything else you can tell me?"

Annoyance flashed across his face. "Obviously, yes. If you'll let me speak, I'll tell you."

Hatred sparked to life in my gut, but I stayed quiet, letting him gather his useless thoughts in silence.

He swallowed. "So... He won't come out. He never does, but I believe—I believe he'll have his daughter with him."

"You *believe*, or you *know*?"

Something weird happened with his mouth, like a twist or a sneer. It tried to betray his feelings, but didn't quite get there.

"It's...been mentioned that she may be given to one of us," he said.

My brain glitched. "Uh... Given?"

"As a...bride." A muscle in his jaw twitched. "She's sixteen. I thought y'all might take exception to that."

Bile rose in my throat. "To be clear, you're telling me the leader of the NAO's army is coming here to give his teenage daughter to one of his faithful subordinates?"

His eyes cut to mine. "It's an act. A show of proof he believes the NAO's stance on *family values*. I believe she's meant to be a reward to the NSF for service and loyalty."

"I see. And which of you has he deemed most loyal?"

My heart thudded several times before his wooden voice filled the ominous silence. "Me."

Silence fell.

His gaze locked on a point below my eyes—my chin, maybe—and he remained utterly still.

I crossed my arms. "You're being given *another* sex slave? Exactly how many of those do you need?"

The muscle in his jaw spasmed again. "At least one more." Then, a hateful smirk spread like syrup across his face. "But to be fair, I didn't ask for her. I only asked for you."

Was he *trying* to provoke me?

"What happened to *not interested*?" I asked, annoyed by the rasp in my words.

That condescending expression on his face only deepened. "Still don't believe me, do you?"

"What else could you want? I have nothing to give." The anxiety surrounding the unknown ate away at my brain like cancer.

"I can tell you what I *don't* want. I don't want a child bride. So let me explain my next piece of information." He placed both arms on the table, interlacing his fingers. "Taking her will both save her and piss him off. It's a power play more than anything. I think I could be persuaded to escort Miss Wyatt to the gaming strip on the Friday following her arrival. I think I might also be persuaded to take her the way through Riverside. Say, around ten that night?"

"Could you be persuaded to be alone?"

"I could not. I anticipate a group of maybe...twenty-five?"

Twenty-five. I committed that to memory.

"I'll warn you though—if his daughter is taken, the general will order attacks."

A bitter laugh bubbled to the surface. "He's okay with her being screwed by you, but not okay with her being in the company of Defiants?"

Lucas shrugged. "I'm not sure why you'd expect him to be sane."

Fair enough. Resting my elbows on the table, I hid my face in my hands. *This is the world I live in.*

"I have something for you," he said.

Something for me? Was that some sort of innuendo?

He tossed me a plastic square I barely caught.

"A pager?" I asked.

He nodded toward it. "It still works."

Right. But what was I supposed to do with it?

"Do you know how they work?" he asked.

"No."

His gaze darted over me again, studying. "How old are you?"

"Twenty-four," I snapped. "What's with the judgy tone? How old are *you*?"

He rubbed his face like talking to me tried every strand of

patience inside him. "It's set to vibrate. If I need you, it'll vibrate and a message will display telling you when to meet me."

"What if I'm busy?"

"You're never too busy for me."

Rolling my eyes, I asked, "What if I need *you*?" I tried to imagine a situation in which I would need this man. No such scenario presented itself.

He stood. "Follow me."

For one puzzling moment, I thought he might offer his hand to help me, but then he merely turned and left. I trailed him through the house until he reached the master bedroom. My eyes fell on the bed, and I froze.

Wait. He said he wasn't interested.

Fear crashed through me in a tidal wave.

I knew... I had *known* this would happen. So why couldn't I breathe?

He glanced back at me and followed my gaze to the bed. Heaving a sigh, he grabbed my elbow with enough force to jerk me forward and drag me through the closet door. "If I want to fuck you, I'll make it obvious."

I shot him a distrustful scowl. "How obvious?"

If he answered, I didn't hear it. I was distracted by the wonders behind the door. He'd converted a walk-in closet into a communications room. Monitors sat on the shelves, screens displaying live feeds of various locations. Radio devices and books littered the shelves, and every spare surface was covered in wires, circuit boards, and parts I didn't even recognize.

My gaze darted everywhere as I entered. Communication was such a difficult dilemma for the Defiance. Many cell towers had been destroyed, and satellite phones were hard to find. Overhead telephone lines were razed at an increasing rate. The internet was nonexistent.

The NAO didn't struggle like we did, so Lucas likely had no idea how magical this room seemed to me. He directed my attention to a square lamp in one corner, glowing with a soft white light. I approached it, and he pointed to a set of buttons at the base. "It has a sister at my house. If you change the color on this one, it'll change the color on mine. I've made a color key."

He pointed to a piece of paper pinned to the wall above the lamp. Blue for *Non-urgent message*. Yellow for *Urgent message*. Green for *I couldn't stay*. Purple for *I'm waiting*. Orange for *On my way*. And red for *Emergency. I need you now*.

"I suggest not using red unless you're dying," he said.

"Can you change the color from yours?"

"Yes."

I exhaled a slow breath, bracing myself against a sudden wave of vertigo. This was real. We were doing this, weren't we? I was his now, at his beck and call, for better or worse.

"Is that it for tonight?" I asked, my voice weak and breathy.

"No." He disappeared into the bedroom.

The closet door swung to close me inside.

Fabric rustled outside the door. "Take off those clothes."

What? Now?

My stomach filled with lead. Was this what he meant by *obvious*?

My shaking, hesitant hands moved to the waist of my leggings, pushing them down my legs. I left them in a pile on the carpeted floor. Same with my shirt. I paused at my underwear.

The closet door swung open again to allow his hand entry. He threw some black fabric onto the ground. "Wear that."

The door clicked shut.

I stared at the clothes he'd given me. Men's clothes. *His* clothes, judging by that weird incense smell.

Not the clothes he'd been wearing. No, these were...sweats?

I seized the pants and pulled them on, then grabbed the shirt.

It was a hoodie.

A fucking hoodie!

Engulfed by the infuriating sense of being managed, I tamped down the impulse to rage-scream. When I opened the door again, his eyes scanned my outfit. "Now *that* is a beautiful sight. I can barely tell you're human under all that."

Was that *sarcasm*?

"You seriously want me to wear this?"

"I want you to avoid attention. Hide yourself, Sophia. It's the only way to survive."

Was that what he was doing? Hiding? Surviving?

Either way, the grave glint in his eye twisted inside me. We both knew too well the horror that would become of me if I were captured. All at once, my head filled with the memory of Daniela's screams.

Panic clawed up my throat. An iron band tightened around my chest.

No! I couldn't have an attack here. Not now.

Breathe!

My ribs expanded, yet my body screamed at me for more oxygen. My chest hitched. I turned from him as my vision darkened. I tried to shove it away, but the memory stabbed at me with all the subtlety of a combat knife.

Her scream splits the air.

Alarmed, I try to stand, but my injured leg protests. Mahmoud darts to the window, using one finger to slide a curtain to the side. He swears under his breath.

"What is it?" I whisper, cursing the throb in my leg. We were raiding an abandoned neighborhood for supplies when the rotten stairs in this old home gave way beneath me. Daniela had been trying to get help. She was out there for me.

Because I am fucking clumsy.

"Hunters caught her a few houses down," Mahmoud says.

"No, go help her!"

His tortured eyes meet mine. "I can't."

"What the fuck, Mahmoud? Go help her!"

"I can't," he insists.

"Why the hell not?" I lurch off the chair he found for me and hop to the

window, ignoring the waves of agony in my leg.

"No, Sophia. Stop! You don't need to see this—"

My heart rips clean from my body when my gaze lands on the horror outside.

Six of them.

One has Daniela bent over a car's hood, his hand tangled in her hair, wrenching her head back while he—

"Oh my god." My breakfast rises into my throat. It takes everything in me not to vomit all over the window.

Two other men hold her down, while the rest laugh from the sidelines. A knife handle juts from her side.

Rape as a weapon of war. The Hunters use it the same way one would use a gun or a grenade. Efficient and brutal.

My good leg gives out, and I hit the floor. The pain is a distant thing, like waves on some faraway beach.

Another of Daniela's screams fills my ears.

I returned to myself gradually, and only when I realized I was sitting on the floor in his closet, my knees drawn to my chest, did I dare look at him.

He stood like a soldier, hands behind his back, regarding me with an inquisitive stare, not a trace of pity in his eyes. "Do you have panic attacks often?"

I cleared my throat, thankful he was so callous that he hadn't tried to help—or worse, *comfort.* "Often enough."

"Who's Daniela?"

Annoyed that I'd let her name slip in my panic, I forced myself to stand even though my legs weren't quite ready. "No one."

He took a step closer, his gaze penetrating me in a way that made me think he could see far more than what I showed him. "It seems you have firsthand experience with what happens to women who don't hide from Hunters."

I gave him a faint nod, unable to meet his eyes.

"Then *take my advice* instead of fighting with me about it."

I scowled, but he ignored me in favor of ushering me to the front door.

"I have something else for you," he said, taking my hand. A set of metal knuckles slid over my fingers. Not the typical metal hoops. Each circle came to a sharp point. The four shark-tooth daggers would puncture skin with very little pressure. I'd seen the weapon wielded by other Hunters. I'd treated injuries dealt by it.

These were Hunter knuckles, and if anyone saw me with them, there would be questions.

"Are you right-handed?" he asked.

I nodded.

"If you ever need to use this, you go for the throat." He held the blades parallel to his trachea, then dragged them toward his chest. God, that maneuver would kill a man in seconds. "If the throat isn't accessible, then the stomach. And for godsake don't let them get you on your back." He paused. "And don't cut yourself with it. You seem... clumsy."

For once, I couldn't take offense. It was true.

He opened the door and pushed me into the gathering darkness. "Protect yourself. I need you alive."

The door slammed in my face.

7

CHEST PAIN

 ...however the forms of government may be changed, or the principles of it altered, violence is always despotism.

— THOMAS JEFFERSON, INAUGURAL ADDRESS

Back at headquarters, I sank into a corner of my bedroom and struggled to breathe for several minutes while panic tore through the fragile stability in my mind. My meditation—the forest, the warm rain, the smell of cypress—none of it mitigated the alarm bells singing through my veins, shredding them open from the inside.

Memories crawled over me like a horde of spiders.

Aching with fever, staring into a pair of beautiful dark eyes. "I'm Zara Akbari. I'm going to take care of you."

Unified News spreading the NAO's recruitment efforts. "Freedom is earned, not given. Join the NSF!"

Nia Williams, standing at a podium. "They're bigger than us. They have more weapons and better supplies. But that doesn't mean we're weak. We have the heart. The brains. We will stop this madness!"

Bodies hanging from a ceiling, the Brotherhood Cross carved into their backs.

A safe house in flames, innocents jumping from windows to escape, only to meet their end on the cement below.

Prisoners heaped over each other in Unity Square, the blood from their bodies staining the wall behind.

I tried to breathe, to excise the images from my mind, but they always attacked when I was at my weakest, my lowest. The only way out was through the quagmire.

Eventually, my head cleared. The tears dried. Drained and weak, I made my way to Theo's office.

"Twenty-five men?" he asked after I told him the news of Wyatt's daughter.

"Yes."

He tapped his chin. "I wonder if there will be other women we'll need to consider."

"He didn't mention it."

Theo pursed his lips. He hummed, distracted, clicking his pen against his desk. Normally, I would let myself out, but something niggled at my thoughts.

When Theo looked up, his eyebrows lifted. "What's wrong?"

I released a sigh. "He's different from what I thought he'd be."

Chandelier lights sparkled in his dark eyes, full of grim acceptance. "Even monsters can be complex creatures. Not everything is black and white, Soph. You know that."

I pinched the cotton of my new sweatpants between two fingers, rubbing back and forth. The faint scent of frankincense wafted toward me.

"Are you...okay?" Theo asked, almost as if the words hurt to say.

My gaze shot up, and I wondered if now was the time he'd finally ask. *What does he do to you?*

And I could say, *Nothing, but I don't know why and I don't know what he wants. He's maddening.*

But Theo said nothing, so I didn't either. Instead, I swallowed my disappointment. "I'm okay. Did you know he's the one in charge of sentencing the prisoners?"

Theo nodded.

"I don't understand why he's doing this," I whispered. "None of it makes sense."

"I know. We need to be on guard. I worry there'll be a catch. He'll trap us when we least expect it."

Tears sprang to my eyes. Some part of me had wanted him to deny it, to tell me Lucas Scott would prove to be an asset, that he'd never hurt us. But of course he didn't say that. It wasn't true.

However, if Lucas could deliver Tekqua back to me, I'd suffer any amount of betrayal. I'd suffer his hands. His body. His brutality. Anything.

I wanted her back.

"I miss Tekqua," I said.

His voice roughened. "I know."

"Have you ever considered raiding the House of the Rising Sun, Theo? We could save them."

He shook his head. "They guard the House as well as they guard their headquarters. I've looked into it."

I swallowed to stifle the tears. She hadn't been publicly executed, and her body hadn't been recovered in the field, so she had to be a prisoner.

A slave.

She was at the House. I was certain.

His face softened. "It's a scare tactic. They're sowing uncertainty and panic through extreme cruelty, just like when they stopped using guns for their executions and started choosing their own weapons instead."

The image slipped through the cracks in my memory vault of

Colonel Jack Miller standing at the podium in Unity Square, where they performed all their public executions.

"To conserve ammunition for the Security Restoration Campaign in our northern territory, capital punishments will no longer be served by firing squad. Instead, executioners will choose how the sentence is carried out. In accordance with Executive Order 16389, in an effort to maintain unity and stop the corrosion of peace in our great nation, convicted traitors of the Unified States of America are sentenced to execution by the hand of the National Stability Force. Let this act serve as a reminder that unity prevails. All hail the Commander!"

That was the day we started calling them Blood Colonels.

It was a mockery. A humiliation. A deep wound to our pride. They wanted us to suffer in full view of the entire country. The entire world.

This is what happens when you defy us.

"But if they make us fear them, then they control us," Theo said now.

I nodded, not trusting my voice. My fear definitely controlled me. It dictated my every action. It influenced each thought.

"Is there any more information?" he asked.

I shook my head.

"You can go then. I need to think."

Standing to leave, I made it to the door before he murmured my name. When I glanced at his face, a rare mask of grief had settled over it. "I miss them, too."

Right. Didn't seem like it.

I wandered downstairs, trailing through rooms full of people without stopping to speak to any of them. After meandering aimlessly, I made my way to the café for a snack, choosing a seat alone at the back of the room to wallow in my darkness.

Devon spotted me and took the place across the table. "You doing okay, Soph?"

"Of course." I faked a smile and lifted my dried apple slices. "Remember the beginning, when we had those food expeditions?"

He pulled a face as he sat, drumming his fingers on the table. "I hated slaughtering the cows."

"Better than slaughtering humans," I muttered.

Solutions to the food shortage had developed over time, primarily through vegetable gardens and hunting, but those early days of hunger still haunted us.

"Where's Isaac?" I asked, referring to his boyfriend, one of our lieutenants.

"Upstairs. Asleep. Late night for him."

Whatever I said next made him laugh, but my heart and thoughts floated far away.

Distant.

Distracted.

Scared.

When it grew late, I forced myself to my bed.

As usual, my mind wrapped itself in dark, anxious thoughts, my eyes wet with tears. When I managed to sleep, I dreamt of my old squad, plagued by the belief that it should have been me. None of them had deserved what had happened to them. They'd been better and stronger than I ever was, and yet mine was the only heart that still beat. How did it do it when it felt so utterly demolished?

The grief was like cancer, hidden, invisible amongst the valves and ventricles and arteries. It weaved through each muscle fiber, strangling them one by one. Slow and deliberate and cold.

My chest hurt.

The ache was constant, ebbing and flowing like waves on the shore. Sometimes the tide receded, and my thoughts cleared, but then a storm surge would drown me. It weighed on me, stealing my breath from my body.

My chest *hurt*.

Tekqua had always been my rock.

When the tears came, she chanted my mantra. When I couldn't sleep, she sang. When I needed distraction, she talked until I'd forgotten why I was hurting to begin with. In the summer, we'd laze in the coolest parts of headquarters while she mocked my hair's ever-expanding entropy. When snow coated the overgrown gardens in a sparkly white blanket, Tekqua dragged me into the cold for snowball fights. We would shiver and laugh until our stomachs ached, then trudge inside to drink cinnamon moonshine Adam had stolen from who-knew-where.

Without her, I was stumbling on unstable ground, and everything hurt—my heart, my skin, even my fingernails. My mind was a mess of hopelessness, my soul missing pieces shaped like the people I'd lost. In every spare moment, I wondered whether I'd ever be normal again.

But I already knew the answer.

No, there was no going back to normal after this.

8

SAFE HOUSE RED

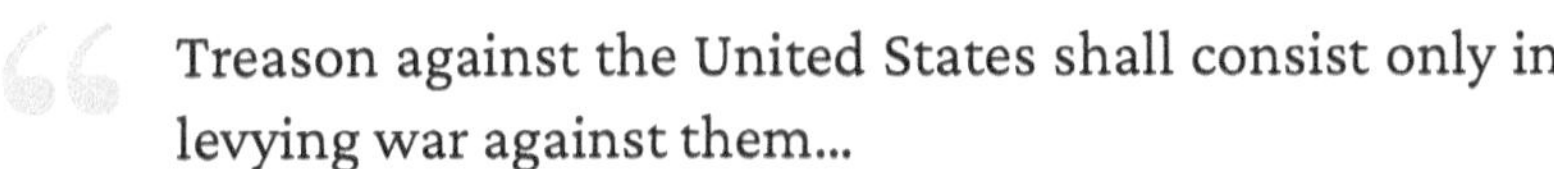

Treason against the United States shall consist only in levying war against them...

—ARTICLE 3, U.S. CONSTITUTION

*O*ur van jerks to a stop, and my squad hustles into the afternoon light. The air reeks of smoke and gunpowder, and shots pop in a metallic wheeze through the skies. Cherry Street had been a trendy nightlife spot prior to the war, and the road is narrow, with the abandoned shells of bars and restaurants standing on either side—the ghosts of normalcy.

Safe House Red used to be a glamorous luxury apartment building.

Now it's on fire.

Several blocks down the street, black smoke billows into the sky. Even from our distance, I can see the residents jumping from windows and balconies, trying to escape the flames.

My squad is meant to keep the combat soldiers armed, but in the mayhem, that goal melts to the concrete beneath our feet.

Sergeant Taylor whips around. "Change of plans. Keep safe. Stay together. We head to Safe House Red to evacuate civilians, got it?"

Time slows as I peer around, the world tilting while the colors shift. It takes on that darkened texture, that film that tells me this isn't real.

Not anymore.

But I have been here before. I didn't like how it ended.

Maybe I can change it this time.

Stray bullets ricochet off brick and metal. Glass shatters as soldiers dive for cover. The brick face of one building explodes, rattling my teeth. Debris sprinkles over us in a deadly rain.

"That way," Sergeant Taylor shouts, pointing toward a blown-out Mexican restaurant.

"Stay together!" Rodrigo yells as we run.

Pistol in one hand, blade in the other, I follow Rodrigo inside the building, then scramble over the bar for cover. Tekqua plops next to me, breathing hard.

"Assess your surroundings," Sergeant Taylor says. "Where's the closest exit?"

Daniela pops up to peer over the bar and through the front window. "I think there's a squad of Hunters across the street."

Princeton and I lift our heads. The world outside is a mess. Soldiers dart everywhere, some brawling in the street, others jumping for cover. The jewelry store across from us is missing its door. Inside, a slew of men in Hunter black aim firearms at Defiants.

"We can't just sit here," Tekqua says. "We have to do something. They're burning alive!"

"We need to get out of here," Daniela says, crawling on all fours to a crumbling wall near the back corner of the restaurant. We follow.

In the alley outside, a Defiant jogs past. "There's about twenty of them in the gastropub down the street. Safe House Red is done."

Done? What does that mean, done?

The seven of us slip behind a trattoria and press our backs to the brick. An explosion tears open a nail salon nearby.

"Fuck!" Rodrigo throws his hands out to protect us.

"We need cover," Sergeant Taylor says. "Everyone armed? Stay together!"

We sneak along the wall single file. At the building's edge is an open street with no cover. The parking lot of a Catholic church spreads out wide on the other side. Sergeant Taylor assesses our surroundings. At the sharp jerk of his head, we follow.

At the corner, Tekqua squeezes my hand. "Stay with me if you can."

We take off at a run. Bullets sail our way, chinking through abandoned cars and bouncing off the concrete. Together, we jump through the broken glass into the pub. Overturned tables and chairs transform the place into an obstacle course. We dart through the maze, the kitchen, and out the back door into a small parking lot.

I'd just set my foot on the asphalt when—

"Get down!"

Sergeant Taylor, Rodrigo, and Tekqua fire their weapons toward a gourmet burger shop, and a half dozen Hunters fire back. Something ricochets off an air conditioner unit and embeds in Mahmoud's leg.

"Agh!" He staggers backward.

I raise my gun, and with a couple lucky shots, snag one Hunter in the pelvis. Princeton and Sergeant take out another.

"Right there!" one Hunter yells. "Defiants twelve o'clock!"

My legs have never moved faster. Past a pizzeria. Across a side street. Behind a sub shop. We topple into an empty building next door.

Mahmoud slides down a wall. I lift his pant leg. A jagged piece of metal protrudes from his calf. I yank it out, and he hisses.

Time slows again, and I take the moment to stare at his face.

He's right here in front of me. Alive.

They all are.

I want to tell them to stop, to go back. It's not worth the sacrifice.

But my mouth is stuck, and nothing comes out.

In slow motion, Mahmoud grimaces at the pain in his leg. Rodrigo confers with Sergeant Taylor. Daniela looks down on Mahmoud, her bottom lip between her teeth. Princeton checks his weapon.

And Tekqua.

Tekqua is looking at me.

Bright gaze. Hard mouth. Determined brow.

I want to reach for her, to hug her.

My arms won't move.

"Alright, squad," Sergeant Taylor says as time resumes. "Let's regroup."

Outside the small space, another explosion rocks the street, close enough to shatter the front windows of our building. The coffee shop across the way is pandemonium, the fight spilling into the street.

Screams for help rise above the bullets and explosions.

"We push now," Sergeant Taylor barks. "Hit 'em hard!"

No, *I think.* We can't go in there.

But it's no use.

Weapons in hand, we burst into the fray. Inside the shop, Hunters outnumber Defiants two to one. They fight with hands and knives, their firearms likely discarded or empty. Bodies litter the floor.

Two Hunters corner one soldier. He raises his hands to surrender, and one Hunter sinks a blade into his stomach while the other laughs and spits in his face.

I shoot them both.

Then I run, barely skidding around the corner to the bathroom before the bullets chase me. I try to sneak a peek at the fight, but my gaze falls instead on a grisly sight.

Bodies hang from the ceiling. At least a dozen, stripped bare, with Brotherhood Crosses cut into their backs.

Bloody Brotherhood Crosses, *meaning they were carved while the victims were still alive, while their hearts still pumped blood to the injuries. These are residents of Safe House Red. An old man. A female amputee. Two—no, three—children.*

If I had anything in my stomach, I would puke it all out.

This isn't just cruel.

This... this is atrocious.

Gunshots jerk me back to the present. Princeton enters my field of vision, retreating from a Hunter who has him at gunpoint. My heart throbs twice in my chest, and I rush forward. Gun raised, I watch the Hunter's eyes widen.

"Wait—"

My bullet snags his throat.

"Thanks," Princeton wheezes.

The word has barely left his mouth when Rodrigo shouts, "On your right!"

Two Hunters have firearms trained on Princeton and me. "Fucking traitors!" they spit.

My brain sticks on that word.

Traitors.

I'm not the traitor. They are. They'd declared war against the United States and destroyed it. How could they not see that?

Sergeant Taylor leaps onto one, and his bullet goes wide. Princeton and I duck as Rodrigo darts in front of us.

The second bullet finds a home in his chest.

I scream.

I'd known it was coming, but still, I scream.

The rest of the battle fades away as I crawl to Rodrigo and take his face in my hands.

He doesn't move. Doesn't breathe. Doesn't blink.

"Rodrigo!"

His eyes fix unseeing on a point above my head.

"Wake up!" I shake his shoulder even though I know it's pointless. He won't wake up.

Princeton lays a hand on my back. "Sophia, he's gone."

I look up at him.

So are you, I want to say. You're all gone, and you left me here.

Colors swirl, and I think I might be crying.

The dream pulled apart at the edges, though I fought to hang on to it. It wasn't a good memory, but it was the last time we were all together. Rodrigo had been alive, and then he just...wasn't. A moment in time. A split-second decision. His entire life, distilled to nothing.

He'd died saving my life.

When the tears came for Rodrigo, they flowed in torrents. It was like a jagged piece of glass had been inserted into my heart. It hurt to breathe, to swallow, to exist. Only now did I recognize the normalcy of that reaction. I was still whole and unbroken, a stranger to heartbreak. Rodrigo's death was the first time I suffered even a hint of the pain I was capable of feeling.

The naivety of those who have never known grief was a beautiful thing, I thought. A little like a snowflake—unique, but fragile. Once destroyed, it could never be recreated the same way. If someone had tried to explain to my innocent self how it would feel to lose Rodrigo so suddenly, so violently, I wouldn't have believed them. When it happened, I thought my heart would never heal, and I had no concept that things could ever be worse.

I was so naive.

On the evening of that battle, I sat on the floor of the common room, using Mom's legs as a backrest while she stroked her fingers through my curls. Tekqua remained a comforting presence nearby, her hand squeezing mine every so often. After a time, the dulcet tones of a guitar thrummed through the room. At first jumbled, the chords gave way to a song I recognized.

Tears in Heaven sprinkled over my consciousness, and liquid filled my eyes once more. The chord progression raised goosebumps on my arms. Above me, Mom hummed the tune. I joined in the lyrics, as did many others. When I craned my neck toward the guitarist, I found Adam Ambrose's grieving face.

Adam, who thrived on camaraderie, who fostered unconditional companionship amongst us all, did what he did best: he brought us together again. The song filled the room—his guitar and our voices. Tekqua squeezed my hand and didn't let go. Mom laid her cheek on my crown. Dad squeezed my shoulder.

The music played on.

It had been a terrible day, and yet, I longed for it now. Cheeks wet, I turned over in bed and forced myself to go back to sleep. In my dreams, at least they were alive. My dreams, it seemed, were the only safe spaces left.

9

GOOD GIRL

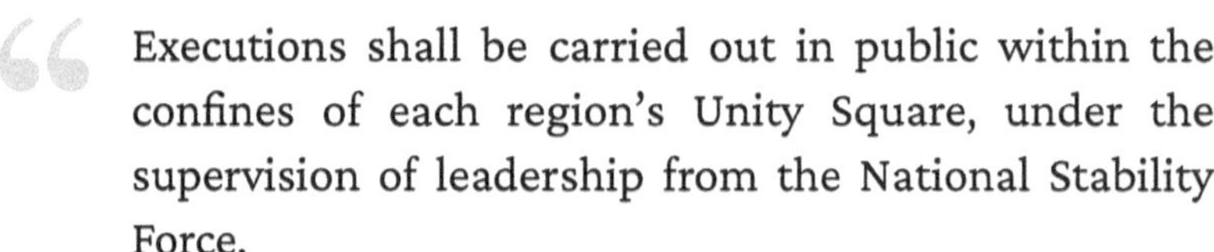

Executions shall be carried out in public within the confines of each region's Unity Square, under the supervision of leadership from the National Stability Force.

— CAPITAL ENFORCEMENT AND EXECUTION ACT,

N.A.O.C. 18 § 4709

The morning of my third meeting with Lucas Scott, trepidation returned. The whole affair was wearing on my flimsy rationality. I hated the lack of control, and in a dark, unhealthy part of my mind, I wished he was the man I'd been expecting, the one who would use and abuse me, the one who'd enjoy my pain. It would have been a relief to let pain erase the sadness for a bit, to let my hatred of him cloud all the other negative emotions.

But no.

He couldn't even give me that.

As I headed toward the underground exit, Zara caught me.

"Sophia, wait!"

I turned slowly, already dreading the encounter. Other than a few superficial exchanges, we hadn't spoken much of late. Not that I was avoiding her. I just... Grief had stolen my ability to small talk.

Her brown eyes turned luminous as I met them. "Where are you headed?"

"Just need a walk."

She smiled. "Want some company?"

"No." At her confused look, I added, "I-I'd like to be alone."

She gripped her elbows, frowning. "You're always alone. I'm here if you want to talk, Soph. Like we used to."

Like we used to.

Before Tekqua had been captured. Before everyone had died.

Managing a smile, I bobbed my head. "Maybe tomorrow?"

Her smile lit up her whole face. "Yes, that would be wonderful."

Guilt flooded me. I'd had no real intention of seeking her out tomorrow, but that joy on her face was like barbs in my overburdened soul. She was so kind, and I was so, so broken.

Muttering some acknowledgement, I hurried away before she made it worse.

I'd dressed as Lucas asked me to, wearing a pair of black scrub pants and a loose hoodie—*not* the one he'd given me last week. The warm weather broke a sweat on my back beneath the unseasonal clothes, and the roots of my long curls were damp by the time I arrived. I rushed up the steps and slipped into the house without knocking, refusing to surrender to the desire to run the other way.

Lucas was sprawled on the sofa, flipping through a book. He didn't even bother to look at me. "You're late."

"No, you're early."

"It's 7:04." He stood and tossed the book onto the cushions, then scanned my outfit with a hint of surprise. "Look at you. At least you know how to obey."

"*What?*"

"You seem like the kind of woman who prefers noncompliance over intelligence."

Glaring at him, I managed a slow inhale for patience. "I'm wearing the clothes you wanted me to. I showed up when you asked me to." I pulled the knuckles from my pocket. "I'm armed with the weapon you chose for me. I've done everything you asked, like I promised I would. Can you stop insulting me and just give me your information?"

His eyes flashed, but not with anger. No, it was something...else. "I did some research on you this past week."

All the blood drained from my head. He did *what*?

With a nearly imperceptible smile, he lifted one eyebrow. "Sophia Elena Reeves. Twenty-five next month. Born in Virginia. Joined the Defiance mere weeks after the Fracture. Been at the center of the resistance since its inception. Soldier turned medic, though the records aren't clear why."

My mouth fell open. Did they have that much information about all of us? "How...?"

"Did you think I wouldn't research the woman I'm entrusting my life to?"

Where would he even find that information? I hid my unease with a snort. "Entrusting *your* life? What about *my* life?"

"What about it? Do you feel endangered, Sophia?"

"Yes," I said, even though it wasn't technically true. "You are the most dangerous man I've ever met."

He had the gall to laugh, bitter and disbelieving. "This from a woman in close contact with Theodore Harrison?"

"I've seen you murder people on live TV."

His jaw went rigid. "No one forced you to watch."

I fought the urge to stomp my foot. "Would you just give me your fucking information?"

He offered no indication whether he wanted me to sit or go to the kitchen like before. His head canted in a silent show of interest.

"They're planning to move on your base near Knoxville in the next few weeks. Warn your people to reinforce."

I remained quiet, waiting for more, but he gave nothing else. "That's it? That's all you got?"

"Yes," he said simply. "Now I'm going to teach you how to fight."

My breath caught in my throat. "Wait. What? No."

"*No*? You don't get to say no to me."

Well, that was a really great way to get me to fight him, the asshole. Miraculously, I held myself back. Not silently, though. "Fuck off, Blood Colonel. That wasn't the deal."

He stole the tiniest step toward me, and I took a larger step back.

"I'm adding a requirement to my cooperation."

"No, I'm not fighting you."

He hesitated, his colorful gaze examining my resistance with curiosity. "Last week, when I realized how poorly trained you are, you asked if I wanted someone else."

Prickles woke along my spine. "Yeah, so?"

"If I demanded a new contact, what would Harrison do?"

"He'd find you someone else."

His eyes narrowed. "And what would he do with *you*?"

I started to answer, then paused as I realized I didn't know what to say. Theo and Williams had been explicit that this assignment with Lucas was top secret. Other than the three of us, no one knew about the traitor Blood Colonel handing over information through me. If Lucas requested someone new, that would make me superfluous. It would mean I knew something I shouldn't. It would make me a liability.

Theo wouldn't punish me for that.

Williams, though?

I said nothing, but Lucas seemed to see the answer on my face. He smirked. "You will take my training, or I'll ask for someone else, and we can both learn how the Defiance deals with information spillage."

My shoulders fell as I surrendered to his logic. "I don't like training."

"It's more appealing than the activities you *imagined* would happen between us, right?"

"No activity with you sounds appealing, Lucas," I said, scowling.

His brow raised.

I threw my hands up. "Fine. You're right. Fighting you is better than fucking you."

We stared at each other a beat, unmoving.

After several breaths, he finally spoke, his voice like satin over a razor blade. "Remember what I said about thinking before you speak?"

I clenched my teeth so tight they hurt.

"If you challenged any other NSF soldier like that, he'd shove his dick so far down your throat, you'd suffocate."

A muscle near my eye twitched as I imagined it. "Good thing I have teeth."

He sighed and squeezed the bridge of his nose. "Are you brave or just stupid?"

"Impulsive and reckless."

My mind threw a memory at me as I said it, a day in the field with my squad, when I'd been deployed far too soon after recovering from the flu. I'd known I was too weak for the mission, but stubbornness compelled me anyway. We were nearly caught by a Hunter patrol, and I fell behind as we ran for cover.

Tekqua was the only reason I lived that day. She covered me while I was too breathless to speak, resting my hands on my knees. She'd let someone braid her hair into badass zigzagging plaits that hugged her scalp, and wore a tight black turtleneck and tactical pants. Armed, straight-backed and strong, she was the very picture of a Defiant.

And I couldn't even stand upright.

It was the first time the notion had drifted through my brain that while Tekqua Madden had grown into a competent soldier, I didn't *want* to be good at it.

And I never would be. Not even with this predator's training.

In Lucas's endless silence, I murmured, "They're not ideal traits in times like these."

He did nothing but watch me, and the fabric of my scrubs strained in my fist until he turned toward a hallway leading to the back of the house. "Fine. Let's see if I can train them out of you."

My breath released, and I followed, trying and failing to decipher the title of the book he'd been reading. Was he a novel sort of guy? A history buff? What books did Lucas Scott the psychopath read in his spare time?

The mystery boggled the mind.

We wound up in a room near the back of the house—a dark, empty bedroom with an expanse of cushy gray carpet compressed in places by the furniture that used to be there.

He toed off his shoes, and I did the same.

With his expression hidden in the darkness, the deep resonance of his voice vibrated through my spine. "You ready?"

"No."

He slammed into my shoulders hard. It knocked me backward, and we fell. His leg pinned one of my arms, and his hands were free to choke me. They slipped around my neck, but as soon as he had the position, he let go.

"Wow." He ran his hands through his wavy hair. "You're terrible."

"I am not!"

"You didn't even move. You just stood there and let me maul you."

I scowled and rose to my feet, resetting my position as he did the same. "You surprised me."

"Attacks don't come on a schedule." Before the words had left his mouth, he pummeled me again. I threw one foot back to brace the blow. When I lifted my arms to fend him off, he pressed his hand to my face. My head jerked to the side. I stumbled. He grabbed my curls and shoved me face-first against the wall, his body molded to my back. "It would be *that* easy, Sophia. Even if you don't fight back, you have to know how to get away."

He retreated, and we did it again.

And again.

Once he learned my skill level, he slowed and showed me techniques to evade him. It worked fine in slow motion, but when he put in some effort—any effort at all—I found myself disadvantaged and helpless beneath him.

But what did he expect?

He was a ranking officer in an army created solely to commit human atrocities. I would never be like him.

After an hour, he stared at me with those extraordinary eyes, their color finally visible now that I'd adjusted to the low light. "This is worse than I thought. You resort immediately to fear and panic."

Still breathing hard, I swiped a hand over my sweaty brow. "That's a normal reaction to being attacked by someone like *you*," I snapped. "How did you even learn all this?"

His head cocked as if that was the stupidest question he'd ever heard. "I've fought in a war for the last three years. What the fuck have you been doing?"

I sent him a death glare. "Not all of us can be cold-blooded killers."

His expression grew frigid. "Pity," he spat and leapt at me again.

We sparred until long after sunset. Though the night was chilly, the exercise and my poor stamina had me sweating in my hoodie. I growled and yanked it off my body, baring the tank top I wore beneath. Throwing the sweatshirt to the side, I faced him again.

The merest flicker of his eyes to my breasts, and ice flooded my veins.

What was I doing?

Had I forgotten who this person was? Had the unfavorable power dynamic between us slipped my mind? Why was I showing him parts of my body when he was a Hunter, and he was a man, and he was *clearly* attracted to women?

And even though he'd saved my life, even though these lessons were meant to protect me, I *still* expected his next assault to be genuine. I expected to be laid out and threatened by the man he'd been in my head before he'd flustered me with this guy who...wasn't terrible.

Lucas Scott was a violent executioner. A Blood Colonel. Being pinned beneath his lean body should have been the most dangerous place in the world, but once again, he trapped me without pain. No threatening advances, no careless grazes against body parts he shouldn't touch. I tried to escape him, but I failed.

He sat on my hips, holding my wrists. "Your panic makes you make stupid decisions. Did you have *any* training?"

I scowled. "My first drill sergeant died. After that, I got... complacent."

"How'd you survive?"

"Dumb luck." *And protective friends.*

"You have the instincts of a cocker spaniel. Do you like to cuddle and be petted too?"

Such an asshole. My teeth clenched as I gritted out, "Depends on where you pet me."

A brief pause.

He blinked, and then a sound burst from his mouth.

No, not a sound. A *laugh*.

His face transformed, and a genuine smile appeared like some lost treasure. It was definitely a more pleasant expression than his cold frown.

I glared at him.

"Do you have a *shred* of self-preservation in there?" he asked.

"You're *attacking* me. I'm allowed to be pissed about it."

He released my wrists and stood. "You made a deal with the devil. Suck it up and follow through."

I laughed, mirthless and bitter. "Why? What more could you do to me? I'm already in hell."

He eyed me. "This isn't hell. And you lack imagination." The dire tone in his words had me hesitating. I studied his face for answers, but it had reverted to its mask.

Slowly, I stood, my jelly muscles barely holding me up.

Tekqua had always been far more dedicated to her role as a soldier than me. When she advanced to sergeant, she took command of our squad with determination, arranging daily exercise routines and training maneuvers. With her hours of working out, she gave herself a body I envied but didn't want enough to work for. Meanwhile, I could barely handle a combat knife, and I'd resigned myself to scrawny arms and my mother's hips.

With Tekqua gone, my stamina had dwindled to nothing, and now it flaunted its absence with shaking limbs and a pounding heart.

"My imagination is just fine, thanks," I said.

"There are worse things than spending a single evening with me every week, Sophia. Trust me."

Trust him? No way.

He scrutinized my trembling legs and sighed. "Good thing for your patients you're a better medic than you are a soldier."

I crossed my arms. "How do you know whether I'm a good medic? Was that in my research file too?"

He did nothing other than offer that tiny smile I wasn't sure even existed.

"I'm not that good at it," I admitted to him, then wished I hadn't. Lucas Scott didn't need to know my weaknesses or insecurities.

His head cocked, curious again. "Everything you learned about the human body, you learned through sheer will and determination. You can fly under the radar in med school. There's no skirting by in the field. You know how to save lives when there's no electricity and barely clean water. You're better than a doctor. You're a combat medic. Own it."

"Yeah," I said with a roll of my eyes. "What a respectable title to have."

"Better than cold-blooded killer," came his answer, icy and sharp and edged with bitterness.

I forced my aching body to straighten as I looked him in the eye. "You earned that title."

"No," he bit out. "Many titles I've earned, but *that* one I did not."

My heart raced at his sudden intensity. A million questions soared through my head, but would he answer any? I chewed on my lip and asked the only one he might. "What title have you earned then?"

His bare expression morphed, now absent of the cold. "Doctor."

I narrowed my eyes. "No way. I don't believe you."

He shrugged and struck once more.

When my endurance finally imploded, he walked me to the door. "I have something for you."

Once again wary of innuendoes, I faced him.

He wiggled a silver key in my face. "It goes to the front door. In case you arrive before me again."

Suspicious, I tested it. The key slid into the knob and turned without a catch. Hmm. Alright, then.

A crease formed between his eyebrows as I pocketed it. "Why do you always assume I'm lying to you?"

"Because you're a traitorous murderer."

He expelled a long breath. "Keep that key on you at all times."

First the knuckles, and now the key. "Are you always this bossy?"

"Yes." He patted the top of my head like a dog. "And you're such a good girl."

My teeth snapped with how hard I gritted them. "You have no idea how much I hate you."

"Mm-hmm. I hate me too. Have a good night." He pushed me into the darkness and shut the door in my face. I left sore and nursing several bruises, questioning every moment I'd spent with him.

Less than a year ago, this same man had arrived at Unity Square a newly minted colonel. On our television screen, three dozen condemned men and women stood against the familiar blood-stained wall, bound at the wrists and ankles. Each month, the execution changed locales, but that one was ours.

Those people were ours.

And Lucas Scott was assigned to kill them.

Like every other execution day, we'd gathered in the common room, jostling for the best view of the screen, each of us desperate to look, but scared to see.

Tekqua had gripped my fingers, her gaze riveted to the screen.

When Lucas appeared, tall and sharp, his features cut from stone, his dead eyes stared straight into the camera. "Good evening," he said in a robotic voice. "I am Colonel Lucas Scott. In accordance with..." He droned on with the same speech they all spoke before those unlawful executions, pretending as if an executive order was enough to forego all due process. After he finished his address, and the unseen audience echoed the *All hail the Commander*, he stepped toward the line of prisoners.

But he had no weapon. I remember my perplexity with crisp clarity. Normally, the executioner chose from the torture devices on the table, but Lucas Scott had appeared empty-handed, as if he planned to kill three dozen people with his bare hands.

But then he paused.

The image was still etched in my memory. He stood beside the first prisoner and cracked his neck, a spark of silver flashing at the tip of his finger. I'd squinted at the screen, my stomach falling when Adam whispered, "Is that a *scalpel*?"

In the next several seconds, I discovered that the method a man chose to deliver a death sentence told me everything I needed to know about him.

Catlike movements brought Lucas Scott before the first prisoner in line. He gripped the man's shoulder and punctured his neck. A quick crank of Scott's wrist, and he moved to the next one while the dying man dropped to his knees.

My head spun at his indifferent efficiency, less messy than his fellow Blood Colonels, but more cold-blooded.

Ninety seconds. Twenty breaths. Fewer than two hundred heartbeats.

He'd killed them all. Like a robot. Wholly inhuman.

I'd never seen anything like it.

On the screen, bodies littered the ground, pools of blood spreading through the dust. Pale as death, Lucas Scott twirled his scalpel around his fingers like a pencil and tossed it over his shoulder. He'd disappeared offscreen, leaving us to stare at the carnage he'd left behind.

Now, that same man had me beguiled. Who was this person who killed like a machine but took time out of his life to train me to survive? I wanted to understand every word he said and action he took. Why was he doing this? Why take this risk when he didn't seem to hold the Defiance in any esteem, when he had no problem murdering us in broad daylight?

They hurt my sister.

Where was his sister? Did she live in this city with him?

I brought my concerns to Theo, and he confirmed he still didn't know the whereabouts of this mystery girl despite several attempts to locate her.

Still, regardless of his motives, Lucas Scott's information was on point. Over the next several weeks, while I struggled beneath his deadly hands, he passed along guarded NAO secrets. Upcoming plans, battle tactics, locations of interest—all in Theo's grasp. We learned their food and supply routes, the many locales of the Stability bloc, how they rotated women through the House.

Week by week, the infrastructure of the NAO made its way to Theodore Harrison, and a notorious NSF Blood Colonel, the man who'd greeted us with the coldest execution in the NAO's history, became the greatest asset we'd had since the start of the war.

IO
CRIPPLED

 The greatest enemies in a combat survival and evasion situation are fear and panic.

—U.S. ARMY FIELD MANUAL

The guilt over ignoring Zara boiled over the next day, and I met her at the quarantine house. Given that the local hospitals were either abandoned or only treated loyalists of the NAO, we'd been forced to commandeer a roadside hotel to provide more privacy for the patients who needed long-term healing. All medics took weekly shifts at the facility. They were like a breath of clean air compared to the suffocation of the hospital wing at headquarters, where the injuries proved endless. The patients at the quarantine house needed little more than TLC.

It gave Zara and me plenty of time to chat.

That used to be something I looked forward to. Now, I couldn't stifle the fear that gnawed at me as we settled into our usual chairs in the old check-in lobby.

What would the next loss do to me? Who would it be? Would it be Zara?

Which of my friends would I hug goodbye, only never to see again?

I first met Zara Akbari when she'd cared for me during a flu outbreak more than a year ago, but the woman had taken me under her wing when Theo assigned me as a medic. Twenty years my senior, she'd been a practicing physician for at least a decade before The Fracture. She'd taught me pathophysiology and pharmacology while Dr. Grayson schooled me on the nitty-gritty of field medicine.

While Dr. Grayson was quick and dirty, Dr. Akbari was all nuance and gentility.

"Why do we still call it the quarantine house?" I asked as I sank deep into my chair.

She laughed. "I suppose it's a misnomer, given it isn't used for quarantine any longer."

"Nor is it a house," I said with a forced chuckle.

"Old habits, I suppose."

We used to find whatever bags we could for tea and spend an hour or so chatting after a shift. It had been months since I'd let myself do this, and I pulled my feet beneath me in the chair, looking everywhere but her eyes.

She set my teacup beside me, then took a sip from hers. "How are you doing today, Sophia?" She had always asked this question first, as if it were a therapy session.

And maybe it was. She'd helped the cuts that used to be fresh and bleeding scar over to something cold and stiff.

Still painful, but different. Chronic.

"I'm fine," I answered, even though nothing was ever fine. Nothing would ever be fine again.

My lie was met with a pitying gaze. "I don't think that's true."

I shrugged. None of us were okay, and we both knew it. We were treading water in a vast, violent ocean with nothing to hold on to. I longed to sink beneath the surface. I could marvel at the sanctuary in drowning. Either way, I couldn't breathe, so why not just... submerge?

There was tranquility in death.

No prayers. No words. No oxygen.

Only peace.

"You've been keeping busy?" she asked.

"Yeah. As much as I can." I took a mouthful of tea. It tasted of bitter ash.

"I heard you've been meeting with the general regularly," she said. "I'm so glad. Things had seemed strained between you two for a while."

Would it sadden her to know that I was only meeting with Theo to relay the information I gathered after he sold me to a spy? My gaze trailed over the check-in desk nearby. Behind it, the blue decorative tile that had once been trendy was now chipped and dusty.

"He's your only family left, right?" Zara asked, voice gentle.

My throat constricted. "I guess. What about you? Do you have any family, Zara? We never talk about them."

She took a sip of tea. "My parents passed long ago, but I had a husband once."

"Where is he?"

She offered a sad smile and set her cup aside. "Sometimes we fall in love with the wrong person."

I considered that, wondering whether it was truly possible. "Maybe it wasn't love, then," I finally said.

She gave a slow nod, thoughtful. "Have you ever been in love, Sophia?"

I shook my head.

"When you fall in love, you'll see. Even when it ends badly, it was still love."

How had it ended badly? Was the man dead? Or worse, a Hunter? "Do you miss him?" I asked.

"No. I miss being in love, though. It's like flying and falling all at the same time."

I thought of the swooping sensation that attacked during times of turbulence in an airplane. I hated that feeling—flying and falling and completely out of control.

"Sounds scary," I muttered.

Her smile warmed. "It is. But it's also wonderful. There's nothing like it."

Something uncomfortable poked at my heartstrings. "I wouldn't want another person to care about."

Her gaze dropped. "There aren't many left, Sophia. I understand how hard that is, but if you care for no one, what's the point of anything?"

I sighed. "Maybe there is no point."

A long silence passed before she said, "I want to help you through this."

I finally met her gaze. Within it, I could see the compassion, the desire to fix me. "I don't know how you could. Maybe... With some time..."

Her eyes grew bright. "Well," she said, her voice a bit more wobbly. "At least you're here now. I've missed you. Being with your people is good for you."

A powerful urge to spill it all washed over me. I wanted to open my mouth and tell her everything—my thoughts of death, my panic attacks, my secret mission with a Blood Colonel whose mysteries had become my sole reason for living. I wanted to explain to her why my muscles were sore and where I'd obtained the suspiciously finger-shaped bruise on my arm.

What would she do?

Would she pity me? Tell me to stop? Wish me well?

Would she worry over me? Thank me?

I'd never know.

Because I couldn't tell her.

The secret was mine, and spilling it would lose the Defiance its biggest advantage. In this, as in everything else, I was utterly alone.

I set my teacup down. "I think I should go."

She straightened. "No. Please stay. We can talk about anything you'd like."

Easing back into my chair, I studied her hopeful face and nodded. She turned the conversation to bland matters—a novel she thought I'd like, the patient in room four who never failed to demand a glass of orange juice, a commodity we didn't have. I actually giggled when she confessed that the soldier in room six came on to her every time she checked on him.

"His lines are so cheesy," she whispered, a glint of humor in her eye.

"Tell me his best one," I said through a round of genuine chuckles.

She bit her lip and leaned closer. "Yesterday, he said, 'You must've went a long way when you fell.' And I just looked at him, so he said, 'Because you're like an angel in hell.'"

A bark of laughter burst from my mouth, and I slapped a hand over it. "Is he cute?"

"He's your age! He looks like a baby."

As the conversation wore on, the knot in my chest eased, and smiling grew easier. It was only later, when I lay in bed and decided that my day hadn't been terrible, that I realized Zara had been right. Being with my people was good for me. My body felt lighter. Brighter.

But it wouldn't last. It never did.

And *that* was why I avoided them. If I didn't care, their deaths wouldn't hurt so much. I was terrified of the pain my heart was capable of suffering.

There was a reason they called it crippling fear.

I was utterly crippled. Ruined.

But maybe...

Maybe I wouldn't always be. Maybe reopening myself to Zara was the first step in regaining my humanity.

Or maybe we were all doomed.

II

BLINDSIDE

> To question authority is to lend your voice to the
> hypocrites of the Defiance. Every voice raised for them
> is a stone thrown at all true Americans.
>
> — NEW AMERICAN ORDER, A HANDBOOK

Every Thursday, Lucas beat the shit out of me. Or, he would have if he hadn't pulled his punches. Each move I made, he was twelve moves ahead. If any of the bouts were real, I'd have been dead or captured within minutes. He offered advice about areas I could improve, but I suspected he enjoyed watching me struggle. He chuckled a few times, fueling my frustration.

I missed his fury. Furious Lucas was scary, but predictable. The sarcastic self-defense instructor he'd transformed into had me second-guessing my entire life. After a full evening of battering me, he crossed his lean arms and frowned. "I hope you're at least remembering everything I tell you since you're incapable of doing anything I say."

I didn't bother to hide my annoyance. "Every time I try, you throw some new move at me and it fucks up my concentration."

He cracked his neck. "Do you think an attacker will allow you to concentrate before he attacks?"

"Of course not."

"Then—"

I threw up a finger, and his mouth snapped shut. "I'd expect my *trainer* to allow it."

A small laugh escaped through his nose. "You need me to hold your hand through it?"

"How were *you* taught? It couldn't have been like this."

"See one, do one, teach one." His casual one-shoulder shrug had my hands itching to strangle him. "That's how I learned everything."

Sweating in the stuffy room, I resisted the temptation to growl. As spring melted into summer, sparring became a venture in heat endurance, and my hair defied gravity. "Can't we at least open a window?"

"Not if you're going to yell at me." His voice lowered to a whisper. "You might wake the neighbors."

The growl rumbled deep in my chest, and I exploded. "What neighbors? No one lives in this neighborhood."

He dropped his head. I glared at his hair before he glanced up, *laughing* at me. "Is that a *temper*?"

"I'm hot and hungry." *And maybe I'm also on my period.*

"Want to stop early today?"

"*Early*? You've been battering me for two hours."

"*Battering* is a bit strong." He gestured toward me. "You don't even have bruises."

I threw out my arm and showed him a tiny bruise near my wrist.

He perked an eyebrow. "Really?"

"When I arrived, my arm was pristine, and now..."

"Now you're deeply and irrevocably flawed."

He was unmoved by my flat stare. "Have I mentioned that I hate you?"

"Once or twice."

"Can we *please* open a window?"

With a toss of his hand, he motioned behind me. "Go for it."

Pane up, I sat on the floor beneath to catch the breeze. He took a seat against the wall three feet away, and we peered at each other through the dark. When he leaned his head back, my gaze traced the outline of his throat. Such a vulnerable place, the throat. If I had a knife, I could kill him instantly.

I shook myself.

Why had *that* thought popped into my head?

I was spending far too much time with a murderer.

Desperate to think of anything else, I shifted my focus to something irrelevant. "Why do we sit in the dark? You have solar panels."

"I don't want people to know about this place. Lights are suspicious. Candles work fine."

"Then why are there no candles in here?"

His skeptical gaze slid my way. "Didn't you *just* say you're hot? Do you ever stop complaining?"

Damn, this guy was good at pushing my buttons. "Do you ever stop being an ass?"

A dramatic sigh escaped his lungs.

"If I'm so annoying, why don't you report your information directly to Theo?"

"Who the fuck is Theo?"

"Harrison."

Vibrant eyes grew penetrating and curious. "You call your general by his first name?"

I mentally slapped a hand over my eyes. *Clever, Sophia. Good cover.*

He waited for my explanation, but I gave none, so he widened his eyes...questioning, expectant.

I groaned. "Fine. He was a friend of my father's. Growing up, he was just Uncle Theo. It's why I've been in the Defiance since the beginning. Theo's always been by my side."

Lucas blinked at me. "No."

"No?"

He raised a hand, fingers splayed, all *pause-while-I-reason-through-this-difficult-dilemma*. "Let me get this straight. Your entire ideology is based on the concept that we're all equal and free, and yet *the leader* of that ideology chose to sell his adopted niece—like a pimp—to what I'm sure he thought was a woman-hating rapist for information?"

Could I burn him with my gaze alone? "He didn't *sell* me. I volunteered."

"And he allowed you to just...walk into my arms? Without issue?"

I opened my mouth, but what could I say? Memories of Theo flitted through my mind, and I had no idea how to answer his question.

"You said you'd bring her back!" I scream at him. "You said she was alive!"

His mouth opens, but nothing emerges.

"You promised!" I yell.

Theo hurries around his desk and takes my arm, but I shrug out of his grasp.

"You promised, Theo! Mom— She's dead!"

"I tried," he says, his tone thready and desperate.

"You should have tried harder!"

Outside his office, a crowd gathers. A soft voice—Zara's?—cuts through my anger. "Sophia, let's get you some water, okay?"

I ignore her. "You refused to let me go with them. I could have—I could have helped her!"

"You'd be dead," he says, brow creased.

"Maybe that would have been better!"

A gentle hand touches my shoulder. "Sophia—"

I yank away from Zara's grip.

"It's alright," Theo says, looking over my head. "She's just upset."

Just upset?

An inhuman wail erupts from my mouth, composed of nothing but loneliness and pain. I launch myself at him. My fists pound his solid chest as I scream You promised! *over and over.*

After a moment, Theo restrains my wrists.

"I hate you!" I yell. "I hate you! Get off me!"

"God," Lucas said, interrupting my reverie. "And I thought my side was bad."

"Your side *is* bad, and you're avoiding the question."

"I'm sorry." He drew his knees up and draped his arms over them. "I was too distracted by my absolute revulsion. What did you ask?"

"Why don't you report your information to Harrison instead of me?"

He cocked his head. "How would I go about that, Sophia?"

"Well, I mean, how did you contact him in the first place?"

His smirk appeared. "You didn't ask him?"

"He wouldn't tell me."

The chuckle that burst from him had me stiffening. "I'm not surprised."

Embarrassing for Theo then?

"You could've met him here," I said.

"He would've never allowed that, which is laughable, considering he let you traipse in here with no escort. Would he be upset if I murdered you?" He threw a hand up. "No, don't answer. I don't want to know. If he'd come here, he would've brought a dozen people as backup. He'd have the whole neighborhood swarming. It would've raised alarms, and we'd be discovered. And even if he hadn't, what if I was followed? How would I explain meeting secretly with the general of the Defiance?"

"You couldn't, I guess." I studied his face, his guarded expression. "You're a planner, huh?"

He nodded. "I didn't want physical evidence, and I needed a mediator of his choosing so he could trust her. I wanted someone who wasn't on the front lines so she'd outlast me."

Outlast.

I shook off that word. "And you wanted a woman."

Something off-putting lurked deep in his eyes. "Yes."

I wanted to ask him why, and he waited, eyes gleaming like he knew my thoughts. But I couldn't do it. What if the answer was the obvious one?

It seemed unlikely, but possibilities sifted through my mind. Maybe he thought if I trusted him, I'd be more into it. Maybe he was trying to seduce me so I'd give him information. Maybe he liked my second-guessing everything.

Or maybe he didn't want anything at all.

Then why was he doing this?

I straightened my spine. "Do you have information tonight?"

His head tilted, and he chuckled under his breath before giving me several points to take to Theo. When he finished talking, he stood and offered his hand. My heart thumped in my chest while I considered refusing him.

Had I ever voluntarily touched this man?

With a shaky hand, I reached for him. Warm fingers closed around mine, and he yanked me to my feet. I tried to let go, but he held tight and pulled me close. "You still think I'm going to hurt you, don't you?"

I swallowed. "Hurting people is what you do."

His brow raised. "Why would I spend all this time trying to keep you alive just to hurt you in the end?"

"I don't know. You've been playing mind games from the beginning."

His eyes flared with surprise, there and gone before I could investigate it. "Have I?"

"You—you purposely mess with me."

He shook his head and dropped my hand. "I think you hear what you feel. Not what I say."

Was that true? Though the man had lost some of his terrifying aura, he still chilled my blood to ice. Every time the memory of his first execution popped into my head, the fear would wash over me like acid rain.

I'd witnessed Lucas Scott kill dozens without mercy. It was only a matter of time before I was next.

"What do you want from me?"

His voice softened as it sometimes did, almost brittle in its exhaustion. "I don't want anything from you, Sophia."

"Then...why are you doing this?"

"I told you. They hurt my sister."

My throat thickened, and tears burned behind my eyes. It would be so easy to trust him, and yet, "I—I just don't believe you."

His gaze grew distant. "That's good. You should never take someone's words at face value."

My stomach dropped. "Are you saying you're lying?"

"No." He held an arm out as an invitation to leave. "I'm not."

THE FOLLOWING WEEK, we sparred as usual, but his concentration lingered more on the walls and windows than on me. After almost an hour of struggling to best him despite his distraction, I snapped. "What's with you tonight?"

"Mmm?" He'd been gazing out the window, but his attention drifted to me.

"You got something on your mind?"

He took a silent moment to examine my face, thoughts whirring behind his eyes. The flicker of two candles accentuated the amber freckles hiding in the blue of his irises. So pretty, those eyes. The man was lightning—dazzling, but deadly.

"What sorts of things do sixteen-year-old girls think about?" he asked.

My lips parted. Uh... "What?"

"Lily Wyatt. I'm not sure she's a normal sixteen-year-old."

"Why?"

A subtle flush of color appeared over his sharp cheekbones, and ravenous curiosity attacked me. What horrible thoughts could be happening in that jaded, murderous mind to make him *blush*?

He cleared his throat. "I think maybe they...groomed her."

"Groomed? Like they brushed her hair?" My thoughts, however, lingered much further south than the girl's head.

"No. Not like that." He pressed his lips together. Took a breath. Then...said nothing.

"Like what?" I prompted.

He released that breath. "Like they...*prepared*...her for me."

Several seconds of silence passed while color crept further across his face. I fought down the rising nausea. "That *cannot* mean what I think it means."

He shuddered, expression contorting. "She knows things I don't think normal sixteen-year-olds know."

I lifted an eyebrow. "You'd be surprised what sixteen-year-old girls know."

A beat passed.

His mouth opened with a *tsk*, and he pointed at me. "Okay. Definitely going to have to elaborate on what you mean by *that*."

I shook my head, chuckling. "Tell me what she did."

Another few seconds elapsed in which he did nothing but trail his attention over the popcorn ceiling. I waited, ensuring he sensed my impatience with the whole crossed arms and tapping foot bit.

"She's very...affectionate," he said eventually.

"Ugh. Okay, stop." That was *not* what I was thinking. "I don't want more details."

He grimaced. "I think she'll need help once she's with you. She thinks her only worth is in what she can offer a man."

Ew. The NAO ideals were just the worst. Men and their worship of the almighty dick were going to ruin this planet. "That's disgusting. And yet I'm not surprised these are the things you people teach your children."

Everything about him sharpened. He stepped closer, gaze dropping to me. "She is the product of a timid, obedient mother, and a psychopathic father. *I* don't have children. I don't fuck children. And if I ever had a daughter, I certainly wouldn't allow her to act like *that.*"

I snorted in his face—probably not smart. "*You* are a Blood Colonel in the NSF."

"Only Defiants call us that."

I ignored him. "That isn't an easy rank to reach. You really expect me to believe you're different from them?"

"I don't care what you believe. I'm telling you the truth—like I always do."

We stood an arm's span apart, glaring at each other, assessing.

The silver spark of the scalpel he used to execute people flashed across my mind. Cold crept across my skin. I lifted my shoulders. "I can't trust you."

"I don't need your trust."

"You *do*, though. You don't want anyone else to play this game with you." I motioned to the room around us, as if it encompassed the entirety of my relationship with him.

He said nothing.

"You've armed me. Hidden me in giant clothes. Killed your own men for me. You've done everything in your power to make sure I continue to be the one to receive your information, even though you think I'm incompetent and reckless. For some reason, you only want me, and you won't tell me why."

His gaze flickered over my face, but his silence screamed into the void between us. Pressure built, crushing, like sinking to the bottom of the ocean.

I let it embrace me, pushing harder on his hidden buttons. "What would you do if I were killed?"

He stiffened. His expression hardened, then iced over entirely. Those remarkable eyes fixed on mine, raptorial as a jaguar.

"Would you accept someone else?" I asked.

"That won't happen."

My heart jumped into my throat. "It might—"

"No. It won't." His tone was final. Commanding. *"You will stay safe."*

The choked sensation from when I first met him washed over me. Full of threat and danger, the sarcastic man I'd grown accustomed to transformed before me into the ruthless Blood Colonel—a killer hiding behind pretty eyes...

Coveting my safety.

"Alright." My voice was barely more than a breath.

His intensity faded by degrees, and he watched me as a predator might, like he thought I might run. "I'm not sure who convinced you that you hold no value, but let me be clear about something. Your life matters, and if you continue to act as if it doesn't, we're going to have a problem. Do you understand?"

No, I didn't understand at all. I was no one to this man, just some Defiant who served as a glorified text messaging service.

He stepped closer, and his voice honed to a sharpened blade. "Do you understand, Sophia?"

My throat closed up at the implied threat in his words, so I merely nodded. He kept insisting he wouldn't hurt me, so what was this? If I told him right now that I was worth very little to the Defiance, that losing me wouldn't affect them in the slightest, what exactly would he do?

It was a simple truth.

"Is there a plan for tomorrow?" he asked, changing the subject entirely.

Still reeling, it took me a moment to remember what was happening tomorrow. Ah, right. Lily Wyatt's rescue. "I assume there is. It's not information they share with me."

"And you won't be there? They're not sending you out into the field to die again?"

Bemused, I shook my head. "I'll be in the hospital wing, like usual."

His gaze narrowed. Did he think I was lying?

"So maybe try not to kill anyone," I added.

The ice around him melted, his muscles relaxed…and I drowned in the confusion. What *was* that? His head canted to the left, thoughtful. "But if I kill them, won't that ensure you an easy shift?"

My mouth fell open. "Was that a *joke*?"

"No. Of course not."

Something behind my belly button pulled tight, and I floundered in the bewilderment. Was he…teasing me? Right after he scarily declared I must somehow become immortal?

Who *was* this man?

Lucas sat cross-legged on the floor and patted the carpet.

Okay, so we'd just ignore it all, then. I could do that. I was excellent at the head-in-the-sand option.

I settled before him while he detailed once more his itinerary for the following night. He gave tips and suggestions about ways to help us succeed. Knowing his ideas would wound Theo's pride, Lucas wanted me to present them as if they weren't important or he was trying to keep them secret.

"Tell him I 'let slip' that the river will be low enough to cross that night."

"Oh, mention the part about the empty warehouse off-handedly."

The man understood how to exploit people's weaknesses, and I couldn't help but wonder which of my flaws he was sucking dry. When the time came to leave, he opened the door for me. "Until next week."

I allowed myself to give him a cheeky smile. "Mission tomorrow sounds dangerous, and you'll be the primary target. Will you even be alive for me to meet you next week?"

"With any luck, no."

My smile fell.

He clocked that reaction with a smirk of his own. "Aw, cheer up, darling. As long as I'm alive, you still have to tolerate me."

I rolled my eyes.

"And hey, as a bonus prize, if I die, this castle of dust"—he spread his arms to indicate the house—"can go to the girl who would most enjoy my death."

"I'm sure there are some who'd enjoy it more than me."

His smirk turned wry.

A moment passed in which we stared at each other, and unlike all the other Thursdays, I hesitated to leave. "So that's the last will and testament of Lucas Scott?"

"Mm. A celebratory document the nation over, I'm sure."

I patted him on the shoulder. "Sad little murderer. No one likes him."

His expression flickered, his lips pressed together, and I startled when a smile broke over his face like sunshine emerging from heavy rain clouds. Real and bright. Even teeth. Shallow dimples.

And then he laughed. Pinching the bridge of his nose with his eyes squeezed shut, he laughed.

He just...*laughed*.

Logic told me he was made of flesh and blood and therefore capable of the full range of emotion, but this introduced a whole new side to him. I didn't want or need this proof that he was human.

"Your mouth is going to get you killed," he said.

Despite my suddenly pounding heart, I shrugged as if I routinely stood at Hunters' doorsteps to witness their fits of hilarity.

Vivid eyes found mine, full of mirth, sparkling like the Caribbean Sea. "I have something for you."

"*More* presents?"

Motioning for me to follow him into the night, he led me to the side of the house, where a bicycle leaned against the brick. He wheeled it to me. "They can't catch you if you're faster than them."

He brought me a bike? I never bothered to check one out from headquarters because the walk was so short. Lucas, however, had no way of knowing that, and even if he did, I suspected he'd prefer me on the bike.

I stared, mystified by this further evidence that my safety

mattered a great deal to him. "Why are you so obsessed with my being caught?"

"Call it a personality flaw," he said without looking at me.

The bike was a simple black cruiser, one speed with a coaster brake. "This is in good condition. Where'd you get it?"

"It's mine."

I glanced at him, but he refused to look at me. The evening air around us was cool, scented of flowers and petrichor from the rain earlier. A half-moon lent only tinges of silvery luminosity to his face. I could barely make out his expression, but his eyes? His eyes picked up the low light, and in my silence, they finally darted in my direction.

"I can't take your bike," I said.

He raised his eyebrows, all stern like he was about to start bossing me around again.

"It's just," I said before he could start, "why would you give me this?" My chest burned with a flaming desire to understand his motives and grasp his objectives. I wanted to know *why*. All the whys. I needed them.

My focus bounced between him and the bike.

"Shut up and take the bike, Sophia." He said it like a plea, a friend begging another to do something for their own good.

My stubbornness reared, and I crossed my arms. "Don't tell me to shut up."

Something changed. His stance, maybe. Or perhaps the sharpness of his expression. Or maybe part of me was hard-wired to respond to internal changes in him—a protective instinct brought on by the danger he represented.

He didn't move, but suddenly I felt crowded by him. Suffocated. Not threatened, exactly, but overwhelmed, and I couldn't pinpoint why.

Then his voice dipped into that satiny, razor-ish register that sent tingles down my legs. "Maybe I will when you stop saying stupid things."

The insult stiffened my spine, and he practically lit up, waiting for my response.

Did he *want* to fight with me?

I hesitated, staring into eyes that were far too pretty to belong to a man. "You may be the most confusing person I've ever met."

A crooked smile spread over his face like honey, further confirmation of his humanity. "And it only gets worse from here."

Definitely true. He wanted something from me. Maybe it wasn't my body, but there was a reason he'd asked for someone like me, and the anxiety of waiting for the next blow to land had my entire life rattled. I left him, ignoring his taunt of *Don't crash!* as I rode away.

The bike cut my commute by several minutes. I stored it with the other bikes and headed straight to Theo.

I ran into Adam near the stairs.

"Nice bike," he said.

I kept walking. "Yeah. I know, right?"

"Where'd you get it?"

I spared him a glance as he rushed to keep up. "Theo gave it to me."

His grin was so familiar, I found myself reciprocating despite that my heart was still pounding with confusion and nerves.

"I won't ask Harrison whether that's true if you do my KP duty next week."

I could probably have asked Theo to corroborate my story, but Adam and I had been playing this game for years.

"Deal," I said.

He wiggled his eyebrows at me. "I hear there's a big mission tomorrow. You know anything about that?"

I pasted on a bewildered expression and hoped it was believable. "Why would I know anything?"

He eyed me. "Come to the meetup tonight."

"I'm not in the mood."

His hand ghosted over my shoulder. "Soph, don't do this to yourself."

I slowed. "Do what?"

"You're locking yourself away. You don't have to. It's me."

His words tugged at something deep inside. The remains of my heart, maybe. Adam was one of the relics from my past, one of the only ones still living. His presence should have been comforting, but looking at his face made me ache.

We stopped in the hallway near Theo's office, where I tapped my hand on the permanent bronze dog statue by the door in silence.

"I hate that you're so alone," he said.

"You sound like Zara," I muttered.

What did it matter if I was alone, or if I pushed them away? I wasn't going to make it out of this intact, even if I lived, and neither would they. Caring for people only caused pain. Hadn't he figured that out by now?

Still, Adam had always been strong for everyone. He'd held us together time and again. Who held him together? Had anyone ever offered him solace?

I blinked several times to stave off the tears and stared down the hall to avoid the disappointment in his eyes. But in the end, he broke me.

"Sophia." His tone was so soft, so sad, that the tears finally tore through my resolve. "None of them would have wanted this for you."

I still hadn't found the courage to ask Lucas about Tekqua, fearful of what he might find, and my heart twisted from guilt and grief. "I miss them, Adam."

His face crumpled when I glanced his way.

"Why is no one helping us?" I whispered through the tears.

"I don't know," he said, because it was an unanswerable question. Was Haynes stopping any foreign aid from reaching us? Was the world siding with him? Did anyone care about us at all?

Adam touched my arm. "What can I do?"

"Nothing." I turned and said the next words as I walked away from him. "They're dead, and I may as well be."

I STAND under a bridge in the pouring rain. Lucas faces me, silent, twirling his infamous scalpel around his finger like a simple pencil.

"Why are we here?" I ask.

"I told you to stay safe."

I look up and down the roadway, heavy rain obscuring the distance. The world is nothing but wet smudges of gray and green, soundtracked by the din of the storm. No immediate threats pop out, but I search for them anyway.

When I find none, I turn back to him. "Protect myself from what?"

He says nothing, but his eyes gleam bright in the gray. The scalpel spins and spins.

How can someone so innately treacherous be this magnetic? One small move with that scalpel could end me, but I drift toward the danger regardless.

What stays his hand? Why is this predator not attacking his prey? If I turn, will he haunt my steps? Will he stalk me with that blade until it finds my throat?

What do you want from me? *I long to ask.* What are you looking for? Why are you doing this?

I take a single step toward him.

His brow lifts. "Behind you."

I barely turn before Lucas grabs me, his familiar hands yanking me against him as a faceless stranger arcs a blade where I'd been standing. Lucas buries his scalpel in the stranger's neck. The guy falls dead at my feet, his blood mingling with the rain and asphalt to create a morbid watercolor.

"Watch your blindside, Sophia," Lucas whispers against my ear.

Heart fluttering, I bolted awake. My hands clenched the blankets while I blinked in the dark, trying to ignore the image of a knife swinging my way.

He'd saved me. Even in my dreams, Lucas Scott protected me. Why on earth would my subconscious seek him for sanctuary?

Ignoring the implications, I forced myself to go back to sleep, then woke anxious the next morning, my stomach in knots for everyone heading into the Lily Wyatt mission. Jayden took me in his arms before he left, and only then did it occur to me we hadn't slept together in weeks.

"A kiss for luck?" he asked.

I smiled through the nerves and gave him a quick peck. The team set out, and I couldn't hold back one last warning to be careful, even as a pair of intense, multi-colored eyes flashed across my thoughts, paired with a bolt of unease.

Was I... I couldn't be *worried* about Lucas?

I tried to laugh at myself, to talk myself out of my own stupidity, but really, I was just trying not to throw up.

Later that evening, our team returned safe and healthy, gloating at their success. Only one of ours had fallen—not Lucas's kill—while nine of theirs had. They took Lily Wyatt to a safe room for holding. I barely caught a glimpse of her screaming as she was escorted upstairs. My ears perked for news while the soldiers debriefed, but since no one gloated in ecstasy, I assumed none of the Hunter deaths included a certain shifty Blood Colonel.

Relief and confusion stirred, along with something else. Something dangerous and warm. Foreign and unwanted. If I were forced to put a label on it, I would've fought that label with every word and weapon I possessed. Lucas Scott was not someone who engendered this sort of emotion. Or at least, he wasn't supposed to. Not *this* emotion.

But at night, when I closed my eyes, it flashed in neon across my mind.

Hope.

12

COMMON GROUND

 The Brotherhood Cross is not just an emblem. It is the heart of our unity. Under its shadow, defiance is crushed.

— RICHARD HAYNES, CAPITOL HILL ADDRESS

Lily Wyatt was the worst person I'd ever met—and I kept regular company with a man who could, by definition, be accurately termed a serial killer.

The girl had been fully indoctrinated into the intolerant NAO culture. Hateful and brash, she lashed out at us like a petite blond snake. She was irate she'd been rescued—or, to use her term, *kidnapped*—and spat insults at us designed to disparage our lifestyles, our religions, our sexual orientations, even her own gender. She kicked and hissed at anyone who came near, while her pleas to return her to her father fell on deaf ears. Sobbing, she beat her fists on her locked door, yelling we'd stolen her from her purpose in life.

I tried not to dwell on the psychological damage that went into a sixteen-year-old thinking her *purpose in life* was to serve a man.

Prior to relocating her to a base further from the active combat zone, we kept her in a small room with a twenty-four-hour guard. Her enraged screams echoed through the entire sleeping wing, day and night. I loathed her. Maybe it was unfair, but it didn't matter. I couldn't wait for the day I never had to hear her voice again.

That Thursday, the house on Evanston was locked and empty. Extracting the key Lucas gave me, I checked over my shoulder before letting myself in.

The house was dark, the windows allowing for scant bits of summer evening light. I waited for Lucas for two minutes before taking the opportunity to explore. The house was a large ranch-style, mostly still furnished. The kitchen and back bedroom were familiar to me, as were the master bedroom and large closet Lucas had converted into a communications room. The rest, however, remained a mystery.

I strolled the hallway, glancing at the pictures on the walls—paintings and dusty portraits of a happy family. I wondered where they'd gone. Maybe they found a safe place far away from the war.

Or maybe they were dead.

The end of the hall opened into a cheerful den lined with shelves full of books, vinyls and knickknacks. A plush sectional dominated the center of the room. Off in the corner, almost as if it had been forgotten, stood a shiny black grand piano, the only part of the room not covered in dust.

Sheet music was propped on the music rack. My fingers trailed the keys.

"That's why I chose this house."

I spun with a gasp, my heart in my throat. Lucas leaned on the doorjamb, arms crossed, shadows playing hide-and-seek across his face.

"Don't sneak up on me!" I said.

He raised a lazy hand. "I'm not sneaking. I'm walking."

"You walk like a jungle cat."

His brows raised. "You startle like a deer."

With my hand pressed to my chest, I willed my heart rate to return to normal. Only then did I register what he said. "The piano? That's why you picked this house?"

"Most of the abandoned neighborhoods have been gutted or burned, but this one somehow survived. I *suspect* it's because we're close to the Defiance center of operations?"

I crossed my arms, silent.

He chuckled at my nonresponse. "Yeah. That's what I thought. Dangerous territory for a Hunter, but the grand piano was hard to resist."

"You play?"

"Sometimes."

"Play for me?"

His eyes narrowed. "No."

I gazed down at the piano, dragging a finger over one key. "Someday?"

"Tell you what, if you can ever pin me in a fight, maybe I'll teach you *Chopsticks*."

"Finally!" I said, a grin pulling itself to the surface. "Some motivation!"

The edge of his mouth flickered like he wanted to smile, but he just shook his head. "Is *staying alive* not motivation enough for you?"

"Obviously not."

With a sigh, he motioned me toward our training room. After he lit the candles, we faced each other.

"So...about the other night," I said.

"What about the other night?"

"It went exactly like you said."

His gaze flickered over my face, curious. "As has everything else I've told you about."

"But you didn't kill anyone."

He paused, head cocked. "You asked me not to."

I blinked. "I— You did that for me?"

A moment passed in which his expression morphed from impassive to incredulous, like I was the stupidest creature on the planet. "No. I did that for me."

Butterfly wings fluttered in my chest while I searched his face for a telltale twitch, any sign of a lie.

He let out a long exhale. "Contrary to what you might believe, I don't *like* killing people, Sophia. Didn't realize that needed to be stated out loud, but I'd like it on the record."

Words stuck in my throat. What did one say to an executioner who admitted to disliking it? I stammered out, "Right. I didn't think...you—"

He raised a hand. "Just stop. How is she?"

I took a breath and shook myself. "Extremely annoying, if I'm being honest. There was a desperate moment in the middle of the night when she was screaming at us that I wished we'd let you keep her."

He chuckled. "Bad enough I had her for three days. She's a handsy little creep. No one taught her about personal space. I had to order her to sit in a corner so she'd stop touching me."

"She called me a bushy-headed whore."

His lips pressed together, but the amusement escaped anyway, in little crinkles around his eyes and twinkles in the aquamarine.

"You think it's funny?"

"Just...picturing your response."

I stomped my foot. "She's the worst! She kept referring to us as *dirty sluts*, so I told her she was a waste of her dad's spunk."

His laugh was a sudden, powerful thing, like a crash of thunder. "She's just a kid. You're insulting her with...semen?"

I rolled my eyes. "She clearly has no problem with jizz, Lucas, since she was so intent on getting yours."

The laughter died as he shuddered.

"Do you realize she believes she'd be happier as a slave to you than free with us?" I said. "She begged us to give her back to you."

He shrugged. "She's been brainwashed. She's young enough. She'll see the truth eventually."

"The truth?"

He ran a hand through his hair. "Yeah, I mean…"

I waited, but he didn't elaborate. "You mean…?"

He made a gesture like I was supposed to connect dots I absolutely couldn't see. "Come on. We're all different, but we're still human. Still equal." Then, under his breath, he added, "Still savages."

"Equal?" My mouth gaped. "*That's* your truth? You're a Hunter!"

A lock of hair fell to hide the largest scar on his forehead when he cocked his head to the side. "Sophia, we've spent weeks together. Do you really still think I believe the NAO's doctrine?"

Well…

He fought on their side and executed innocent people. But he'd never treated me like I was beneath him for being female, had he? And the things he said…

"No, I guess I don't. I don't know who or what you are."

"I'm the guy teaching you how to not die. You ready?"

I rolled my eyes but nodded, nonetheless.

I fought and lost to him for more than an hour before he let me breathe. If only I'd trained more with Tekqua when I had the chance, maybe I wouldn't be so winded. Still, each loss on my part was met with a small piece of advice. When I tried to utilize that advice, however, he countered it with another way to disable me. My improvement was masked by his unbeatable excellence, and I grew tired and sweaty, my mood settling somewhere in the dregs of outright waspishness.

But…

Every time he showed me how to free myself from a certain grasp or attack from a disadvantaged position, the information shuffled through the catalogue in my brain, filing into a section entitled *Survival.*

I growled when I'd finally managed to trap his arms behind him, and he gave a sharp twist. I ended up on my back, blinking at him.

His silent laughter burst my last bubble of patience. I aimed a kick at his ankle, but he hopped back to avoid it.

"Help me up, you evil bastard."

He grabbed my wrist, and I clutched his forearm, but he hissed and pulled away. He shook out his arm a couple of times before offering his other hand to help me, murmuring a soft apology.

"You okay?" I asked, studying his arm.

His face blanked. "It's nothing."

"It's not *nothing*. If you don't want to tell me, just say it."

"Fine." He raised one eyebrow. "I don't want to tell you."

I gripped my hips. "Tell me anyway."

Wincing, he shook his arm again. "Has anyone ever pointed out the sheer idiocy of your stubbornness?"

I fastened on an innocent smile. "You could always request someone else. I'm sure there are less stubborn girls itching to spend every Thursday night wrestling with you."

A hint of the smirk appeared. "No. It's you or no one. Deal with it."

"Then you deal with me. Tell me what's wrong."

"Why?"

"Maybe I can help."

His gaze grew bright, his eyes wide. "Help?"

"Yeah," I said, shoving away the sudden flare of self-conscious-ness. "I—I'm a medic."

"You want...to help me?"

Did I want to help him? Why on earth had I offered it? I didn't care that he was in pain.

Except...I did care.

"I think I do," I said as heat climbed my cheeks.

He scratched his neck. "Right. They, uh, weren't exactly happy I managed to lose the general's daughter. She was in my care when she was taken. I was...questioned."

"Questioned," I repeated, tone flat.

He said nothing.

"You mean *punished.*"

Still nothing.

My heart thumped, and my gaze shot down his body, searching for injuries. "What did they do to you?"

"It doesn't matter. I'll survive."

"But they hurt you…"

Lucas released a heavy, bitter laugh. "It's nothing compared to what they've done to my soul."

My entire body froze at that admission. I wanted so badly to believe he wasn't the man I'd expected in the beginning. Would he give me proof?

"I can't fix your soul," I said, voice raspy. "But maybe I can fix the rest."

The room went utterly still while he examined every inch of my face, and whatever he saw there urged him to surrender. He extended a hand toward the wall, an invitation to sit. Only after I was settled did he take a seat next to me.

I curved my fingers in the universal *gimme* sign. "Let me see."

He proffered his arm. "There's nothing you can do."

With a quick tug of his sleeve, a gasp clawed through my throat. Three familiar brands marred the radial aspect of his forearm, two long healed and one bright red, fresh.

The Brotherhood Cross.

"Why?" I whispered.

He glared at them. "They're a reminder of what we're fighting for."

I swallowed my pity. "It's an odd place to put them."

His gaze drifted to mine, and he offered his hand like he wanted me to shake it. I set my palm against his, and my attention dropped to his forearm. Every time he greeted someone, the marks would be visible.

An announcement.

This is who I am.

But he hadn't chosen these signatures of ownership. These reminders to hate.

What had he done to earn the other two?

I released his hand and traced the scars. When I reached the fresh wound, I found no signs of infection or necrosis, though I could only imagine the pain. I started to ask what he'd been using to tend it, but his gaze was hyper-focused on my mouth.

I dropped his arm like it zapped me and wet my suddenly dry lips. "Do you have antibiotic creams?"

"Yes, Sophia. I'm not an idiot." How was his voice so controlled when that look on his face was...not?

"Could have fooled me," I said, "since you're serving a regime that thinks branding is an appropriate punishment for a mistake."

Mercifully, he moved his attention to the ceiling. "He lost his daughter. You'd want someone punished if you lost a loved one."

"I *have* lost loved ones. I'd never brand the people responsible."

I willed him to look at me again, and he did. Ocean eyes alight, he trapped me in a silent staring contest, one I was determined to win.

Determined, that was, until the corner of his mouth lifted in a twisted smile, and something corkscrewed in my chest.

My gaze dropped to my lap.

Coward.

"We have something in common," he murmured.

"That's impossible," I said, just to be stubborn.

Chuckling, he rose to his feet and extinguished the candles. "Come on. I have something for you."

I followed him to his communications closet. Inside the small room, with the lamp glowing softly in the corner, he handed me a sheet of paper. The writing flowed freely in dark ink, with a funny little curve to the Ds I found endearing.

"Is this your handwriting?"

"No," he deadpanned. "I have a scribe."

Irritated, I flicked a cross expression at him. The smirk was back, and he pointed toward the title of the paper. *Jack Miller.*

"What is this?" I asked.

"A psychological profile."

I read through the first few lines. It detailed intimate characteristics of his fellow Blood Colonel—habits, weaknesses, and most intriguingly, his schedule.

"You want us to target him?"

"He was injured yesterday. Fell hard onto asphalt, scraped up his arm pretty bad, jacked his shoulder. He won't be able to fight the way he normally does."

I perused the information with a little more interest.

"He's still vicious, but if you wanted to kill one of us, this is your best chance."

I leaned against the shelves, continuing to read.

"How good is your memory?" he asked.

"Pretty good, but there's a lot here. This'll take me a while."

"Take your time." He left the room, and I meandered behind him, scanning each line three times before closing my eyes and trying to recall.

Adaptive charisma. His men are loyal to a fault. Beware they will die for him.

Sleeps little. Often patrols southern parts of the city close to midnight for fun.

Thinks of humans only in terms of utility. Has no one he cares about enough to sacrifice his honor or rank. Do not be fooled by his 'dedication' to his men.

Obsessive preoccupation with the subservient role of females. Will always underestimate a woman.

I curled up on one sofa in the living room while he read a book on the other, ignoring me. Midnight had passed before I lifted my tired eyes.

He shot me a wry grin. "I was wondering if you were going to nod off."

I blinked a few times, struggling to keep my lids up. "Aren't you sleepy?"

He shook his head. "I don't sleep well."

"Why not?"

He stretched out on the couch and shut his eyes. After a long moment, he said, "When I close my eyes, I hear voices begging me not to kill them."

Instantly awake, my gaze snagged on his face. With his eyes closed, I could study him as long as I wanted, and I stared hard, trying to find answers to his mystery in the lines of his profile— straight nose, tense jaw. He still had those shadows beneath his eyes, likely caused by the ghosts of his past haunting him at night.

It had never occurred to me he didn't *want* his job. So what compelled him to keep doing it? Why would he support the NAO in the first place if he didn't believe in their cause?

Had something happened to change his mind?

They hurt my sister.

Maybe he thought they'd hurt her again if he didn't stick around.

"Where is your sister, Lucas?"

His jaw clenched. "She's dead."

I sucked in a breath, my heart tripping. "What? She died? When?"

No answer came, but a muscle in his cheek twitched. Recent, then? Perhaps the grief still cut at him.

"Wait. Did she...die, or was she killed?"

A click filled the quiet between us when he swallowed. "What do you think?"

I bit my lip, unwanted pity settling deep inside me. "Why was she killed?"

His gleaming eyes snapped open and found mine. His voice went hard and dark, like sharpened steel. "She defied them."

Defy.

She...*defied* them.

Was she a Defiant?

Eerie sorrow unfurled in my chest, a night-blooming flower right in the center of my heart. The amount of pain in those three words severed an artery feeding my hostility toward him.

Lucas wasn't *protecting* his sister, but *avenging* her. He wanted retribution.

A scary thought. The receiving end of Lucas Scott's vengeance was a fatal place to be.

"What was her name?"

His face softened, and the amber flecks in those blue-green eyes burned in the scant candlelight. "Her name...was Sophia."

We stared at each other in the silence that followed. A current came to life along my nerves, hovering the border between pain and pleasure. Was he lying? He was messing with my head, right?

He shifted as if the sofa had grown uncomfortable. "I called her Sophie."

The current pulsed as pieces of the puzzle began to shift into place. Was this why he wanted me to survive? Why my life mattered to him? Maybe he thought he'd failed to save his sister, this other Sophia.

Sophia Scott.

One day, I wanted to learn all about Sophia Scott.

"Do you have it memorized?" He gestured to the paper in my hand.

My face contorted into a grimace. I'd forgotten some lines in the midst of this new revelation.

He chuckled. "I'll take that as a *no.*"

"Maybe just a little more time."

"It's the middle of the night. You're not going home this late."

I figured he'd say that. The route to headquarters was short, but it was by no means safe.

"Take as much time as you need. I'm going to try to sleep. Don't leave this house unless the sun is up, please." Instead of using one of the beds, he sprawled on the sofa, throwing an arm over his eyes. I returned to the paper, and after a while, my eyes drooped again.

Darkness took me, and even in sleep, I swam in a sea of ever-expanding questions, most of them centering around *why*.

Was his sister's death really why he'd betrayed them? Or was there more to it?

Why was it so hard for me to believe? Wasn't I angered by my own losses? Didn't I resent the Defiance for taking everyone I loved away from me? Unlike me, Lucas had simply decided to do something about it.

Warmth touched my face. "Sophia, I need to leave soon."

Groaning, I turned into the warmth. Fingers?

I jolted awake.

He'd been stroking my cheek, probably hesitant to touch me anywhere else. My eyes landed on him as he leaned over me, freshly washed and shaven, hair damp. The watery morning light underscored the shadows under his eyes.

He jerked his hand away at once, but his fingers left invisible, burning lines on my face. "Time for you to go back to your people."

Touching my cheek, I wasn't sure if I wanted to wipe his touch away or press the heat deep into my skin. I sat up and rubbed my eyes, yawning. The paper I'd memorized fluttered to the floor.

He snatched it up. "Hope you got it all."

I nodded, and he ripped it into tiny pieces.

Taking a moment to stretch, I ran my fingers through my curls. Morning usually wasn't a great look for me. Jayden called it my just-fucked hair.

"You can't hide the mess from me now," Lucas said without looking at me. "I've already seen it."

I choked on my disbelief. "Insulting a girl's hair is a good way for a man to get maimed."

He glanced at me out of the corner of his eye. "Who said it was an insult?"

My whole body flushed. I spun on my heel, aflame under his scrutiny as I replaced my baggy clothes. Before I could flee, however, he approached me, expression wiped clean. He raised my hood, tucking in stray curls with gentle hands and unfocused eyes. "Hide these, please. Too tempting to grab."

Who was tempted? Was *he* tempted?

I bit my lip. "Do me a favor, yeah?"

He lifted an eyebrow.

"Antibiotic ointment and moisturizer, twice per day."

His small smile clawed its way into my good graces.

I started to leave, but turned back, finally gathering the courage I should have mustered weeks ago. "Lucas, does—does the name Tekqua Madden mean anything to you?"

Those arched brows drew together. "No. Why?"

My insides shrank to nothing. What had I expected?

It doesn't mean she's gone.

"No reason."

It meant nothing. How many prisoners did he deal with every week? He couldn't remember each one. He probably didn't even pay attention to the names.

But...now what?

A QUICK BIKE RIDE LATER, I headed to Theo, but slowed at the security detail outside the door. I traded glances with them as I gingerly entered his office, then stilled when I found the Prime Delegate sitting across from him.

My skin turned to ice even as my heart broke into a heavy sprint.

It was like being in the same room as the president. Once, when Williams gave us a motivational speech after a particularly bad loss, Tekqua had leaned in and whispered, "I want to be her when I grow up."

I had laughed and laughed.

But now I saw what she'd meant, as Williams sat there with her pristine power suit and perfect hair. The authority she possessed radiated from her very pores. The influence she held pressed down on my shoulders, making me feel small and inconsequential. This woman negotiated with foreign nations, commanded our armies, upheld our beliefs.

She was an icon, and I was no one.

"Sophia!" She stood to greet me.

I was frozen in the doorway. "Miss Williams."

"I'm back from Aota's area," referring to the commanding officer on the eastern lines. "I'll be here for a few weeks."

I closed the door with a loud snap. "Any news from their neck of the woods?"

Her close-lipped smile was small but genuine. "Rumor is Russia is thinking of joining the fight against Haynes."

"Really?"

She glanced at Theo. "The tides are truly turning, and this informant is a godsend. The NAO *knows* we're a threat now. Our ranks grow by the day, and their loyalists have discovered the regime doesn't taste quite right. If my sources are correct, Haynes's Security Restoration Campaign is losing ground in Canada. With Russia in the mix, the NAO won't have a chance. Haynes's administration is falling apart, piece by piece. We keep up this fight, and we *will* have victory in our hands."

"That's...great." I tried to muster some enthusiasm, but it rang hollow.

Theo's deep voice brought my gaze to him. "I expected you last night."

"I had a lot of information to memorize. It took hours."

His eyes roamed my body, searching. Did he think Lucas would leave marks? He could just ask.

It'd been weeks.

He *still* hadn't asked.

Instead, his mouth tightened, and he tapped his fingers on the desk. "Very well. Tell us what you know."

"Yes," Williams said. "I'm very interested to hear what sort of information he gives you."

I swallowed and sat beside her, proceeding to list every fact I'd learned about Jack Miller.

13

MINE

Patriotism means to stand by the country. It does not mean to stand by the president...

— THEODORE ROOSEVELT

Yanking up Lucas's sleeve the next week, a smile tugged at my mouth. The burn was healing well. "You did as I said!"

"Yes, as I continue to not be an idiot, I did tend to my injury."

The sarcasm was easy to ignore while I shed the infuriatingly warm clothes he made me wear. Taking off my outer layers no longer intimidated me. Perhaps I was stupid to trust him, but if he ever attacked, I'd lose anyway. Might as well be comfortable in the meantime.

I faced him that night with the same vigor as usual. As time passed, my discomfort with him faded. I grew familiar with his body in a way I had with no other man, not even Jayden. Not *intimate* per se, but I learned the shape of him. I memorized how he moved. I'd begun to decode the mysterious colors in his eyes.

Not only that, but I luxuriated in the protection my name provided me.

His sister was Sophia, and she had died. I was Sophia, and I was still alive.

I wasn't afraid to exploit that psychological advantage to the edge of his sanity. He *wanted* me alive. The power dynamic had shifted just slightly in my favor, and we both knew it.

But still...

Why had he willingly handed over such a telling truth?

That question festered, and I knew I'd never get the answer.

Around the summer solstice, I finally convinced him to play me the piano. He avoided and diverted me every other week, but I was tenacious. I needed to see his hands do something other than hurt or kill things. He sat at the piano only because I dragged him into the room and forced him onto the bench. Back straight, he stared daggers at me.

I leaned my elbows on the piano's lid. "You can either play for me now, or listen to me complain every week until you do."

"Your stubbornness is going to get you killed someday," he said with the barest shred of humor.

I pointed at the keys. "I wrestle with you for you. You will play for me."

He glanced at the ceiling. Taking a deep breath and donning a victimized expression, he set his hands to the keys, and played—

Chopsticks.

"Do it right!" I flicked his ear. He glared at my hand, and it occurred to me that he had killed people for lesser slights. "Please?" I added in a small voice.

After a moment, he replaced his hands on the keys, and out poured the most melodic, haunting song I'd ever heard, one that pulled his fingers up and down the keyboard like a wave.

Fascinated, I followed his hands.

Practiced. Scarred. Talented.

And it occurred to me... This music was beautiful. These hands were capable of great things. If he wanted, he could probably paint masterpieces or skillfully operate on the most delicate structures in the human body. Sadness crept over my skin with prickles and goosebumps as I ruminated over the horrors he'd chosen to create with them instead. The song curled about me, stirring something deep inside. Something evocative—almost graphic—in its hopelessness. It crooned my ruin until tears pricked my eyes.

When he finished, he peered at me with nothing other than a raised eyebrow. I cleared my throat and wiped away the rebellious tear, hoping he'd mistaken it for something else.

"I wrote that for Sophie," he murmured into the silence.

My mind conjured an image of a younger Lucas playing songs for the enjoyment of his little sister, and a spark of heat erupted in my chest, reminding me of the warmth he'd buried in my cheek.

"You...wrote that?" What emotions did Lucas keep hidden behind his tiny smirks and aquamarine eyes? Powerful ones, if that song was any indication.

His hands spread over the keys, but he didn't play any of them. "Before she died, obviously. She—" He cleared his throat. "She called it her sad girl song."

I fought the urge to reach for him. His grief gleamed in the barely visible cracks and crevices he couldn't hide. It united us, that sadness. Grief was something I could relate to. It was universal. This war had taken from all of us. I'd lost *everything.*

But losing everything meant I had nothing left to fight for. He was still fighting, which meant that, deep down, Lucas Scott still had a shred of optimism.

I wondered where he'd gotten it.

I wondered if he'd share.

IN THE FOLLOWING WEEKS, I distracted myself in the hospital wing or the quarantine house—busy, bloody hands tending wounds on autopilot. As one of the quickest, I treated a lot of the serious injuries.

Lieutenant Isaac Johnson—Devon's boyfriend—was brought in one afternoon with a gunshot wound near his collarbone. I was the first to assess him, shushing Devon's panicked pleas so I could concentrate.

"You are a lucky son of a bitch," I said, smiling at the location. "It missed your chest cavity, and there's an exit wound."

He groaned out a laugh. "Doesn't feel lucky."

Dr. Grayson stopped by, listened to my assessment, then let me treat him. After I'd cleaned the wound and dosed him with pain meds, the tension in his body eased.

"Damn, girl," he said after I finished tying his sutures. "I barely felt that."

Clipping the remaining thread, I smiled. "Fast hands."

At first, I'd been a hesitant medic, but after mere weeks in the hospital wing I'd realized that no amount of attention I gave a wound could make it worse. Now, I sped through it all just like Dr. Grayson and his years of experience as an army physician taught me.

Isaac gripped my hand. "Thank you."

Dev hugged me, and they left after a few hours, Isaac's arm around Dev's shoulders. Pride welled in me as I turned to the next patient.

A while later, a woman was escorted into the hospital wing, shaking and half-dressed. Zara and I exchanged knowing glances. With a creased brow, she took a paper bag from our supply closet before leading the woman to a private exam area.

"What's that?" I ask Dr. Grayson on my first day as a medic, pointing to a stock of paper bags in the top corner.

His gaze clouds over. "Ah, yes." He takes one from the shelf and hands it to me. Inside are a few pills, two vials, and a single foil packet that stares up at me with the words hCG Rapid Test Device (urine).

I swallow.

"It's a rape kit," he says unnecessarily.

"How often are you handing these out?" I whisper.

"More often than I like to talk about. If you need to distribute one, ask if they want an exam. Sometimes there's tearing."

Swallowing, I shoved that memory away to focus on my task—the next injury to patch up.

As days passed, the stories from the injured soldiers painted a darker picture of the outside world than even I experienced in my time as a soldier. Yes, Hunters were cruel and awful, but the Defiance response bordered on merciless.

In early July, I treated an acid burn on a soldier whose hands wouldn't stop shaking. He said his unit had come across a group of children near a combat area and tried to move them away from danger. A throng of Hunter women attacked with squirt guns full of some caustic substance, and the soldiers had been forced to retaliate.

He covered his eyes with one trembling hand. "I killed two of them. Someone else got the others. In front of the children."

A smattering of memories from my days as a foot soldier crossed my mind, and I shied away from the fear and hopelessness in them. I touched his hand. "They hurt you. What else were you supposed to do?"

"I could have—I don't know—I could have knocked them out. They kept spraying. Got Phelim in the face. He might be blind now. But they didn't want us touching the kids, even though we were trying to help. Didn't want us near them. Like we were dirty."

After thorough irrigation, I dressed his acid burns with ointment and gauze, ignoring the two silent tears that crawled down his cheek.

"The world's gone mad around us," I whispered, "but we're going to win this." Unsure whether I believed my own words, I couldn't look him in the eye.

A bitter scoff answered me. "And then what? The country's decimated. Nothing will ever be the same."

"We'll—we'll rebuild it. Better than it was."

He rolled his eyes.

I found his body among the dead brought back from a mission two weeks later. I lifted his dog tag.

MORIN
CARTER P.
739 80 2831
B NEG
PROTESTANT

Hands shaking, I dropped it back onto his chest. The sight of him motionless sent me into a tailspin. The panic attack slammed into me like a sheet of glass, shattering everywhere as I fell through it. I collapsed in my bedroom, praying for air.

Tall trees.

Warm rain.

Scent of cypress.

It didn't help.

I curled in on myself on the floor and bawled.

That place inside my heart where sadness resided had expanded to touch every nerve, every cell, squeezing the life out of me. The pain of being the one left behind ached like a deep bruise. Why was I special? Why hadn't I been the one to die? When would it be my turn?

Lucas went easy on me that night, but distracted and upset, I still lost. Afterward, as I reached for the door to leave, he grabbed my wrist. "You okay, Sophia?"

"I'm fine."

"You're not *fine*. But are you okay to ride home?"

"It's only a five-minute ride."

His voice grew terse. "A lot can happen in five minutes."

I stared at his throat, afraid I'd cry again if I said anything.

He didn't let me go. His focus drilled into my face for a long, silent moment. "I need you alive."

I couldn't help my gaze as it strayed to his eyes. Heat from the long fingers around my wrist spread up my arm. He didn't care about anyone else's life, not even his own, but he cared about mine. I opened my mouth, but words stuck in my aching throat. When it finally escaped, it was barely more than a whisper, a hope that he would give me the truth. "Why?"

A flare of warmth appeared in those ocean eyes before he dropped my wrist and my gaze. "It's just...something I need."

"But *why*?" I pushed, wondering whether he'd admit it.

I couldn't save my sister, but I can save you.

He shrugged. "Willful stupidity."

Sighing, I left.

WITH LUCAS'S INFORMATION, the Defiance had gained a distinct advantage in the war. The rapid-fire wins meant things had begun to snowball in our favor, and the NAO's response escalated the violence. The air thickened with the aura of an impending battle. A big one.

Perhaps it was finally ending. What would I even do if the end came? I couldn't go back to a normal life after this. The scars ran too deep. If this war ever finished, I feared it would live on forever inside me, a mushroom cloud where my heart should be.

"Sophia?"

I startled, almost falling off my bed before turning toward the voice.

Devon stood in the doorway of my bedroom. He lifted a hand in apology. "Sorry. I said your name four times."

I tried to smile. "Oh. It's alright. I'm a little distracted."

"I know. You want to come downstairs with me and Isaac?"

"No, thanks." I settled deeper into my bed, flaunting my desire to stay put.

His tone gentled, turned coaxing. "Come on, Soph. It'll be good for you."

Would it? Maybe it would distract for a while, but the thoughts would inevitably return, and I'd be right where I started. Regardless, I had to meet Lucas in an hour.

"I'm good," I said. "Have fun, though."

He hesitated, but eventually nodded and shut the door.

Later that night, I stood in the back bedroom of the Evanston house, dripping in sweat.

"One wrong move could be the difference between life and death, Sophia," Lucas said.

"I *know*." I fanned my sweaty face, glaring at him.

"That sassy attitude isn't going to save your ass from death or torture. Learn to protect yourself."

"I'm *trying*!"

"You're failing."

His lectures had been annoying in the beginning, but they'd eventually torn apart my defenses. His concern for my welfare established itself with increasing dominance as each week passed. Every time I left the house, he gazed at me like he wanted to hide me under a blanket until the war was done. I tried not to let it sway me in his favor, but anyone would develop a soft spot for a person who spent so much energy caring.

How had he wound up a Hunter? He never answered when I asked, choosing silence over lies, so I drilled him on NAO logic instead. Back against the wall, I sat beside him on the floor, gazing at the stars outside the window. "How do they justify their cruelty?"

"You have to be raised with the othering, I think. When it's that deep, when it exists in everything you do, it has to come from something you learned as a child."

"What kind of people teach their children to think this way?"

"The NAO was bred from a love of tradition and obedience to the norm. I mean, come on, Sophia. You know this. These people fear what's different. Humans don't like change. Haynes preyed on all the right things at exactly the right time. Loyalists want to live in a world where what benefits the majority dictates the rights of everyone.

They call it *unity*, but what they mean is *hate*. There is us and there is them, and there is nothing in the middle."

I stared at his profile. The words came quickly to his lips, like he'd thought on it often. He always classified the NAO as *they*, separate from himself, as if he'd never been part of them at all.

"It's crazy," I said. "How are there so many of them?"

He laughed without humor. "If you recall, the NAO didn't start out pushing a dictatorship. Commander Haynes took baby steps. His ultimate rise to power happened over the course of years, and now, they kill anyone who speaks out. Do you have any idea how many people are trapped out of fear?"

Like...him?

"They're deranged, Sophia. I can't fathom how they justify their treatment of women. If you're female, you must be meek, obedient, and ready to spread your legs. You can't travel on your own. Can't hold your own job. Can't even exist without the permission of a man. If you try, then you must be *corrected*."

The deep furrow between his brow, the anger in his eyes—they gnawed at me, so I turned on my teasing tone. "What about me, Lucas? Do I need correction?"

He turned to look at me, his gaze raking over my face. "You just need a hairbrush."

Over the next few weeks, the number of soldiers in the area tripled, and injuries increased. Servicemen thanked me as I patched them up, only to greet me the next day with new injuries. We took hold of a Hunter safe house at the end of July, and several injured Hunters wound up in our care. We dealt with the hatred of many. Frequently, however, we received wary kindness.

Do you have any idea how many people are trapped out of fear?

My head throbbed. I spent a lot of time in my forest. Tall trees... warm rain...scent of cypress...

Lucas proved relentless during a heatwave. We struggled for hours, me throwing full-force punches while he pulled his. Trying to catch my breath, I braced my hands on my carpet-burned knees. "I have a theory you were sent to torture me slowly into madness."

He snorted. "I'm the one suffering. It's been, what, four months? The only change I see is the size of your hair. Does it have self-awareness? Can it see me?"

When I lifted my head to glare, his gaze darted down my loose shirt. I straightened as he jerked his head away. A tinge of red spread across his fair cheekbones, along with a self-mocking smirk. "This is why you wear a hoodie."

"Mm-hmm. You try wearing one when it's one hundred degrees outside."

He pointedly lifted the hood of his sleeveless hoodie, dropping it over his head. It shadowed his face, but his eyes glimmered.

I shot him a scathing expression. "Okay. Can I have one with no sleeves then?"

"Maybe." He crossed his arms. "If you're a good girl." A black bracer covered his right forearm, hiding the hate brands. He always wore it with short sleeves and annoying pangs of sympathy stirred in me. His hair was damp and curling from the sweat, stubble darkening his jaw.

Even in my thin undershirt, the house was stifling. Sweat dripped down my temples and neck, and salted my lips. My baby hairs curled around my face. Lucas wasn't wrong about my hair. In humidity, it tended to take on a life of its own; the curls expanding even in my topknot. Self-consciousness attacked me as I dripped and frizzed, and he leaned against the wall, managing to remain poised despite the heat. For the first time since meeting him, I became aware of him not as a Hunter or as my enemy, but as a man.

He looked good.

What?

No, he didn't.

"They're trying to find your headquarters," he said.

My eyes widened. "Really?"

"They aren't getting very far, from what I understand. Been looking on the other side of town."

I sent him a flat stare, then rolled my eyes. "That's spectacularly worthless information."

He blinked, unmoved. "Crabby Sophia is not my favorite version of you."

A slap of heat bloomed on both my cheeks. "I'm not crabby!"

His brow lifted. A bead of sweat from his temple made its way over his jaw and dripped down his throat. I followed its progress. What would it feel like if I dragged my finger over the path it took? Would his skin be soft? His stubble scratchy? Would his Adam's apple bob when I trailed my fingers over it?

"—is that fair?"

"Hmm?" I snapped to attention. "What was that?"

A pulse woke between my legs as my traitorous body decided it wanted things that *I* absolutely did not. It sickened me, this proof that he'd gotten under my skin.

"Hello?" He snapped his fingers in front of my face. Candlelight flashed on the gold ring around his pinky. "What is going on in there?"

The end of the world, apparently.

"I'm tired."

He angled his head, all skeptical and leery. Shadows appeared under the planes of his cheekbones. The effect was...

The throb pounded.

And I hated myself.

Months—*months!*—I'd spent rolling around with him on this very carpet, and not once had it struck me that he was handsome. He was a scarred psychopath. A brutal murderer. Maybe—*maybe*—a rogue vigilante.

He wasn't handsome.

He—

He was talking again. What had he said?

"Are you okay?" Exasperation sharpened his features. It should have been off-putting, but instead, it flipped the pole of his magnet. Where once I'd been repelled, now I was lured closer.

"I'm just tired!"

"Fine. Why don't you go home before you black out, and Uncle Theo comes at me like a rabid dog?"

I sighed. "Please don't call him Uncle Theo. He'd kill me if he knew I told you that."

"Pretty sure he tried to kill you by sending you here to me."

"I'm still alive, aren't I?"

He huffed. "Only by the grace of some phenomenal luck."

If I could have scorched him with my gaze alone, I would have done it.

His head jerked back. "Damn, girl. What th'fuck did I do to you?"

Hatred burned in my chest—for him, for myself, for this ache low in my belly that shouldn't belong to him, but somehow did. "You started by existing, and it's only gotten worse from there."

"I did warn you that would be the case."

"Do you have to be so—so—" I threw my arms up.

Face a mask of bewilderment, he raised his brows. "So *what*?"

"Argh!" I marched from the room.

He followed me. "Did you just stomp away like a child?"

I whirled on him, my voice a high-pitched screech. "Do you have a death wish?"

He looked at me like I was stupid. "Yes, obviously."

That stopped me in my tracks. "Wait. You do?"

He rolled his eyes. A particularly stubborn curl flung itself above his left eyebrow.

My fury exploded as I fought the desire to touch it. "You're impossible!"

"I'm not the one making zero sense."

"Why am I here if you have no information today, Lucas?"

"Not every week will be a goldmine," he said. "We've been fairly successful so f—"

"If you have no information, why didn't you page me? I didn't have to come tonight. I look at that damn pager every day, and it hasn't once gone off."

"I—"

I threw up a hand. "I don't want to hear your excuses."

"You asked—"

"Ah! What did I just say?"

He blinked several times. Pretty eyes. Dark lashes. Then he stepped closer, danger glinting at the edges of his expression.

I swallowed against a suddenly parched throat. An instinct buried deep inside screamed at me to run away. He was a fox, and I was nothing but a dumb bunny locked within his sights. Still, my anger refused to relent, and I remained glued in place while he stepped closer.

Then closer still.

"You come to me," he said, voice low and even, "because I asked for you. Because I am committing treason for you, and the only thing I asked in return was that you be here every Thursday night to learn whatever I choose to teach you. You seem to have forgotten your role here, Sophia. You are mine to command. Mine to instruct. Just *mine*."

By the time he finished his speech, he was standing so close I had to crane my neck to look him in the eye. My heart pounded against its bony prison as he stared down at me, unblinking. My fury had only grown hotter, sparking in my skin like a live wire. "I don't belong to you," I said, but it emerged all wrong—thready and cracked, like even I didn't believe it.

He smirked, humorless. "You're mine. Just ask Uncle Theo."

My hand curled into a fist. Before I could rethink it, I swung.

He caught it, then twisted and jerked my arm behind my back. In a flash, my front was pressed against the wall, his body a cage around me.

"Never attack in anger," he said beside my ear, his peppermint breath ruffling strands of my hair. "You will always lose."

"Let me go, you bastard."

He pushed a little closer—a warning—then released me. I fled toward the dark living room.

"Next week, drop the attitude."

I stared daggers at him through the darkness. When I pulled my attention back to my full-coverage clothes lying beside the front door, I shuddered at the idea of smothering myself in the suffocating heat. "I'm not wearing these."

"Yes, you are."

"No, I'm not! It's more suspicious to be wearing winter clothes in the summer!"

"You will cover yourself, or you're not leaving." His tone was final.

"Like hell I'm not leaving." I stomped toward the exit.

With a *whack*, a knife whipped through the air and buried in the wood of the door, right in front of my face. Frozen, I watched it vibrate, the silver glinting in the low light, before spinning toward him, eyes wide. "Where the fuck were you storing a knife? You could have killed me with that!"

"Put on the hoodie."

I crossed my arms. "No. It's too hot."

His jaw clenched. With sharp, precise motions, he jerked his sleeveless hoodie over his head.

He took off his shirt.

He *took off his shirt.*

He just...took it off.

And threw it at me. I barely caught it.

"Wear it. Now."

A vicious wave of heat rolled over me, paired with the sensation I'd edged too close to a steep and dangerous precipice. I tried to avert my eyes, but the gloom wasn't deep enough to keep my gaze from touching his mouth...throat...chest...all the way to the happy trail disappearing beneath his joggers.

I was broken. Defective. Self-destructive and sickeningly attracted to things that could hurt me.

I forced myself to put on his shirt. My skin had grown too tight for my bones, my ribs too narrow for my heart. I wanted to run and collapse and cry and scream all at the same time.

"Hood up," he said.

My desert-dry throat constricted as I lifted the hood over my head, hiding the curls.

His low voice slithered through the shadows. "Your life is worth more than your comfort. Never forget that."

"You could have hit me with that knife. Do you realize that?"

A pause, and then, "If I wanted to hit you, you'd be dead."

A blink was the most coherent response I could manage. I slipped away in silence, heart thrashing like a wild animal.

When I arrived home, I gave my lack of information to Theo, showered, then found Jayden perusing the café for a snack.

"I want you," I said into his ear.

Brows lifted, he let me drag him to my room. I ripped off our clothes and fell into bed. Closing my eyes, I ran my hands along strongly muscled arms, trying to get lost.

He kissed the right places, making me squirm. Shivers of pleasure arced through my nerves.

He parted my legs, settling between them, but as the frenzy built, bright eyes flashed across my mind. No! I shook my head, trying to evict him. It worked as Jayden's deep, honey voice rumbled my name against me.

Then, the bead of sweat attacked my consciousness. In my thoughts, I acted on my fantasy, pressing close to Lucas, touching his vulnerable throat. He spun me against the wall.

No.

I lost the momentum and tried to rebuild.

But there he was again, his lips wandering down my neck… chest…stomach.

He dropped to his knees, gazing at me with a crooked smirk and those ocean eyes.

Burning near the threshold, I turned to breathe in Jayden's skin.

He smelled...expensive. I suspected he had a hoard of old colognes he'd stolen from homes he'd raided. He smelled good, but he didn't smell like—

The rhythm changed, and Lucas eased my shorts down my legs, fingers stroking while his lips kissed up my thigh.

"Oh, god," I murmured.

The thoughts couldn't be banished, not as he picked up my leg and hooked it over his shoulder, not as his pretty eyes met mine while he teased me with his tongue, not as he held my gaze when I came apart against his mouth.

I spasmed in real life. The wave crashed hard, and the picture in my mind embedded, carving a permanent, secret place in my fantasies.

My joints went lax until Jayden finished and rolled to the side. I stared wide-eyed and unblinking at the ceiling.

What... what did I just do?

A dark chuckle whispered through my head, like he knew exactly what he'd done to me.

No, no, no.

I shook myself and focused on the man in my bed. "How was your day?"

He laughed. "Better after that. Been a *while*, girl."

"I've had a lot on my mind. Tell me about your day."

I closed my eyes as he described a successful raid he'd expected to go poorly. My mind drifted through it.

"I'm telling you, it's like we know every move they'll make right before it happens."

My eyes snapped open. "Maybe it's a coincidence."

"I don't think so. Someone's spilling secrets. I wish I knew who. I'd like to shake the man's hand."

If Jayden suspected we had a spy, then maybe the Hunters suspected it too. Worry squirmed inside me. "If he has secrets to spill, that means he's a Hunter. You want to shake his hand?"

"A Hunter traitor? Hell yeah, I do." He yawned. "You mind if I sleep in here? Ryan's in my quarters tonight, and he snores."

I was lucky that no one had taken my private quarters from me after my parents died. It was only fair to share with him. "Sure," I said, but I stayed awake long after he'd fallen asleep, contemplating my situation and general lack of common sense. By the time I drifted off, I was convinced it had been a mere glitch.

I didn't want Lucas Scott.

I didn't.

Did I?

14

PROXIMITY GAME

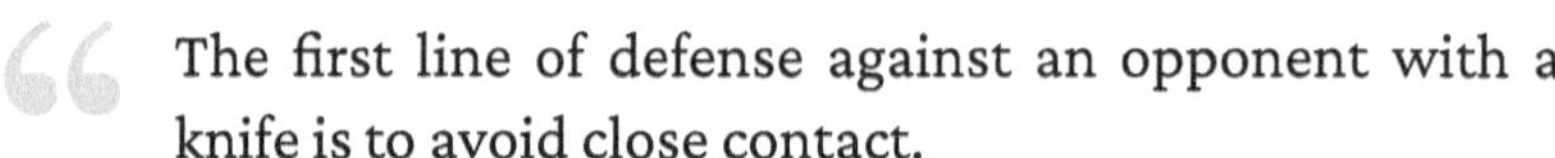

> The first line of defense against an opponent with a knife is to avoid close contact.

— U.S. ARMY FIELD MANUAL

Proximity. Dangerous curiosity. Stupidity.

These were the reasons I woke at night, Lucas Scott's face in my mind.

It had nothing to do with the lethal glint in his eye when he said I belonged to him.

...Right?

Thoughts of him consumed me, and I wanted to go back to the beginning, when I'd been wary and suspicious and incessantly worried he might rape me.

How laughable.

I could no longer imagine any situation in which Lucas would harm me. He spent such an inordinate amount of time wanting me protected that I'd come to equate him with safety.

Lucas Scott, my safe harbor. I was fucking insane.

Questions and arguments fought with each other in my head, and I retreated to my imaginary forest to escape it all.

The next week, pretending I'd never gotten off with Lucas at the forefront of my mind was easier than I'd anticipated. He threw a hairbrush at my face; a few wavy black strands caught between the bristles. My eyes flicked up toward him. "A hairbrush? Really?"

His brow lifted. "Today, you're going to learn how to kill people with knives."

"I didn't realize stabbing someone was difficult."

"The difficult part is *staying alive*. Knife play is a proximity game."

I held up the hairbrush. "Is this supposed to be my knife?"

He pressed his lips together, and I suspected a suppressed smile hid somewhere in there. "It's for your protection. I had a dagger for you, but imagined you falling on top of your own knife."

I shot him a nasty scowl and kicked off my sandals. "Thinking of me when I'm not around, Lucas?"

You're one to talk.

He moved into a defensive position, eyes twinkling. "Only a little. Come at me."

I stabbed inexpertly with my hairbrush. He slammed his palm hard onto my wrist. The hairbrush fell from my grip. I froze, surprised, then backhanded his shoulder before retrieving it.

He blew out a noisy breath. "Okay, you need to use both arms. Your non-dominant arm protects your body. Grip that knife so I can't knock it from your hand."

I nodded.

"Focus on your footwork. Stay far enough away so I can't get you with a sweep of my arm. You never attack first. When he makes his move, you move on his recovery."

He motioned what he wanted from me, and I mimicked him.

"Good. Be deliberate because you may only have one chance. You want my secret? Go for places that bleed fast or supply vital organs. This is the *only* reason I'm good at this."

My mind flashed to the executions I'd watched him perform, the lethal precision of his scalpel. He lifted my hand, poking my hairbrush into every artery or organ on his body that would result in serious injury.

Since becoming a medic, I'd focused on how the body healed rather than the ways it was prone to die. My face pinched in greater distaste with each new location he unveiled.

"If for whatever reason you can't get to those places, go for the dominant hand. He can't stab you if he can't use his hands."

I tried a couple of times, him moving my hands for me.

"Remember, your attacker doesn't need to be skilled to hurt you. If it's possible, you should run. Few people walk out of a knife fight."

"*You* do."

"I was trained to survive. I wear the scars as proof."

My gaze lifted to the scar above his eyebrow. "I could try to disarm him."

"You could try. Probably be the last thing you ever do."

What?

He lifted one finger, leaving the room and returning with a permanent marker. He pulled off the lid and tossed it behind him like one would throw salt to ward away evil spirits. "Take off your shirt."

I gaped. "Uh. What?"

"You have something under there, right? Take off your shirt."

Hesitant, I obeyed, then stood before him in nothing but my sports bra and shorts.

Unperturbed, he didn't glance below my eyes, and I grew *immediately* annoyed. He held up the marker. "Try to disarm me."

My gaze zeroed in on the black cylinder in his hand, and I leapt at it. All my energy focused on ripping the marker from his grip. Twisting and grabbing, we ended up on the floor, where I struggled until I got both my hands around his, and pried his fingers from the marker. "I did it!"

"Congratulations," he said dryly. "Now get up." He led me to the bathroom next door. His hands came to rest on my shoulders while we looked in the mirror. I chuckled at my reflection—striped with black ink.

"Imagine that had been a real knife, Sophia. All the black would be red and dripping. You think you could have survived?"

Ah, well, okay…

"Point taken," I said, meeting his eyes in the mirror.

"If you can, you run. It will save your life."

I fingered a long ink stroke over my abdomen. "How am I going to explain this at home? You made me ugly."

He snorted and left the bathroom, muttering under his breath. "Right—" *something, something* "—impossible."

Quelling the compulsion to grin, I followed him back into the room and retrieved my shirt, covering most of the ink.

"How many people see under your clothes anyway, Sophia?"

Lie!

"Only you, sadly."

"No Mr. Sophia waiting back home?"

"If I had a Mr. Sophia, I wouldn't have agreed to be yours." I slapped a hand over my mouth as soon as the words emerged. Why had I said it like that?

His eyes brightened, and a joyless smile spread over his face. "I'm glad you finally understand the situation here."

"I didn't mean it like that."

"Then explain how you meant it." He dipped his head, peering closer at my face. "I'd love to hear in great detail exactly what you meant and why you're blushing."

"I'm not *blushing*." I flicked my fingers regally and lifted my chin. "I'm warm and have flushed delicately from the heat."

"There is nothing about you that's delicate."

I scowled. "There's nothing about *you* that's likable."

His eyes sparked again. "Then why aren't you trying to kill me?"

The question gave me pause. Is that what he'd been expecting? Murder attempts? *Real* ones?

"I am," I said, though it emerged weak and petulant.

"You're not," he said, like it was an incontrovertible fact.

So I tried harder.

We fought for the next few hours. Pride surged at my progress until an embarrassing moment in the middle when he tripped me and I fell on my hairbrush. I peeked up as he speared me with a pointed lift of his eyebrow. "This is why we don't play with real knives."

"I hate you."

"I'm aware. Do something about it."

I hopped to my feet and let him attack me again. We continued in that vein until sweat drenched us once more.

"There's hope for you yet, Reeves."

We lay side-by-side, panting on the carpeted floor.

He launched into his weekly information. As I'd already known, he told me the NAO's major supply line for both the NSF and the US Army stemmed from the area north of the Ohio River. Hunters had taken up defensive positions along the river, protecting the northern banks and their position behind it. They formed a barricade all the way to Pennsylvania, where they dove southeast toward the coastline to control the entire eastern seaboard. The NAO had a firm grip on everything north of that line.

As soon as Lucas said the words, my mind shuttered, pushing away the pain that still smarted from the loss of my parents last year. Lucas didn't notice. He described a plan he'd devised for the Defiance to safely cut off those lines.

"We already tried that," I said, my gaze frozen on the ceiling above me. "We had to pull back after months of heavy losses."

I sensed his attention on my face. "I remember. Max Aota kept sending his soldiers on suicide missions."

I turned to look at him, brows raised.

"Luckily, I have information you didn't have last time."

He explained what he knew—weak points in the outer defenses, timetables for guard changes, key bridges we could destroy. As he spoke, I couldn't help the little spark in my chest, the one that whispered *maybe*. Maybe it would work this time. Maybe we could do it. When he fell silent, I inhaled a stuttered breath. "Lucas. This—this could end things. If they have no supplies—"

"I know. Isn't that the point? If we cut off their lifeblood, it could all end."

We.

That word.

I thought of the precipice that loomed last week, when he'd stripped the shirt off his back so I'd have something cooler to wear home. The night he'd claimed me as his. The cliff drew closer now, but I couldn't pinpoint what made me keep walking toward it. This man had killed innocent people. He'd slaughtered POWs with little remorse. At what point did I begin to look at Lucas Scott and see not a callous murderer, but a strategic antihero?

"You have ink everywhere," he murmured, taking in my stained skin. His finger brushed my temple, where ink marred it. "There's rubbing alcohol in the master bathroom if you want to get it off before you go home."

"Thanks." I didn't stand. Instead, I stared, trying to uncover his secrets through those sea-blue eyes that said more than any other part of him.

He didn't deflect.

"Why are you doing this?" I whispered.

"They hurt my sister."

I wondered why he kept saying *hurt* when he'd admitted she was killed. Did he not like the reminder of her death? Was the pain they caused her worse than the death she experienced? It couldn't be the entire reason he'd given up everything, could it?

"There has to be more to it than that."

"There really isn't."

I shouldn't have done it, but I touched him. My thumb grazed his forehead as I wondered what thoughts hid just beyond my finger. "One day, I'll understand you."

Aquamarine disappeared behind expanding darkness. "I wish you wouldn't try."

"Why?"

"Because you *will not like* what you discover."

I frowned at the certainty in his answer.

"Listen." He sat up and made me do the same. We sat cross-legged, facing each other, and he looked me straight in the eye. "That picture you've created in your head of that man who turns traitor for some noble reason? Sophia, he doesn't exist. Remember how scared of me you were in the beginning? That was the correct reaction. That's the man I am."

I shook my head. "If you were anything like the man I thought you were, you'd've fucked me with a knife to my throat and given me no information."

"I never said that's what I wanted from this. You assumed."

The frustration came to a head. "You didn't ask for immunity. You don't want to be saved. You only said you wanted a woman. What else was I supposed to think?"

His brows lifted. "Did it occur to you to ask *why* I wanted a woman?"

"The answer seemed obvious."

He sighed. "Never look at what's obvious, Sophia. Look for the details *beside* the obvious. You'll find a lot more information there."

I fought the urge to roll my eyes. "Fine. Then what *do* you want?"

"Nothing," he said.

I stared hard into his eyes, wishing I could see into his brain and understand every puzzle piece he'd laid before me. "Nothing?"

He didn't respond.

"So you're only doing this because they hurt your sister," I said.

He nodded.

"*How* did they hurt your sister, Lucas?"

Something happened then.

Something soft.

A smile broke over his face, gentle, almost relieved. The tiniest laugh puffed out of his mouth, and he took my hand to hold between his. His thumb stroked the inside of my wrist, waking a trail of goosebumps across the surface of my arm. "Congratulations. You finally asked the right question."

My spirits sank. "You aren't going to answer it, are you?"

He released me and stood, breaking the spell between us. "Nope. And it's time for you to go."

15

JUDGE, JURY, EXECUTIONER

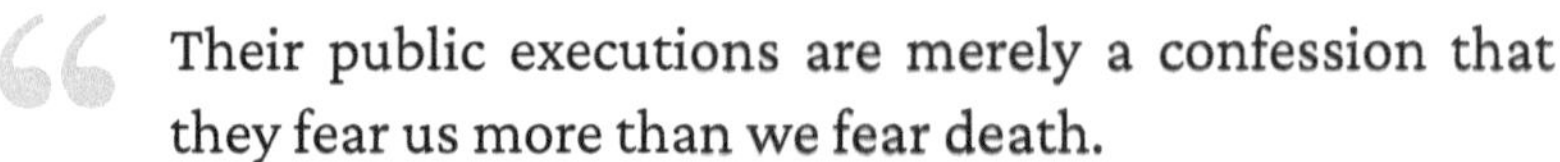

> Their public executions are merely a confession that they fear us more than we fear death.
>
> — NIA WILLIAMS, IN RESPONSE TO EXECUTIVE ORDER 16389

Week by week, I adapted to the whims of the Blood Colonel who dominated my Thursday nights. He gave me chores after he wearied of my poor endurance. I was to jog every day—"*at least* thirty minutes, Sophia, and *only* during the day"—and he wanted me to take time to work out. I grumbled, but obeyed, remembering how Tekqua had always wanted me to exercise more. This was the least I could do for her.

His information bought the Defiance a distinct advantage, and the NSF brought in recruits trying to manage it all. Theo was thrilled, greedy for Lucas's intel. He mentioned more than once that we might end this thing.

Yeah, I'd believe it when he got us there.

We failed to kill Jack Miller before he healed, but we got several lower officers in the attempt. Lucas wasn't surprised by our failure.

"He's a hard man to pin down," he said when I told him they'd fallen back.

A few times, Theo or Williams asked me to approach Lucas outside our weekly meetings, and I biked to the house on Evanston to turn the lamp purple.

I'm waiting.

When the light glowed orange—*on my way*—in response, butterflies fluttered inside. Those meetings were short, and Lucas was always in a rush to return.

Twice, I received a page to meet him at a different time than usual. On both occasions, he gave information that led us straight to a timely win.

During those weeks, Devon tried to approach me many times, but I kept my distance. I declined Zara's invitations to chat. People gossiped, especially once I started exercising on a regular basis. They smiled like they thought I might snap, and the pitying darkness in their eyes made me squirm. What theories had they developed about the lonely orphan, afraid of human touch and affection? The only person who didn't treat me like a fragile china doll was Lucas Scott.

He treated me like a rag doll.

And yet, every spare thought focused on his mystery. Nothing made sense, and my curiosity would not be slaked. The day Lily Wyatt was transported from headquarters, paranoia set in. I spent a solid two weeks spiraling, convinced it was some elaborate ruse to infiltrate us. Perhaps he was a great actor, winning me over so I'd lead him into the fold, and that's when he'd strike—literally killing me with kindness.

Those suspicions disappeared on the first of August.

"Remember when they used to use guns?" a man asked as we settled in the TV room to watch the executions.

"I miss those days," a woman replied.

Brandon Sikes, the anchor of Unified News, announced the event as he usually did, then the feed cut to Unity Square.

My stomach vanished.

It wasn't his turn.

It should have been Jack Miller.

Why was it Lucas?

Unity Square was a simple gray courtyard composed of concrete and dust. The camera always faced a wall of cement blocks, and a wooden podium stood to the side. Above the darkened bloodstains on the wall, the Brotherhood Cross gleamed on a flag of pristine white.

Only the Defiance flew the US flag anymore.

An audience sat behind the portion we could see, but the camera never panned over them. We only knew they existed from the chanted *All hail the Commander* that accompanied every execution.

Lucas approached the podium dressed in military finery, as if this was something to be celebrated. His unsmiling face peered at the camera, a mask of ice as he read the verbiage of the executive order that forced him to do this.

To me, the tightness of his mouth and tension in his body were obvious signs of his discomposure, but the people around me disparaged him, told stories of times they'd witnessed him on missions.

"...kills without mercy..."

"...soulless..."

"...cold-blooded..."

"...inhuman..."

Lucas's calculated ability to steal life with minimal effort had garnered him a reputation of detached viciousness.

"Iced bloodlust," Tekqua had once whispered when his silver scalpel ended yet another dozen lives. As I watched him walk offscreen that day, not a speck of blood marring his skin, I couldn't help but agree. The man was nothing but ice and blood.

Now, I knew those eyes, that face—scorched with grief.

Not cold-blooded, after all.

Lucas's voice whispered through my head. *When I close my eyes, I hear voices begging me not to kill them.*

The man was a chameleon, able to wear whatever skin he needed to survive in the moment. I turned away as he stepped toward the condemned, the scalpel already in hand, unable to watch him do it.

At the Evanston house that night, I'd barely stepped inside when the color of his eyes caught my attention, gleaming like polished aquamarine. He stood in the middle of the living room, skin ashen, his movements slow and hesitant, like he thought I might be afraid.

Should I have been afraid?

He was dangerous. He'd ended lives not three hours ago. But he stood still, holding himself back, his hands useless at his sides.

No fear surfaced.

Instead, I forced a smile. "I've been told remorse is a sign of a healthy mind."

"Yeah? Who said that?" His voice was different. Strained.

I took a few steps closer. "My father."

"And where is your father, Sophia? Why didn't he keep you from running into the house of a murderer?"

A silence passed. "He died trying to cross the Ohio River."

Lucas's throat bobbed.

"As did my mother."

He studied me a moment. "What else did your father say?"

"When you're faced with a choice between two bad options, you can only choose the better one. Remorse is a sign you understand there's a wider context to your decisions than the obvious right or wrong."

His face drained of color. "Are—are you trying to *absolve* me, Sophia?"

"I could see you didn't want to do it. I can see the pain on your face now."

He shook his head. "You're reading into things."

I'd considered that. All afternoon I'd argued I was excusing his actions to make my time with him more palatable, but my instincts told me otherwise. I took another step closer. "It wasn't your turn. Why'd they make you do it?"

His unblinking gaze was so intense, I fought the urge to look away.

"I volunteered," he murmured.

My heart skipped a few beats. "What? Wh-why?"

"Because there was a kid."

I froze.

"A boy. Thirteen." His hard expression turned curious. "Didn't you see him?"

Too busy watching Lucas, I hadn't paid attention to the prisoners lined up to be executed. In truth, I hated looking at them. It engendered too much pain.

"You killed a *kid*?" I whispered. Not only killed him, but *requested* to do it. How could the NAO possibly have justified the execution of a child? A myriad of emotions sped my heart—disbelief, disgust, horror, sadness, fear.

He studied my face carefully, and his voice lowered. "Still want to absolve me?"

There had to be a reason. Maybe I didn't understand it, maybe I would *never* understand it, but there had to be a reason.

Still, a poisonous wave of anger washed over me, hot enough to make me reckless. My feet moved before I knew what I was doing, flying toward him. My palm connected with his face in a vicious smack, the sound like the recoil of a rubber band. Scarlet bloomed over his cheek, not unlike the patch he wore on his shoulder when he'd committed those murders.

Wrath exploded inside me.

I attacked, using all the training he'd bestowed upon me. My fingernails clawed at his face, scraped gouges into his skin. I tightened my hand into a fist and slammed it into his jaw, flinching at the pain that bloomed in my knuckles. Still, I kicked, punched, screamed.

He could've gotten away. Stronger, bigger, faster—if he'd wanted to hurt me, to kill me, he could have done it. But he didn't fight, not even like when we sparred.

I hit him as hard as I could, ignoring the throb in my pinky as a gash opened at his mouth. I grabbed his neck and hair, trying to cause as much pain as possible, to leave marks others would see. His lip bled freely, staining my skin. It fueled a blind fury inside me.

How dare he bleed? As if he were human enough to do it. As if he possessed a heart.

I shoved his shoulders. He slammed into the wall beside the brick fireplace. At his throat in a flash, I didn't fumble when I wrested the weapon he'd given me from my pocket. The sharp points of the knuckles balanced atop his carotid.

He lifted his hands to either side, slow and submissive, and we stared at each other. My chest heaved, but his barely moved. Something in his eyes screwed confusing tendrils of ice into my chest. Something like...a plea.

A breath escaped him, and with it, I thought I heard a single word.

Please.

Was he pleading for leniency or begging me to kill him? Maybe the greatest mercy I could give him was ending his miserable life.

Did it matter which it was?

He'd surrendered to me. To *me*. This predator stared at me with no plan to attack, no recourse for escape. If I desired, I could end his life, and he'd let it happen.

Do it, I told myself. *Just do it!*

But I couldn't.

The rage inside me buckled and broke. Sparks exploded in my head, showering over every preconceived notion, burning them to ash. He wasn't the man I'd originally thought, but he also wasn't the man I thought I'd begun to understand.

He was an enigma.

One thing I knew for certain. Hidden beneath layers of mystery and snark, there was a *reason* he'd turned traitor. A profound one.

A reason he killed like a robot.

A reason he volunteered for executions.

A reason he'd asked for a woman, but wanted me safe.

A reason he wanted to die.

And I needed to know it.

"*Why are you doing this?*" My voice was laced with desperation, begging for an answer.

But I didn't get it. At least, not the one I wanted.

"They hurt my sister." He said it so softly, and I—

I believed him.

I could find no other motivation. He didn't want me. He didn't want clemency. He didn't want to live. He only wanted vengeance.

Breathing too fast, I studied the silvery scar above his eyebrow. No fury, no ice. Instead, pain engulfed him, suffused by a cloying, hopeless exhaustion, the bone-deep kind that couldn't be relieved by rest. It radiated from him like the heat that burned in his touch.

"It's what I deserve," he whispered when I hesitated.

I yanked my hand back and dropped the knuckles to the floor. *Did* he deserve to die? What was I missing?

It didn't matter. His death wouldn't be at my hand, not when he offered it to me freely. I wouldn't play judge, jury and executioner for him. If he wanted to die, he could do it himself.

I backed away. "Tell me your information. I want to leave."

A brief silence passed in which he stood motionless, staring at my face with flagrant disappointment. His mouth opened, and words fell out—the precious information Theo wanted so much that he'd been willing to let me die for it. I memorized it and left.

Only after I returned home and gave the information to Theo did I realize I still had Lucas Scott's blood on my hands

PART TWO

16

GRIEF

 Grief is like snow.

— LUCAS SCOTT

I couldn't get the idea of Lucas stabbing a scalpel into a kid's neck out of my head. For days, the image attacked at random, and I'd flinch so hard that people stared. I retreated to my safe space to get away from it. *Tall trees...warm rain...scent of cypress...*

Still, the horrid image would skewer my meditative state at the worst times.

Several days passed before I understood the weight on my chest was *betrayal*. Why had I thought better of him? I'd *seen* him kill innocent people. I'd somehow convinced myself he wasn't evil. He'd proven me wrong, and it was almost as if he'd broken a promise.

Then the look in his eyes before he did it would flash in my mind, his willingness to let me kill him afterward—no, not just willingness, but *desire*—and I'd spiral out of control. I turned the riddle of him over so many times that my head ached.

What was I missing?

The secrecy, the mystery—they were driving me mad. My hands shook, and panic attacked when I least expected it. I could barely eat, which made my workouts agonizing, and my sleep was punctured by rude awakenings from violent dreams.

What was the point of living when this was what life would be?

Three nights after I nearly killed Lucas, a sweet scent eked through the air, like burning wood and petrichor, drawing me outside. The summer sunset passed in shades of candy pink and ember orange. The incongruous beauty clashed with the ugly emotions inside.

I stood in the overgrown gardens of headquarters and sobbed until I laughed, a maniacal soundtrack to the night. The laugh finally gave way to a black fury. It struck like a fork of lightning, and I fantasized about laying waste to the NAO, burying them so deep that they suffocated.

It wasn't fair, I thought, that they'd done this to us. These deaths, these tragedies, were on them, and they didn't even care. They reveled in the devastation.

I wanted them to burn.

I wanted them all to burn.

The next day, Dr. Grayson pulled me aside to ask after my welfare, but I waved him off. Jayden caught me one night after he returned from a raid, expression soft as he took in my face. He ran his hand over my curls and gave me a reassuring smile. "It's going to be okay."

How could he possess optimism when I drowned under an entire ocean of hatred and terror? I turned from him, loath to find comfort in his arms when my very soul felt as if someone had taken a hacksaw to it.

And yet...

I returned to Lucas the next week and pretended nothing had changed. After all, I couldn't *stop* seeing him just because he'd proven himself a killer. It was a fact I should have remembered from the beginning.

"Let's just move on," I said when I entered the house.

Hesitant, he handed me the knuckles I'd left on the floor. "It's going to keep happening. You know that, right?"

"I know. It's my fault for wanting to think better of you."

A muscle in his jaw flickered, but he said nothing.

The cut on his lip healed by the second week, and August had almost passed before we reestablished our normal routine. The days sizzled with heat, and my scuffles with Lucas became feats of misery and sweat, but I put in my all because otherwise he complained.

Week after week, he remained his mysterious self. He griped when he thought I was childish, pointed out every instance of my incompetence, and refused to answer the questions I most wanted to know. He continued to gift me with things he believed would keep me safe, the most ridiculous being a pair of tennis shoes after he complained I showed up every week in sandals.

I eyed the gray and purple sneakers. "Are you serious?"

He shoved them at me. "You need reasonable footwear."

My scowl didn't deter him.

"Is *reasonable* beyond your capabilities?" he asked.

"Is it *reasonable* to want to kick you in the knee?"

He pointed at the shoes. "You'll do a lot more damage if you're wearing those."

September arrived in a haze of sweat and my own increasing endurance, and as my reservations finally vanished, I gathered the courage to ask about Tekqua.

We sat sweating as usual, both of us on the floor on opposite sides of the room.

"You want me to search for her?" he asked. "We keep records of prisoners."

I nodded. "Maybe you could help me find her."

His curious eyes met mine. "Who was she?"

"My best friend."

I recounted the story of the man I'd shot in the head to save her life—the first person I'd ever killed. After that, it all spilled like water from a tipped jar. I gave him too much information, but I couldn't stop. I hadn't spoken of Tekqua to anyone since she'd been captured, and emotions I'd repressed for months flooded the rocky terrain around my heart.

The day she'd disappeared was the only one I couldn't force from my mouth.

"Where's Tekqua?" I whisper to Isaac, who'd been on patrol with her.

They'd been missing for days, and he'd just returned—alone.

Isaac flinches at Dr. Grayson's prodding of his leg. "Captured."

One word.

Two syllables.

But it has no meaning. I understand it, but it makes no sense.

Everything goes gray about the edges. Shouts burst around me. The floor rises to hit my knees. All the oxygen flees the room, and I'm pulling nothing but poison into my lungs.

My forest is gone.

My life is meaningless.

There is nothing left.

I'm falling, falling, falling, with no end in sight.

This is the NAO's most deadly weapon, *I think.*

They have the ability to use love against us. They can take what we care for most. They can systematically remove the things that make us human.

Without them, we have nothing to fight for. If we have nothing, why would we fight?

This is how they get what they want.

By breaking us.

I swallowed hard, ripping that memory apart before it had a chance to drown me in yet another panic attack.

When I finished my story, silent tears dripped, and Lucas regarded me with an impassive face. "What happened to her?"

I sighed. Of course he'd ask that. I cleared my throat. "She—she was captured."

"How long ago?"

"January."

A pall fell as we both silently acknowledged what that meant. If she'd been captured, then he'd been the one to decide her fate. He dropped his head, hiding his expression. His voice broke the silence, mellifluous and soft. "I don't remember her."

I nodded, both relieved and upset. "I've been scared to ask you. Scared of what the answer might be."

"She's pretty?"

"Beautiful."

"I usually have to send the pretty ones to the House."

I swallowed. Tears rose.

"That means she could be alive, Sophia."

My bitter laugh replied. "Death before slavery."

His head rested against the wall, and he regarded me through his lashes. "There are shades of gray."

My eyes snapped to his. "What would you know about it?"

"I'm very familiar with the brothels. They're better than torture and death."

"Rape *is* torture, Lucas. Even if it doesn't hurt."

He sighed. "If they're executed, they're tortured to death. If I send them to the Stability bloc, they starve. If I send them to the House, yes, they're raped, but they're fed, and they have beds to sleep in, and if they behave, the men aren't allowed to harm them."

"So it's torture, starvation, or debasement."

He lifted an eyebrow. "Physical scars or psychological ones. At some point, everyone has to decide which is worse."

I cursed under my breath.

He regarded me closely. "What did you do, Sophia? When she didn't come back?"

It poured from my mouth. Every broken, self-destructive action I took. I'd been reduced to uncontrolled panic attacks. Engaged in unsafe sex. Shut out everyone and everything. I'd careened through wild guilt and dark desires for death, wishing something would come along to end the pain.

I omitted nothing, including the part that led me to him.

He nodded like he not only understood, but expected it all. "Your psychological wounds are worse."

I frowned. "What about you?"

His teeth flashed in the dark, a wry smile appearing. "You know the answer to that."

Yes, I did. His entire body was riddled with scars. Some days, he came to me with fresh, nasty injuries. None of them bothered him more than whatever darkness haunted his past.

"Both of us are scarred," I said.

"Seems so."

"I'm broken and you're beyond repair." I motioned between us. "Maybe we deserve each other."

He stared for a long moment, and the air thickened. Eventually, he spoke, his voice barely audible. "No," he said. "You deserve better."

A COUPLE OF WEEKS LATER, a chain of violent thunderstorms struck. We worried about a tornado when the sky turned green and the clouds dipped low, but I booked it to the house on Evanston during a break in the storm.

The rain returned in the last minute of my ride, soaking me in a downpour. Upon my entry, Lucas took one glimpse at me dripping onto his carpet and sighed.

I scowled. "Don't even start. Let me have some of your clothes."

"*Now* you want my clothes?"

"Obviously," I snapped.

With a small chuckle, he ushered me into the master bedroom and dug out an outfit. Clothed in his dry cotton, I headed toward the back room, but he didn't follow.

"Wait, Sophia. Come here." He sat on the couch and patted the cushion beside him.

My limbs froze as my abdomen filled with lead. What was that tone in his voice? Was that...concern?

I studied his face, attempting to parse what was coming from his expression alone, but it was guarded. Carefully blank. Dread bloomed in my chest as I sat.

He took a breath, and in the strangest move of all our time together, he placed his hand atop mine. "I'm not sure I should tell you this."

My breath snagged in my throat. "Tell me...what?"

His gaze dropped to his hand over mine, but no words emerged. "Lucas?"

"I found your friend," he said, eyes slicing up to mine.

Time stopped.

My ears rang. My head swooped. The world closed inward. For several seconds, his face floated in a sea of hazy black.

"Where is she?" It came out as a hoarse whisper.

"Sophia..."

"Tell me, Lucas."

His hand tightened on mine. "She's dead."

I blinked several times, trying to make sense of those words. She couldn't have died. She was taken to the House. I'd pictured her in a brothel.

Ice spread through my veins, froze me in place. My lips and the tips of my fingers tingled.

He was talking, but my shock smothered the words. My body shook as I visualized her beautiful face, smiling, always watching over me.

"—Sophia?"

I focused on his eyes. "How?"

He hesitated, worry softening his expression and brightening the aquamarine. "Are you sure you want to know?"

"Yes."

He pressed his lips together, and after a tired sigh, he said, "She was captured with several others. I remembered her as soon as I saw the cause of death. I was going to send them to the Stability bloc, but she spit at me, and the other colonels decided she needed correction, so they—" He shook his head, closing his eyes a moment and swallowing.

"I tried. They—they're—I did *try*, but they wouldn't stop. Afterward, they decided she should go to the House. She was hauled off toward the transport truck. They pushed her around as they went. She was limping after they—" He shook his head again.

His hand gripped mine so tight his knuckles blanched, and his other lifted like he thought to wipe my tears. Except he didn't. He let them fall. "Paul pushed her toward the ramp to the truck. She stumbled and caught her foot on the edge. Her hands were tied behind her. She had nothing to brace her fall. She hit her head on the metal platform. We thought she'd knocked herself out, but I went to check on her, and she had no pulse."

My throat closed, and I couldn't catch my breath. Stifled and smothered, I gasped for several seconds before I jerked off the couch to run for the door, the open air, the rain. I had my hand on the doorknob before he caught me.

Strong arms circled me, pinning mine against my sides, unbreakable as I struggled to free myself.

"You cannot go out there."

But I needed air! I needed it.

"*Breathe*, Sophia!"

I couldn't. I *couldn't*.

"You can't go outside like this. It's storming. It isn't safe."

A strangled breath caught in my throat as I choked on the absurdity of the word *safe*. None of us were safe. I'd never be *safe*.

Tekqua's voice echoed in my head.

"*You my girl.*"

"*Sisters?*"

"*Sisters.*"

Lucas wouldn't release me, as if he believed with absolute certainty that his arms were safer than the world outside. His front pressed against my back, body chained around me like iron bands, voice trickling through my panic.

I tried to picture the forest. Warm rain. Cypress.

His scent drifted into my nose instead. Peppermint. Incense.

"Shh. Just breathe. It's okay to be upset, but you have to breathe. Focus. In. Out. Good. Like that, okay? Keep breathing."

The air came easier as I focused on his voice, his scent, the pressure of him everywhere, holding me together. His arms loosened, but I yanked them back around me, scared I'd fall apart without the support. Eventually, we stood in silence, his arms encircling my shoulders, my hands gripped on his forearms. Eyes closed, I kept my attention on the beat of his heart against my back, the rise and fall of his breaths.

He let me decide when to break the embrace.

And it was *definitely* an embrace.

Tears fell and dripped onto his arms. I relaxed back, my head resting on his shoulder. He bore my weight without comment, even though my wet hair was probably soaking through his shirt.

Had I known deep inside that Tekqua was dead? Why wasn't I surprised?

The worst part was the sense of normalcy. It had grown easier to grieve with each death that passed. Was I growing callous, or had I gotten used to the loss?

The storm thundered loud enough to match the crumbling foundation inside my chest. Cracks of lightning bleached the darkness surrounding us.

"I'm sorry," he whispered close to my ear, and his lips found my temple.

His lips...were touching me.

Lucas Scott's lips, on my body.

But he didn't kiss me. The pressure was there. Nothing else.

I should have yanked away, but I couldn't because it *helped*. Something inside unknotted, and it felt as if I'd taken a breath after spending far too long underwater. My worst fear had come to light—

Tekqua was gone, never to return—but Lucas Scott stood there, volunteering to anesthetize the pain.

I seized that offer without qualms.

Turning, I clung to him, burying my face in his neck. He tensed before his arms settled around me, his steady pulse giving me a drumbeat to follow. My traitorous heart sighed in relief, like this was where it wanted to be all along. It just...clicked into place like an interlocking puzzle piece.

I ignored the hell out of it. Pretended it didn't exist at all. Because I was simply upset, and he was offering something to make the pain go away. *Of course* I wanted to stay in his embrace.

But I couldn't ignore his finger as it drew shapes on my back, couldn't stop myself from gripping him like he held me to the earth. Minutes passed before I managed to lift my head from his shoulder, unable to meet his eyes. "Thank you. You didn't need to do that."

His hand gripped my chin, lifting until I couldn't avoid his gaze. The blue-green band of his irises had thinned behind the expanding blackness at the center. He studied me from behind a guarded expression. "You're going to be all right."

Not a question. Not a command, either. Just a statement of fact. *You're going to be all right.*

Maybe I was and maybe I wasn't, but in that moment, I thought it might be possible. I could be all right. Someday.

I stepped away from him and sat on the couch. He chose the seat across from me, and we stared at each other in silence. Lightning flooded the room, erasing the golden light from the candles for a beat.

"Do you have any information?" I asked.

"Nothing that can't wait until next week."

My shoulders fell. "You—you're not going to tell me?"

"You deserve the brain space to process what you just learned," he said in his softest tone. "Be selfish, Sophia. You deserve it."

Those words unlocked the dam, and I burst into tears.

His eyes widened, and he leaned forward like he wanted to touch me again. "Don't cry. I'm sorry. I'll tell you if you really want to know."

I shook my head. I didn't care about his information. My heart was mangled, tortured, and I clutched at my chest, weeping into my knees.

"Tell me what to do," he said, voice strained.

I sobbed and kicked the table between us. It extinguished the candle, and the light halved.

"I'm going to kill him. Paul, you said? Paul Kingston, right? Another Blood Colonel?"

"Yes."

"I'll kill him."

His brow crinkled with worry. "Not tonight, you won't."

I scowled because he was right. There was nothing I could do. "Someday, then."

"Sure. Someday," he said, like he was mollifying a child.

He let me cry for several minutes, and I finally squeaked out a watery, "What am I even doing here?"

"You're trying to stop the bad guys."

I sniffled. "It isn't working. Things keep getting worse."

"You're wrong," he said, and my blurry gaze rose to his. "It's definitely working, Sophia. You won't have to do this much longer."

My tears stalled. "You think so?"

He dipped his chin in a small nod.

"What happens to you when this all ends?"

The corner of his mouth lifted in a small smile, but he didn't answer. In the silence that followed, I rose to leave, but he stood at once. "What are you doing?"

"Going...home?" I gestured to the door.

He pointed at the window. "The storm isn't letting up."

"I don't care."

His expression hardened. "It isn't safe."

I was beginning to hate that word.

With a sigh, I glanced around. What was I supposed to do?

Wrung out and exhausted, I needed sleep. When I met his eyes once more, he offered me a hand. "Come on."

He took me to the master bedroom and pulled back the covers on the bed, inviting me to lie down. I blinked at it, then at him. "You want me to…"

"Sleep," he said. "The storm will pass by morning."

Too tired to argue with him, I slipped into the bed. Into *his* bed. Dressed in his clothes. Coated in his scent. Wearing the invisible tattoo of his lips against my temple.

"I'm less safe here than I would be at headquarters," I said.

He pulled the covers over me. "No, you're not."

"There's safety in numbers," I said with a yawn.

"There's safety with me."

I paused in my effort of finding a comfortable position to look at him, brow raised.

"For *you*, there's safety with me," he corrected, rolling his eyes in that *why-are-you-such-an-idiot* way.

"Yeah, yeah. You need me alive. Why's that again?" I asked, already knowing he wouldn't answer.

He pivoted toward the door. "Just know I'm not leaving, so the monsters won't get you tonight."

I might have smiled if my face were capable of it. Instead, I drifted to sleep.

After a dreamless night, I woke with tear tracks dried on my cheeks. Tekqua's face was the first thought in my mind, and her dedicated space in my heart gave a painful throb.

Gone.

She was gone.

And if she was gone, if they were *all* gone, what was the point of anything?

My sore eyes cracked open. Morning sunlight filtered through the sheer curtains in soft gold, illuminating the dust in the air. It took a moment to place my surroundings, but when I did, I sensed the emptiness of the house.

He wasn't there.

When had he left?

I sat up. The air smelled of incense, and I caught sight of a burned stick on the nightstand.

Two items sat beside it: a note and a handful of tea bags. I snatched the note, unfolding it to find Lucas's familiar handwriting with the funny-shaped Ds.

Sophia,

I know this hurts. I know it feels like it will last forever.

Grief is like snow. Harsh and cold. Destructive and unforgiving. It comes in silence, and it buries everything.

But snow doesn't last forever. You're the one who taught me that. No matter how dark and cold the night, the sun will always come out.

Don't hide in the darkness. You belong in the light. You are made of it.

—L

P.S. Peppermint tea helps me with anxiety. Take it.

P.P.S. Please destroy this note before you leave.

I stared in wonder, reading and re-reading. Heat simmered in my chest, deep inside parts I wasn't aware existed. How could he possibly believe that I had taught him anything about healing from grief? My grief was still burying me, destructive and icy, just like he described.

I wasn't made of light. I was made of shattered glass and broken hopes.

Still, I refolded the paper, smaller than the single crease he'd left down the middle. When it was no bigger than a pack of matches, I slid it into the cup of my bra. It stayed there, and when the time came for me to remove my bra back at headquarters, I transferred the note to my sock.

It became kindling for the flames he'd ignited in my heart last night, burning me from the inside out. I kept it on me, day after day, reading it before I fell asleep at night to remind myself I wasn't alone.

I treasured it, and never once, despite his request, did I consider destroying it.

17

HANDCUFFED

>  The primary function of the National Security Force is to safeguard and defend true Americans from all domestic enemies.
>
> — NEW AMERICAN ORDER, A HANDBOOK

I wanted to tell my friends what happened to Tekqua, but how would I convey the information without disclosing how I'd learned it? Once the war ended, I could give them the entire story. To his credit, Theo hugged me tight, murmuring condolences into my curls.

Dad's hugs were better, I decided. He'd never been so stiff.

The following week, Lucas was careful with me, but I took out all my grief on him by using his body as a punching bag. I threw myself into trying to pin him down.

I failed.

We didn't discuss the note, or touch on the embrace we'd shared, the one I'd relived in my head dozens of times.

Far too intimate.

I'd never held anyone like that, as if he was the only thing that mattered. Like letting go might hurt me.

We ignored it all, and sweat-drenched in our practice room, I stood across from him, panting. "I'm never going to be better than you."

"Nope." He popped the *P*, which only made me scowl.

"Then what's the fucking point, Lucas?"

His mouth did that thing, that lopsided almost-smile wanting to weave itself into my favor. "Staying alive is the point."

I flung an arm at him. "Why can't you teach me to fight like you?"

"You'll never be able to do it, Sophia. You don't think like I do."

Was that a jab at my intelligence? I gripped my hips and glared.

Something warm tinged his eyes as he took in my anger, a bare hint of indulgence. "Is that what you want from life? To be good at seeing the weaknesses in people so you can kill them?"

Oh, my glare cooled.

"To face a man with nothing but a knife, to see his poor grip, his favored right leg, the little tremor in his shoulder telling you he's tired, and instantly know the best way to end his life? To be so many steps ahead of him that he may as well already be dead?"

"I—"

"—will *never* think that way. You think like someone who still has a soul they don't want damaged. It's why—" His mouth snapped shut, and a slow flush of color spread up his neck into his cheeks.

Curiosity stabbed at me. "Why...?"

"Why...I teach you defensive strategies."

Oh, you fucking liar. That wasn't at all what he was going to say.

"You aren't a killer," he continued. "Your goal isn't to be better than me. Your only goal is to be better than you were."

I groaned. "Fine. Let's go again."

My endurance had improved since I'd started exercising, but I couldn't keep up with him. I swept the stray hairs from my face and waited for him to attack. He grabbed a wrist with one hand and my throat with the other. I yanked at his grip to keep from choking.

Once free, I reached for the pretend knife in my pocket, this time a comb. He smacked my hand away.

Together, we tripped, and my back hit the wall. He squeezed off my air supply.

I panicked, both hands scrabbling to get his fingers off my throat. He loomed over me, and I raised my eyes, pleading for mercy. Our gazes clashed.

He faltered.

His long fingers spasmed, releasing me, and I sucked in air. "Why'd you stop?" I asked, trying to catch my breath.

Instead of answering, he took hold of my chin to lift my face, turning from one side to the other while he inspected my neck. "I don't think it will bruise."

I swallowed. He'd never been worried about bruises before.

"Next time, knee me in the groin. Don't panic when you can't breathe. Cause pain until I let go."

Snared in the web of his attention, my body stilled. The green in his eyes came out to play, the outer rims like storm clouds. His gaze drifted from my neck to my face.

Electricity crackled to the surface of my skin, and my entire world tilted off its axis. He had *never* looked at me like this. Not when I examined his hate brands. Not when he claimed me as his. Not even when I clung to him, desperate for comfort.

I tried to hold his stare, but I failed. My focus sank instead down, down, down to his mouth, and longing tore through my common sense.

I do not want this.

I should not want this.

I cannot want this.

The mantra chanted through my mind, ever quieter until the truth smothered it.

I want this.

I tipped closer.

He drew a breath.

A knock pounded on the front door. Our heads snapped toward it, both of us freezing as a man entered the house.

"Colonel?"

"You didn't lock the door?" I whispered.

He *always* locked the door.

"I did."

My stomach dropped. "Who is that?"

"He's trouble." Lucas's sudden curse was quiet, but harsh. He pushed me toward the door, whispering, "Do what I say and pretend to be scared, do you understand?"

Every nerve iced over.

What was happening?

He shoved me toward the bedroom across the hall, still furnished, and I didn't have to pretend. Terror flooded my body with adrenaline. While my skin went cold, the muscles beneath poised to spring and flee.

Lucas remained focused, his ear cocked toward the man searching the home.

Boneless and shaking, I let him tear my shirt over my head, leaving me in a bra and cotton shorts. Before I understood what was happening, he was on top of me in the bed. He yanked something from the bedside table, and suddenly, both my wrists were cuffed to the iron bed frame.

I tugged, trying to shove down the panicky sense of entrapment. The metal only dug into my skin, stinging.

Tears blurred my vision.

I was chained to a bed beneath a Blood Colonel. This wasn't a situation most women survived.

"Hello?" the voice called, closer.

Lucas dragged my shorts down, then wrapped my legs around his waist. I obeyed every silent command, petrified by the tension in his stormy gaze.

He paused just long enough to look me in the eye. "Trust me," he said, and his eyes begged me to obey.

His lips crashed against mine, one arm encircling my waist to draw me flush against him.

My mind blanked.

I hated that I'd wondered what this would feel like. I hated that he was kissing me under duress. I hated that I now knew *how* he kissed, what he tasted like.

Mostly, I hated that I really didn't hate it at all.

"*Struggle*," he ordered against my ear. He pinched my waist hard, and I whimpered, squirming to escape him. He only pulled me closer.

A throat cleared somewhere near the door, but Lucas didn't stop. His hand curved around my thigh, sliding to my hip, waist, breast. I yanked my face away, trying to catch my breath, and he scraped his teeth down my neck, then pressed a covert kiss where his hands had choked me earlier.

The throat cleared again, louder this time, and Lucas put on an affected sigh. He lifted his mouth from my skin and glanced behind him. "You better have a fucking good reason for being here right now, Lieutenant."

The man stood at attention. "Sir, Colonel Miller requests your presence urgently."

"It's Thursday," Lucas said, tone flat. "This is his night to deal with emergencies."

"Yes, Colonel. These were my orders, sir."

I thought Lucas might stand, leave me tied down and exposed to this Hunter officer, but he didn't budge from his place atop my body. My own personal bodyguard.

The thought didn't calm my heart in the slightest.

"How'd you find me here, Lieutenant? You following me?"

"No, sir. Your quarters were empty, sir. You have no comms on you. Found this address on your desk." The man's gaze darted to me. "I guess your Friday nights are getting tame?"

What did *that* mean?

And why would Lucas leave this address on his desk? That wasn't like him.

Lucas's voice dropped to a lethal register. "Watch yourself. Why are you going through my desk?"

"Colonel Miller's orders were to find you *now*, sir. There's a... *situation*."

The fear turned rancid in my gut. What could that mean? Did it involve the Defiance? I peered closer at the man's face. Sweat had gathered on his brow, and his jaw ticked. Was it Lucas who had him so nervous? Or was the mystery situation dire?

Lucas appeared unfazed. "And the *seven other colonels* present at base are not enough to handle it?"

The man did not reply, but once again, his attention dipped to me and our eyes locked.

With a rough hand, Lucas cupped my jaw, jerking my head to match his gaze. "Don't look at him. As far as you're concerned, I'm the only man in the world. Got it?"

I nodded, frantic. My heart slammed against my ribs, and we were pressed together so tightly that he had to feel it like a hammer against his chest. Eyes squeezed shut, I fought to keep breathing, to push away the growing panic.

Because in that moment, Lucas Scott was the only shield I had, and I *knew* what was about to happen. To protect his cover, he'd leave with this soldier, and I'd either be taken with them as a prisoner, or I'd be left alone, handcuffed to this bed.

I prayed for the latter, even though prayers didn't work. At least in this house, the possibility of survival existed. If they took me with them, I'd wind up executed or a slave at the House. Funny, when I'd agreed to be a Hunter contact, I thought Lucas would be the greatest threat to my life. This kind of situation hadn't even entered my awareness. Clearly, it had entered Lucas's, since he kept a pair of handcuffs prepared for me in a bedside drawer.

Releasing his tight grip on my face, he pushed off me. Without the warmth of his body, I became aware of my near nakedness. I lay before these two Hunters in nothing but a strappy sports bra and neon blue bikini underwear. I tugged at my restraints, desperate to cover myself. Metal links clinked against the decorative iron, giving not an inch.

One last time, the officer's gaze found me, but this time, a flare of heat lit behind his eyes. Whether it was lust or hate, or some combination of the two, I couldn't tell, but it pulled goosebumps to the surface of my exposed skin.

Lucas's dangerous stare locked onto him. "See something you like, Lieutenant?"

"No, sir," the man said, returning to attention.

"Good. Because I plan to come back and finish what I started here, and if everything is not exactly how I left it, I'll know who's to blame."

"Yes, sir."

"At ease. Where is the rendezvous point?"

Lucas followed the officer from the room as the man began his brief, but I couldn't stop the fearful whimper that escaped me. Metal clanked as I struggled to free myself. "Let me go," I whispered.

At the door, Lucas's ocean eyes emptied of all emotion as he stared down at me. "You *do not* make demands of a man. Your only value is in obedience. That's your first lesson. When I return, I'll teach you your second."

With that, he disappeared.

18

MERCY

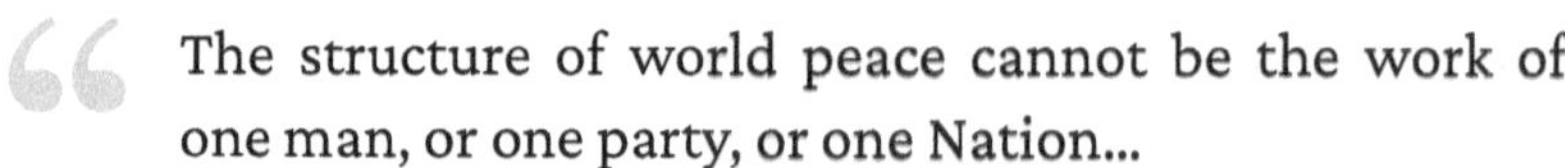

> The structure of world peace cannot be the work of one man, or one party, or one Nation...
>
> — FRANKLIN D. ROOSEVELT

Hours passed, and my arms ached with the effort to break the bed apart and free myself. The cuffs rubbed raw spots into my wrists, and my fingers had long since grown numb. Eventually, I curled into a ball at the head of the bed, trying to ignore the chill against my bare skin.

What if Lucas never came back? What if he died out there and I was left chained in his house?

With those thoughts, I'd redouble my efforts to break the bed frame, but it was antique cast iron, thick and strong. Why couldn't it have been Ikea junk?

I drifted in and out of consciousness, dreaming fitfully of my capture—sometimes by Hunters who wanted to use my body as a toy, but other times by the man who'd chained me here. Those latter dreams were strange. Soft. Slow. In one, he released my arms only to draw them tight around his neck, then held me like he thought he'd never get the chance. In another, he left me handcuffed while he lectured me on my inability to escape.

I jolted awake at the telltale thunk of the front door closing. Dread bloomed, dampening my palms, speeding my pulse. I made myself small and quiet, but I couldn't stop the images of that lieutenant returning with the heat blazing in his eyes, ready to punish me or rape me or do whatever the hell he wanted.

Light preceded a body into the room.

Lucas paused at the doorway, holding a lit candle and a pile of fabric. Tears filled my eyes again, this time from relief. My shivering frame jiggled my cuffs against the metal, the only sound between us. When I could hold back no longer, his name spilled from my lips on a sob.

He drew closer, and the candlelight shed a golden glow over dark spatters on his skin. His searching gaze darted over me.

"What if he comes back?" I asked, trying not to let my voice tremble.

"He won't." He set the candle on the bedside table and reached for my wrists.

"You don't know that. He knows where we meet—"

"He's dead."

One wrist released, and I was finally free to move my arms. I stared up at him, but his gaze was focused on my other wrist. My voice shrank. "You killed him?"

He nodded. "He was lying. I've never written this address anywhere. He's clearly been spying on me. He knew this location when he should have never found it. He knew I'm keeping secrets." His eyes touched mine, then dropped again. "He knew your face."

My breath caught as I rubbed the ache from my wrists, free of the metal. "How do you know he didn't tell anyone?"

His mouth twitched, and his hand spasmed into a fist. "I just know."

Did he *torture* that man for information? "That's the third person you've killed for me," I said.

"I'm certain it won't be the last." He replaced the cuffs in the bedside drawer and handed me the items he brought—thin sweatpants and a hoodie. More of his clothes.

I pulled them on while my mind whirred. Why would Lucas assume he'd have to keep protecting me? More importantly, why would he bother?

Fully dressed, I sat at the edge of the bed, examining every plane of his blood-spattered face, scrutinizing his expression. He hadn't even bothered to wash up before he returned to me. Had he been worried?

His gentle thumb wiped the moisture from beneath my eye, and something inside me reached for him. My hands found his shirt of their own accord, and I pulled myself closer to his safety, straight into his bloody embrace. "This is why you wanted a woman, isn't it? You were prepared."

His arms surrounded me like they had in my dream, forming a protective barrier, and I tried to nuzzle closer. "I should have warned you," he murmured against my hair. "I'd planned for it, but I never thought anyone would find us here. You were just so scared of it I couldn't bring myself to tell you."

"Nothing about you scares me anymore." I lifted my head to look at him. "You just saved my life."

He pressed his forehead to mine. "You wouldn't even be here if it weren't for me, and I will not tolerate threats against your safety."

What about threats against *his*? What had this risk cost him? Another tear fell while my throat dried up. He'd committed a second act of fratricidal treason for me. He kept risking his life, marring his soul, for *me*. He'd been protecting me from the very beginning— training me, arming me, hiding me in his clothes.

Killing for me.

I buried myself in him, let his heat soak through my skin like sunlight, and suddenly I was warm and safe...enfolded in the arms of a murderer.

The familiar smoky incense clung to him, but more powerful than that was the tang of gunpowder and blood. That only made me clutch harder, because it was proof that he placed himself in lethal situations every day and the odds were stacked high against his survival.

He winced when I squeezed, and I released him. "Did you get hurt?"

Silence.

I swiped at my tears. "Let me see it."

With a small hesitation, he lifted his shirt and showed me a knife wound stretching from his collarbone to the center of his chest, weeping blood. "One of yours. He went for my throat."

I touched the healthy skin surrounding it. "I assume he's dead now?"

More silence.

"Let me help you," I said. He wavered, but I tugged on his hand, forcing him to lie on the bed. While I grabbed the medical supplies he kept in the master bath, I called out, "So what happened?"

"Uncle Theo thought tonight would be the best time to raid the armory I told him about."

I filled a bowl with water from the sink, then headed back his way. "Did he succeed?"

"They took losses."

My eyes widened as I reentered the bedroom. "Heavy ones?"

"Not as heavy as us." He winced when I wiped a rag near the wound to clean away the blood. "They got John White."

My hands stilled on his chest. "One of the other Blood Colonels?"

He nodded, and glee spilled into my bloodstream. "Wow," he said, clocking my reaction. "Who knew you were so bloodthirsty?"

I scowled at him. "You all murder innocent people on live TV. John White favors a hammer, Lucas. A *hammer*."

His eyes fell shut, and a slow breath left his lungs. "I know."

I reverted my attention to his wound. "I'm turning on the lamp."

He didn't argue.

Bathed in light, the wound looked worse than it was. I set about cleaning it with the antiseptics in his first-aid kit. "Do you have anything to numb it? It needs a few sutures."

"It will be fine." His hand stopped mine, and I met his eyes, fervent in a way I'd never seen. "You're okay?"

I set my palm over his heart. "I'm okay. I was just scared. I thought I might be trapped here, and I couldn't escape."

His eyes scorched as he sat up and took my face in his hands. "I will always come back."

Longing blazed through my chest.

"I won't allow harm to come to you, Sophia."

My every sense locked onto him, and my voice dropped to a mere whisper. "Why not?"

His gaze fell to the bed, and he released my face.

I pushed closer, begging silently for answers. "Lucas? I need to know why. Please."

Jaw clenching, he took a steadying breath, like he needed the strength to look at me again, as if barely healed wounds inside had ripped open, and he was watching them bleed out with no way to stop it.

His attention moved to me by degrees, and the aquamarine turned liquid. Bottomless. Full of pain.

He said nothing, but the truth was there, sparkling in his eyes. He looked at me like he was staring at the rest of his life—tenuous and easily taken—and the realization didn't please him.

I tried to swallow, but my mouth had gone dry.

Without thinking, I surrendered to the urge of my body and tipped forward. My lips touched his in a single, slow kiss, worlds different from the frantic, fake kiss from last night. This one was soft, brimming with an understanding that something pivotal had shifted between us, even if neither of us would ever admit it.

When I pulled back, the blue in his eyes was on fire, flames devouring the restraint that always leashed him. Still, he didn't move. Instead, his mouth opened and formed words that looked as if they hurt him to say. "You need to go home."

He was right.

I *knew* he was right.

I couldn't make myself move.

"Sophia," he said, gaze still latched on mine. "It's nearly dawn. You need to go home."

I nodded—a strange, jerky movement—then stood. Before I could leave, his hand seized my sore wrist, holding me in place.

I looked down at him. "Lucas?"

Staring at his hand, he started to pull me back, then abruptly let go. "Be careful."

"I will." I made it to the door before I turned back to him, curiosity staying my feet. "What happens on Fridays, Lucas?"

He lifted an eyebrow.

"That officer said your Fridays were getting tame. What happens on Fridays?"

His mouth—the mouth that I'd just voluntarily kissed—tipped up at the corner in the smile buried deepest under my skin. "Maybe one day I'll let you have my secrets."

"But not today?"

"Not today."

"He chained you to a bed?" Theo demanded after I rehashed the entire story, rage blazing across his face.

The impulse to defend Lucas could not be ignored, and I stiffened in the chair before Theo's desk. "He was trying to keep his cover. For *you.*"

The general's eyes narrowed, and he templed his fingers under his chin. "For the *Defiance.*"

I slumped back into my chair. "Yeah. He was just protecting me."

"*That* is protecting you?"

"It's more than what you've done," I snapped.

Theo froze, and I regretted my harsh words at once. He hadn't wanted me to accept this position as Lucas's contact. I'd agreed to it willingly.

"You're right." He dropped his head. "I should have done more for you. After your parents—"

I raised a hand. "Stop, Theo. I don't—I really don't want to hear it."

His lips pursed, and he offered one stiff nod. "Right. Did he have any information for us?"

"We were interrupted before he gave me anything. He had to deal with the *situation*."

Theo's gaze darkened. "Yes. I'm aware. Luckily, he arrived after we'd already fallen back, so he couldn't do much damage."

"Why would you plan it on a Thursday night when you knew I'd be with him?"

Releasing a breath, Theo relaxed a bit. "I was hoping he'd be otherwise occupied. The fewer of them we have to deal with, the better."

I picked at a frayed seam in Lucas's sweatpants. "Were you successful?"

"We were. His information was good."

I eyed him, challenging. "It always is."

He hummed noncommittally. "I keep expecting a bait and switch."

Sorrow dragged cold fingers across my heart at Theo's callous admission. It made sense that he held little trust in Lucas. Theo was still picturing the man I'd expected in the beginning—the killer with the iced bloodlust. But Lucas wasn't that man at all, and the absurd need to argue on his behalf attacked my self-restraint. Lucas had done nothing but help us from the moment he approached Theo with this arrangement. He didn't deserve Theo's distrust.

"He isn't going to do that," I said. "You can trust him."

Theo's brows lifted, making it clear he thought me naive, even though he didn't say it. "Why don't you get some rest, Sophia? You had a long night."

THE FOLLOWING Thursday I found Lucas perched on the armrest of the sofa in the living room, waiting for me. I opened my mouth, but he interrupted me before anything emerged. "It's healing fine."

Crossing my arms, I sent him a scowl. "That isn't what I was going to ask."

He dipped his head, eyebrows raised in skepticism.

I shut and locked the door. "Okay, it was, but I was worried. You didn't let me sew it."

He stood and strolled toward our training room. "Don't waste time worrying about me, Sophia. I'm either fine or I'm dead."

I shot a glare at the back of his head as I followed, tugging off my outer layers as I went. We faced each other, and for a brief moment, I wondered whether he'd address the misshapen elephant that had entered our midst in the form of a soft kiss haunting all my waking thoughts.

But no.

The corner of his mouth quirked, and he leveled me with a pointed stare. "Today, I'm a rapist. Save your innocence."

A laugh caught in my throat. "Lost that a long time ago."

"Humor me."

In seconds, he had both arms around my body, slamming his full weight into me, knocking the breath from my lungs. I tried to knee him, to dig my elbows in, but he upended me, and we landed together on the plush, carpeted floor. My back spasmed, but I tried to fight my way from beneath him. His hairbrush-knife pressed into my throat.

I went limp and huffed in frustration.

He jerked away, and I rose to take the beating again. At one point he managed to hold both my wrists in one hand, his legs straddling my hips. He had one arm free to do whatever he wanted, and I was helpless.

"Are you even trying?" he demanded.

"Yes!"

"Once you're pinned, you're fucked. Literally. You need to do everything you can to prevent it."

"I know."

"Then do it. Don't let me get your wrists."

He jumped off me, and I tried again. I wound up with my arms locked above my head, my legs hooked around him.

"Don't spread your legs."

"*You* spread my legs."

He rolled his eyes. "Obviously. Your goal is to keep me from doing it."

My brain stuttered.

Because...

I didn't think that was my goal at all, and wasn't that just proof of my infinite lunacy?

We did it again. I managed to keep my legs closed, but I was still trapped beneath him.

Again and again.

I would have stomped my foot if I'd had the mobility. "I'm smaller than you, and I will never be as strong. *Show me* how to beat you."

"Slide your right hand above your head."

I did.

"Plant your right foot outside my ankle."

I did that too.

"Now push your hips up and roll."

We rolled together and our positions reversed.

I scowled. "Why couldn't you start with that?"

Impatience flittered across his expression. "I've shown you this before. I was hoping you'd figure it out on your own. You need to learn to fight dirty. You'll never be stronger than the man attacking you. You're on top now. Find your knife. If you don't have one, hit my face. It wouldn't take much for me to get you on your back again."

"Okay. Here I am. How do I get away?"

"Think about where your knee is. Jerk it up."

I started to, but he twisted to avoid it. "Don't actually do it. Jesus!"

Chagrined, I pulled back.

"I'd still like to be able to use that portion of my anatomy when we're done."

Blood rushed to my face, staining my skin, as images poured through my mind of him *using* that portion of his anatomy.

"Sorry," I muttered, then mimicked the move. He fake-flinched, his grip loosening. I scrambled to get away, darting to my feet. At the door, his hand gripped my ankle, and I fell hard onto my stomach. After sliding me toward him, he leapt onto my back, his weight pressing me into the carpet. I wriggled in vain and gave up with a sigh.

When he laughed, I jerked my elbow back, catching him hard in the side. He *oof-ed* and chuckled.

"Get off me, Luke!"

"Ah, have we officially reached the nickname stage of our relationship? Can I call you Soph now?"

"I hate you. Get off."

He rolled onto his back beside me. I stayed on my stomach. A tinge of mirth danced in his eyes. "I should point out an assailant would likely not obey you."

I offered a scathing glare. "Thanks for those *poignant* words of advice."

"Alright. That's it for today. Once you start spitting at me, you're useless."

Quelling the fiery desire to punch his arm, I rose to sit cross-legged beside him. "Do you have any information?"

He rubbed a hand across his face. "They're moving a load of prisoners from the Stability bloc in a month. You may be able to intercept them."

"Where are they taking them?"

"Executions. They're running out of resources to keep everyone alive." He said it so blasé, like we were discussing which of his coworkers stole his favorite pen.

"Who will perform the executions?"

"Me."

Right. Of course.

Why did I always forget this about him? The man was an executioner.

"They're painting it like a celebration. A huge win for the NAO. They know the Defiance is getting closer to toppling everything, and they want to get under your skin, prove they still have all the power."

"So if we fail, how many people…?"

He shrugged. "I think around two hundred."

Two hundred?

My head swooped. A moment passed before I could speak. "How—how can you be so calm about potentially murdering that many innocent people?"

"Potentials are not actualities." His gaze cut to mine. "And I'm not calm. I'm pissed. This shit always falls on me."

I paused on the bare creases between his eyebrows, the flush of red in his nose and cheeks. Expressive this man was not, but I'd finally learned to parse out the subtle tells in his face.

This was Lucas Scott, angry.

"It does," I said, puzzling out his reaction. "Why?"

He shook his head, withholding an answer.

"Could you refuse to do it?"

His mouth twisted. "So we can watch Jackie Miller do it instead?"

All the blood drained from my head as another piece of the puzzle snapped violently into place. The NAO took away their option to use firearms for executions solely to degrade us. They wanted us to know the horror that would happen to those who defied them.

But unlike his comrades, who tortured before they killed, Lucas didn't inflict pain or make the deaths linger.

Perhaps Commander Haynes had realized how this treatment of his POWs would look to the rest of the world. Not even fascists enjoyed overt human suffering.

"Holy shit," I muttered.

His arched brows drew together. "What?"

How could I not have seen? Not only did Lucas offer the most merciful death, he also did it in the most terrifying way. With Lucas and his scalpel, Commander Haynes got exactly what he wanted—terror and a humane death.

"You... You're... You..."

"Are you having a stroke?"

"This is why you volunteered," I said, my voice all raspy and weak. "This is why *you* wanted to be the one to kill the kid."

Understanding washed over his expression. "Oh, *god*," he said like I was about to put him through something torturous. "Don't glamorize this."

"You can't save them, so you kill them as painlessly as possible."

I couldn't reconcile the man I'd originally imagined with the one lying on the floor next to me. Every new fact transformed my opinion of him into something less dark than before.

Lucas was a man whose ethics had been molded by the atrocities of war, who believed worthy ends justified shady means. He did what he had to, even when it ripped him to pieces to do it.

He was a champion cloaked in shadows, a sinner bathed in light.

In one swift move, he sat up and gripped my hand in both of his. "Why are you still looking for something to redeem?"

"You are tearing your soul apart to save people from torture!"

"They still die, Sophia," he said, incredulous. "I take their lives."

I narrowed my gaze on him. "How long does it take to die from a severed carotid artery?"

His jaw clenched. "Longer than it takes to pass out from it."

"So if it isn't mercy, what is it?"

Face hard, he glared at me, and in that moment, I knew he wouldn't admit it. He'd never see himself the way I saw him because he'd never existed on this side of things, watching his own people be skinned alive simply for wanting to be free.

"No one should suffer for a death they don't deserve," he said eventually. "Being humane doesn't make me merciful. It doesn't make me good. I don't care about these people I kill."

I glanced down at his scarred hands holding mine. The gold band on his pinky glinted at me. "Yes, you do. You hear their voices at night, begging for mercy."

He deflated, and when he spoke again, his tone was resigned. "You're making me out to be better than I am."

"I know what I see."

With a long exhale, he whispered my name like he couldn't believe the sheer extent of my stupidity. I lifted my gaze to him, unable to stop myself from snagging on his mouth, remembering how it felt against mine.

"You are the most stubborn woman I've ever met."

"And you're the most confusing man," I said. "But I think... I think I'm beginning to understand you."

He shook his head and stood. "If you really understood, you would have killed me a long time ago."

19

TRAITOR

>  Whoever, owing allegiance to the United States, levies war against them or adheres to their enemies, giving them aid and comfort within the United States or elsewhere, is guilty of treason and shall suffer death.
>
> — U.S.C. 18 § 2381

Over the next couple of weeks, Theo's shock over the possibility of saving two hundred prisoners had him making lists of questions to ask Lucas, who rolled his eyes at most of it.

"This is obvious," he would say. "Does Uncle Theo really need me to spell it out for him?"

"He's just trying to be careful."

In the midst of it all, Lucas told me the Hunters had long suspected a traitor among them. "The other colonels and I are interrogating soldiers," he said as we sparred. "I'm trying to find the rat."

I laughed, imagining him searching for himself, but then the reality of the situation settled. "They don't suspect you, do they?"

He blocked my punch. "Not that I know of, but they'll figure it out eventually."

I reset, fists in front of my face. "Not if you're careful, right?"

"As the Defiance wins more ground, they'll consider higher levels of rank."

A bolt of fear shot through my chest, and I dropped my hands. "What does that mean?"

"I can't do this forever. I'm surprised we've gotten six months."

The fear spread down my limbs. "No. You can't... What do you mean?"

He sank to the floor, inviting me to join him. We sat mirroring each other, knees up, elbows draped.

"This is how it was always supposed to happen, Sophia."

I studied the blue-green, searching for hints of his emotions. "You think they'll catch you?"

He opened his palms as if to say, *What do you think?* "I told you from the beginning I didn't expect to survive this."

Something inside my chest squeezed tight. Back then, I hadn't cared if he died doing this. Now that things had shifted between us, I couldn't slow the attachment growing inside, and the knowledge that someone else I cared for might be ripped away...

Lucas treaded up steps that grew increasingly more narrow and steep, but I refused to acknowledge the possibility he'd slip. His life mattered to me, and I wouldn't entertain the idea he might lose it.

"Luke—"

"Soph—"

"You act like you're a lost cause," I said.

His head cocked curiously. "Think about it, Sophia. *Really* think about it. No matter which side wins, I'll be executed. I'm either a traitor or a war criminal."

I huffed. "But..."

There was that stupid quirk of his mouth. "But what? What logic are you going to apply to get me out of it?"

"You're on our side!" My voice grew testy. "They wouldn't execute you."

"I never asked for clemency. I didn't want any kind of immunity. Uncle Theo hinted heavily that I'd never get a pardon."

How could the Defiance execute him as a war criminal after everything he'd done to help?

"I won't let them kill you," I said, setting my jaw.

He stared, mystified. "Is there any woman on this planet more stubborn than you?"

"If you ever find her, I'd love to meet her."

His perturbed expression spoke volumes. "I have my hands full with one of you."

"You aren't my keeper, Lucas. Though you certainly act like it sometimes."

He scoffed. "I do not."

"Cover yourself, Sophia," I mocked in a deep voice. *"Wear a hoodie, Sophia. You're mine, Sophia."*

Unimpressed, he shook his head. "I don't sound like that."

"I'm evil, Sophia. I deserve to die, Sophia."

He pitched his voice high and whiny. *"I'm* tired, *Lucas. It's hot, Lucas. I don't believe you, Lucas. I wasn't ready, Lucas."*

I dropped my jaw and shoved his shoulder. "I hate you."

"Yeah?" he asked. "Then why do you want me to live?"

Rolling my eyes, I refused to dignify that with an answer. Instead, I left.

As I entered headquarters a few minutes later, I ran into Adam and his huge grin. "Hey, Soph."

I tried to skirt by him without conversation, heading for the main stairs.

He followed me. "Where ya been?"

"Bike ride."

"Isn't it *interesting* that you go on a bike ride at the exact same time every Thursday, but never any other time of the week?"

I froze halfway up the stairs, but didn't glance his way. My hand found a decorative column to steady myself. "I don't know what you're talking about."

"Come on, Soph," he said, tone chiding. "We both know you're lying."

I continued up the stairs. "Why don't you talk to Theo, then?"

"I did."

I stopped again at the landing, turning to glare at him.

Usual grin absent, his expression was a cross between concerned friend and suspicious officer. "I've been watching you for months, but Harrison was pretty tight-lipped."

I dismissed him with a wave of my hand. "I just like bike rides."

"Where'd you get the bike?"

"I stole it."

He narrowed his eyes. "And where do you go?"

"To the other side of the neighborhood."

"Are you *alone* wherever you go?" He trudged up the stairs to meet me at the landing.

"Yes."

His voice lowered even though no one else was near. "You're lying."

"I'm not!" I matched his challenging stare with some degree of difficulty.

His gaze dropped to my pockets. "Show me what weapons you're carrying."

The blood drained from my face. "I'm not carrying any."

He snorted. "Bullshit."

I shoved past him toward the remaining flight. "What does it matter to you?"

"Because I have a feeling whatever you're carrying is Hunter issue."

Butterflies swirled in my stomach as I paused on the second stair. "W-why would you think that?"

"I saw the knuckles." He grabbed my elbow and marched me up the last steps. We ducked into an alcove at the top. "You leave here in weird clothes and come back with new bruises. You walk around looking all haunted. You're distracted and isolating yourself. And *suddenly* we are winning this war. Coincidence?"

"Why are you watching me so closely?"

He rubbed a hand over his face. "What are we giving for information? It better not be what I think it is."

Insult washed over me even though his assumption was fair. "Maybe he just wants exoneration," I hissed.

Adam lifted a skeptical brow. "Is that what you're giving him? Exoneration?"

"This isn't any of your business," I said, scowling.

He leaned closer, his hand forming a gentle cup around my shoulder. "The general took advantage of you. After Tekqua, you… you don't have to do this."

I shot him an *are-you-serious* expression. "Who else would?"

A moment passed while we measured each other. Eventually, his shoulders slumped, and he rested his weight on the wall. "Tell me who it is."

"No." I mirrored his pose, staring at the opulent stairs and wrought-iron railing across the hall.

"This war might actually end thanks to him. He's a goddamn savior, whoever he is."

I turned toward him, scrutinizing his face. "You wouldn't say that if you knew who he was."

He paled, his gaze sharpening. "Are you *safe*, Sophia?"

I thought of Lucas using a hairbrush to teach me knife play, giving me weapons to keep me safe, protecting me from Hunters invading his house, killing men he considered threats. I thought of his smirk, the yearning in my chest when I left him, the taste of his kiss.

I hid my expression by dropping my head. "No. I don't think I'm safe. Everything is out of my control."

"Can you get it back?"

Staring at the hardwood floor, I told him the truth. "I don't want it back."

A long silence passed. His hand touched mine, fingers gripping. "We used to be friends."

I lifted my gaze to his, melting into brown eyes that had once carried so much humor. "All my friends die."

Lips pressed together, he exhaled through his nose. "Well. You're going to need someone when shit hits the fan. I'm here when you're ready."

A COUPLE OF DAYS LATER, I sat on a couch beside Devon while we waited for Isaac to return from a mission. At some point, I sensed his gaze boring into me. "Something's going on with you."

I shrugged, eyes glued to the book in my lap. "It isn't anything I want to talk about."

"If it's about Tekqua—"

"It isn't." I closed my eyes. "I'm just—I'm tired of this, Dev. I want to be somewhere else."

He blew out a long breath.

"Isaac's been busy lately," I said.

Dev waved his hand toward the covered window. "He's preparing for some huge rescue mission. They always send him on the most dangerous missions. Meanwhile, I get sent to find canned corn."

Chuckling, I threw my book onto the table between us. "It's because he's so good. And besides, we still need food. Your job is important too."

"Yeah, his gives me palpitations, though."

I studied the small grin that graced his lips. "You really love him, don't you?"

"Yeah, girl."

His smile made me smile. "Describe it to me."

Dev met my eyes, a hint of intrigue sparking in his own. "I used to think I was happy until I met Isaac. But then— One conversation, and I knew I'd never be the same. Nothing about me changed, but my threshold for happiness had drastically risen. Isaac's like a key to a lock I didn't know I had."

I thought about that, about my own happiness threshold.

Devon's features went all mushy. "We fit together."

And deep down, fear ate at me.

No part of my connection to Lucas Scott was healthy. He was obsessive and unscrupulous. I was desperate and lonely. The damaged combination didn't lead to happiness.

But maybe I didn't want happiness.

Maybe he didn't deserve happiness.

Maybe happiness was a myth told to children to give hope that the cruelty and unfairness of life might end.

I thought of that conversation with Zara.

When you fall in love, you'll see. Even when it ends badly, it was still love.

I wasn't naive.

He was the wrong person. I was looking for comfort in the wrong places. All of this would end badly.

But the electricity in my heart burned. The hotter it grew, the more I liked the pain of it.

Psychological cutting.

I let the metaphorical blood drip over my mind, painting my thoughts red. The color of warnings and anger and violence, of passion and sin and love.

That week, I headed to the house on Evanston with the chill of fall curling about my limbs. I hustled up the steps and slipped through the red door, locking it behind me. The familiar incense scent of the house enveloped me—the fragrance of Lucas's attempts to control his anxiety.

He entered the room and leaned in the archway to the kitchen.

After a sip from his cup—probably peppermint tea—he raised a brow. "Still want me to live?"

"Yep." I shed my modest outer layers, tossing them to the floor.

With a sigh, he set his cup aside. "Fine. Come try to hurt me."

After only forty-five minutes of scuffling, I managed to get my hands around his throat securely enough that I thought I might win.

Then he flipped me, reversing our positions, and I gave up. "You know all my weaknesses. It isn't fair."

"You should know a few of mine by now."

A scornful snort was my reply as he pushed away from me to stand. "What weaknesses?"

"Um. I have a trick knee." He pointed to his left knee.

I narrowed my eyes at his normal-appearing knee. "I don't believe you."

"Of course you don't," he muttered.

He offered me a hand up, then cursed when I karate-chopped his *weak* knee. He fell to the carpeted floor beside me.

I burst into laughter at the shock on his face. "You weren't lying?"

"I'm never lying, Sophia. For fuck's sake!"

Curled into myself, I laughed until I couldn't breathe. "All this time, I could have gone for your knee?"

He braced a hand against his eyes. "Can we just go over the plan one more time?"

"Sure," I said, still laughing.

We moved to the kitchen and settled at the table. He reiterated the finalized strategy he'd tailored with Theo for the prisoner transfer, the one they'd edited through me for weeks. Once finished, he took a deep breath. "I'd really like this to go well."

"Me too."

His hand covered mine where it lay on the table, and my gaze lingered on the gold band. "If it doesn't, I don't want you to watch it."

I glanced at him, puzzled. "Watch...it?"

"The execution. Please don't watch it."

A pulse woke in my temple. Most of the time, his face was a curtain hiding everything inside, but the suppression of his emotions tonight, the pained little notch between his eyebrows—they struck like an icepick into my chest. I'd begun to fantasize about a way for him to defect, to get away from all of this, but where could he go? Besides, he had some goal in his head, something he was working toward that would repay his sister's maltreatment. Lucas called me stubborn, but I wasn't the only one. No amount of begging him to stop would change his mind.

"I've seen you do it before," I said.

His mouth tensed, and he didn't look at me. "Just... Please, Sophia?"

Swallowing, I nodded.

"Promise me."

"I promise. I won't watch."

When it came time to leave, he touched my throat, his thumb brushing my jaw in a random pattern. My body responded to that small caress as if it were something far more intimate. Tingles spread down my chest and arms, and I fought the urge to lean closer. We hadn't broached the subject of the night he handcuffed me to the bed—the night he'd looked at me like I was all that mattered. Maybe I'd made it all up in my head.

"Next week?" I said.

His finger drew a shape over my pulse. "Next week."

20

AND THEN YOU

 *Persons taking no active part in the hostilities... shall in all circumstances be treated humanely...*

— GENEVA CONVENTION (III), ARTICLE 3

I tried not to think about Lucas when the soldiers left a couple of days later. Devon and I held hands while he fretted for Isaac. He didn't know I was fretting too. I nearly cried when the first freed prisoners arrived wearing ragged clothes, dirt caked in their creases and under their fingernails. They came in waves, shaking and weak, shuffling their feet, eyes downcast.

Pasting on a smile, I helped distribute small portions of food. I treated and dressed raw wounds from lashes. I organized a shower system so they could each wash themselves in private.

One girl stopped me as I cleansed a festering sore on her leg, laying a bony hand over mine. I glanced up to find tears sparkling in her eyes.

"Thank you," she murmured.

Shame slithered through my chest, weighing me down. I didn't want to be thanked for things that shouldn't need to be done in the first place. Still, I smiled and nodded, then returned to my work.

When Theo entered headquarters, dark circles ringed his eyes.

I snuck up on him. "Did his plan work?"

Theo tilted his head back and forth, wishy-washy. "I had to modify it. We left some prisoners behind."

My stomach fell. "What?"

"The last leg didn't make sense. I suspect he was trying to lead us into a trap."

Anger exploded. "*What*? He wouldn't do that."

"I don't want to talk about it, Sophia." He walked away, and I stared after him, shocked. What the hell? They'd curated that strategy for weeks, and Theo changed it on a whim? The plan had been flawless.

I couldn't dwell on it long. The prisoners needed attention.

A count the next morning tallied two hundred and fifty-six freed people.

We celebrated. Hard.

Adam led the charge, and champagne was brought from some stash I hadn't known existed. Most of the stunned prisoners avoided the ruckus, but those who joined us managed a few smiles.

As for the rest of us, we couldn't stop smiling. It was our first major victory in a long, long time. We danced and drank and partied in a way we never had. Devon and I giggled drunkenly as Isaac reenacted his part in the rescue. Jayden tried to get me alone. I avoided him.

"May we live to see our glory," Adam shouted, holding his glass high as he leapt atop a table.

Cheers rallied around him while I snorted. "An honest hope in a world gone mad," I muttered to Devon.

"We're going to win this," he replied, expression resolute. "I'm sure of it."

I smiled as he took Isaac into his arms, planting a long kiss on his mouth.

We stayed up late into the night and woke hungover to continue the celebration. By the time I left to meet Lucas again, I was exhausted but overjoyed. He'd helped us save so many. He deserved acknowledgement for what he'd done, even if only from me.

I bounded through the cracked front door of the Evanston house, grin in place, bolting the lock behind me. With only two candles lit, the room flickered with shadows. My gaze fell on Lucas.

He leaned on the table behind one couch, weight braced on both hands. Next to his hand sat a lowball glass, a finger of amber liquid inside. He wore the dress uniform of a Blood Colonel, but he'd shed the scarlet-shouldered jacket and tie. His head lifted, and unsmiling, he traced my body from top to bottom. "I see you've forgotten your lessons on how to be discreet."

I glanced at my shorts and crop top. In my haste to see him, I'd left behind my baggy clothes. "I'm sorry."

He waved away my apology and took his cup in hand, eyeing me over the rim as he stole a sip.

"Where'd you get...whiskey?"

The edge of his mouth twisted, and he gestured to a sideboard I'd never noticed before, all heavy wood and decorative carvings, where an open bottle of liquor sat. "A gift. For services rendered."

Ice water seeped through my veins. How could I have forgotten the executions? We'd rescued many, but some were left behind. Those people had been executed today.

By Lucas.

"The price of my soul is a fifth of fine whiskey," he said with an acrid edge to his voice.

I advanced into the room. "Lucas, you saved so many—"

"I killed thirty-two innocent people today." He hurled the glass at the wall, where it shattered in an explosion of glittery silver shards, leaving the liquor to drip down the dusty paint. "Why am I doing this? I should be dead by now."

Despite his warning glance, I closed the distance between us. "You saved more lives than you took."

He shook his head. "Christ. How are you still so innocent?"

"You make the hard choices no one else wants to."

His gaze sharpened on me. "This isn't a choice. This is *obedience*. This is *exactly* what they want. They're punishing me for the misdeeds of my family."

"Wh-what?"

He ignored me. "I am their servant on broken knees."

"That's not true."

"It is." His hand landed on my neck, his thumb stroking up and down the column of my throat in random patterns and shapes. Aquamarine eyes took me in, growing more curious, more intense. "And yet you're still here. Why are you still here, Sophia?"

I pressed my palm to his cheek, rough with stubble. "Because you helped people survive, Lucas. It's *our* fault we couldn't save them all. You're too blinded by the sin to see the good within."

Stepping closer, he slid his hand into my hair. Fingers anchored until my neck arched and I was looking straight up into his face. "My sins are so vast," he said, "that no amount of good could compare. It's like a vat of poison with a drop of antidote."

My lips parted as I gazed into his eyes, trying to follow his meaning.

"It still kills you. It just does it slower."

An invisible fist reached inside and twisted, begging me to make that pain in his voice go away. His face was nothing but sharp lines and shadows—the arch of his dark brows, the cut of his cheekbones —but it was the fractured bits of teal in his eyes that captured my full attention.

"Nothing is killing you, Lucas," I said.

His hand tightened in my hair, dragging us closer together. "What other way do you see this ending? There is no hope. No way out. Nothing but darkness with no clear direction."

"We—we just keep moving forward."

"Which way is forward?" he demanded, releasing me. He dug his fingers into his hair and paced away. "I had *one reason* to keep going, even though avenging her won't change what happened to her. I just wanted retribution, and I figured I'd do as much damage as I could before the NAO discovers I've betrayed them and executes me." He looked up and glared at me. "And then *you*."

I froze. "Me?"

"Harrison threw you at me, and you couldn't have been more destructive if you were a fucking grenade."

My breath caught. "What?"

"I won't survive this," he said, making each word clear and sharp, like he thought I might not understand. "I can't do this forever. I don't *want* to do this forever. I can't keep killing people like this, and I have weeks at most before they discover me."

I needed to argue, to plead even, but the raw anger in his voice, the sheer agony in the cracks of his mask forced me to stillness.

"I was fine with it," he snapped, eyes flashing. "I *wanted* to die. Until *you*."

My throat ached with a fresh wave of tears.

"What's going to happen to you when I'm gone?" he asked. "You're untrained and reckless, and *no one* watches out for you."

I swiped at a tear. "Then don't leave. Stay here, with me."

"I can't *stay*, Sophia. There is no route of survival for me. It's just all going to hurt a lot more now."

Frustration built inside, at his unwillingness to seek another avenue. "You haven't even tried—"

"What?" He prowled closer again, still glaring, his predatory steps silent in the expanse between us. "Tried *what*?"

My voice shrank. "I don't know, but this isn't fair to me. You're mad because you care whether I live or die. I didn't do that to you."

He laughed then, bitter and angry. In a sure move that sent tingles spiraling down my legs, he hooked his fingers through the belt loops of my shorts. I was tugged into the hard plane of his chest. "Yes, you did," he accused. Fiery hands gripped the bare skin of my waist, his fingertips creeping under the hem of my crop top. His eyes were like gemstones—cracked under pressure, barely holding it together. He dipped closer, and the graze of his lips near my ear woke goosebumps all along my spine. "You make everything so much worse. You make me want to live."

Heat blossomed in my chest, rapid and all-consuming, and I moved on instinct. Our lips met in a hard collision, half desire, half resentment. It was a sigh of relief and a scream of frustration all wrapped inside a powder keg. We needed but a single spark to light it, and the kiss detonated.

His arms circled me so tight I couldn't breathe.

My hands clenched on his shirt until the fabric protested.

His tongue drew a line across my lower lip, and I opened for him, deepening the kiss beyond anything that was smart or sensible.

Reckless, he'd called me, and I'd never felt it so acutely as in that moment, with Lucas Scott's deadly hands jerking me hard against his body, his mouth doing wicked things to mine. I tugged at the buttons of his shirt as he pushed, pushed, pushed until my low back hit the sideboard where his execution prize sat.

He swiped the bottle aside, and it fell to the floor, spilling liquor onto the frayed carpet. The air grew thick with the fragrance of aged whiskey and bad decisions.

Lifting me to sit atop the sideboard, he wrapped my thighs around him, dragging me right to the edge until what he wanted and how much he wanted it became unbearably apparent. My blood sang in my veins at the feel of him pressed against me, awakening even the numbest parts inside—the places that hadn't felt alive in months, that I thought were gone forever.

The places that hoped for more.

They ached with the stinging prickles of restored circulation, painful but necessary. I'd been half-alive when I came to him last spring, and unbeknownst to him, he'd spent the better part of six months waking me up...only to admit he planned to die despite it all.

Why did that only make me want to hold him tighter?

His mouth demanded submission, and I relented to the faint traces of peppermint and whiskey tickling my senses. Every breath held more of his scent, his very essence. Heat zapped down each nerve ending. Frantic need took the place of my common sense.

I tore at his shirt while he ripped mine over my head. He yanked the straps of my bralette down my shoulders until it circled my waist, then palmed one breast. His thumb dragged pleasure over the peak until I arched into his touch. Sound collected in my throat, some combination of a moan and a plea. He swallowed it with another bruising kiss. My nails made red lines down the strip of exposed skin between the panels of his shirt before I attacked the buckle of his belt and the zipper beneath.

Fevered and feral, I threw my head back when his mouth dipped to my neck, exposing the most vulnerable area of my body to this lethal predator. He kissed the spot my pulse pounded hardest, where the life-giving artery coursed just below the skin. His tongue trailed over it, then his teeth as I tightened my legs around him.

I wanted him closer. Needed it. Around me, on me, deep inside me.

And he knew it.

He felt it too.

I could sense it in his manic, possessive touch.

The tension between us ratcheted up. His vicious hands dove beneath the hem of my shorts, and I helped him drag them down my legs. They landed somewhere behind him as he took hold of my waist, holding me still so his gaze could rake down my body—bare chest heaving, legs spread wide for him.

God, that look on his face. I could get addicted to that look.

I recalled that day so long ago, when I'd been terrified of what he might do to me. I remembered his answering frustration.

If I want to fuck you, I'll make it obvious.

This was obvious.

This was a man desperate for the relief my body could give him.

This was Lucas Scott screaming his desire into the void.

My heart pounded in my throat, in my head, deep in my center where my blood turned to molten gold, glowing at that hunger on his face. I was captured by the savage want in his eyes—the want for *me*. I couldn't look away from it. Not when he caught his lip between his teeth. Not when he pulled himself from his briefs, fisting his length. Not when he braced his hand on the wall behind me. Not even when he took my hip in a tight grip and thrust deep inside me.

I sucked in a breath at the invasion. Exquisite and excruciating at the same time. Wrong. Right. Black. White. I didn't care about the dichotomy. I wanted to dive into him and mix us both into gray.

Through it all, I kept my eyes on his, and finally, aquamarine lifted to mine.

Slow. Dark. Greedy.

He moved, dragging in and out, painting his name all over me with each thrust. His mouth touched mine again, but not in a kiss. It was as if he couldn't help himself, like he needed to breathe me into his lungs, just like I needed him.

We existed in a desperate place, a dangerous place, one we likely wouldn't survive. But Lucas Scott held out his hand, and instead of running, I took it. I gripped tight and let him pull me right to the edge of his knife.

The precariousness of it all wracked me with foolish despair, and I wrapped myself around him, arms and legs, fingernails clawing to keep him there—right there—even though it was impossible. A powerful arm encircled me, and his thrusts grew longer, deeper, harder, hitting a spot I didn't even know existed.

The glowing spot.

I didn't want to come.

Not like this.

Not when I knew the end would come shortly after, and with it, the destruction of the tentative peace we'd forged between us. There would be nothing but friction between us now, and I didn't want to learn whether we would strain to keep away from each other or fight to stay together.

But just like every other encounter with Lucas, my desires surrendered to him. He wanted my orgasm, so he got it. He ripped away the shreds of restraint I still possessed and tossed me onto a new plane of fiery, torturous pleasure.

The intensity took me by surprise, like a gunshot to the heart. The air wrenched from my lungs to make room for a sizzling wave of ecstasy unlike any climax I'd ever known. It burned down to the very core of me, installing something inside that belonged solely to him.

Waves of pleasure swelled and crested, and I rode each one to its peak, mindless with the desire for *more...now...forever.*

I was breathing hard against his neck when I returned to myself, and he used my body to find his own release, withdrawing and spilling onto my abdomen with a low groan.

Foreheads pressed together, we breathed in time with one another, letting the seconds stretch and snap around us.

Then he looked down.

He stared at his spend, dripping down my skin. His thumb dragged through it, smearing it across the indents from the band of my shorts.

I peered into his face as it grew paler and paler, and the last thing he said drifted through my mind.

You make me want to live.

His focus trained on the mess he'd made while I closed my legs and hastily pulled my bra to cover myself. Any rays of vulnerability I might have glimpsed disappeared as he stepped back, tucking himself away. The bleakness in his eyes gave way to something utterly dispassionate, and he met my gaze.

"This isn't a love story," he said in a dead voice.

I crossed my arms and ankles, wishing for more cover, but my clothes were strewn across the room. "I know."

"This is a tragedy."

I swallowed, and my reply emerged thready. "I know."

Retreating further, he scraped his fingers through his hair, the gold ring flashing in the candlelight. Ocean eyes latched onto me. He looked caged. Hunted.

"Lucas—"

He raised a hand to cut me off, sharp and precise. With one last glance, he turned and left, closing the front door softly behind him.

I blinked at it, waiting for him to return, but seconds and then minutes passed with nothing but silence. When goosebumps chased themselves over my arms and a small shiver wracked my frame, I slid from the sideboard, but I didn't reach for my clothes. Instead, I fled into the master bedroom and checked whether Lucas had found a way to power this house's water heater.

The stream from the sink ran for thirty seconds before it warmed, and illogical tears sprang to my eyes. My bra landed in a mangled heap on the floor, and I stepped into the hot shower.

Only then did I allow myself to cry.

The tears were silent but profuse, dripping to mingle with the water as it made jagged rivulets down my body. It washed away all evidence that Lucas had ever been there, and my heart didn't know whether to sigh in relief or cry harder.

When the warmth faded, I stepped out and raided his drawer of Sophia clothes, using a T-shirt to dry myself, then throwing on the sweats he liked best. After retrieving the note I always kept on me from the pocket of my shorts and tucking it into my bra, I sank onto the bed, uncertain what to do.

My mind wanted to relive it—every burning moment, each desperate kiss—but my heart wasn't so sure. It seemed to sense I'd stumbled into something far out of my depth, and it whispered to be careful.

You've suffered so much, it said. *This will end in pain.*

Eventually, I crawled into the bed, curling up in the same spot I'd lain after Lucas told me about Tekqua. As I shut my eyes, I thought of the Lucas from my dream all those months ago.

He'd warned me to watch my blindside.

Why didn't I realize that he was the one standing there?

THE NEXT MORNING, I woke alone, and my heart sank. Had I really expected him to return? What deranged reality was I living in, seriously? Before the disappointment could morph into more tears, I forced myself out of bed and into the morning sun. My bike sat in the exact place I'd left it, and on my ride, I let the chilly fall air serve as a slap to the face. A wake-up call.

Lucas was right.

Last night changed nothing. It just made me face some hard truths.

I didn't want him to die. I wanted to keep him.

A dreamer's hope, of course—nigh impossible—and my abused heart had already begun to ache at the impending loss.

When I returned, headquarters looked the same, yet entirely different. Prisoners had been given cots that lined the hallways. Eventually, they'd be taken to safe houses, but each needed an examination and treatment before being cleared for transfer.

I tiptoed through the hall, hoping to reach my tiny private sleeping space before anyone saw me. Theo, however, caught me at the top of the stairs. His stern face took in my appearance—oversized sweats, ratted hair—and his mouth turned down.

"I expected you back last night," he said.

"I got distracted."

His penetrating stare saw far too much, so my gaze dropped to his feet. Hiding like a coward.

"My office," he said and turned.

I followed him with hands wringing, wishing I'd at least had a chance to brush my teeth. He shut and locked the door of his office behind him, then took his place at the desk.

He didn't sit, so I didn't either. "Does he have any additional information for us?" he asked.

"He...wasn't exactly in a good state of mind last night."

His attention lingered on my mess of hair. "Celebrating, was he?"

Heat spiked through my nerves. "Mourning," I snapped. "Actually."

A skeptical wrinkle formed on his brow. "Mourning? You believe that?"

"Unequivocally."

Disgust and pity warred in his expression. "How many people did he execute?"

My eyes narrowed. "The same number you failed to rescue." A vicious satisfaction coursed through me when his eye twitched. In his silence, I asked, "Have you ever considered why Lucas performs so many executions, Theo?"

"Because he's efficient, obviously."

I rolled my eyes. "Right. Why do you think he chooses to be efficient when the others torture first?"

Scoffing, he brushed me off with a wave of his hand. "Don't start acting like Lucas Scott kills innocent people as some kind of, what, *charity*?"

"Those people are condemned to die, regardless. At least he—"

"If he were truly decent, he never would've risen to a position to do it at all. He didn't stumble into his rank, Sophia. You're forgetting who he is and where he came from."

How dare he patronize me? I hadn't forgotten anything. Theo was the one who didn't understand the full picture. "You don't even know who he is. You're such a hypocrite."

"This is war, Sophia." He rapped his knuckles on his desk to emphasize *war*. "They're a regime that supports totalitarianism. Supports subjugating women."

I crossed my arms. "I know, but this isn't black and white. Lucas Scott isn't purely evil. His actions have reasons."

"What could possibly excuse—"

"How many people have *you* killed?"

Theo's mouth tightened. "That is irrelevant."

"Irrelevant when it's convenient for you."

"That is enough!" he barked. He looked at me like he was staring at a stranger, like I was some NAO sympathizer who refused to see the error of my ways. "I never should've let you do this. Look at you, coming home after hours alone with that pathetic excuse for a man, agreeing to do God-knows-what with him, then defending him as if the blood on his hands and the desecration of your body aren't unforgivable sins."

I blinked, shocked into speechlessness. Desecration? Lucas had done nothing but try to protect me from the moment I met him.

Theo would know that if he'd ever bothered to ask.

He never had. That was his problem—assuming he already knew.

"What would your parents say?" he asked as I gaped. "I promised your father I'd watch out for you, and this is what I've let you become."

A wave of affront passed over me, hot and cold all at once. I pitched my voice low, daring him to insult me. "What have I become, Theo?"

He said nothing.

I stepped closer to the desk, supporting my weight on the tips of my fingers. "Are you insinuating I'm a whore?"

His silence spoke more than words ever could.

Whore. Damaged. Compromised.

Maybe he was right.

I stood before the general of the Defiance, wearing a Hunter's clothes, armed with his weapons, his taste still saturating the back of my tongue. Lucas killed thirty-two people yesterday, and I'd rewarded him by inviting him inside my body.

Why had I done it? For the hope he'd keep giving me information? Keep allowing himself to live? Keep looking at me like I mattered to him?

But Theo had *asked* me to do this, and now he was judging me for it. If I was damaged, he was the one holding the weapon. If I was a whore, he was the pimp who sold me.

Rage erupted, scalding my skin. "You gave me away for the mere promise of useful information, and you have the gall to insult me for doing exactly what you wanted me to do?"

"I never wanted you to do it. Williams—"

"You didn't use the words, but you begged me to fuck him into compliance. Are you happy you got what you wanted? Did I play my part well enough for you?"

He winced. "Sophia—"

"Don't! You don't get to stand there and accuse him of being an unforgivable sinner and me a dirty whore when you *gave* me to him. You sacrificed me to the slaughter, and all he has ever done is try to protect me."

Theo snorted. "*Protect* you? Is that how he protects you?" He gestured toward my mussed hair, my rumpled clothes. "You have teeth marks on your throat."

My breaths deepened as fire spread through my cheeks, and my heart pounded in my chest. "I wanted his marks on my skin."

His eyes widened.

"Ask me what he makes me do for him. Go ahead, ask me."

He didn't.

"Ask me if I like what he does to me."

He ground his teeth. "Stop it, Sophia."

"Ask me, Theo. Don't you want to know if I've been a good little slut for him?"

Theo stared at my face for a long time. "I'm not sure what you're implying here, but let me remind you who this man is. In the last year, he has personally executed dozens of people, and that's not including the people he killed in battle."

"Again, I ask, how many people have *you* killed?"

His jaw hardened.

"How many soldiers have you *ordered* to kill people?"

"Sophia—"

"It isn't black and white. I know exactly who he is. You're the one who doesn't understand."

He sighed. "I'm not sure I can allow you to keep doing this."

I smiled with rancor. "Try sending someone else. See what he does. I don't think you'll like the outcome."

Theo's jaw went slack. "This is not a tenable situation."

"You're getting your information. Isn't that what you wanted?"

"Yes, but at what cost?"

I sneered at him. "You're not paying any price. You gave me away and lost *nothing*."

"I lost *you!*" he yelled.

"Oh, don't pretend you give any fucks about me, Theo."

"Williams... But I-I gave you the option. I didn't want this for you."

"Could have fooled me. But it doesn't matter because I'm not stopping now."

"Sophia," he said in a low voice, evening out the rough edges of emotion. "The fact that Lucas Scott has a conscience doesn't negate who he is. Maybe I'd feel more charitable toward him if he didn't need to test that conscience so frequently."

The injustice of it all—Lucas's position he didn't want, Theo's preconceived notions—they ate away at my patience. "Lucas suffered yesterday because *you* failed to follow the plan he'd spent weeks strategizing with you. If you had, those people he had to kill yesterday wouldn't have died. You can't blame him for following the orders he's given when you want him to keep his position. It was *your* decision to abandon those people. We didn't blame our own soldiers for your mistake."

With a sneer, he dropped his gaze to his desk, his papers, everywhere but my eyes. "You really shouldn't speak to me that way, Soph."

I deflated, and my voice softened. "If you weren't there to kiss away my boo-boos when I was a little girl, I probably wouldn't."

A faint smile smoothed the lines of his face, and he placed his hands on his desk. "Perhaps there's more to this situation than I understand, but you need to be careful."

"No, I don't, Theo. He'd never hurt me."

"Yes, well, he's more than willing to hurt others. Remember that.

Because when his usefulness has expended itself, he *will* be discarded."

My jaw clenched at that word. Discarded? Lucas wasn't some tool that could be thrown out when broken.

But Theo went on. "Williams believes he's a liability. She won't allow him to live. If the NAO doesn't execute him, she'll order it herself."

A liability? In what sense? Was she *ashamed* of working with him?

"Besides," Theo continued, "his death will be a great win for the Defiance. A morale boost before the final blow. Scott is used to you. He lets his guard down with you, right? When the time comes, you're the weapon Williams will choose to end him."

Time slowed. A sudden deluge of ice water pumped through my veins with every heartbeat. He could have stabbed me in the chest and I'd have been less shocked.

"Wh-what?"

"Lucas Scott will not survive this war, Sophia. He didn't ask for immunity, and I was clear with him he'd never receive it. He knows what will happen when we win. I thought you understood it as well."

"I..." But I had no words. Nothing.

"Williams plans to finish him before the end, in case he decides to disappear. She'll get as much information as she can, and then it's over for him. You're the only one who can get close to him."

"Why didn't you tell me?" I whispered because if I attempted anything louder, my voice would break.

Pity bled through his hard expression. "It was obvious, Sophia. I'm sure Scott has been expecting you to attack since your first encounter."

"If he expects we'll double-cross him, why would he do this at all?"

He finally settled into his chair, his shoulders dipping in a rare display of exhaustion. "That's what I've been asking from the start. The catch is coming. I just hope Williams gives the go-ahead to end him before that happens. We're getting closer. A few more strategic wins and the NAO will be in our hands, and you'll never have to deal with Lucas Scott ever again."

"Because you'll order me to kill him?" I said, not bothering to hide the weighted despair in my tone.

Theo dipped his chin in a stiff nod, and a fresh wave of tears thickened my throat. I spun to hide it, and he didn't order me to stay.

When I made it to my bed, flares of panic stole my breath, too great for even my forest to disband. I wouldn't do it. I refused to take his life. They couldn't make me do it.

...Could they?

21

THREE POINTS

 I hate war as only a soldier who has lived it can, only as one who has seen its brutality, its futility, its stupidity.

— DWIGHT D. EISENHOWER

You're the weapon Williams will choose to end him.

The words haunted me for days. When I wasn't reliving those moments of foolish ecstasy in Lucas's arms, I was imagining how I'd tell him they planned to kill him.

Should I tell him?

He deserved a head start, at least, but I could already imagine his response.

I wouldn't stop you, Sophia...

Despite his perpetual mystery, I was certain of that. If I attacked, he wouldn't defend himself, just like that day he killed the kid. I'd set my blade to his skin, and he'd raise his hands in surrender.

Every time I imagined plunging a knife into his throat, I was assaulted by the serrated agony in his voice when he said, *You make me want to live.*

There was something ironic in dying at the hand of the only person who sparked the will to survive.

I wouldn't do it.

They couldn't make me do it.

I was so distracted that I leapt in surprise when someone touched my shoulder in the hospital wing. Hand pressed to my chest, I ignored my racing heart to turn.

Dr. Grayson shot me an apologetic smile. "Sorry, sorry! Didn't mean to scare you."

I set aside the supplies I'd been organizing and tried to smile. "No, it's my fault. I was deep in thought."

He nodded. "I just wanted to make sure you were okay. You've seemed...a bit out of sorts recently."

My mouth opened, but I had no response.

"Zara says you've pulled away?"

Heat seeped into my face. She'd asked me to chat several times, and I always found an excuse not to.

He raised a hasty hand. "Not that I'm prying. I really just want to make sure you're all right." His sincere smile plucked at emotions that lived far too close to the surface. I swallowed down the ridiculous urge to cry. Why couldn't Theo be more like Dr. Grayson or Zara? I *wanted* to talk. I wanted to spill it all the way I used to with Tekqua, yet the only people available were my judgmental fake uncle and a Hunter who'd fucked me and walked away without a word.

No matter how much I wanted to talk, Lucas's role was still top secret.

"It's just been a hard few months," I said. "Lonely."

He squeezed my shoulder. "War is a terrible thing, and we see only a portion of it within these walls. It takes a large toll on our hearts to see so much senseless death."

Senseless.

Such a good way to describe it.

Where was the sense? What was the point? Why were we still killing each other in the streets? I could no longer remember what we truly fought for, and wasn't that a terrifying truth? Did the soldiers on the other side feel the same?

We were all pawns in the game of war.

"My heart feels…disfigured," I muttered because at least that was true. Truer than silence. Truer than *I'm fine.*

"I know, Sophia. I'm here any time you need to talk," he said and gave me a smile. "Zara as well. She misses you."

With a stiff nod, I returned to the supplies that needed organization, still distracted, grateful to the schedule that I had no patient responsibilities that day.

THE FOLLOWING THURSDAY, I headed to the house on Evanston under a lovely fall sunset. The trees had transformed into a rainbow throughout the neighborhood, and the air caressed me with the unique notes of autumn—dying leaves and burned wood.

The smell of death.

Despite the beauty, my stomach twisted into knots. What would I walk into? Would Lucas even show? Last week had been a series of mistakes that we couldn't undo. Would he pretend nothing happened or pick a fight with me about it? I'd played out this encounter so many times in my head that it felt as if I'd already lived it.

I'd argued with him. I'd brushed it aside and returned to the status quo. I'd leapt into his arms. I'd dropped to my knees. Any scenario was equally likely, yet each one had a single thing in common: I had no idea how it would end.

With nerves tingling in my stomach, I opened the front door to find Lucas standing in the middle of the living room, waiting. His unblinking stare latched onto me while I shut the door and leaned against it. Before I could speak, he crossed his arms. "I have three pieces of information for you to take to Harrison today," he said in a clipped tone. "You ready?"

Narrowing my gaze, I searched his face and found a well of bewildering anger. He stood straight, cold, military-stiff, and I fought the urge to shrink away from this version of him. Why was he so furious? Was it with me or the situation at hand?

"Lucas," I said, a plea and argument all at once.

"Three things," he repeated, eyes bright in the candlelight. "Are you ready?"

I hesitated, unsure how to navigate these unfamiliar waters. Of all the scenarios I'd imagined, incandescent rage on his part wasn't one of them. "Is—is this how it's going to be?"

"Moving forward, this will be a transactional relationship. You will arrive on time and safely deliver my information to General Harrison. In exchange, I will provide the most accurate information I can."

My shoulders slumped despite my desire to stand tall. "That's what I wanted in the beginning."

"And now it's what you're getting."

"But I don't want that anymore."

His jaw clenched. "I don't give a fuck what you want."

The tiniest flame of resentment ignited. What the hell had I done to deserve *this*? Fury wasn't a fair reaction on his part, and why did he always get to make the rules?

I was so tired of the power imbalance between us.

"I can see you're gearing up to say something that flaunts your suicidal stubbornness," he said, "so let me stop you now. There will be no argument. From now on, this will be the arrangement."

A thick sensation surrounded my throat, making it ache. "I don't understand."

"Yes, you do," he said. "You're not a stupid person."

The sudden impulse to throw things at him was a difficult one to suppress. "Then explain it to me like I am," I snapped.

His expression didn't change, but something brightened about him, almost as if he found me funny. Fiery anger sizzled deep in my belly.

"If I'd known about you from the beginning," he said, "I never would have done this. I would rather have died."

My entire soul went slack. He couldn't have meant how that sounded...

He would have chosen death over me?

The corrosive anger spread through my chest and poisoned my bloodstream. "Why? What changed?"

His flat stare spoke volumes.

"Are you *ashamed* that you fucked me, Lucas?"

A tinge of red appeared on his cheekbones, but other than that, he yielded no reaction. "Not ashamed. Disappointed."

The insult was like a slap to the face. Sudden, stinging pain spread through my nervous system, and I fell victim to the shock of it. Everything went prickly—my heart, my emotions, even my words. "Was I not as good as you imagined?"

A joyless smile appeared at his lips. "You were more willing than I imagined."

"*Willing*? Do you prefer to take women against their will, Lucas? Are you disappointed to discover women actually have desires of their own?"

I wanted to hide from his sudden scrutiny, like he could read my every feeling as it shimmered across my face.

Embarrassment. Anger. Shame. Confusion.

"Disappointed that you have desire for *me*," he said eventually.

I blinked, at a loss for words.

His voice lost a smidge of its sharpness. "You are deeper in this than you should be, Sophia."

"I'm not—"

"You used to guard yourself from me," he said. "Do you remember that? Every week, you'd show up terrified that would be the day I collected what you thought I wanted. I'm not sure when that fear stopped, but last week, you willingly gave me the one thing you never wanted me to have. Why would you do that if you weren't invested?"

My throat dried up like desert sand as I recognized the truth in that statement. I could blame passion or the heat of the moment, but I'd slept with him because I wanted to. Because I felt something for him I knew I shouldn't. "It doesn't mean anything," I croaked.

He shook his head, surveying me with a regret I hated. "Don't lie to me, Sophia. It's insulting. I am a dead man. They will hunt me down and destroy everything good that has ever touched my life, including you. Why are you giving your soul to the devil? You don't hang with a hunted man if you want to live."

Theo's words crept into my brain—*You're the weapon Williams will choose to end him*—but I shoved them away. "That's not what—"

"No!" He went sharp as a blade again. "There is no arguing with this. What have I been telling you from day one? *Protect yourself.* That includes your heart. Guard your fucking heart, Sophia. It's the most sacred part of you."

"Then why the fuck did you carve your name all over it?" The words flew out before I could stop them, heated and desperate, and I slapped my hand over my mouth.

He blanched, but it only made the blue-green gleam brighter in his face. After a long silence, during which I considered melting into the floor, his words punctured the escalating tension between us. "I didn't."

Words deserted me.

"Not intentionally," he added. "This is a losing game, and I refuse to be another thing that hurts you."

I rolled my eyes.

He marked that reaction with a flash of his eyes, and the fury returned. "What will you do when I die, Sophia?" As I started to answer, he cut me off. "Do you remember the months of self-destructive grief you described to me after Tekqua died?"

I fell victim to silence, wishing he wasn't right. Perhaps I'd grown too attached to him, but losing him to this sudden code of ethics wouldn't hurt any less. I was free-falling, and if he didn't catch me, if I didn't land safe in his arms, I'd crash over jagged rocks. "It isn't your job to protect me from that," I finally ground out.

We stood in the stillness, facing off, until eventually, he opened his mouth. "I have three points for you to take to Harrison. Are you ready?"

My spirits sank. It felt as if he'd started a chess match, but he was both more patient and a better strategist. What else could I do but play the game?

"Fine," I said. "Yes."

"Russia officially joined the fight in Canada. If we don't end up in a nuclear war, it looks like Haynes is finally outnumbered. He's already started pulling back. If that war ends, he'll have more manpower domestically."

I nodded, perturbed by that information.

"There has been talk of a counter-invasion into the US. You are particularly vulnerable located here so close to Canada. We're aware your Prime Delegate has been in talks with the Canadian prime minister. She needs to establish a peace treaty with Canada, the European Union, all of them to protect—"

"Yeah, okay. I got that."

He nodded, then hesitated. His gaze dipped to my throat, my feet, my hands before returning to my eyes. "While Haynes is alive, the Defiance will never have more power than the NAO." He ignored my glare. "But I think I've found a way for the Defiance to get to Haynes. You could end his entire cabinet."

I blinked. "Wait. Are you serious?"

His tone dipped to a careful, almost apologetic register. "Giving this information will compromise me. Once the Defiance acts on it, I'm dead."

"What?" I demanded. "No! We aren't doing that."

His eyes fluttered closed. "Sophia."

My anger finally burst to the surface. "Don't *Sophia* me, Luke. You can act like you're doomed, like I'm stupid for caring, like sleeping with me was a mistake, but I don't care about any of that. We will not be willingly leading you to the slaughter. You're not some sacrificial lamb."

"I am a spy with a winning hand. If you keep that information from them, they'll try you for obstructing the war effort."

"I don't care," I said.

We stared, neither of us giving an inch. With a concise, emotionless voice, he relented. "We can discuss it later. I need more intel anyway. You got the rest of it?"

I nodded again.

"Good." He pointed at the door. "You can leave."

I gave him an icy stare. He lifted a single brow in response, and I was struck again by the desire to throw things at him. How could he dismiss me so easily?

Annoyed by the sharp pang of sadness, I left.

When I made it back to my bedroom, I stared at the wall and tortured myself by reliving the conversation over and over. With each replay, one detail grew hideously more apparent. His words had been laced with a thread of steel.

He wouldn't give in.

He knew I'd begun to feel something for him. He'd admitted that he didn't want to die, that he wanted to live for *me*. But it didn't matter. He still planned to offer his life in service to this war.

His days were numbered.

Soon, I would lose him, and he'd taken away our last days together in some sort of bid for morality.

It was only then, with the certainty of his voice ringing in my ears—*they will hunt me down*—that I realized how deep my feelings truly dove.

I hadn't been lying when I told him his name was carved on my heart. I wished I could remember at what point he'd taken his scalpel to it. When had he laid claim to this part of me I'd never given anyone?

Why was it so one-sided?

I fell to my knees. "Shit." My hand pressed over the abrupt black hole in my chest.

I knew better than to get invested in anything these days, so how did this happen? With no emotional currency available, I couldn't afford to want people this way. Caring for Lucas Scott exacted an agonizing toll on my bankrupt soul. Fierce and strange, the pain cut deep. Like grief, but worse because he wasn't dead. Not yet. He was alive but indifferent. Warm but untouchable. *Right there*, but so far away.

I knew how to grieve. I was an expert at it. What I didn't know was how to grieve for someone still alive.

22

FIELD DUTY

 He who knows when he can fight and when he cannot will be victorious.

— SUN TZU, *THE ART OF WAR*

Weeks passed. Every Thursday I'd arrive to Lucas waiting for me, yards of space between us. He'd give me his information and refuse to engage if I tried to speak of anything else. In turn, I declined to listen to any points of information that might lead to his immediate demise, something that frayed his patience with each vanishing hour.

I wanted so badly for things to go back to how they were before we slept together. Strangely, I missed wrestling with him. I kept up my workouts in case he ever changed his mind, but each week I was sent on my way without even a lecture.

To keep from brooding, I took more medic shifts. Zara was thrilled when I agreed to sit down for a chat one afternoon. We stole a small area of the sparsely populated café, far from the riveted windows where cold air leaked through.

She handed me a cup of English breakfast tea and settled in the chair beside me, elbows on the table. "It has been too long."

I chose to stare at the table instead of looking her in the eye. "Sorry. Been busy, I guess."

"Oh? Have you made new friends?"

I thought of Lucas pinning me to the ground. Lucas throwing a knife at the door to keep me from leaving. Lucas doling out life advice like a mother hen.

Never look at what's obvious, Sophia.

"Not really," I said.

She smiled. "Well, time gets away from us sometimes, doesn't it?"

"I can't believe we've been dealing with years of this."

Her smile dimmed. "It seems as if things are improving a little."

I shrugged, and Zara shifted the conversation to happier subjects —the rookie medics she was training, the soldier who always hit on her, a new interest in sketching the oak tree just outside the quarantine house.

I asked questions, but was at a loss to volunteer anything from my own life. I had no new hobbies or interests, nothing to speak of that wasn't top secret or debilitatingly depressing. She must have sensed my growing discomfort, because her hand squeezed mine where it lay listless on the table.

"I'm here for you, Sophia," she said. "I hope you know that."

My lips rolled between my teeth as I battled the tears that always sat so close to the surface. I stared at her hand atop mine. "Do you remember when you told me that sometimes you fall in love with the wrong person?"

In her silence, I glanced up. Her dark eyes sparked with interest, and she set her cup aside. "I do."

"Do you think it's possible to make yourself fall *out* of love?"

She studied my face as a crease deepened between her brows. "I'm not sure it's a decision that can be consciously made."

"But what if—what if it's doomed? Like, there's no chance for a happy ending?"

A short silence, and then, "Have you fallen in love, Sophia?"

I jerked my hand back. "No. It's just theoretical."

"I—"

"Reeves!" barked a voice outside our sphere.

I jumped and turned toward the stranger, hand pressed to my racing heart. A soldier stood near the café entrance in combat fatigues, the rank on his chest declaring him a Second Lieutenant, though I'd never seen him before.

I stood and saluted him. "Yes, sir?"

"New mission orders. You're on rotation for field duty. Briefing in the rotunda in five." He spun and left me gaping.

Field duty?

But...I'd been exempted from field duty by Theo.

I turned to Zara. "I'm so sorry. I have to go."

She nodded, her expression a mask of concern. I sprinted from the room, heading straight for Theo's office. When I reached it, the handle didn't budge.

Locked.

"Theo!" I banged on the door, ignoring the strange looks from passing soldiers.

No answer.

"Hey, hey," came a familiar voice, and I whirled to find Adam wearing a confused smile. "Need something?"

"Where's Theo?"

"The general is out until tomorrow. He had a meeting."

My heart stalled, then picked up its pace. If Theo wasn't there, he couldn't stop them, and I didn't have the rank or authority to refuse a mission.

"What's wrong?" Adam asked.

"They're sending me into the field."

He laughed. "You go into the field all the time."

But I didn't. Not for months.

If they waste you, they lose me. That is non-negotiable.

Lucas had made it clear that *he* was my only field duty, and Theo had agreed with that request. If I went out and something happened, I wasn't entirely certain how Lucas would respond.

But he'd been so cold of late that maybe it wouldn't matter to him if I was hurt.

Besides, as medics, we were always kept out of direct battle. The last time had been a fluke.

"I have to report," I murmured to Adam.

"Good luck," he singsonged as I walked away.

I sprinted to my room to change into the combat fatigues I hadn't worn in months. The white armband with the red cross stood out starkly against the olive green. I pulled on my boots, then slipped Lucas's knuckles into my pocket. I always had the weapon on my person, just as he'd asked.

When I arrived in the rotunda, it was bustling with soldiers, and many of my fellow medics stood at attention, ready for instruction. I grabbed one of the medic packs and took my position.

"Alright, listen up!" shouted a captain I had recently treated for a scalp laceration. Every soldier fell silent, eyes straight ahead. "We've got a situation at a lookout southeast of command post B," the captain continued. "Friendly patrol got hit—hard. A dozen confirmed injured, with at least that many unaccounted for. It's on us to get in, secure the wounded, and get the hell out. Wounded personnel will be on floors three and above. This is extraction only, but expect enemy presence. We go in fast and stay tight. Only engage if fired upon. Medics, you're lead for triage. Prioritize stabilization. Rally point is here"—he pointed to a map behind him, right at the cross streets near command post B—"and if comms go dark, fall back to Safe House Blue. Exfil once objective is secured. You know your roles, soldiers. Gear up. We leave in ten."

The room exploded into action.

Before I'd taken a single step, Isaac appeared before me. "You're with me, Reeves." He pointed to a group of armed soldiers standing nearby. "This is Maldonado, Khattab, Phan, and Andrews. We're taking the sixth floor."

The soldiers wore scars and mean expressions as proof of experience, but my stomach dropped at the thought of joining them. It'd been months since I'd seen direct action, and the captain said there were Hunters in the area...

Few people walk out of a knife fight.

Luke's voice echoed through my head like a warning siren. He wouldn't like this.

I didn't have a choice, though. With my heart picking up speed, I turned to Isaac. "Yes, sir."

"Stay close," he said. "They'd been on a recon patrol when they were attacked. Hunters are probably waiting for their extraction party."

I nodded.

He gripped my upper arm, right over the red cross. "If they engage, don't hesitate."

I swallowed the sense of doom. Anxiety pooled in my stomach, but I ignored the nausea and my shaking hands.

"We got you, girl," said Phan with a big smile. "You won't have to fight. You're only there to heal."

Was this guy new? What an idiot.

We headed out shortly after, and I rode in the rear of an electric ATV with Maldonado driving. Sunset had just passed, and the brisk November air seeped beneath my heavy gear to chill my very bones. While my temporary squad joked around, I stayed quiet, certain they could hear the erratic pounding of my heart.

Darkness had enveloped us by the time we made it to the location—a six-story glass office building that had apparently been reappropriated as a lookout. Other squads had arrived before us, their footfalls crunching on the asphalt as they marched toward the building, guns in hand.

How many soldiers had received a firearm? How many rounds were they given? Since the Gunlock Law, firearms had grown increasingly harder to find. How the Defiance armed themselves was a mystery to me, though I suspected stealing from the NAO—thanks to Lucas—was the prime method.

I stayed close to Isaac as our squad moved in. The glass of the main door had been smashed in, and we stepped through in silence, following the other squads. I flinched at the crunch of glass under our boots.

We found the stairs behind the abandoned check-in desk. Isaac peeked around the corner before giving us the go-ahead. In the pitch-black stairwell, I followed the bouncing flashlight of the soldiers above and below. The other squads peeled off as they reached their assigned floors, and the familiar sounds of medics barking triage orders filtered from the propped doors. Six floors up, Isaac set his hand over the push bar. Metal scraped against metal as he pushed it in, then peeked into the darkened interior.

Cubicles spanned out with offices at the perimeter. I strove to see through the darkness, keeping my ears perked for suspicious noises, but there were none. Not enemy soldiers, not dying comrades.

Nothing.

We snuck through the gloom, clearing each cubicle and conference room, every office and restroom. The place was empty...except for a break room on the south side of the building.

I stepped in after Isaac and Maldonado, my gaze darting to the dark masses on the floor near the windows. A beam of light grazed over the six bodies lying at strange angles in pools of red.

My heart sank, but I approached the bodies to check each one—riddled with bullets and pulseless. Sprays of blood spattered the windows, now pockmarked with holes. I peered into the dark world outside, wondering what these soldiers had been surveilling. What portion of the Hunter domain had they lost their lives to observe?

"They're gone," I said, voice steady.

Isaac nodded once, all business. "We'll transport the bodies to the rally point. Let's clear the floor and help the other squads with anyone still alive downstairs."

While I waited with him, the four soldiers cleared the rest of the floor, searching for anyone else, anyone who might be alive.

They found no one.

As we regrouped near the stairwell, the walkie-talkie on Isaac's belt erupted in static. "Eyes on enemy. Level one. Over."

My heart jumped into my throat.

Isaac unclipped his device. "Copy that. How many? Over."

"At least twenty. They're at the front, but circling back. Get down here. We're going in now. Over and out."

Isaac glanced at me, visage stern. "Remember what I said. No hesitation." He pulled a pistol from his holster. "Where's your blade?"

Hands shaking, I yanked out my combat knife.

"Stay close to me. I'll cover you, okay?"

"Wait," I said. "What if—what if we just waited?"

"Not an option," he said without further explanation, then briefed the other soldiers. "Shoot to kill, men. We meet at the rally point as discussed."

My body transformed into a buzzing wire as we returned to the main stairwell. Khattab opened the door and motioned for us to follow. Shouts from below bounced against every concrete surface.

Hustling down the steps, we made it to the second floor before I slipped the knuckles from my pocket. Breaking glass and the thuds of fists against flesh greeted us as we rounded the last flight.

I braced myself for the coming fight. My senses zeroed in on a primal, innate survival instinct, one I barely remembered I possessed.

In a flurry, a Hunter dashed through the door to the stairwell, weapons raised. As Maldonado raised his gun and fired, the Hunter hit the floor, and we spilled into the lobby. My stomach dropped.

Outnumbered.

I was transported back to the battle at Safe House Red, the chaos of gunfire and smoke and blood. With a surge of adrenaline, I gripped my weapons so hard my knuckles blanched. Lucas's voice murmured in my ear, guiding me. *If you can, you run.*

I mapped out the quickest route to the broken door we'd come through. Several floor-to-ceiling windows had been smashed, but no matter which I chose, a throng of fighting soldiers stood in my way. I gritted my teeth and picked a window.

With my knife and bladed knuckles in the defensive position Lucas taught me, I darted through a couple of fights without anyone taking notice. One of our men stumbled into me after being shot in the chest. He dropped at my feet. My eyes darted up to find who shot him. The Hunter stood with his back to the broken window I'd been heading toward.

His gaze swept down my body, eyes widening. A cocky grin spread across his face. I backed away and ran toward another window. I was caught around the waist and spun to face a different man.

If you ever need to use this, you go for the throat.

I didn't hesitate, slamming my reinforced fist into vital, life-giving structures. He choked, and something sharp scraped my lower belly.

He fell to the floor, and I turned again, heading for the window, ignoring the pain and blood saturating my clothes.

Two Hunters blocked me.

Never attack first.

I waited.

"Where'd you get those knuckles?" one asked.

The other man lunged for me, and I dodged him the way Lucas had taught me. I managed to sink my knife into him as he retreated. Not a fatal blow.

He swung his arm and sliced me twice more in the stomach below my vest—glancing, shallow blows that burned like fire. I cried out, clutching my stomach.

The one who'd asked about the knuckles shoved me to the

ground. He leapt on me, and his broad hand wrapped around my throat. His smile turned psychotic as he crushed my windpipe. Black sparks burst into my vision.

Don't panic when you can't breathe.

Right hand up. Right foot outside his ankle. Roll.

Our positions reversed just as Lucas showed me. I buried my knife in the man's liver. The other soldier yanked on my left arm, and my knife clattered to the floor.

I jumped to my feet and ran.

The soldier chased me, but the path to an open window was now clear.

I leapt through it.

He followed, calling for help. "The bitch just got Rogers!"

For the first time, I was grateful for Lucas's forced cardio workouts. I ran, but the pain from my wounds turned the asphalt to sand, making each step harder than the last.

Behind, pounding footsteps stalked me.

I flew down the sidewalk into a dark, abandoned neighborhood. They gained on me quickly. I couldn't tell whether there were two or three, and I was too afraid to check.

Taking streets at random, I zigzagged through the neighborhood and hoped my endurance would outlast theirs.

I hoped in vain.

Fingers grasped the medic pack strapped to my shoulders, jerking me backward. I fell to the pavement. A blade jabbed into my left leg.

A scream ripped from my throat. I lashed out with my remaining weapon.

"Shit!" The Hunter backed away just in time.

His partner had almost reached us when he leapt on me, his upper body pinning my legs to the ground.

Don't spread your legs.

On my back, I struggled with him. He seized my wrist in a bruising grip to stay my weapon while his blade sank over and over into my left leg. Excruciating fire licked up my thigh with each stab. He wormed his way up my body, managing to insert one knee between my legs before his buddy arrived.

Think about where your knee is, Sophia.

I jerked my right leg up into his groin, and he released an animalistic groan, falling to my side.

Go for places that bleed fast.

He faced away from me, clutching his groin. His knife clattered out of my reach. I no longer had a weapon that could dig deep, so I took my knuckles to the vulnerable area behind his knee like Lucas taught me.

The other man grabbed me by my hair. "You bitch."

I swiped the knuckles at him, slashing his arm, but it didn't slow him. He wrenched me onto my side hard enough that asphalt eroded the skin of my arm. Blind anger twisted his expression. He raised his hand and slammed a knife through my left thigh.

My vision went black.

Oh, god.

The pain.

Agony sheared through every cell. It shredded my throat with another scream.

But if he was playing with me to prolong the torture, that single decision saved my life.

As he retreated, reaching for another weapon, I went for his throat. I couldn't give him the chance to jerk away, so I threw my arm around his neck in a deadly embrace. It buried him deeper on the blade. His weight hurled me onto my back once more, and he fell on top of me. Hot blood poured over me like bathwater.

When he went limp, I pushed him off me. His partner groaned, weak hands trying to stop the gush from the wound I inflicted. He lay in a puddle of blood, his skin ghostly white in the dark. He paid me no mind as I stumbled away, yanking the knife from my leg. It clattered to the glittering cement of the sidewalk.

Blood pulsed from the wound.

Too fast. Too much.

I limped. Fire burned through every inch of my body, and blood seeped down my leg, soaking my clothes. I clenched the knuckles in my hand so tight it hurt.

Once the man's groans faded behind me, I took stock of my surroundings. I stood on a dark street corner, and I had little time. Dizziness fought my pounding heart as it tried to compensate for the hemorrhage.

Where was I? Where could I go?

I glanced at the closest street sign. Twenty-fifth and Columbia. Seven blocks from headquarters. Fourteen from the rally point.

I wouldn't make it that far. I turned my head, staring down the street that led to Evanston, only three blocks away. He wouldn't be there, but he had supplies. I could make a tourniquet...

I tripped along, trying to keep to the grass to hide the blood trail as my left leg screamed in pain. When I reached the familiar steps to the house, I fell forward, knocking my shins hard onto cement. I had to crawl to the porch, smearing every surface I touched in blood.

Sparkles threatened my vision, obscuring the doorknob. Still, my hand wrapped around it.

Locked.

Numb fingers pawed at my pockets, and I dropped the knuckles on the porch in favor of gripping the key I always carried. Metal slipped into the slot, and the tumblers gave way.

I fell into the living room.

I should stop. I needed sleep. So tired...

I could close my eyes for only a moment.

But...tourniquet.

I whimpered as I forced myself back to my feet and stumbled to one side, catching myself on the sofa. Bloody handprints stained the fabric as I pushed forward and gasped for breath. My energy flagged.

No time to make a tourniquet. Consciousness fled as blackness crept up. I staggered through the master bedroom into his communications room.

I lit upon the lamp, glowing a soft white. My finger grazed the button for *RED* before I collapsed onto the carpeted floor.

23

UNTIL I DIE

—ERNEST HEMINGWAY

I swam in darkness with nothing but stars sparkling above me. Cold water crept into the cracks of my very soul. Like a vacuum, it lured me toward a looming void beneath.

Despite the cold, I burned. Every move stung and scorched, cauterizing me from the inside out. The water grew colder the deeper I went.

The void promised relief, and I swam toward it.

A jolt, a bright flash of pain, had me crying in protest.

"Stay with me, Sophia!"

I pushed the voice away. I wanted the void.

My heartbeat throbbed in my arms and knees, sharper in my leg and abdomen. Agony ebbed and flowed with the waves around me.

"Sophia, can you hear me? Don't you fucking let go."

I sank into the cold ocean, drowning, languishing in the knowledge it would end soon. Meaningless words drifted through the water—a voice I recognized, but couldn't place. I bobbed in and out of the abyss, floating in freezing waves until the burning began to ease. A different sort of warmth enveloped me, enticing me away from the cold.

"Sophia, please. Open your eyes."

I groaned, begging wordlessly to go back under.

"No, sweetheart, don't fight. You'll rip the stitches."

Was I fighting? I let my muscles relax, and the pain of my various wounds eased. Again and again, a warm, worried voice coaxed me into obedience.

I liked that voice.

Comforting.

Safe.

At some point, the timelessness converted back to seconds and minutes. My body beached itself somewhere on the shores of consciousness.

"Please," the voice whispered. "Please open your eyes."

Powerless to disobey, my lids cracked. The world swam into focus. An IV line sprouted from a vein on my hand. The tubing led to bags of fluid hanging on a hook above the bed. I focused on the letters. Saline and antibiotics. The bedside table was littered with empty vials.

"Sophia?"

Disoriented, my gaze traveled toward that voice, the one that had coaxed me back to life again and again.

Unkempt and brittle, Lucas Scott stared with a blank expression and a rainbow of emotion in his eyes. "Can you hear me?"

At my slow nod, he released a breath.

He sank to his knees by the bed, where I lay tucked under covers in his master bedroom. His forehead fell onto the mattress beside me.

"Thank you," he whispered to the floor.

Stiff and sore, I lifted my hand to scratch my fingers into his hair, counting his breaths.

One, two, three...

We stayed like that for a long time, one of his hands resting on my leg, the other on my ribs.

After a while, he shifted onto the bed, his weight dipping the mattress. "Can you speak?"

"I—I think so," I said, my voice rusty.

"Will you tell me how this happened?" The lethal calm in his voice prickled along my spine, surging my veins with adrenaline, but I still tripped over the memories thanks to the drugs in my system. Frozen beside me, Lucas stared at the wall above my head while I stuttered out a mess of a story. When I finished, my eyes fluttered closed, fatigue dragging me back toward the void.

"You were almost dead by the time I got here," he said, tone lifeless. "I was sitting in my living room, and the light turned red, and—"

My eyes popped open. Skin flushed, he wouldn't look at me again. As I set my hand atop his, he turned his palm to grasp my fingers.

"They stabbed you *sixteen times*. Thank god they didn't hit anything important because I wouldn't have— The bleeding—" His words grew harder, angrier. "You were pale as death, your pulse *so* faint. I can't believe I got the bleeding to stop. You're fucking lucky I'm O negative."

"Y-you gave me your blood?"

He ignored me. "You left a trail of red breadcrumbs leading here, so I had to wash away the evidence. When I made it back, you were burning up. I had to steal antibiotics." He lapsed into a long silence, staring down at my hand on his. "You've been in and out for *six days* —and I—" He shook his head. "But I had to leave so no one suspected." His gaze lifted to mine. "What if you'd died while I was away?"

The fear in those words reminded me of a caged animal, threatened and feral. His voice wavered, then neutralized. "Can you please tell me why you were sent on a raid like that?"

I swallowed against my thick tongue. "It was a rescue mission. They needed medics."

"And they were willing to sacrifice you for it?"

My heart lurched a slow, throbbing beat, and I fought against the narcotized confusion. "Theo wasn't there. He couldn't—"

"Is your life worth *nothing* to them?" he hissed, like a cornered cat. "I *told* you. I told you I wouldn't tolerate threats against your safety."

I blinked heavily at him.

"They're supposed to protect their vulnerable, not throw them out to be eaten by wolves."

"Lucas, it was a misunderstanding."

His gaze turned sharp, his voice cutting. "You will not leave this house until I say so. You'll stay until you've recovered."

Nerves tickled my insides. The same danger I remembered from those first weeks with him radiated toward me, but it formed an invisible shield around me. Protective. Possessive.

Those intense eyes focused on mine, furious and devastated. "When you go back to them, you can tell Harrison my continued loyalty depends entirely on your survival. If something happens to you, Sophia, I will kill him."

I blinked as his words filtered through my brain and settled into the place I processed dangerous things.

Because this... this was perilous. If I told Theo that Lucas was issuing threats...

"If threatening him is how I make you matter to him, I will." A bloodthirsty anguish deepened his voice, each consonant honed like a knife raised to protect me.

I attempted to sit up, but I couldn't do it. Healing stab wounds illuminated with pain like neon lights. "You can't do that," I rasped.

"I assure you I can."

I tried to form a counterargument, but it was useless. If he wanted, this man could ninja his way into our headquarters and murder everyone inside. Lucas was the most lethal person I'd ever met, and I had no doubt that if he wanted someone dead, they would be.

His hand was so rigid around mine that my fingers tingled. My voice dropped to a placating whisper. "Lucas—"

"I won't lose you to this war."

I sank deeper into my pillows while the confusion spun my head. Hadn't we been operating under his belief that my presence in his life was the worst mistake he'd ever made?

"I don't understand," I said.

A beat passed while he stared at me, jaw twitching. "You are *mine*. If they take you from me, I'll kill them all."

He'd...what?

This man had spent the last several weeks standing halfway across the room, barking information and ordering me to leave, and now he was promising to murder our general for threatening my safety?

My sleepy, drugged brain couldn't comprehend it. Instead, it threw out a memory I wished it didn't:

You're the weapon Williams will choose to end him.

Mysteriously, my life seemed to be all Lucas cared about, and the Defiance, in all their hypocritical wisdom, wanted me to betray him.

I let go of his hand to grip his face. I wanted to see him up close, needed to understand the emotions that drove these desperate words. Flecks of amber blazed from his eyes like flames, and fizzy heat burst to life in my chest.

Lucas Scott was a perpetual enigma, but one thing was abundantly clear: he cared a great deal about me. Maybe he wished he didn't. Maybe he regretted ever agreeing to let me be his contact.

But I mattered to him.

Lucas had a personal vendetta and a crooked moral compass. He guarded the things he cared for with frank violence. Somehow, in some way, I mattered to him, and he now considered the Defiance a threat to my life.

As the gravity fell on me, hard as a slab of iron, panic followed. He'd tried to push me away, but he couldn't stop me from falling any more than he could stop himself from caring. We'd both wind up dead in our attempts to keep the other safe…

A sob burst free. "Lucas, they're already planning to kill you. They want *me* to do it. If I tell Theo you're threatening to kill him, he'll—"

"Try to end me first," he finished for me, a tad softer. "I don't care what they try with me, so long as you remain safe."

I blinked. "Wait. You *knew*?"

"Of course I did. It's the strategic move. Take my information, then kill me when I've outlived my usefulness. I used to analyze every move you made, wondering when you'd strike."

"Wh-what?"

"If they try to take you out with me, however, I'm going to have a big problem."

I blinked, studying the resigned set of his shoulders. "They wouldn't do that," I whispered, "and I—I'd never do that to you."

He rolled his eyes. "You should have done it the day of those executions, but you were still searching for something to redeem."

"Well, I was right." I tried to sit up again. He took hold of my elbows, helping me into a sitting position. "I'm alive because of you."

We stared at each other long enough that things turned hazy, and his face glowed.

He touched my cheek. "If they let something happen to you, Theodore Harrison is a dead man. The NAO destroyed my country. Commander Haynes shot my father. Jack Miller killed my sister. If the Defiance sacrifices you, I'll burn it all down."

Warmth spread from my chest to my fingers and toes, and I surrendered to the pounding desire to kiss him.

My dry lips met his, and I pulled him as close as I could. Every little movement hurt, but the pain didn't stop me. I wanted it to hurt. I wanted the reminder I was alive, that I had lived because of him, that I would continue to live. *For him.*

I fell backward, and he followed, trying to be gentle. But I didn't want gentle. I only wanted *him.*

"Sophia, you're barely healed." He spoke the words against my lips.

"I don't care. I almost died. You saved me."

"It took me hours to fix you. You're finally getting some color back. Please be careful."

I clawed my fingers into his skin, trying to keep him close, even as he withdrew. Despite the pain medications painting fog over my reality, I still wanted him next to me, on top of me, inside me. I'd thought those wounds would kill me. This dangerous, morally ambiguous man gave me his own blood to keep me alive.

I wanted him.

But he wasn't wrong about my wounds.

"How did you fix me?" I murmured as the pain ratcheted up.

"I told you. I'm a doctor, remember?"

My hazy focus landed on him, and I waited for the joke, but it never came. "You—are?"

His mouth quirked in that wry smile. "Another thing you thought I was lying about?"

Words deserted me.

He pressed his palm to my forehead. "You feel feverish again."

Each blink dragged me closer to the void, my body telling me to rest. "I think it's you," I slurred. "You make me hot." My eyes closed against my will. "Don't leave."

I was almost asleep when he whispered, "You'll never be rid of me now, Sophia."

When I woke again, the light in the room had changed, and he was gone.

He was *gone.*

I writhed on the bed, panicking at the loneliness, the abandonment. At my single whimper, he popped up from the bench at the end of the bed.

My body stilled when I found him, the anxiety drowned by a wave of relief.

He hadn't left.

He'd stayed, like he promised.

His stare froze on my hand when I reached for him. Slowly, he moved to stand next to me, taking hold of my fingers.

With protesting, sleepy noises, I demanded he lie beside me, tugging on his arm with all my failing strength.

Color flickered in his eyes as he caught my meaning. He crawled onto the bed beside me and settled against the pillows while I turned toward him. My fingers interlaced with his on his chest, and exhaustion lulled me back under. I drifted off to him tracing shapes on my knuckles.

The next time, I woke enfolded in his warmth. I'd wiggled my way right next to him, my head on his chest, his arms around me. I turned my face into him, breathing him in.

"Lucas?"

"Mmm?"

"Stay with me."

He kissed my forehead and let long seconds pass in thick silence. Finally, he said, "I will. Until I die."

24

SANCTUARY

 Duty, Honor, Country.

— THE UNITED STATES MILITARY ACADEMY AT WEST POINT

I roused from my drugged fever safe in his arms. Asleep, his face was different. Less haunted, more tranquil. He hadn't shaved, and a deep purple stained the skin beneath his eyes, but still, he held me captivated.

He'd saved my life.

I tried to recall our previous conversation, but it was like grasping at the wispy strands of a dream. Key phrases jumped out at me, the loudest ringing through my now sober mind.

You are mine. *If they take you from me, I'll kill them all.*

How did I become so damaged? I was basking in the love language of Lucas Scott, which coasted along the lines of a sociopath. More than that, I didn't care. A ferocious fire had ignited inside me. He'd claimed me as his, but he also belonged to me.

I'd lost so many, but my heart wouldn't survive losing him. The fickle universe would have to take me with him. Lucas Scott was mine, and I would keep him, or I would die.

There was no in-between.

The aches in my body had faded to tolerable. I started to disengage, letting him sleep while I tested my legs, but as soon as our bodies separated, his eyes snapped open. His arms tightened around me, keeping me close while he stared his fill. After a moment, he tested the temperature of my forehead, then trailed his fingers down the side of my face. "Think you can eat?"

I nodded.

He eased away, leaving me cold, and disappeared through the door. With less pain than I imagined, I scooted to the edge of the bed and planted my feet on the floor.

Then I hesitated.

Injuries aside, I hadn't eaten in days. I'd be woozy and weak on my feet. Lifting my shirt, I peeled at the tape of the bandage near my hip bone. A one-inch closed incision glared at me, clean and healing. Two more defaced my stomach.

I wore no pants, only a pair of his boxers, and I tried not to imagine him cutting through my fatigues to reach my bare, bleeding skin.

I'd begun to peel at the tape on my legs when he reappeared in the doorway, carrying a plate of apple slices with fresh water. The corner of his mouth twitched as he set the plate beside me, the water on the table. "Try to eat. I'll do this."

Cross-legged at my feet, he removed the tape with delicate, skilled movements. Once the bandages lay in a pile beside him, he traced his finger near the worst injury. "This is the one that almost killed you." His voice was lifeless. "I did the best I could, but your leg won't ever be the same."

It was the same leg I'd broken before Daniela died. It hadn't been the same since then anyway.

His eyes flicked to mine. "How are you feeling?"

I rolled my wrists and shoulders, but everything ached, even my head. "Stiff and weak," I said, grimacing.

"You probably need more blood." He stared at my leg like he'd made a grave mistake in not bleeding himself dry for me.

I took his chin in hand, forcing him to look at me. "You did enough. I'll be fine with a little time."

He didn't argue, but that meant nothing. In the end, Lucas would do what he wanted. He always did.

I leaned down to set my forehead against his. "Please don't hurt yourself to shave a couple of days off my healing time."

He sighed. "Just eat."

Several slices of apple later, my stomach was full, and I set aside the plate. I chanced a small smile at him. "Will you help me stand?"

After a staring contest in which I was pretty sure he considered handcuffing me to the bed to keep me from hurting myself, he finally nodded. With him bracing my elbows, I planted my weight on my feet, trying to lean on my right leg. My left sparked with fire.

Still, I was upright.

A satisfied smile stretched. "I did it! Am I allowed to shower?"

His brow lifted. "Can you stand without assistance?"

I glared down at my shaky legs. "I'd really like to feel clean. Will you help?"

After another bout of vexed eye contact, he unhooked the tubing from the line in my hand, taping the Luer lock. "Can you walk?"

"Let me try." Heavily favoring my injured leg, I managed some slow but bearable steps. He started the shower while I brushed my teeth.

Before I could undress, he touched my waist, and I met his gaze in the mirror. The threatened animal vibe had returned, and his hand fisted the fabric of my shirt so tight his knuckles blanched. I thought he might say something, but the words gleamed instead in the desperation of his eyes.

I can't lose you.

"I know," I whispered, and stretched an arm back to circle his neck. He dropped a long kiss on my shoulder.

How had we reached this impossible place, grasping onto each other with broken fingers?

He released a held breath before helping me undress and step into the shower. The heat eased away the discomfort. My left leg throbbed, but it could bear weight.

While he faced away, leaning in the doorway, I cleaned myself. I relished every drop of hot water until it ran cold, then grabbed the towel he left for me. "How are you here?" I asked as I dried off. "Won't they wonder where you are?"

"No. Every other day I've had to leave, but it's Saturday." Under his breath he added, "Fucking finally."

Saturday? My stomach cramped as I considered how long I'd been down. I would have bled to death in his closet if he hadn't come. What were the odds that he'd see the light just as it turned red?

When would my dumb luck run out?

I tried to brush past the sudden fear in my gut. "Heaven forbid wars be fought on weekends."

He shrugged. "Even God got a day off."

Wrapping the towel around my body, I shot an incredulous look at the back of his head. "Are you comparing yourself to God, Lucas?"

He turned to flash me a small smirk. "No. I'm taking two days off."

I almost laughed. I *wanted* to laugh. At the cheek. The absurdity. The sheer impossibility of this situation.

But I couldn't laugh.

My body had forgotten how.

He turned to face me full-on. "It's taking everything in me not to chain you to the bed. You're doing too much too soon."

I looked down at myself. "I'm just standing here."

"You're going to undo everything I've spent the last week trying to fix."

The ache in my leg had begun a steady throb, and my entire body felt vaguely as if it was spinning in space, so I capitulated without argument. "Help me dress, and I'll get back in bed."

He retrieved some of his clothes while I stood in front of the mirror and opened the towel.

I gaped at what I found.

Dehydrated and pallid. Skin stained with bruises. Purple and red dyed my whole thigh, and the deep wound Lucas had sewn shut stood out bright and jagged, the blue stitches a macabre reminder of the violence I'd barely survived.

"How did you save me?" I asked as I took in the extent of the damage.

He flicked a hard gaze toward me. "Luck."

"Or skill?"

Mouth tight, he helped me don an old blue T-shirt emblazoned with *Duke Medicine* in white letters.

"You went to Duke?"

He didn't answer. Instead, he guided me—gently, but forcefully—back to the bed. My hands splayed over the clean cotton. "Did you...change the sheets?"

He swiped up the plate and shoved the glass of water into my hand. "Sorry," he quipped. "I wasn't aware you preferred dirty bedding. Drink this."

"Wow." I took a sip. "Your patients must have loved your bedside manner."

"I was a surgeon, not a babysitter," he said and left the room.

I stared at the doorway, bemused. For *not-a-babysitter*, the man certainly did a fine job taking care of me. He returned with the plate refilled, this time with a bowl of broth, strawberries and three slices of cheddar.

I lifted the cheese between two fingers, eyeing it.

"You need protein," he said as if he assumed I would argue.

I moved my gaze to him. "The NAO has cheese?"

His expression eased. "The NAO has everything."

Anger spilled into my blood, heating it as I tried to remember the last time I'd enjoyed the simple pleasure of cheese. This inoffensive orange square in my hand represented years of deprivation and loss. I ripped into it with my teeth, wishing I could do the same to the NAO.

A soft caress nuzzled my cheek. "Don't waste your energy hating them right now. Just focus on yourself."

"Who are you to give advice like that? All of *your* energy goes toward hating them."

"I didn't almost bleed to death. I have energy to spare."

I glared down at my NAO-infested plate. "I'll make you a deal. I'll eat this whole meal if you tell me why you hate them so much."

He sat at the corner of the bed. "I told you—"

"They hurt your sister. Yeah, I know." I rolled my eyes. "What did they do to your sister, Lucas? How did you go from doctor to executioner? Why did Commander Haynes shoot your father?"

For the third time that day, we entered a battle of stares, and I locked, unblinking, onto the blue in his eyes. His throat worked with a swallow, but finally—*finally!*—he capitulated.

"Fine. Eat."

My heart leapt, but I kept the thrill off my face, opting to shove a spoonful of broth into my mouth instead.

Lucas's sigh was heavy, weighted by memory. He set his elbows on his knees and spoke to his clasped hands instead of me. "I was in my last year of surgical residency when the Capitol Hill Massacre went down. Things moved fast after that. All military officers were called in for active duty, even those of us on an educational deferment."

He glanced up to make sure I was eating, and I shoved a strawberry in my mouth.

"I came from a military family. My father was a colonel when this all started, and he lived and breathed for this country. My mother passed from cancer fifteen years ago. Sophie was ten at the time, and I was already away at college. My father didn't know what to do with her, so he got strict, and she did the typical rebellious teenager thing and learned to hate everything he loved."

"Including this country?" I asked with a mouthful of cheese.

His head fell. "Yeah."

"So, what happened?"

"The war. I thought they'd want me as a medical major, but the Defiance took more men than anyone was led to believe. The NAO was desperate for bodies, and I hadn't finished my medical training. Plus, I had a head for strategy. They shipped me to Ontario for intelligence and command. Dad was promoted to a one-star general once Haynes realized he was losing half his army to a rebellion.

"My sister tried to join the rebellion. She was twenty-five, and Dad had no grounds to stop her, but he tried anyway. He trapped her in DC, where trying to escape would have been suicide, especially for a single woman."

Once again, he studied me, and I diligently chewed.

"I didn't even think to refuse," he said. "In the military, they groom you to fall in line, to love your country before everything else. Duty, honor, country. All that. It was easy to join up when Haynes wasn't president. Plus, it's what my father wanted for me. This country... It used to be great. But when the NAO took over, I hated every second of wearing that uniform, of looking like I supported their hate. I knew what was happening was wrong, but I didn't know how to get out. My father raised me on patriotism, and I was using this country to pay for school. I'd promised them four years of service.

"Sophie, though. Sophie was the smart one. She hated this regime from the very beginning, shaming me and my dad for serving a dictator back before he truly was a dictator. I remember arguing with her that I was just serving my four years and getting out, and she'd laugh and say I sold my soul for med school tuition."

He lapsed into a long silence, and I sat frozen, staring at the hunch of his shoulders.

"I wish she hadn't been right," he murmured after a bit.

"So how did it all go down?" I asked.

He glanced my way as I ladled broth into my mouth, allowing a small smirk to surface that faded as he spoke again. "They shipped me to Canada to fight, and I was there for more than a year. We were given very little information about what was happening back home. I'd heard of the Defiance, but I didn't really understand. I didn't know.

"Then the Defiance got stronger, and Haynes needed more protection domestically. He pulled thousands of troops back into the States to serve the NSF, including me. I was promoted to lieutenant colonel and given a battalion of Hunters to command. My father was promoted even higher. The only good part of it was that I'd returned home to DC."

"Back to Sophie?"

He nodded. "*That's* when I learned about the prisoner camps and brothels. It's when I learned about Executive Order 16389. I had no idea how bad it had gotten. Sophie was miserable. Angry. Dad... It's like he was blind to it. She told me what the NAO was really doing, and I... Christ, I didn't know what to do. The violence in the country was escalating. Civilian riots were killing innocents and soldiers alike. Theodore Harrison was both aggressive and smart, and his losses were nothing compared to the NAO's."

"It didn't seem that way on our side," I muttered.

He shot me a knowing look. "The propaganda is misleading. Again and again, your Prime Delegate approached Haynes for peace talks, but he wouldn't even consider speaking to a woman. The news painted it like he was protecting us from the dangerous rebels. Sophie wanted us all to defect, and I wanted to. I really did. But I couldn't find a safe way to escape."

I sensed a darkness looming in his story, and I almost stopped him. Did it really matter how it ended? Wasn't this bad enough?

"She was serving as a spy," he said, so soft I could barely hear him. "The whole time, she was stealing information from our dad and giving it to the Defiance. At first, I tried to talk her out of it, but then..."

"You helped her, didn't you?"

He nodded. "We did it for months before they discovered her. It was the middle of the night when they knocked down our door. Commander Haynes confronted my father directly. He thought Dad was aiding Sophie. They had no idea I was involved."

Another silence stretched, and I wished I was close enough to touch him, to offer any sort of comfort. "So Haynes shot your father?"

"That's the gist of it. Once Dad convinced Haynes he wasn't a spy, Haynes then considered him an idiot for letting a woman steal from him. They arrested Sophie. I was told she'd be questioned and processed like any other citizen arrested for a crime, so I thought I could bail her out. I'd find a lawyer. I'd free her."

My heart sank.

His gaze slid my way. "I didn't know at the time what the NSF considers due process."

I set my empty plate aside and scooted closer to him. "Which Blood Colonel processed her?"

His eyes flashed. "Jack Miller."

My mind blinked over the pages I'd memorized months ago—intimate details of Jack Miller's weaknesses, his schedule, his entire life—and it all began to make a morbid kind of sense.

"You've been hunting him, haven't you?"

"He transferred her to the House," Lucas said. "For *correction*. One day, I will tear out his heart."

This was far more dreadful than I'd imagined, and nausea churned in my gut. "Lucas, I'm so sorry."

His mouth stretched into a humorless smile. "It gets worse. They put a scarlet patch on my shoulder like it was an honor, then shipped me to the most active combat zone as punishment for my father's crimes. I'd been in combat before, but that first execution was the first time I had ever killed anyone in cold blood. I tried to make it quick, as painless as possible, but instead of leniency, people only saw my inhumanity.

"The truth of it was what hurt. Those strangers dropped at my feet, and I felt nothing. That was the point I began to realize the NAO had stolen my humanity. Nothing mattered anymore. Nothing but getting Sophie out, but I couldn't find her."

I knew the story would get worse. Sophie hadn't survived, after all, and I'd known it from the start. But I wanted a different outcome. I wanted an ending that allowed her freedom. I wanted a life for her.

"It was all so much harder than I thought it would be. I volunteered to take over prisoner registration hoping I'd get some sense of her location. Before me, they didn't keep good records of the prisoners, so locating her was nearly impossible. Still, I prepared. I got food. Gas. Everything we would need to escape to Canada." He swallowed, but the motion looked painful, like the next words would gut him to say. "I found her last February. It turns out Jack Miller took a shine to her. He treats Defiant sympathizers worse than dogs, and he used her like a toy. She didn't survive him."

I stared at his profile, trying to process that. "She didn't...*survive* him?"

"He chokes women while he rapes them. To assert his dominance."

I wished I hadn't eaten that entire plate, as it badly wanted to make a reappearance.

"I might have killed Miller if he'd been anywhere near me when I discovered it, but I was in the brothel, and Anna... She calmed me down."

"Anna?"

"She's the madame of the House in this region." He lifted his hand, where the gold band glinted on his pinky. "She gave me Sophie's ring and helped me use my anger to my advantage. The Hunters didn't know I'd discovered where Sophie was. They assumed I'd stay loyal to protect her, and they abused that assumption. It gave me the perfect opening to go deeper than I ever had. Given my rank, I had access to a lot of information. I learned everything I could, and every Friday night, I go to the House. Anna's network gives me what the women are able to steal from the officers who use them."

"And you bring it all to me," I said. The puzzle pieces finally settled into place in my mind, forming an intricate, complex picture. He'd been a doctor in training, then a soldier following orders, then a brother protecting his sister, and now a vigilante seeking justice.

"My father deserved the death he got," he said. "I deserve the death that's destined for me. Sophie didn't deserve any of this. The NAO can burn in hell."

I scooted close enough to take his hand. "How long after you found out she died did you approach Harrison?"

"A couple of weeks, I think. I hoped he'd kill me on sight. And then I hoped he'd send an assassin to murder me. Instead, he sent you."

"He sent me."

He huffed out a small, bitter laugh, still staring down at the ground as if avoiding my gaze would make it all easier to say. "Another Defiant Sophia. The fucking irony."

That first meeting in March, he'd been furious and cold as the sharp edge of a knife, licking his wounds by lashing out at the woman he thought would kill him—a woman torturing him with his sister's name. He'd come to me in pieces, shredded apart by circumstances beyond his control, broken by years of coercive abuse and fear.

We'd both arrived at this house prepared to relinquish our lives, perhaps even hoping for the end.

Instead, we'd found sanctuary.

I reached for him, and he gave no resistance. He let me pull him toward me, surrendering easily to my pleas to come closer.

"Kiss me," I whispered, and he did.

His mouth molded to mine, urgent and gentle all at the same time. His hand dove into my wet curls, holding me in place while he drugged me with the kind of kisses I'd fantasized about since that night we'd slept together.

When I tugged, he obeyed, sliding up my body as I fell to the mattress. He cupped my jaw, deepening and slowing the kiss like it was some dessert he wanted to savor.

My heart slammed in my chest, pounding to the beat of his own, pressed right against my chest. The kiss was beautiful and terrible all at once, like a diamond ring on a bloodstained hand.

I was falling for a man who existed somewhere between the pursuit of revenge and a traitor's death. Even he knew his days were numbered, and if I handed him my heart, he'd take it to his grave. Still, I found myself on my knees, giving it all to him willingly, and he snatched it with greedy hands. We both needed something to hold on to. The great tragedy was that the thing we'd found to grasp was like crystalline water leaking between our fingers.

Fleeting. Impossible to keep.

His eyes burned bright as he broke the kiss. "You almost died in my arms, do you know that? My hands were soaked in your blood. I spent days begging you to open your eyes, terrified you never would."

Any woman would have melted at the expression on his face, all hot and possessive and needy. I pulled him back for another kiss.

I burned in the fire—pain in my leg, pleasure against my mouth. His lips dipped to my neck, and he murmured endearments against my skin as if he wanted to tattoo them there. As my eyes fell closed, his caresses slowed, grew more calming.

"You're making me sleepy," I muttered.

"That's the point," he replied, kissing the thin skin covering the veins of my wrist. "You need rest."

"I need *you*."

"I'm right here."

My eyes gave up the fight, but my fingernails scraped his ribs, anchoring onto him. "You'll stay with me?"

He found a place beside me, enfolding me in his arms while his fingers traced shapes on my bare skin. "I'll stay with you, Sophia. Until I die."

25

SAY THE WORDS

 ...as they kiss, consume.

— WILLIAM SHAKESPEARE, *ROMEO AND JULIET*

It took days to heal. Lucas only left my side to meet whatever requirements the Hunters demanded of him, but he always returned, greeting me with a kiss and a subtle hand to my forehead, checking for fever. While he was gone, I rested and ate the food he left for me. He removed the stitches after a couple more days, and my bruises faded from violet to yellow. Moving grew easier, and I unsnarled the tangles from my hair with a hairbrush Lucas used to pretend was a knife.

I napped.

A lot.

Sometimes I woke to an empty house; other times, I opened my eyes to him lying beside me, sleeping or reading. It was so *normal*, like a war wasn't happening right outside the window.

But it was.

The war remained the ghost in the room with us, haunting our every second together. I'd never feared ghosts before, but now I was terrified. Lucas Scott was a crisis of my faith. Short of a miracle, a great deal of pain loomed in my future, and I found myself praying to a deity I'd long forsaken to save us both from the inevitable.

No answer ever came.

"I should get back to headquarters soon, shouldn't I?" I asked one evening, drowsing with his finger twirling a curl round and round.

His attention didn't stray from his book. "You'll go back when I say you can go back."

I couldn't stop the sleepy smile. "When will that be?"

"I'd prefer never."

I peeked up at him. "You want to keep me forever, Lucas?"

He hummed noncommittally and turned a page.

"Theo will wonder where I am," I said, scooting close enough that I could press a kiss to his shoulder.

"He knows you're safe."

I stilled, my hand splaying over the pages of his book so he was forced to look at me. "What did you do?"

His brow lifted. "Who, me?"

"Lucas! Tell me."

In a flash, he tossed the book aside and rolled until he had me caged beneath his body. His legs straddled my hips while he held my wrists in a loose grip against the mattress.

"Make me," he said, and his treacherous mouth crushed mine in a hard kiss before he pulled away.

I would have—if I'd had the strength. I would have made him do a lot of things. The heat in his eyes had only grown hotter as the days passed. If he weren't so afraid of injuring me, I was sure he'd have already surrendered to the magnet between us. I had only to stare at him a certain way, and his gaze would light on fire.

Still, he resisted, and my patience waned. I wanted him, but I didn't have the strength to act on it—a frustrating position.

After a week, once I could walk properly, he took me to his

communications closet, where the carpet was stained brownish red with my blood. He'd long discarded my ruined fatigues, but he'd saved the objects in my pockets in a small drawer.

A switchblade. My dog tags. The bladed knuckles I'd dropped on the porch, still bloody.

My face burned as I stroked a well-worn note sitting in the middle of the pile.

Grief is like snow...

I never wanted him to know I kept it.

"I asked you to destroy that," he said.

I nodded.

"But you were carrying it on you."

I said nothing, my eyes cast down.

His voice grew stern. "Look at me, Sophia."

The silence grated while he waited for me to oblige. Gathering every shred of courage, I lifted my chin, ready to argue.

"Do you always carry it with you?" he asked with deceptive nonchalance.

"Yes."

A pained, intense blue flared in his eyes. "Why?"

The seconds slipped away while we stared at each other, and I swallowed down my chagrin. "I think I just...wanted you close to me."

He cupped my cheek, searching my face. "I'm right here."

"Right *now*," I said, hating the sudden sting in my eyes. "But you aren't, really. You're nowhere. And everywhere."

He wiped away the tears, studying me for several long, agonizing moments. His knuckles trailed down my throat. "I can't make that uncertainty go away," he murmured, the words tortured, his inability to give me what I wanted tormenting him.

Against my better judgement, my hands slid up his chest and anchored around his neck. "Just stay with me. It's all I want."

Again, the words slipped from his lips: "I will. Until I die."

"That's not good enough," I whispered.

His forehead rested against mine. "It's all I have."

We stayed like that for a long time, but eventually, he pulled back like always, guiding me to the bed where he liked me best.

"I can't stay tonight," he said, once I was tucked under the covers.

I froze, searching his expression but finding no clues. "Why not?"

"Mission."

I eased against the pillow, but every muscle had grown taut. "Dangerous?"

He shot me that familiar *are-you-an-idiot* face.

I grabbed his wrist, trying to tug him back to me. "No. Stay."

He gave me a few inches, but didn't relent. "I'll come back."

The tears reappeared. "You don't know that."

His hands landed on either side of me. He leaned close enough to kiss me, but he didn't. "I will come back."

Gazing into his eyes, I could see the sincerity etched within, but he could never be sure. I wouldn't know which was my last moment with him until after he was gone.

His attention dipped to my mouth, but instead of kissing me, he retreated. "Rest," he said and disappeared.

I SLEPT in fits and starts, even my dreams punctuated with blood and death. I startled awake sometime in the early morning when a weight depressed the mattress. Lucas sat beside me, barely visible in the dark. He still wore his Hunter black fatigues with the scarlet patch where the American flag should have been. I glared at that patch for a long moment while he stared into space.

When he made no move to leave or come closer, I sat up. His head turned slowly, and the second he met my eyes, I knew he'd returned to me from something terrible. His bare expression was a pale smear in the surrounding blackness, but he looked...fractured. Whatever he'd just done would haunt him, whether it was lives he'd taken or humans he'd imprisoned. They would live in his psyche forever.

I wanted to tell him it was okay, that he was only doing what he had to, but none of this was okay, and he didn't have to do any of it. He could choose death. He would've already chosen death, if not for me. I was at fault here too. I wanted him alive, and in order to stay that way, this was the price.

"Lucas," I whispered, setting a hand on his shoulder to cover the scarlet.

"Sophia," he said, voice like gravel in the darkness.

His kiss took me by surprise, harsh and quick as it was, and I sucked in a gasp. He cupped my neck and kissed me like everything would reset if only he could melt into me instead. The kisses were long and hard and drugging, tasting of the same herbal peppermint as usual—the taste of his anxiety, the show of weakness that only I could see.

Perhaps it was the trauma of the mission or the culmination of days of self-deprivation, but something had unleashed him, and I could tell just by the strength of his grip on my neck that he wasn't stopping this time. He needed an outlet, and I was happy to give it to him. I surrendered to his hands as they tugged me closer, melting into his touch. In a blink, I was on my back, his body a cage above me.

Thrills of pleasure shot down my spine as his hungry gaze swept my face.

"Say what you want," he said. "Out loud."

"You."

He seemed to like that word, or perhaps the needy way I said it, because his breath caught and he dipped closer until his mouth touched mine. "What do you want from me? Tonight? Right now?"

Heat flooded my insides, turning everything molten, and I hooked my good leg around him so he wouldn't gain a sudden conscience and try to retreat again. "You know what I want, Lucas."

"I need you to say the words." He kissed a trail across my jaw to that sensitive place beneath my ear. The tingles were almost enough to distract me from his words.

What exactly had he witnessed this evening that had him begging for my consent?

"Lucas," I grabbed his face, forcing him to look me in the eye. "I want you to fuck me."

The aquamarine studied me closely, every hint of my expression and crevice around my eyes, but he made no attempt to comply. Heart pounding, I counted twelve beats before he finally moved. He dove under my loose T-shirt, hands greedy when they met my skin to slide the fabric up and away. My obedient arms lifted as he stripped it from my body. I lay beneath him in nothing but a pair of his boxers, while he remained fully dressed in Hunter fatigues.

I attacked the buttons of his evil shirt, wanting to tear that scarlet patch from his shoulder. He distracted me with a kiss to the notch beneath my throat, then climbed the slope of my breast and took the peak into his mouth. Pleasure arced, and I gave up on his buttons to thread my fingers into his waves.

He groaned when my fingernails raked over his scalp—the sound of a man starved for affection. He palmed my other breast, and my hips bucked into him, seeking friction. Desperate for more, I tugged harder at his shirt, but he ignored me. His mouth released me, dipping to nibble the edge of my ribs and trail his tongue to my belly button and below.

Air whooshed from my lungs as I realized what he intended to do. My subconscious had woven fantasies of this into the muscle fibers of my heart, but I'd barely allowed it purchase on my reality. Now, fire scalded every surface of my skin as his fingers hooked around the elastic band and peeled it down my legs, careful of the healed wound. Open-mouthed kisses trailed up the inside of my thigh as he spread my good leg wide and tugged me right to the edge of the bed.

As his knees hit the floor, I found myself whispering—prayers, wishes, encouragements, all wrapped in his name. Moonlight shimmered over the raven waves of his hair, and I was hypnotized by the beauty of it, by the sight of his head between my thighs, by the naked desire in his ocean eyes when they traveled up to meet mine.

The tiniest quirk at the edge of his mouth spoke of a dark knowledge, like he knew exactly where he was about to take me while I wasn't sure whether we were climbing to paradise or descending to the most wicked circle of the underworld.

With a single teasing swipe of his tongue, my whole body shuddered in pleasure, and a terrible, wonderful truth dropped a curtain over my reality: I couldn't tell the difference between heaven and hell. This was torture and ecstasy. Fire and rapture. He made me want to open wider and shut down forever.

But he gave me no choice. He subdued my body the same way he had for months—with deft proficiency. Lucas Scott was a master at getting what he wanted from me, and when the euphoria climbed my spine and escaped my mouth in a cry shaped like his name, he didn't stop. He kept up the soft rhythm until a second, stronger wave crashed over me.

Heart fluttering, lungs breathless, every thought scattered in the wake of the pleasure. I was barely aware of his heat retreating, but I reacted on instinct to keep him close. Still tingling in every nerve ending, I jerked to sitting and gripped his shirt. Standing between my spread legs, he relented to my wild kiss. He still tasted of peppermint, but now he also tasted of me, and that lit a new flame deep inside.

This time, my fingers worked the buttons of his shirt without fumbling, and I ripped it from his body. He stood tall while I pressed my palms to every ripple of muscle, every jagged scar, and finally the hard ridge still hidden by his clothes.

I loosened his belt. Unbuttoned his pants. Tugged them away until he stood before me in nothing but his tented boxers. Tipping forward to kiss his chiseled abdomen, I coaxed him closer. Fingers tangled in my hair as I pulled him free of the cotton, my hand gripping him at the base.

I glanced up, but I was unprepared for the open hunger, the raw adoration on his face. Deep in my belly, the flame blazed, and a new, insistent throb woke between my legs. His fingers trailed down the turn of my jaw, thumb brushing over my lips before exerting pressure on my chin to open my mouth.

Obediently, I leaned forward to lick a bead of liquid from his tip, and the hand in my hair tightened. I allowed myself a small smile as I took him into my mouth, slow and deep, letting him suffer the same as he had done to me. I relished possessing this power over his pleasure. So often, he held the upper hand, but with this, I *owned* him.

I felt his gaze on me as I worked, and I hoped this would ink a tattoo into his mind. I wanted this to be the image that surged the next time he wrapped his own hand around himself, seeking release. As the minutes passed, my throat relaxed, and I let him sink deeper, then deeper still. He grew even stiffer in my hand, and I sensed him try to pull back, but I took more of him instead.

His breathing went ragged, and an involuntary whine of protest escaped my throat as he jerked away before he came. He cupped my jaw in one hand, forcing me to look up at him. I licked the salty taste of him from my lips.

His gaze followed my tongue. "You like that?"

I nodded. I'd wanted him to succumb to me, wanted to watch him give in solely because of what I was doing to him.

"You'll like this next part more. Lie back."

Nerves alight with anticipation, I did as he asked, my legs still dangling off the edge of the bed. He spread them wide, then braced his weight on one elbow and slipped the other hand between my thighs again, right to the place that throbbed hardest. He drew tight feathery circles, and I sucked in a breath at the shimmery waves of ecstasy that rocketed me to the edge within seconds. Need pounded inside—to be invaded, filled, to have *him*. My legs wrapped around him, a desperate bid to pull him closer, but he waited.

He tortured me.

Circle, circle, circle.

My breath came in pants, and I reached blindly for him, my mouth reckless and messy against his.

"Please," I begged. "Please. Now."

Just as the waves began to crest, he pushed inside. Sunlight dawned with rays of pleasure, and I threw my head back with a thankful moan. I rode out the orgasm on his steady rhythm, my nails buried into his back, pulling him right against my chest. With just a few more thrusts, he found his own climax, spilling his pleasure onto my breasts.

While our foreheads pressed together, his rapid breathing mixed with mine, and my mouth sought his again. The kiss was softer now, lazier, and he stayed there for long minutes, savoring. I grew drowsy in his embrace, and when he finally pulled away, it was only to retrieve a towel. He wiped up the mess he'd made—both on my chest and between my legs—and coaxed me back into my usual spot in the bed, where I curled onto my side. He slipped behind me, pulling me deep into his arms.

"Will you sleep?" I asked, remembering his haunted look from when I'd first woken.

"You're the one who needs sleep. Don't worry about me."

"I always worry about you, Lucas."

His hand slid up my stomach to rest between my breasts, over my heart. "I'm right here, sweetheart. Just rest."

I gripped his forearm, my thumb brushing over the ridges of the brands there. Quiet descended, but before I fell asleep, I whispered his name.

"Hmm?"

"I'm sorry if something bad happened tonight."

He pressed a long kiss on my shoulder. "You happened tonight. That's all that matters."

26

THE RETURN

 You're lucky she's not dead.

—— LUCAS SCOTT

Lucas was insatiable.

So was I.

After he decided no amount of sex would rip open the wounds he'd so carefully sewn back together, he took to worshipping my body with his mouth. For days, I was drunk on him and dead to the world outside. Like an addiction, every moment he wasn't with me was spent fantasizing about when he'd return. I wanted to map him with my tongue.

Funnily, Lucas as a lover was not much different from Lucas as a sparring partner—he still kept me pinned beneath him, but the result was far more enjoyable. I always let him spread my legs.

But eventually, I healed enough to leave the house. As I stared at the faded bruises on my leg, greenish-yellow in the early morning sunlight, I fought the urge to cry. Was it too much to ask to stay inside our bubble, to lock the door and hide, disappear into the fantasy we'd created?

But I had to return to the real world, and we both knew it. I had a job to do, and without Lucas's information, the Defiance was operating in the dark.

When Lucas entered the bedroom, already dressed in Hunter black in preparation for the day, he caught me examining my leg, and his mouth tightened.

"I have to go," I said.

His head dipped, and he busied himself with straightening his cuffs. "I disagree."

"I can't stay here forever, Lucas."

"Why not?" he asked, lifting his head to glare at me. "What have they ever done for you? Tell me what they can give you that I can't. You are so much safer—"

"I'm *hiding*," I said.

"You're healing."

I pointed at my thigh. "I'm healed. I'm better. Because of you."

"And if I return you to them, they'll throw you right back into the firing line."

"I agreed to this," I said, taking his hand. "This is what I signed up for when I agreed to be part of the Defiance."

He shook me off and sat at the edge of the bed, dropping his head into his hands. Raven waves fell forward, hiding his expression. Morning sunlight glinted over the silvery scars on his knuckles, the sharp angles of his body. He was a study in melancholy, armored with trauma and sorrow.

And I loved him.

So much.

It almost hurt, this love, knowing how it would end. Part of me wondered why I'd even consider leaving him when we had so few seconds left together.

But what if there were a path for us?

What if I found a way for him to live?

It was only possible if the Defiance won.

He let out a sharp sigh, then pinned me with a stare. "You sure?"

I nodded and slipped closer to run my fingers through his hair. "I'll always come back to you."

He grunted.

"And you'll stay with me, right?"

He tugged me down for a kiss. "Until I die."

Until I die. The only promise he'd make. He wouldn't admit to any feelings or imply we had a future. I could have him until the day he died, and he believed that day approached with unfailing speed.

The thought was like acid in my veins.

"I want you more than once a week, Sophia," he said against my lips.

I gave in to the urge to climb on top of him. "I'll come to you," I said between kisses. "Every night."

He spun me onto the mattress, and both of us relinquished our words.

THE WALK back to headquarters was both terrifying and painful. I hadn't anticipated the vulnerability of the outdoors after being safely harbored with Lucas for weeks.

Golden sun. Singing birds. Death hiding in every shadow.

My leg throbbed relentlessly by the time I arrived, but I drew little attention despite my limp. Adam, however, stopped me at the top of the stairs with a slack stare.

"Sophia?"

I gaped at him, unprepared for such a quick run-in with someone who might have noticed I was missing.

He scooped me into a hug. "General kept saying you were okay, but I thought you'd been captured," he said, tone full of giddy relief. "Where have you been?"

I told him the planned story—I'd been injured and taken to another safe house until I healed.

He released me, his expression morphing into confusion. "Which one?"

I said nothing, and Adam's confusion faded to wary understanding.

"Ah. Are you...okay, then?"

"I'm fine." I backed away. "I have to see Theo."

"Right." He swallowed hard. "Let me know if you need anything."

I needed a miracle, but I doubted he had any of those. With a smile in his direction, I hurried toward Theo's office.

The curt "Enter!" after I knocked made me hesitate. What would I tell him? Why hadn't I cooked up a solid story? What would he do with the truth?

I took a deep breath before poking my head in. At his desk, Theo shuffled through some documents, but his gaze lifted as the door opened, and his eyes froze on me.

"Sophia?" He jumped from his seat and grabbed my shoulders for a hug. "You're okay? Where have you been?"

When he released me, I shut and locked the door. "I was wounded and ended up at the house on Evanston."

"Evanston? I thought you—" Theo blinked a few times, forehead wrinkled, eyes wide. "You've been gone three weeks."

"I was unconscious for a week." I tugged my clothes to show him the healing knife wounds. When I lifted my sweatpants and showed him my leg, he hissed.

"Shit. What happened?"

"I nearly bled to death. Lucas—he saved me, Theo."

A long silence followed my words, and Theo sank into one of the chairs before his desk.

I perched on the one beside him. "I woke up stitched and healing. He was a surgeon, apparently. Before all this. He stayed with me, treated the infection, gave me his blood. He saved my life."

Theo remained quiet, digesting that information. I let the silence stretch.

After a time, Theo stood and opened a drawer in his desk, extracting a small piece of paper. "I received a note."

I recognized Lucas's handwriting. "*Uncle Theo, you're lucky she's not dead,*" I read aloud. "That's all he said?"

Theo sneered at the note. "The guy is a dick. I don't know how you stand him. I received this a week after you disappeared."

Pressing my lips together, I tried not to react. "How did he get that to you?"

"It was found in the pocket of a dead Hunter dropped off in the middle of our territory. Someone brought it to me, asking questions. It's funny. Multiple Hunters have been found dead in our streets. Most of them traced back to the fight at that lookout."

Given Lucas's irrational anger at my injuries, that tracked, but I didn't know what to say.

Theo sat in the chair behind his desk. "I have questions."

I swallowed my apprehension and nodded.

"You've been with him this whole time?"

"Yes."

"Doing what?"

"Healing."

"Healing." Theo's voice was thick with disbelief, his dark eyes narrowing on me.

"Among other things," I said.

"Care to elaborate?"

"Not especially." I hesitated with the next part. "But he said he won't help you anymore if something like this happens to me again."

I neglected to mention the death threats.

Theo's gaze sharpened, suspicions forming in his eyes. He folded his hands on his desk. "Why?"

"I think he feels...protective of me." Understatement, yes, but Theo didn't need to know that.

"We're talking about the same man, correct?"

I glared at him.

"I don't get it. You're just a contact." He raised his eyebrows. "Right?"

I fidgeted with a hole in my sweatpants. "Maybe I'm not *just* a contact to him."

"Then what are you?"

I took a breath and scratched my face, uncertain what to say.

"Is he forcing you, Sophia?"

Now he chose to care? Where was this concern months ago when I was terrified each Thursday about what Lucas Scott the Blood Colonel would do to me that night?

"Would it matter if he was?" I asked. "Isn't that what you wanted from me? Weren't you under the assumption I'd end up with my legs spread for him?"

Theo flinched.

"You never even asked. I gave you the opportunity to ask, and you buried your head in the sand and changed the subject."

"I didn't want to hear about it. You said you asked him for it. What was I supposed to think?"

"You should have asked! You abandoned me and offered no support. Even Lucas knew what you thought would happen to me. You should've seen his disgust when he realized who I am to you."

Theo's jaw hardened. "I fought Williams to give you the choice. I thought you'd say no, but you didn't. I never wanted this for you. Scott is a monster, and before this is over, I will kill him for what he's done to you."

Not *I will kill him for being a Hunter*, or *I will kill him for how many people he's murdered*, but *I will kill him for what he's done to you*.

Something shifted in my mind as I realized the source of Theo's hatred. With how much Lucas had helped us, Theo should have been singing his praises, but he wasn't. He'd offered me as collateral, but he hated Lucas for accepting it.

Voice softer, I leaned forward. "Theo, do you know what he's been doing every time I meet with him?"

"I can imagine."

I shook my head. "He's been teaching me how to fight. His training is the only reason I survived that mission. The man you see on TV doesn't exist, Theo. The real Lucas Scott never wanted any of this. His sister was a spy. She got caught and killed, and he took her place."

Theo's frown creased his entire face. "His sister was...a spy?"

I nodded.

A long moment passed before he gave a hesitant, "Even if that's true, it doesn't make it right."

"There isn't right and wrong in war. You know that. There's only hope and what we do to survive."

Theo relaxed into his seat, studying me. "So he never touched you?"

"He never touched me unless I asked to be touched."

Brows raised, Theo narrowed his eyes.

"We're sleeping together," I clarified.

He blanched. "So that's why he won't work with us if you're hurt? He'll lose his toy?"

I tried not to take offense at that. I wasn't the target of Theo's anger here, but being referred to as a toy wasn't winning him any points. "Not exactly," I said.

Fingers tapping a rhythm against his desk, he stared at me with a curious edge, like he knew I was holding back. "Then explain."

"I'm in love with him."

His eyes went wide. "What?"

"I tried not to be, but he's a good man, Theo. A good man who's had to make hard choices."

He gaped at me.

"And Lucas...feels similarly." The words tasted strange in my mouth, and I realized I didn't like stating something Lucas had never admitted to himself. He didn't need to say the words, though. The sentiment glinted at me from the depths of his eyes.

"That can't be true. He's—he's *inhuman*."

I sighed. "I don't care what you think. I love him, and I won't give you any of his information if your plan is to kill him. I won't help you hurt him. In fact, I want immunity for him."

The words burst from me, and it wasn't until that moment that I understood the bargaining chip I possessed. Lucas had failed to secure his own clemency, but I could do it for him. If they wanted his information, they could only get it through me.

And I needed Lucas Scott to live.

Theo exploded into incredulous laughter. "That's impeding the war effort, Sophia. It's illegal."

"You think I care? Imprison me then. You'll lose your informant, and I'm not sure you want to see what he'll do if you take me from him."

His mouth opened, but he said nothing.

"I'd like your promise, Theo. And I'd like it in writing."

He ignored me. "*Take* you from him?"

I gave him a slow, Lucas-style smirk.

Theo's skin went gray. Chandelier lights glistened in his dark eyes. "What will you do if I refuse?"

"I won't give you any of his information."

Another laugh boomed deep in his chest. "He's the only reason we've gained an advantage. We're getting close to the end, Sophia. You'd jeopardize that for this monster?"

"Yes."

I had something of extreme value in my hands, and if I played my cards right, he'd give me what I wanted.

His voice went faint. "Who are you? You're not the girl I saw raised with morals and integrity."

Something snapped inside me. How dare he use my upbringing against me? I'd lain to rest every person I'd ever loved, and now he chastised me for trying to hold on to someone who made me feel whole again?

I stood, towering over him. "That girl died with her parents. She was buried when her best friend was taken and killed. The dirt was laid when her only remaining family sold her as a whore to a spy. Would you like to put flowers on her grave, Theo? *Here lies Sophia Elena Reeves, a girl with integrity.*"

Stricken, he glanced away from me. Silence rained over us.

"You said Williams wants him dead at the end of this," I murmured. "I'll do anything I can to stop that, even if it kills me. If you care about me, you'll find a way to make this happen."

Theo blinked at his desk a few times and sighed. "Alright, Soph. We'll talk again later." I started to leave, but he stopped me. "From now on, I will make sure every officer knows you are unavailable for missions. That never should have happened."

"Where were you?" I asked. "I looked for you."

"Classified," he said. "But we're getting close. We're going to win this thing."

I gazed into his hopeful eyes. "Is there any winning after all this?"

He dropped his gaze to his desk. "Dear god, I hope so."

27

HURRICANE

 Men are ambitious, vindictive, and rapacious.

—ALEXANDER HAMILTON, FEDERALIST NO. 6

I went to him every night, just like I promised.

Sometimes, his smiles came easily. Other times he'd crawl into bed, desperate and reckless, long after I'd fallen asleep. He'd kiss me awake and use my body to erase the memories of whatever had happened, the things he'd been forced to do. I always offered what he needed, whether it was hard and fast or excruciatingly slow.

Every day, as the days grew shorter and the nights colder, the risk he took heightened. Each new piece of information had to be catalogued and scrutinized so it couldn't be traced back to him.

I wanted to hide from it all, but now that I'd returned to headquarters, Lucas's paranoia over my safety intensified, and he redoubled his efforts to make me a competent fighter.

In our training room one evening, he handed me a throwing knife. "They're spreading false information now."

I held it by the blade the way he'd shown me, flinging with a snap of my arm. It bounced off the wall like all the others, landing on the carpet.

My shoulders fell. "What did I do wrong that time?"

"You're putting too much force into it."

I sighed, wiggling my shoulders. "So they're trying to ferret you out?"

He shrugged, handing me another knife. "I'm staying ahead of it for now."

Another toss. Another knife on the floor.

"But?" I lifted an eyebrow

"I'll slip up eventually, Soph."

My heart cracked a little more each time I imagined him taken from me. His downfall was coming, and he gripped me tighter and tighter every night.

He crossed the room to scoop up the knives. Dark waves fell into his face as he bent forward, and he tossed them away with a sharp jerk of his head. It said something that the NSF's soldiers weren't keeping to the strict military grooming standards—just another small clue that they were falling apart, all thanks to him.

It was like waiting for a hurricane. The storm grew more powerful as it inched toward us, and I had no way to evacuate. No wish to. I sat helpless, prepared to drown.

When the December executions arrived, Lucas was up to play hangman, and he turned silent in the days leading up to it.

Sitting at the kitchen table the night before, he stared blankly at the wall.

"Lucas?" I slid a hand over his shoulder, trying to spark some life into him.

His eyes lifted, face blank.

"What can I do?"

A slow breath expelled from his lungs. "I'm just so tired."

My throat ached. Tears slipped from my eyes. I hugged him close.

As requested, I didn't watch, but he came home haunted by darkness and jerked awake six times that night.

The sixth time, he squeezed me tight. "I thought I'd be dead by now. Why am I still doing this?"

"Because I need you. We all need you to help end this." I kissed him hard and gripped him as if he could be ripped from my arms any second.

Because he could.

He'd backed himself into a deadly corner, and I sensed the ties that held us together fraying. He never said it, but a bleak and biting sense of hopelessness ate at him. No good options remained for him. Everything would hurt until the end.

At night he'd bolt upright and freeze, reaching until his hand closed around some piece of me.

"Shh," I'd say. "I'm right here."

And every time, his tourniquet-tight grip would tug me as close as possible. As the nights passed, his embrace grew so rigid it hurt, threaded with filaments of desperation and fear.

The new year had dawned before Theo presented me with a signed statement of Lucas's absolution. Provided he continued to offer aid and didn't undermine or hinder the Defiance, he was granted a pardon from war crimes.

"I'm only doing this for you, Sophia. Williams doesn't know." Theo pressed the document into my expectant hand. He didn't let it go. "I love you, Soph. I hope you understand that. I never wanted any of this for you." He released the paper.

I studied his brown eyes, the lines creasing his forehead. "Thank you for this, Theo. Can I trust it's real?"

He sighed. "I'll do what I can, but if you two are smart, you'll steer clear of Nia Williams."

I didn't tell Lucas. Fancy piece of paper or no, if I stood between him and the Defiance, they'd slaughter me to reach him, and Lucas knew it.

When I wasn't with Lucas, I kept busy in the hospital wing. After hearing my cover story, Zara had examined my leg, her gaze clouded in confusion over who had treated it. "It looks better than what I could have done," she said. "Who did you say took care of you again?"

"I didn't," I said. "It was someone at Safe House Green."

The notch on her brow only deepened, and she peered closer at my leg, then into my eyes. "Sophia."

I flinched.

"You weren't really at Safe House Green, were you?"

I swallowed and said nothing.

She nodded. "Please tell me you're safe."

"I'm safe," I whispered. "It's just...classified."

At that, she released a sigh, and we returned to our shifts.

Devon asked repeatedly where I went every night. I finally took him aside to explain.

"Classified?" he said, eyes wide.

"Yeah. Theo's orders."

He gripped my shoulder. "But you're okay?"

"I'm okay. I promise."

Since the summer, my involvement with Jayden had dwindled to nothing. He'd tried to sleep with me twice, but he'd been rebuffed both times.

After the third time, he frowned. "Something wrong, Sophia?"

"I just don't want to anymore."

He sighed, defeated. "Alright. Yeah. It was fun while it lasted, though."

"Yeah."

"Friends then?" He gave me a smile.

I paused. "Friends?" We'd never been friends...

"Yeah, girl." He brushed my cheek with his thumb. "I'll take what I can get."

I blinked in confusion. "Sure. Friends."

Adam continued to throw me his big grins, but he rarely approached. The lingering glances we exchanged made me think he was just waiting for the maelstrom to hit. Of all my friends, he was the one who seemed to understand my predicament the best.

I was certain he knew.

He just didn't know *who*.

Following the completion of Lucas's plan to cut NAO supply lines, the eastern and western Hunter forces divorced. Rumor had it that the Security Restoration Campaign was failing, and the fighting had pushed all the way to the eastern seaboard. As Lucas predicted, Haynes turned his attention to the civil war.

He wanted us gone.

We wanted this over.

The aggression escalated. Tension overtook headquarters, like we walked on tightropes that could snap at any second. Soldiers marched into missions and never returned. Safe houses fell on both sides. Civilians lost their lives trying to flee the urban battlefields.

"I just want it to end," I whispered into Lucas's chest while he held me one night in January.

"I know, sweetheart."

Why did there have to be such pointless hate? I told him about my forest, and when panic clawed at my lungs, he'd murmur into my hair, "Tall trees. Warm rain. Smell of cypress."

It usually helped, but every day the disquiet would rebuild. Men and women came back from missions with fear and anguish on their faces. I treated their bodily injuries, but I could do nothing for the wounds in their minds. Even if the war ended, another would begin —the fight to heal.

Scars existed deep inside all of us—the unhealing wounds of lost faith, broken integrity, bone-deep fear. We'd been so bright and shiny at the beginning, full of life and conviction. We had no idea. None of us had suffered. None of us had known genuine terror.

Good triumphs. That's what we told ourselves. And we believed it, too.

So stupid.

Now we only wanted to survive, and some of us didn't even want that.

Medics struggled to keep up with the injuries, and most days we held each other while we sobbed our failures onto a sympathetic shoulder. I lost my own share of patients, and I numbed myself to their deaths as best I could, but I sometimes vomited up my dinner from anxiety. Zara would always hold my hair back, and when she asked if I wanted to talk about it, I never had the words to explain.

"It's alright, Sophia," she said. "I get it. Can I give you a hug?"

Her hugs reminded me of Mom.

Lucas was the rock I stood upon, but as he gave more information, the rock crumbled. We held each other with brutal force, leaving behind fingerprint bruises. The fear of loss sharpened, like a knife poised at our throats, caressing while it cut. I sensed it every time we touched, with each deep look into each other's eyes...

The end drew near.

A heavy snow fell in late January. Trapped for days, Lucas assured me no missions would take place in such weather.

"Sometimes I think I'd sacrifice myself if it meant ending this war," I whispered to him as we lay under cover of darkness.

His fingers danced absently over my skin. "I'd sacrifice ending this war if it meant saving you."

I turned toward him, but his eyes were closed, as if that admission wasn't shocking. He'd just said I mattered more to him than anything else. How could he say that like it was nothing?

His fingers moved.

Down. Right. Curve. Curve. Diagonal.

Always the same pattern, seemingly random, but my heart thudded as I connected the motions to familiar symbols.

These touches weren't absent at all.

They were letters.

L-U-C-A-S-S-C-O-T-T

He... He was signing his name on my skin.

Thrills of electricity shot down my nerves, chased by warmth.

How long had he been doing this? I replayed the dozens of times he'd touched me like this. When had it started? When had he grown possessive enough to sign his longing into my skin?

Why did I love it so much?

The NAO thought women a subspecies, and living under that regime made me crave independence above all. I never thought I'd want a possessive man, but there I was, *needing* to be possessed by him. I wanted to be his on a deep, biological level. It was a basic instinct of survival.

Stay with him. He loves you more than himself. He will keep you safe.

The world had gone mad.

Darkness reigned over us.

But the connection between me and Lucas glowed, a tenuous light of hope. As his fingers traced his name across my skin, I wished those letters could be seen, that some part of him could mark me permanently.

Because I feared—I *knew*—the light wouldn't last. Hope never amounted to anything, and he walked the fine edge of a knife that grew thinner every day. Eventually, he'd fall, the slice fatal.

I scooted closer, nipping his shoulder. My hand pressed over his heart. "Can I have this?"

A tiny smile materialized as he nodded. "Whatever's left of it."

I kissed his chest. "It's all in there. Maybe a little damaged, but I can fix it."

"I'm sure you're stubborn enough to try."

We fell asleep wrapped in each other, and the next morning, I floated in the nebulous world between sleep and consciousness. He played with my hand, his finger dragging over each of mine, from knuckle to tip. At my middle finger, he paused, and something caught around it.

I blinked my eyes open as he slid a gold band onto it. His sister's ring. He twisted it twice before meeting my eyes.

"You wanna wear that for me?" His voice was husky from sleep.

I melted into the earnest desire in his eyes. "For how long?"

"As long as you want to."

I touched the band, following the delicate filigree before matching his gaze once more. "Why?"

"I don't want anyone else to have it." His fingers laced through mine.

My fragile heart finally shattered.

He didn't want it to end up in the wrong hands. After his death, he wanted his sister's ring to stay with someone he cared for.

"Lucas—"

"I know, Sophia. Just...don't."

Tears burned my eyes, but I held them back. "I'm scared."

He touched my face, drawing his thumb down my jaw and throat. "You don't have to be scared. I'll make sure you're safe."

"I'm scared for *you*."

Mouth tense, he didn't answer.

"I don't want to be alone," I whispered.

His eyes squeezed shut. "We're all alone."

I gripped him, the sheets bunching beneath us. "I'm not alone now. Stay with me. Forever."

"Until I die. That was the deal."

My hand swiped at the defiant tears. "That isn't g-good enough!"

His voice thickened. "I'd give you anything, Sophia, if it were possible."

"It is, Lucas." I sniffled. "We could hide."

"Where?"

"I don't know!" The desperation clogged my throat.

"Don't do this. Breathe, sweetheart."

I couldn't.

"Breathe!"

My fingers clawed into him, but he was used to wearing the marks from my hands.

"Now, Sophia! Breathe."

A bit of air made it in with a gasp, and then I was breathing too fast. He kissed my forehead.

"I don't want to lose you," I said through my choking tears.

He tried to soothe me, but terror had me in its claws. I could already imagine the pain of his loss, and I wasn't certain I'd survive it again. His would be worse than the others. Before him, I hadn't known this sort of love, hadn't believed it existed. It was possible to survive losing it. People did it all the time. They loved. They lost. They moved on. I didn't want to be one of them. My fatalistic desire was to die with him.

What was the point of living when everyone else died?

Savage and painful, I kissed him like it was my last chance. I would've been perfectly happy to fade into him, even if it hurt to do it.

Tasting the salt of my tears on his lips, I fought my way on top of him. We grasped each other, clawing to get closer. I straddled him, and he sat up. As I sank down onto him, I shut my eyes to revel in it. My arms wrapped around his neck while his hands clutched my hips, guiding the rhythm.

We were usually careful. Even in our most desperate moments, he'd been sure to protect me from consequences.

But we weren't careful that morning. I climaxed with a hard shudder, and his fingers gripped me, driving himself deep as he came inside me.

I didn't care. Reckless as always, I wanted every bit of him and any repercussions that resulted. When it was done and we both panted in the afterglow, he pressed a kiss to the rapid pulse at my throat, and I stared at the gold glinting on my finger.

His kiss on my skin. His seed in my womb. His ring on my finger. This was the last will and testament of Lucas Scott.

I gave in to the tears

PART THREE

28

KISSING DEATH

No person shall… be deprived of life, liberty, or property, without due process of law…

— 5ᵀᴴ AMENDMENT, U.S. CONSTITUTION

Several days later, news of a serious attack came mid-afternoon, leaving hundreds injured. The wounded were transported to the quarantine house for treatment since it was closest. Every medic at headquarters was called to help, so we threw handfuls of supplies into packs and hauled out.

When I arrived, chaos and blood prevailed. The injured had been dragged inside and left abandoned in the lobby, and not all of them were soldiers. They littered the floors, the chairs, the old hotel check-in desks. Some moaned, but others were so still, I feared we'd arrived too late.

In a team of medics, I set to work organizing and classifying the wounded per our usual protocol. I grabbed colored flags, throwing greens on the minors, reds on the majors, and blacks on the fatals.

So many black flags.

Body after body crammed into every nook and cranny of the building.

"Do you know what happened?" I finally asked another medic as we worked on one man with a fractured femur.

"I heard Hunters bombed one of the refugee zones outside the city," she said.

My hand slipped on the stabilization board. "What? Why?"

She shoved hair from her face, leaving a streak of blood on her temple. "They probably heard Defiants were living there."

My stomach cramped as I imagined being bombed by my own government just because an enemy lived nearby. Would Theo allow such a thing?

Would Williams?

I really wasn't sure.

We finished stabilizing the man's leg and left him for new patients. My hands grew slippery with blood as I tied off tourniquets, stabilized snapped limbs, removed objects impaled through flesh and bone.

The screams in the lobby slipped into whimpers and moans as people were moved to rooms further in the hotel or succumbed to their injuries.

"Don't leave me!" a soldier cried when I rose to help someone else, giving him up for dead. His insides spilled through a slash in his abdomen.

Shaking wildly, he grasped for me, and I leaned close to his sweat-drenched face. The smell of burned flesh and blood was thick around us. Dark eyes held mine, fear making them glisten until the light died behind them, and he breathed his last breath.

I turned to the next patient, shoving that memory down with the other soldiers I'd failed to save.

We worked for several hours, my body overloaded by death and blood. Fatigue slowed me, and my bad leg ached. I wiped the back of my hand across my brow, taking a stuttered, steadying breath while I stared around at all the work left to do.

A scream ripped through the room.

The main door burst inward, a metal object tossed inside.

My body knew what was happening before my brain did. I spun toward the hallway leading to the back exit right as a grenade exploded, shrapnel flying. Thrown forward along with the mangled debris of chairs and the shredded remains of corpses, my shoulder slammed into the wall. A yelp tore from my throat, and I crumpled to the ground.

The injury in my left leg locked up, my thigh cramping. I couldn't stand.

Blurry anarchy descended. The tinny ringing in my ears deafened me. Dazed, I lifted my head to find throngs of Hunters invading the room. Adrenaline spiked, tingling in my fingertips. The pain in my leg disappeared.

I reached into my pocket, fingers hooking into the metal hoops of the knuckles. Screams pierced the ringing as Hunters wrangled prisoners, slicing the throats of the dying. I scrambled to my feet, using the wall as a brace.

I started toward the back door with several others, tripping over dead bodies in my effort to move quicker.

The deadly tattoo of gunfire added to the pandemonium, and the man next to me dropped to the ground.

I ran faster.

First to reach the door, I crashed into the push bar. The metal slid beneath my sweaty, bloody fingers, but I managed to escape into the cold air.

As I straightened, my heart stalled, then beat overtime. Hunters had surrounded the property. Several pairs of eyes landed on me.

My stomach dropped, but my grip on the knuckles tightened. Searching for an escape, my gaze darted over each Hunter, settling on one with kind eyes.

His face lit up. "Well, well. Look at you." He called over his shoulder, "Hey, Colonel!"

A spike of elation drove through my chest. Could he mean Lucas?

Fleeing Defiants poured from the door behind me, pushing me forward. They were wrangled by the awaiting enemy.

My attention zeroed in on the man now walking toward me.

No.

No, no, no.

Jack Miller smiled, clasping Kind Eyes on the shoulder. "Good job there, soldier."

Panic tore through every fiber of my being.

I ran.

Two of them grabbed me before I made it even a few feet. I cut one of them, but he wrenched my weapon from me.

"Where the hell did you get Hunter knuckles?"

They held my arms and turned me to face Miller. He sauntered toward me. When his gaze slithered over my face, it widened, and a flame caught behind his eyes.

"Fuck me, gents, I think I found me a keeper." He reached out to touch my cheek, and I snapped at him. "Feisty little thing." He seized me, fingers digging into my upper arms.

"No!" I jerked away, trying to dislodge his grip. A fleeting spark of hope lit when one hand released me, only to be extinguished as he punched me across the face, breaking the skin of my cheek.

Exquisite electric shocks sizzled into my eye and ear, dazing me.

"That's better," he said above the buzzing in my brain. "Why don't you give us a smile, sugar?"

I spat in his face.

His fist landed a blow to my temple, knocking my head to the side. Stars danced in my vision, and the world tilted dangerously to the left.

He stepped closer. The sandalwood in his cologne and the winter air mixed, poisoning those scents for me forever.

The third punch knocked me out cold.

Light speared through my eyelids, slicing into my brain like a cruel knife. The pounding in my temple swelled first, but then came an array of other stings and aches. My left thigh throbbed, but that wasn't new. My ribs smarted with each breath.

I ached between my legs.

Groaning, I turned my face from the light.

"That you, sugar?" called a male voice.

My eyes snapped open.

That voice.

The smell of sandalwood swarmed me, and my gaze landed on a man in the doorway.

A raspy scream erupted from my throat. I jerked away, but got nowhere. My wrists were bound above my head, cuffed to the headboard of a bed.

Jack Miller swaggered toward me, a smile lighting his face. "Welcome home."

I yanked again, trying to free myself.

"Now, calm down. You'll like it better here than with the other prisoners. Trust me."

My body stilled as tears rose to my eyes and the enormity of the truth crashed over me.

Prisoner.

"That's better." He reached the edge of the bed, cool green eyes sweeping my face and body. "Why don't you tell me your name?"

Anger mangled all sense of self-preservation. "Go fuck yourself."

He chuckled, then slapped me across the face. The sting spread through my cheek and into my nose, but before I could process it, a vice clamped around my ankle.

Lungs fought for air, but the panic... It rushed through my veins.

The world spun.

Cold hands on my legs.

Rough fingers between my thighs.

I compartmentalized. Blocked it out.

Hours passed. Or was it years?

Goosebumps took up permanent residence on my naked skin. The cuff burns on my wrists grew numb.

Don't think about it.

The pervasive scent of sandalwood suffocated me. Always followed by torture.

Pressure. Burning.

Don't think about it!

How long now? Light then dark. Sleep and tiny sips of water. Timed trips to the bathroom, like I was a dog being potty-trained.

Don't think about it.

Fuck! Teeth?

Try to forget.

Trees... Rain... Cypress...

Please stop.

Please save me.

I tried not to think of Lucas. It hurt too much. My tortured heart was halved by the knowledge I'd never see him again. He'd never know what happened to me.

Where was he now?

Was he searching for me?

Would he find me?

Don't think about it.

Time elapsed. Interminable amounts of it, marked only by my dwindling wish to survive.

My thumb touched the gold ring encircling my finger.

Try to forget.

The tears came, sliding down my temples into my hair. Raw, aching hunger struck. I clenched my fists.

Don't think about it.

At some point, the door slammed open, jolting me awake, and Miller stormed in, hair windswept, blood spattered across his pale skin.

I cringed when he reached for me.

Rough hands positioned my body face down, my wrists still cuffed to the headboard. "Forty men lost today. Good men. God-fearing men." Taking hold of my ankles, he looped a rope around them. "Can't find the traitor who's screwing us. You got any ideas who it might be?"

I whimpered as the rope tightened around my ankles, and he attached me to the footboard.

"Of course you don't. Fucking useless whore."

He crawled on top of me, straddling my hips. His cold hand grazed my spine. A horde of spiders would have been more welcome. His scent once again punctured my consciousness. Weren't villains supposed to smell bad? Jack Miller was always clean, his nails trimmed and dirt-free.

The crisp point of a blade touched my upper spine, and cut deep into my skin. A sob burst from my mouth. Sharp, electric agony detonated across my skin. Screaming, I tried to buck him off, but his weight and my position made it impossible.

Over and over again he dug the knife into my back, cutting for the mere pleasure of watching me bleed. The blood dripped around my sides and pooled on the bed beneath me.

By the time he finished, I was heaving great sobs.

The knife fell to the floor with a thunk. He lifted my head up by my hair, pulling out strands. "Now everyone will always know who you belong to." He spoke the words against my cheek, his breath hot and minty.

My whole body shook with adrenaline and the burgeoning agony of the cuts.

Miller hopped off the bed. I tried not to weep as he left the room, but the tears fell anyway. When he returned many minutes later, he was clean and dressed in the familiar uniform of a Blood Colonel, complete with the scarlet patch on his shoulder. He fetched the bloody knife and cut my ankles free. My wrist cuffs were unlocked, and I was finally loose.

"Stand up."

I obeyed, wobbling next to the bed with his crimson blade at my throat.

"Put those on." He pointed to a couple of clothing items.

Following me with the knife, Miller motioned me to hurry. Hot drips of blood rolled down my back and legs as I lifted the first item —the underwear I'd been wearing when he took me. Disgusted he still had them, I slid them onto my legs with a gag.

I shimmied the second piece of clothing—a slinky red slip—over my head. The silk hugged every curve, the back dipping low to display the wound on my spine.

After I dressed, he tied my wrists with rope, then bound my ankles so I could walk, but not run. "Now you look like what you are. All you need is a little correction."

I met his eyes with all the hatred coursing through my body, but he only smiled. I gathered he was taking me somewhere, but couldn't summon the energy to dread whatever came next.

He pointed at the door. "Walk."

I hesitated, and he drove his knuckles into my bleeding back, forcing me forward. Crying and tripping, I tried and failed to detach from the fiery torture on my spine.

Bloody footprints followed me through the house to the garage. He popped the trunk of his car and forced me into it. I was locked in darkness as we took a drive, every jostle a hot poker against my skin. When the car stopped, the trunk unlatched, and fresh sunlight in a clear winter sky startled my senses. He grabbed me by my bound wrists and jerked me upright, banging my shins hard into the metal of the car. Once I was standing, I swayed, my head swooping with hunger and blood loss.

We stood in a parking lot dotted with cars, and he marched me toward a building of red brick. The tiny rocks on the pavement stabbed into my feet. The cold bit into my bare skin. A few other men headed toward the main doors.

Inside, several glanced at us, chatting in small groups before a day of work. Some wore black Hunter fatigues; others dressier uniforms. They stood at attention as we passed, saluting Miller.

They disregarded me.

We descended to a colder, windowless level, and an armed soldier stood guard at a large metal door. He opened it for us, greeting Miller with a salute, and we passed through it.

This wasn't an office building, I realized. It was a jail. Or at least it used to be. The Hunters had commandeered it for their own purposes.

The cell was filled with people, about fifty of them. Another guard unlocked the sliding bars and Miller shoved me inside.

"Was fun gettin' to know you, sugar." He gave me a calm smile while I cursed his existence. The bars clanked closed and locked. He left, and the guard returned to his watch, ignoring us.

I stared at the people around me, all bound.

"What's going on?" I whispered to a woman slumped nearby.

"Registration," she said without looking at me.

In a flash, sweat bloomed under my arms. Butterflies swirled to life in my stomach, kicking up a mixture of hope and dread. My body went slack, and I sat hard on the floor.

Registration.

Lucas was *here*.

What would he do? What would *I* do?

He might snap. He might give himself away. We might both die today.

And what if it wasn't him? What if another colonel registered me?

I ignored everyone around me as the minutes stretched, imagining the horrors that awaited me. Panic rose from the very depths of my soul as I envisioned myself being marched with a line of prisoners before that bloodstained wall in Unity Square.

Just like Mahmoud.

When the camera panned over the condemned that day, and he

stood at the end of the line, my heart stopped. I thought he'd died on our last mission, but no.

He'd been captured.

His head was high, his gaze straight ahead. His ankles and wrists were tied like the rest of the prisoners. His mouth moved, just barely, and tears had filled my eyes when I realized he was praying. Before I'd accepted his fate, a Blood Colonel I hardly recognized stepped forward and read the executive order like always.

He left the podium. He accepted the weapon. He aimed the gun.

Bullets soared through the air, finding purchase in bodies that had been fully functional only seconds before, bodies that were born to grow and heal and flourish.

And then Mahmoud was hit, and he crumpled like the rest, wasted.

Grief and fear had risen like a tide, but next to them burned a budding flame of fury. It blazed brightly now, right beside my anguish. With my freedom gone, the NAO had taken *everything* from me, and the harrowing need for vengeance wrenched hard inside. I wanted them dismantled. Demolished. Dead.

I wanted to watch them suffer.

But instead, there I was, locked in their prison, suffering for *them*. I'd continue to lose, and they'd continue to win until I had nothing left, not even my life.

After a long time—long enough that the bleeding finally slowed —the large metal door opened, and several knife-wielding Hunters filtered in. One of them shouted orders for us to arrange ourselves in a line. I forced myself off the ground, little prints and puddles of red marking my position. Blood had soaked through my dress and the ends of my hair, dyeing my legs, caking in the creases of my ankles.

It was disgusting, but more than that, it was horrific, and Lucas had never taken the sight of my spilled blood well.

The bars slid open, and we marched through the bleak facility into another large, windowless room. A single desk stood at one end, but it was otherwise empty. The men spread us into rows, then took their positions at the room's periphery. Scarlet stained the ground at my bare feet.

I almost cried when Luke's familiar voice echoed through the room. He sat at the desk, his gaze on the papers strewn across it.

"Welcome. In accordance with the Unity Protection Directive, you are hereby informed that your case has been reviewed, and your evaluation and sentencing today will be deemed lawful and final." He took a sip from his mug and continued with his memorized speech in a droning voice. "No appeals will be made. You have been granted the rights afforded to you under the National Stability Act. You will now receive your sentence, and any resistance will be interpreted as an admission of guilt and met with immediate force."

A beat of silence passed. Not a single soul breathed.

Lucas set his mug down. "Take the men to the Stability bloc."

A round of gasps and sniffles followed.

"None for execution?" a soldier asked.

"Not today." Lucas stood from his seat behind the desk, eyes still scanning the paper in his hand. As he did, another door opened, and Jack Miller walked in, moving to stand at attention behind Lucas's desk.

He winked at me.

My heart pounded, and shivers wracked my body. The male prisoners shuffled from the room, leaving twenty women. When Lucas finally lifted his eyes, he assessed the first row of prisoners.

He looked both terrible and terrifying. Like he hadn't slept or eaten in days. Like he didn't care one way or another what happened to the people in this room.

Inhuman. That was how he looked.

My empty stomach cramped, and my gaze fell to the floor, unable to watch.

His slow footsteps reverberated across the tiles, then paused. An awkward stretch of silence passed.

"Why is that one standing in blood?" he asked.

"That would be my doing," Miller said, pride threading his voice.

"Ah. You brought her? Is that why you're here today, Jackie?" Lucas asked, entirely calm. "Want to see what your prize fetches at auction?"

Miller grinned. "Curious where she ends up, that's all. I have a preference."

My eyes squeezed shut. Sickened by the images of what might happen to me, I wanted to scream. Would Lucas blow his cover? Get himself killed? Get us *both* killed?

The searing throb in my back ratcheted up as his footsteps drew near. When he stopped in front of me, the room stilled.

His voice caressed my skin. "Look at me, sweetheart."

I lifted my head, and tears fell out of my control. His face was as cold as I'd expected, but a whirlwind came to life in his eyes as soon as my gaze met his. Disbelief and dread and shock warred within the blue-green.

He exhaled a slow breath. "There you are."

The words were so innocuous, but they gouged deep crevices into my heart and left them bleeding.

He'd been looking for me.

I *knew* he'd been looking for me.

"She's pretty," Lucas said to the room.

Miller's mouth stretched into a smile. "She's prettier without her clothes on. Had a bit of fun with her before I brought her in."

Lucas looked down at the blood pooling at my feet. "Was it the sort of fun she's going to live through, or should I dispose of her?"

"Eh. She's still good for a ride or two if you want a taste."

Chuckles erupted among the soldiers at the room's periphery.

"Mmm." Lucas's eyes returned to mine. "Sloppy seconds. How tempting."

Miller barked a laugh. "She's still tighter than a drum and wetter than water."

A flare lit behind Luke's eyes, the rapid calculations behind them making the aquamarine gleam. "How long you had her, Miller?"

"Few days."

The fire in Lucas burned, lighting him like neon. Red scorched over the bridge of his nose. A plan was forming in his head, one I probably wouldn't like.

"Why is she bleeding?" Lucas asked.

"Got a little carried away." Miller answered. "Pissed about the raid last night. It's a pretty piece of art, though. Take a look."

Contempt blackened my gaze when I glared at him, and he grinned.

Lucas clicked his tongue, bringing my attention back to him. His brows rose. "Spin."

Wooden and awkward, I pivoted, showing him my bloody back. He brushed my hair aside. Several women gasped, and the soldiers broke into laughter.

"I guess you were never one for subtlety," Lucas said. Could anyone else hear the fury in his voice?

"She needed a reminder."

Lucas circled me. A muscle twitched in his jaw. "What to do with you now?"

"She'll heal eventually," said a man I couldn't see. "Send her to the House so we can all have a taste."

Goosebumps erupted across my body. Tears blurred Lucas's face, but I couldn't look away.

"Anna brings a medic weekly, doesn't she?" Lucas asked.

Panic built in my chest, and I pleaded silently with Lucas.

Please don't let them do this to me.

"She doesn't need a medic," Miller said with a laugh. "You can put those rusty doctor skills to use. She'll thank you on her knees. Ain't that right, sugar?"

The crowd of soldiers turned into a pack of jackals.

"I'll take a turn with her," one said.

"The last one you took had to be put down like a dog," said another. "You can have her last."

They kept going, like it was all one big joke. I wasn't even human to these men. I was nothing more than an object to play with, and they'd play until I broke.

Through it all, I stared without blinking into Lucas's eyes, using that familiar color to steady me.

He wouldn't let these things happen to me. *Surely* he wouldn't let it happen.

Right?

"They're fighting over you, sweetheart," Lucas murmured, egging them on. "Damaged as you are. Don't you feel special?"

My teeth chattered. Why would he encourage it?

Behind him, Miller's grotesque smile widened. "Popular little thing, isn't she? I have an idea. What say we play for her, Scott? Like we used to?"

The corner of Lucas's mouth turned up in the barest smile.

Was this what he wanted?

"Yeah. Let us play for her!" a soldier said.

"I'll join," said another.

Lucas touched the thin strap of the slip, trailing down my chest in an uncharacteristic show of desire. "We playing at the Hangman?" he asked.

Cheers and catcalls poured from the men in the room.

He wanted them to want me. Why did he want them to want me?

A small sob escaped my throat.

What are you doing?

"Yeah," Miller said. "The Hangman. Tonight."

Lucas's finger reached the crook of the V in my dress. His finger moved in a tiny, familiar pattern over my heart. A spark of hope lit in my chest.

"Private game," Lucas said. "Colonels only."

Several officers of lower rank booed and grumbled.

"Interesting," Miller singsonged. "Finally want some new pussy, Scott? Anna will be so disappointed."

Lucas didn't bother to look at him. "She'll live." A beat passed before he added, "Or she won't."

Miller laughed like they were old friends. "Alright, alright. Tonight, colonels only. If her judgment is settled, I'll escort her to her life sentence."

He strolled forward, and panic shot through me like electricity. I stumbled backward, and Lucas did nothing to keep Jack Miller from grasping my elbow. I struggled, but he gripped my arms in a vise.

"No!" I wrenched away, turning to one of the other women. "Help me! Please!"

None of them looked at me.

Miller took hold of my bound wrists and forced us toward the door.

"Please!" I seized Miller's shirt. "Just kill me! Please!"

My legs gave out, but Miller took my weight easily, laughing in my face. "You don't need to die. You just need a little correction."

Dizzy, my head fell. "Please. Please don't do this."

He laughed harder, holding my arms to keep me upright. "Look at you. Just a few days and your manners are already improving." He dropped his voice to a whisper. "But I'm glad I had you when you still had some fight in you."

"*Please.*"

"I kind of like the way she begs, don't you, gents?"

A chorus of agreement.

"Think you can do it for us tonight?" Miller purred.

I changed tack. My legs found strength, and I turned. They all stared, but Lucas froze. I tripped toward him, and Miller let me, grinning.

"Lucas, please. Kill me. Please. *Please.*" I fell to my knees. "Death before slavery."

Except for a flickering muscle next to his mouth, he was motionless as a statue.

"Please," I whispered. "I'll do anything."

Every soldier in the room laughed. They *laughed.*

Someone to my left snorted. "The sluttiest ones always think you'll save them, Colonel. It must be something in your face."

The tears poured, but I kept my eyes open to stare at Lucas. "Please."

"I envy you, Scott," a faceless soldier said. "I've never had a whore beg me like that, and you get at least one a week."

Miller strolled toward me. "He ain't gonna save you. He's a heartless bastard. Ain't that right, Scott?"

Lucas said nothing.

"You'd be safer with me, sugar," Miller said. "Better hope I win tonight. Scott's a killer to the end."

Lucas riveted those blue-green eyes to mine, the color bright. "To the very end," he said. "Until I die."

Miller made some joke about Lucas being indestructible, but I cried so hard I couldn't breathe. Hysteria clawed at me, the oxygen refusing to enter my lungs. I gazed at Lucas, silently pleading, unable to speak or draw in air.

He observed me without any expression, but his aquamarine eyes splintered like gems compressed by tremendous weight. "You have your sentence. I won't kill you, so you should probably breathe."

Blackness crept into my vision.

"Do you hear me? Breathe!"

I couldn't.

"Breathe!"

Their voices faded.

The shadows took me.

29

RESCUE ME

...give me liberty, or give me death!

— PATRICK HENRY

When I woke, I was slung over a shoulder.

My eyes opened to find Miller's backside staring me in the face. Cold air snaked around my bare arms and legs. My bound wrists dangled below my head.

The car trunk popped. He tossed me inside. A fresh heartbeat woke in the wounds on my back, pulling a moan from my lips. I retreated into my mind and lived in a make-believe world where things like this didn't happen.

Tall trees...warm rain...smell of cypress...

He'll come for you.

He'll always come for you.

Lucas had a plan. He *always* had a plan. But I had no idea what to expect. Lucas Scott was not a hero. He was a realist. A pragmatist. He knew if he timed his rescue poorly, we'd *both* die, and in the interim, who knew how much more torture I'd be forced to endure.

The Hangman turned out to be some sort of luxury home transformed into a gaming hell. Miller yanked me from the trunk and marched me to an opulently appointed room, all leather and mahogany. A felt-covered poker table served as the centerpiece. We passed by it on the way to our destination—a silver cage at the corner of the room, large enough for a single human. Miller shoved me inside and slammed the door shut. The padlock secured with a click.

"See you tonight, sugar," he said with a wink, then left me alone.

Until that point, I thought I could survive it, but being given to Jack Miller by the man who'd told me my life mattered more than anything to him did horrid, soul-shattering things to my psyche. The core of me had cracked like safety glass struck hard, webs of fractures spreading out, distorting everything.

A single window provided me company, and I stared at the square of sunlight as it traveled across the room, the ache in my back dulling. I dozed for a time, and as I drifted in the pain-free state of oblivion, the thought floated through my mind that I wanted to stay there. It would be lovely, I decided, if the oblivion never spat me back out.

I was sitting in a cage awaiting a group of men who planned to gamble for the rights to my body. This was what my country had reduced me to. Currency. Something to be used and traded and wasted away.

And I wasn't the only woman to have found herself inside this cage. I was one of many who had come before, their blood staining these bars, and my heart shredded to confetti as I imagined what had become of the rest of them.

I wanted to die.

Now, before anything else bad could happen.

But I wasn't that lucky. I didn't get death. I got slavery.

I startled awake sometime later at the slam of a door. The sunlight had faded, leaving me shivering in the dark.

Male voices filtered through the air outside my room.

At the squeak of a door hinge, low light flooded the room. Sconces along the wall came to life.

Two men entered, chatting, laughing. Chilling recognition settled over me as my mind replayed the various executions they'd performed, the people they'd tortured and killed live on air. Miller joined next, his swagger oozing from his pores. He gave one man a good-natured shove, and patted the other on the shoulder—a brotherly, affectionate gesture.

I wanted to throw up.

They ignored me, continuing to chat and pour drinks from the nearby wet bar. Slowly, a handful of other Blood Colonels joined the room, and my hateful gaze tracked Paul Kingston as he sipped from a glass and chatted with his buddies. I knew so few of the Blood Colonels by sight alone, but that man had killed Tekqua.

I hoped he died today.

Eventually, one of them peeked out the door and muttered a curse. "I can't believe you showed. We finally got the house to ourselves, thanks to you. You should sentence private games more often."

Lucas entered the room wearing a black long-sleeved tee and tactical pants. My heart went wild trying to beat out of my chest.

"You're all shit card players." Lucas accepted a glass from one of the others. "This was too good an opportunity to pass up."

Several heads turned in my direction, and I shrank into the smallest corner of my cage. One of them—Nicholas Blake, maybe?—strolled toward me, leering. Revulsion boiled in my stomach, and I glared at him.

He held my gaze while his fingers curled around the bars. "You're not the first Defiant to grace this cage, baby girl, but you're definitely the prettiest."

My jaw clenched.

"Nice little dress you got here." His gaze traveled across my hunched body. "Looks like you're asking for it."

Rage spilled out. "For what? Dick? Do you even have one of those?"

His mouth quirked in a smile. "You need proof?"

"Nicky," Miller said with a chuckle. "Should I remind you she's not yours yet?"

"Bitch needs a lesson in manners," Blake muttered.

"And one of us will get to teach it to her," said another, chortling.

I hung my head as he retreated. If any of them tried to hurt me, I could only guess what Lucas would do, but there were five of them and only one of him.

Would any more Blood Colonels show? How many were stationed in this area?

Tears dripped from my chin, splashing onto my lap. The pain in my back was a constant friend now.

Chairs scooted across the floor. Chips and cards were distributed. A game of Texas Hold 'Em began.

"You playing to win, Scotty?" one asked.

"Is there another reason to play?" His voice was bored.

Cards shuffled.

Another one snorted, voice mocking. "Never been interested in playing before. What changed your mind, Scott?"

"Jack seemed to think she's tighter than a drum. Isn't that why you're here too, Jamie?"

Kingston grinned widely. "First time for everything, isn't there?" He raised his voice. "How do you feel about that, sugar? You feel special?"

My head shot up. Lucas sat facing me. His blue-green gaze was unwavering, making my heart race, my breaths deepen.

"Aw, she's scared of you, Luke," Kingston said.

"She didn't seem scared earlier when she was begging on her knees for mercy."

Miller chuckled and threw some chips to the middle of the table.

"You've got that pretty face to hide behind. The whores don't realize you're worse than the rest of us."

Lucas's smirk promised pain. "I think she'll figure it out soon enough."

Couldn't they see the bloodthirst behind his expression? Maybe he always looked that way around them, but his eyes shone with murderous wrath, and I silently begged him to do nothing.

He returned his attention to the game, and their conversation drifted. They spoke of their irritation with the Defiance and speculated about the traitor. They complained about their general, gossiped about lower-ranking Hunters, and bragged about the women they'd fucked. Every once in a while, one would turn toward me and wink or leer.

Laser-focused on the game, Lucas didn't look my way again. He became a shark in a pool of fish. The blinds raised, and his strategy aggressed.

A balding man who looked to be the oldest of them was the first to bust. He leaned back in his chair and shrugged, taking a sip of his whiskey. "Too bad, sugar. You and me would've had some fun."

Lucas's chips grew. His lowball sat untouched on the green felt. The blinds increased again.

Kingston busted next, followed by one other I didn't recognize.

Tension drew the air taut. I stood, my fingers clutching the bars of my cage until my knuckles whitened and the tips tingled, but I still couldn't see the cards on the table.

The grin on Miller's face was pure delight. He raised, forcing both Lucas and Blake to drain their stacks, but then folded. Lucas won the hand, and Miller was short-stacked. He busted on the next hand, leaving only Lucas and Blake.

"Good thing I already had her," Miller said with a rowdy laugh and drained his whiskey.

Hand after hand played, each man hedging bets, until Lucas raised in the third round. Blake lifted a brow, contemplating. He called. Play continued. In the last round, Lucas raised again. Blake did the same.

The two men stared at each other, neither smiling. The teasing and chatter from the others died.

"Seem pretty confident there, Scott," Blake said.

Lucas didn't reply.

My hands ached from their tight grip on the bars. My face pressed against them, cold metal digging into my cheeks. Luke's eyes flicked to me for half a heartbeat, and he pushed all his chips to the middle.

Blake's brows lifted, and he pursed his lips. "Alright, then." He pushed his own chips to the middle. "Showdown."

Lucas flipped his two cards. Silence stretched while Blake slid his own cards off the table. I held my breath.

Hands revealed, the men at the table burst into groans or cheers.

"You almost had him," one said.

Who did he mean?

Lucas stared at the cards on the table, and Blake stood, a gloating grin alight on his face.

No.

The giant of a man stalked toward me. I retreated, my back meeting the frigid bars behind me. Sparks lit in my skin with the contact.

He reached for the key to the padlock, lying on a table out of my reach. "Mine now. Bet you're wishing you hadn't mouthed off, huh?"

I pressed further into the bars as the lock fell away and the cage opened. Blake tugged me forward by the rope holding my hands together. "No! No, please!"

"There's that begging I love," Miller called as Blake dragged me toward the door.

"No! Help me! Please!"

I fought and cried, but Blake only laughed. I tried to find Lucas, but Blake jerked me off my feet and threw me over his shoulder, rounding the doorway.

He took me upstairs, through a hallway, into a bedroom, and tossed me on the bed. Wasting no time, he pressed my knees open, but the rope around my ankles impeded him. I tried to kick him, and he caught my ankle, twisting until electric stabs shot up my leg.

"Try that again, and I'll break it in half." He flipped me onto my stomach and pulled until my feet met the floor. Bent over the bed, I cringed as his hands slid down my sides to my hips, and lifted the tiny slip.

"Please," I whispered.

"Please what?"

"Please don't do this."

His hands stilled. A small gurgle emitted from his throat. His filthy touch slipped away from me, and a heavy thump hit the floor.

I twisted in time for Lucas to slide my dress down and haul me to my feet. Nicholas Blake lay dead, bleeding from his neck onto the carpet.

Lucas set to work cutting through my restraints with the bloody knife in his hand. The ropes fell away, and for the first time in almost a week I was free to move my body however I wanted.

He gripped the sides of my head and stared into my eyes, expression strained, voice wavering. "I searched for you everywhere."

Crushing my fingers into his shirt, I brushed against a multitude of oddly shaped objects underneath. "It's you, right? I'm not hallucinating?"

"It's me, Sophia. I'm here."

I crashed into him before he'd finished speaking, throwing my arms around his neck, burying my face in his shoulder. Thanks to the wounds in my back, he couldn't hug me the way I wanted, but his hands gripped my ribs as I cried in silence. He kissed my hair, the side of my face, anywhere he could reach. Over and over again.

"I'll get you out," he whispered. "Okay? You have to do everything I say. This— It isn't going to be pretty."

I lifted my head.

Wait. What?

"Lucas, you're not going back down there to face four men by yourself."

His thumb grazed my cheek. "There's no other choice."

Flashes of images scorched my mind, of Lucas trying and failing to fight them off...him fatally wounded...me trapped as a Hunter prisoner, Luke's blood staining my hands.

Him dead and me wanting to be.

"Tie me back up," I said. "I won't let you do this."

"You won't *let* me?" He whisper-yelled, stepping away from me.

Fresh tears fell, and I reached for him. "You can't die. I'll be alone. What if I can't get out?"

"You'll never sneak out with them alive, not even with my help. They're trained killers." He gripped my arm too tightly. "You really think I'm going to let them live after this?"

"I'm fine, Lucas!" I choked around the tears. "But I won't be fine if you die. It's just a few cuts."

His eyes widened. "Just a few cuts?"

"Yeah—"

He manhandled me until my back faced the vanity mirror on the far wall. "Have you even seen it, Sophia?"

He moved my hair, and I stared at the mutilation on my back. I thought they were random cuts meant to disfigure me.

Not random though.

The Brotherhood Cross.

Speechless, I gawked at the bleeding hate emblem that would forever scar my skin, thinking of the lynched bodies hanging from the ceiling during the siege on Safe House Red.

"Don't even try to tell me what happened to you wasn't that bad."

Tears clogged my throat. "We—we could sneak out."

He scoffed at me. "*You'll* sneak out. I'll provide a distraction."

"You're only one man." My voice broke. "Against four."

Luke's death would disintegrate everything inside me, and if I couldn't escape, it would be in vain. I'd be theirs.

"I've had worse odds," he said.

"I don't want you to die for me. I'll be trapped here."

Lucas took hold of my upper arms. "I won't let you be trapped here. You got on your knees and begged me to kill you today. You have handprint bruises around your throat. Argue all you want, but if I have to die to get you out, to save your life, I will." He pressed the knife into my hand. "You know what to do. If you have to use this, you aim to kill. None of them have firearms. They're prohibited here." He handed me a key. "If something does happen to me, there's a Jeep down the street. Use the kitchen door, Sophia, okay? I killed the guards there, but there are two at the front. Turn right at the sidewalk and run. In the glove box is a loaded gun. Use it only if you need it. Get back home as fast as you can."

He removed his long-sleeved shirt and helped me pull it over the dress. His scent wrapped around me like a warm embrace. He left me, heading for the door, extracting something from beneath his thin undershirt.

"Wait!" I rushed across the room. "Lucas, wait." I threw myself around him.

He wreathed his arms around me, gentle. "Sophia." His lips dropped to my ear, his voice barely a whisper. "Do you know how much I love you? You disappeared, and I never even said the fucking words. I love you. Forever. Until I die."

He could die. Tonight. My blood froze. "Say it again."

"I love you. Let me fix this." He kissed me once and pulled away. "This isn't the end for you. There's a clear path to freedom. Stay out of sight, or you'll distract me."

He peeked through a crack in the door and stepped into the hall.

Too fast! My mind couldn't keep up, and I didn't know what to do. Four Blood Colonels sat downstairs, and while he might take the first one or two unaware, they were all sadists with fighter's instincts.

I flinched as a crash echoed through the house, chased by a bang and muffled shouts. I gripped the knife and tiptoed to the top of the stairs. More cries rang out, some of them screaming questions at Lucas.

"What are you doing?"

A shout, and then another loud thump.

"Th'fuck, Scott!"

Grunts and the unmistakable thuds of fists against flesh emerged from the end of the hall. The picture of Lucas being restrained and beaten flashed through my mind, and I lost it. Slipping down the stairs, I snuck toward the fight.

Fabric ripped, then a clunk vibrated the floorboards.

I made it to the bottom of the stairs and glanced around the corner. One colonel sat slumped at the poker table, throat cut. Another two—Miller and Kingston—scrambled away from Lucas until the table stood between them. Lucas stared into the remaining one's frightened eyes, screwing a knife into his stomach. The man whimpered, falling when Lucas yanked out the knife.

He landed on all fours, and Lucas kicked him hard in the face. Blood sprayed the ground as the thin bones of the man's face crunched and gave way. He fell to his side.

One more kick, and he was gone.

Lucas headed for the other two. He whipped out a pair of karambits. Kingston took a defensive position. Miller had been messing with his shoe, but he straightened, and thrust his knife toward Lucas. Dodging, Lucas entered a deadly dance with his remaining foes.

30
VIGILANTE JUSTICE

Kingston leapt at Lucas with his Hunter knuckles, and the fight disappeared from view. I leaned through the door. Miller jerked his weaponed hand toward Lucas, his knife arcing wide.

Luke pushed them off, twisting to swipe his blade across Kingston's wrist. Blood spewed from the wound, but he held on to his weapon, retreating.

I'd never seen him fight, and I could see why people feared him, why he was known as merciless and cold-blooded. Even outnumbered, Lucas was lethal. Kingston and Miller hesitated before each move, keeping too far for Lucas to do any real damage. He hurled one of the karambits at Kingston, who dove out of the way. Luke leapt at Miller.

His strikes were controlled, powerful.

Forward. Down. Retreat. Repeat.

No frills, no heroism. He fought to survive, and to survive meant to kill.

Miller's practiced defense failed when Lucas drew blood from two swings to Miller's chest. Kingston rejoined the fray. The three of them circled, searching for advantages. I remained quiet, hidden, until Miller landed his blade across Luke's arm, and Kingston lashed at his chest.

Blood spilled, and all thoughts of staying away fled. I tripped into the room, clenching my knife. With a running start, I leapt onto Kingston's back, sinking the point of my blade into the base of his throat.

Blood spurted over my hand. He choked, stumbling backward from the fight, and I dug the knife deeper, refusing to stop when I met resistance. He fell, taking me with him. I landed on my back. Silver sparks ruptured across my eyes with the lightning that struck my wounds. A moan wrenched from my throat.

Still, I yanked the knife from the dead man's neck, and life-giving blood spilled from his body.

For Tekqua, I thought with vindictive satisfaction.

I shoved the body off me. Lucas lashed out at Miller, who defended himself with a quick raise of his arm. "What the fuck are you doing, Scott?"

Lucas advanced. I scrambled behind Lucas, my heart pounding.

Miller's gaze bounced between us. "Oh, you've got to be fucking kidding me. Is *this* why you were such an asshole today? Develop a savior complex?"

Lucas kept his blades out, hands steady.

Miller glanced at his dead friends and spat blood. "I'm assuming Blake's dead?"

Lucas said nothing.

Miller's jaw slackened with sudden understanding. His gaze landed squarely on me. "You had Hunter knuckles."

My heart squeezed tight as he put it all together.

"You had fucking Hunter knuckles." He spat blood onto the floor again and glared at Lucas. "Goddamn it! *You're* the spy? You killed your friends and turned traitor for this fucking whore?"

Still, Lucas said nothing, though I wondered whether he'd mention his sister.

"No pussy is worth this, man. I've had her enough times to know she isn't anything special."

I clenched my fist around my weapon, longing to rip it across his body.

Miller sneered at me. "Though I suppose I did like the way her throat felt around my cock."

My stomach dropped. I had no recollection of that. Had I… Had I lost memories? Maybe he was lying. I was fairly certain I would've bitten it off, even under threat of death.

I expected Lucas to lose his temper, but he countered with, "I doubt it's big enough to reach that far."

Miller's keen green eyes turned calculating, searching. In a flash, Lucas threw his remaining karambit to the floor and pulled something from his waistband. It whizzed toward Miller, catching him above the knee. With a scream, Miller collapsed to a kneeling position. He ripped the throwing knife from his body. Lucas threw another. Miller fell backward, the blade buried in his right chest.

Yanking a spiraled knife from a holster, Lucas dropped to his haunches before Miller, holding the deadly weapon to his throat. "You're lucky. If she weren't here, I'd cut out your intestines and make you eat them."

Miller tracked the blade in Lucas's hand with the focus of a man who knew death hunted him. "Luke, think about this. If you kill me, you're a dead man. You're the only one left? That's suspicious. Leave me alive. We'll play it off like she killed them."

Lucas raised the dagger.

"Or I can get you out!" Miller said, desperate now. "I have contacts. I can hook you up. I'll make sure they don't come after you. You weren't even here tonight. No one will ever know."

The dagger touched Miller's throat.

"Please," Miller said.

"You hear that? He's begging, Sophia."

I smirked at Miller. Vicious pleasure rolled through me. "I like the way he begs, don't you?"

Miller's mouth went slack. "Sophia? Is that your name?"

Lucas's wicked knife whipped through the air and pinned Miller's right wrist to the floor. "You don't speak her name," he snapped, his calm slipping.

Miller screamed. Barely restrained savagery glittered on Luke's face. He wanted to do awful, cruel things to this man before him, and I was the only thing holding him back.

My mind cast back to that sheet Lucas had given me months ago, the list of Miller's strengths and weaknesses.

Will always underestimate a woman.

I snatched one of Lucas's discarded karambits. One swipe, and a bleeding gash opened from Miller's mouth to his temple, barely missing his eye. Blood flowed from the wound, dripping down his neck and reddening his teeth. The split flesh dangled from his face, and his eyes blazed.

Panting with pain, attached to the floor, Miller cursed. He twisted, jerking his pant leg up to his knee and reached down.

Lucas yanked on my wrist. I tripped behind him.

Miller extracted a small handgun from a concealed holster around his calf and aimed. In the time it took Luke to shield me, Miller was able to get off a single shot.

The deafening bang startled my every sense. I screamed. Lucas jumped on him, grabbing his left wrist. It knocked him flat on the floor. Several more shots thundered while they struggled.

I leapt to Lucas's side. He had one hand on Miller's wrist and the other on his elbow. I went for the gun. Once I had the warmed metal in my hands, I pointed it at Miller's forehead, squeezing the trigger without guilt.

Nothing happened.

Miller laughed, teeth scarlet, as I threw the gun at his shredded face. Lucas fell back, gripping his arm to his chest. Blood dripped to the floor, but he pushed himself up. "Sophia, you have to go now—"

A shout from the front of the house caught our attention. "Colonels? We heard shots—"

Miller screamed for help. Still pushing me away, Lucas yanked his spiral blade from Miller's wrist, and rammed it through the most fatal place he could reach. Footsteps entered the house.

Lucas grabbed my hand.

We ran, slipping through the doorway. I met the eyes of one guard, who stared in confusion as Lucas darted past.

His voice echoed behind us as we reached a side door. "Colonel?"

"He attacked us!" Lucas sent them on a false trail. "He's back there!"

Behind us, Jack screamed, "Get him! Don't let him get away!"

The guards headed further into the house as we burst into the chilly night air. We fled down the dark neighborhood street, Luke cradling his arm. I tried not to step on anything too sharp. Adrenaline faded fast, and my back screamed at me. Every jolting step throbbed like fiery knives in my flesh. Rocks dug into my bare feet. My gaze darted left and right, peering at the dark houses.

An engine roared to life behind us, and Luke jerked me to the side. He pressed me against the trunk of a large oak, his arms on either side of me, caging me in.

"Shh."

I struggled to control my ragged breathing, each breath louder than the one before.

A Humvee sped by.

Lucas dragged me onto the street while shouts echoed behind us.

The silver Jeep was parked where he said it would be. I scrambled into the passenger seat and handed him the key he'd given me earlier. We zoomed down the street without headlights, whipping past guards who shouted and ran after us.

Driving in silence, the stress of the last few minutes washed over me. My heart pounded, and the images pulsed with each beat.

Panic set in.

"Hey," he said, voice eerily relaxed. "It's okay. Breathe. You're almost done. A few more minutes and it will be done."

No, it wouldn't! We'd killed five of his fellow Blood Colonels. How would we ever untangle the knots we'd tied? My hands shook. Stained with blood, I tried to wipe them on the silk, but the blood had already dried. I couldn't breathe.

"Sophia?"

I glanced at him. He drove one-handed, his right arm cradled against his chest.

"Breathe." He said it so calmly. "In and out. Think of the forest. Tall trees. Warm rain. Cypress."

I nodded and forced myself to simmer down.

"You okay now?"

"No, I'm not fucking okay, Lucas. I killed a man today. I had a Brotherhood Cross carved into my back today. I've been a prisoner for a week."

He said nothing, his face lined and stiff.

I took a breath. "I need a minute."

He nodded.

I studied him again, lingering over the blood spatters. Bruised and bloody fingers gripped the steering wheel.

"Will those guards find us?" I asked.

"I don't know. They'll have alerted the whole goddamn army by now."

"I wonder why Miller didn't use the gun sooner."

Luke grimaced. "He didn't really have a chance. If I'd known he had it, I would've killed him first."

"Why would you save him for last anyway?"

Glaring at the road ahead of him, Lucas's jaw clenched. "Pride. Stupidity."

Ah, that would probably haunt him until his dying day.

"I thought about you every day," I whispered.

He expelled one bitter laugh. "I thought about you every second."

"You found me."

Surely he'd break a bone if he continued gripping the steering wheel so tightly. "I didn't find you. You were thrown in my face."

My voice dropped to a whisper. "I'm sorry, Lucas. I shouldn't have begged. I only made things harder."

He stayed quiet. I stared at his face without blinking, scared that if I glanced away, he'd disappear.

He slammed his hand onto the steering wheel. "Don't apologize for that. Ever. Ask me for anything, Sophia. Never be afraid to ask me for anything."

"Even death?"

"Even death. I won't give you that, but you can ask me for anything you want." Thick strands of guilt strangled his words.

I wanted to cry again. "Lucas, this isn't your fault."

"All I've wanted is for you to be safe, and I can't fucking manage it." He reached out with his injured arm and grabbed my hand. "I was very clear if anything happened to you, I wouldn't take it well."

"It wasn't a mission. I was taking care of injuries from an attack, and they sieged our healing house."

He cursed under his breath.

"But I'm safe now," I said. "With you."

"You're not safe with me." His voice cracked.

Brows drawn together, I shook my head. "I'm always safe with you."

He glanced at me, taking a deep breath as his eyes darted over my tear-stained face.

"I love you so much, Lucas."

"I love you, too. But that's only going to make the next part very painful."

"The next part?"

The Jeep came to a stop at the house on Evanston.

"You're not safe with me."

31
PLEASE

 Whatever our souls are made of, his and mine are the same.

—EMILY BRONTË, *WUTHERING HEIGHTS*

We entered the house, and Lucas gripped my arms. "I know it hurts. I'm going to need you to bite through the pain, okay? We don't have much time."

Frazzled and scared, my voice shook. "What do you mean? Why aren't I safe with you?"

"I need to make sure Miller is dead."

I gaped at him. "What?"

"He was alive when those guards came. He'll have every Hunter in this territory after us. After *you.*"

"Who cares? You're not going back there." Heat spread across my face and neck as outrage and betrayal corroded my insides. He was thinking of leaving me? After all this?

His hands on my arms tightened, and his voice went ragged. "I'm dead now. Do you understand that? There is nothing that will stop the Hunters from finding me. But if I kill Miller, then *you* are safe. I have to make sure he's dead, Sophia."

"He won't even be there. They'll have taken him for medical treatment—"

"I can sneak into the hospital—"

"No." I stomped my foot. "You will stay here with me. I spent a week being tortured in his house, praying for deliverance, and whoever was listening sent me you. You are *mine*." My voice rose to a hysterical shriek, and I grabbed his shirt. "You're mine! Do you hear me? They can't have you!"

If he decided to leave, I'd have too little strength to stop him. Love was the only power I had over Lucas Scott. I needed him to love me enough to let me save him. Shaking and crying and so scared I could barely breathe, I pressed my hand to my pounding heart.

He raised his hands, placating me. "Alright. Just breathe, sweetheart."

"I *am* breathing."

"Then do it better." He took my hand and led me to the master bathroom, turning on the shower. Using only his left arm, he undressed me. His soiled T-shirt and the scarlet silk pooled at my feet. He stared at the wounds on my back for several moments before testing the water and easing me into the stall.

The water had little pressure, but it stung, and sobs escaped my throat. He gently cleaned away the blood and dirt from my back while I scrubbed the crusty red from my hands and hair.

"Do you really think he would have lived through that?" I asked.

"He's survived worse. The trauma surgeons on base are very good."

I glared at the shower wall before glancing at him over my shoulder. He held his right arm against his chest.

"What happened to your arm?"

He sighed and showed me the hole in his upper sleeve where a bullet had entered. Shocked, I turned, reaching out as he stepped away. "It's fine," he said. "Let me take care of you first. Please."

Staring into those pleading eyes, I nodded, letting him finish. He helped me out and inspected my entire body. Besides the emblem on my back, I had bruises on my throat, teeth marks on my breasts, and lacerations on my wrists. Luke's mouth tightened further with each injury he examined, and his normally bright eyes morphed into a flat blue.

After his thorough perusal, he met my gaze. "I can try to minimize the scarring on your back."

I nodded.

After helping me dress in sweatpants, he disappeared into the kitchen. I eased my aching body face down on the bed, and the day replayed against my closed eyelids while tears gathered.

Lucas reappeared with a plate of food, then gathered an armful of supplies from his closet and dropped them onto the bed next to me. He placed his hands on either side of my waist, beckoning me closer. "When did Miller do this to you?"

"This morning," I said, carefully chewing the slices of apple he'd brought.

Miller had given me so little food in the last week I was worried I'd be sick if I ate too much.

Lucas's finger tapped on my side, and he sighed. "I think I'll try to glue it. You'll need to be careful with your movements." He opened several packets of purple fluid and grabbed one of the sterile packages in front of my face. A pair of tweezers.

"This may burn."

Starting at one end, he squeezed my skin back together and applied the purple fluid, holding it in place with the tweezers while it dried.

Sweat broke across my forehead as my nerves sparked, and I shoved the plate aside. When he squeezed a particularly tender area, I flinched, and his hands froze. He laid a hand over an unblemished portion of my back. "I'm sorry."

"For what? Saving my life again?" Bitterness coated my voice. "Distract me. Where did you look for me?"

He went back to work. "When you didn't show, I told myself you'd just changed your mind about us."

My heart cracked a bit. "You believed that?"

He let out an angry snort. "No. I was lying to myself. You said you'd always come back to me. You promised, and I believed you."

I closed my eyes, squeezing out tears.

"I searched everywhere, Sophia. I went through the prisoners waiting for Registration. I tried to find out if there'd been some sort of evacuation of Defiants. I scoured the brothels. I had Anna searching for you, but she couldn't find you either. Anna's women know everything, so when they hadn't heard anything, I thought…"

Questions surged through me, but he continued in a haunted, wooden voice. "I sent a message to Harrison, and when I got a response, it only said he didn't know where you were. He was searching and hoped you were with me. I sifted through the dead. I followed the lists of casualties, but never found your name. You never came to Registration, so I thought you must have died, that maybe you'd been left behind, or dumped in a mass grave." He paused for a moment, and his voice lowered. "I couldn't give up, though. Not until I knew for sure."

He went silent.

"Lucas?"

"I thought I'd send you to the House. Anna would have taken care of you until I got there. But then I saw how much they wanted you, and I thought if I could get them to play for you, I could win you fairly. I could have gotten you out without anyone knowing. It was the safest way."

"And then Blake won."

He sighed. "Yes."

Nauseated, I let him finish my back, then slid on a loose shirt. "Thank you," I whispered.

"I gambled with your life," he said, sitting next to me. "Don't thank me."

"I'm alive. You saved me. Again."

He shook his head, a jerky, irritated gesture.

With no energy to argue, I reached for his arm. "Let me help you now."

He hesitated only a moment before removing his shirt. The variety of wounds there had my stomach aching with worry—a long slash over his side, bruises darkening his ribs, a puncture wound in his shoulder. The small bullet hole in his upper arm seemed inconsequential in comparison. I examined that one first and sighed my relief when I found an exit wound.

He glared at his arm. "It'll heal. I've been shot like this before. He missed the vital parts."

With no small relief, I marched him to the bathroom, and he showered away the blood just like I had. After he dried off, I took my time gluing him back together, piece by piece. He submitted to my ministrations with only small hisses of pain. When it was done, we sat on the bed side by side.

"What now?" I asked.

He hesitated for a long moment, then fetched his dirty pants to pull out the Jeep key. "Now's the painful part."

"Lucas—"

"You have to leave."

My hand closed around the key. "Leave?"

"Go home, Sophia. Make them keep you safe."

My heart bounced around my ribcage as I stared—then glared—into his face. "I'm not leaving you."

He took my hand. "My cover is blown, and I have nowhere to go. I'm now an enemy to both sides. You stay with me, you die."

"I'm not leaving without you," I snapped.

He remained calm, which only stoked my ire. "We both knew this day was coming. It's time to be brave and accept it."

I gripped his hand. "You're all I have left, Lucas, and I won't lose you without a fight."

"You *have* fought, sweetheart. You've fought and lost. This isn't a debate."

My muscles tensed at his supercilious tone. "You can't tell me what to do."

He sighed. "If you would just listen—"

"I am!"

"You're *not*. I've never been good for you, and now I'm putting you in danger." He grabbed my shoulders almost as if he wanted to shake sense into me. "I just want you to be safe."

"Then you shouldn't have let me fall in love with you."

That killed all semblance of his calm. "Let you? *Let you?* I don't *let you* do anything. You do whatever the fuck you want to do whenever you want to do it." He raked his fingers through his dark waves, his composure cracking. "You were just supposed to be a contact! You've fucked up every plan I ever had. You clawed your way in and won't let go. Why can't you see we've lost?"

"We haven't lost til we're dead." I had nothing but him, and I'd fight for him until my dying breath. "You saved my life today. We haven't lost yet."

"Your stubbornness is going to get you killed."

"No, it's going to keep you alive."

He scrubbed his face hard with his hands. "Please don't do this. Please let me get you out. I can't go back. I can't go with you. Staying together will kill us both."

"Then we die together, Lucas. There's no life I want to live without you in it. You said I could ask you for anything. I'm asking you for this. All I want is you."

Exhausted, desperate and grief-stricken, he squeezed my hand. "Please. *Please*, Sophia," he whispered. "Please don't do this. Just go."

I met those aquamarine eyes, and tried to picture leaving him, letting him face death alone, but I just... I couldn't do it. I leaned closer, holding his anguished gaze. "Would you?"

"What?"

"If our positions were reversed, would you leave me alone to go off and face a traitor's death?"

"Yes." The word was quick, breathless. Full of hope.

"Wow," I said under my breath. "No wonder you don't lie. You're terrible at it."

The amber flecks in his eyes glimmered, warming, but he straightened, and his expression became impassive again. When he spoke, his voice had cooled. "What's your plan then? Do we hide? Do we run? Where do we go? Who would take us in? We have a car with half a tank of gas, a single loaded gun, and two armies chasing us. Tell me how we survive, Sophia."

I turned toward him and took his face in my hands. "You just killed five Blood Colonels to save a Defiant. You've been feeding information to the Defiance for months. You're the reason the tides of the war have shifted. If people on my side knew—"

His eyes widened. "You're kidding—"

"I can take you to Theo, Lucas. He already knows you've turned. He'll grant you clemency."

I thought of the signed paper in my sleeping quarters back home, the one granting Lucas immunity from his crimes.

Then I thought of the doubt on Theo's face when he'd given it to me.

If you two are smart, you'll steer clear of Nia Williams.

"He'll execute me," Lucas said, certain.

"You don't know that!" I wiped the tears from my cheeks, and new ones replaced them. "Let me try, Lucas. Let me save you."

He exhaled, loud and frustrated.

"*Until I die.* That's what you promised me. You aren't dead yet."

He considered me for several seconds. "What will you do when they decide to execute me?"

Heart pounding, I flinched at the images that sprang forth—images of heartbreak and screams and endless torment.

"Tell me, Sophia. When the Defiance sentences me with execution for my war crimes—*as they should*—how will you respond?"

"That won't happen."

His gaze didn't waver. "Tell me what you'll do."

The picture formed, heedless of my desire not to see it—Lucas denied mercy, strung up to suffocate. It burned a fiery wave from my stomach to the tips of my fingers and toes. My hands curled into fists.

He nodded as he stared at my face, like my expression said it all. "I won't be the cross you die on."

"You're the only thing left to live for," I whispered.

His gaze dropped to his knees. "You love me too much. Love isn't supposed to hurt you."

I sniffed. "Isn't that all love is, Lucas? Just another knife buried in our hearts? If you die, it'll tear the knife out. I'll bleed to death."

His eyes squeezed shut. "God. So dramatic."

"I'm serious, Lucas. You're a part of me. I can't live without you."

My name was a soft huff of air, and he dropped his head, lifting my hand to kiss my fingers. His tone lost all life. "I will go with you, but when they apprehend me, that's the end."

Relief washed through me. "Are you saying yes?"

"I'll go with you—"

A smile broke over my face.

"—as long as you *promise me* you'll let them take me, if that's what they choose to do. You will not fight for me. You will not get hurt for me. You will allow them to do what needs to be done. Do you understand?"

I froze.

"I am the devil, and you *cannot* follow me back to hell."

"Lucas—"

He met my eyes. "I'm not bargaining with you."

"Lucas!"

"You fell to your knees and begged me to kill you today, Sophia."

His voice shook. "Do you have any idea what that did to me? If this doesn't work, you *will* stay safe."

"The only times I'm ever hurt are the times I'm not with you."

"I will stay with you," he said. "*Until I die.* It's coming, Sophia. You can't stop this, but you can stay safe. Okay?"

The hard set of his shoulders, the bright, angry blue in his eyes— they told me he wouldn't budge. No use arguing.

So I lied. "Fine."

He eyed me, head cocked. "I'll hold you to that."

"I'll hold you tighter."

He gave a heavy sigh, his hand tightening on mine. His thumb brushed the gold ring on my finger. "This is beyond stupid. I hope you realize that."

32
ASYLUM

 Seeking asylum is not a crime; it is a human right.

— UNITED NATIONS REFUGEE AGENCY (UNHCR)

Under cover of darkness, we drove through the forested road that led to headquarters and pulled up to the gated driveway. Lucas lifted an eyebrow at me. "You've got to be fucking kidding me. *This* is your headquarters?"

I hopped out of the Jeep to push open the gate. A whistle sounded, and I lifted my hand to signal my affiliation. Lucas drove through, and I closed it while he pulled into the circle drive. After exiting the car, he assessed the grand entrance to the rotunda from the shadow beneath his hoodie, all darkened behind the metal window covers.

The watchman left his hidden post to meet us, weapon raised, but when he drew close, he froze, eyes wide. "Sophia?"

The familiar voice iced my nerves. "Jayden?"

"Sophia?" He crossed the distance between us, gathering me in a bear hug. I whimpered and cringed as my glued wounds protested his touch.

He released me, his hands cupping my shoulders, expression concerned. "Are you okay?"

I glanced sideways at Lucas. "I hurt my back. Please don't touch it."

Lucas's narrowed eyes studied us, and my insides filled with butterflies. These two men were never supposed to meet.

"Where've you been?" Jayden's voice cracked. "We thought you... I've been worried about you."

"It's kind of a long story. I can't really explain—"

"Sophia, who is this?"

The deceptive calm in Lucas's voice made my eyes flutter closed. "This is Jayden," I said, forcing a brightness I didn't feel.

Only then did Jayden acknowledge we weren't alone. His attention flickered to Lucas. "Friend of yours?"

The dark kept Lucas's features obscured enough to remain anonymous.

"Yeah. From another safe house. He needs to see the general."

Jayden lifted his chin toward Lucas and lost interest, turning back to me. "God, girl, it's good to see you."

I opened my mouth, not sure what I could say, but he cut me off. His arms slid around my neck, and he pressed his mouth to my hair.

Lucas's expression sharpened into a murderous union of displeasure and rage. "Sophia." His voice was eerie in its softness. "Please make it stop."

Or I'll kill him.

I extracted myself from Jayden's grasp. "We need to see Theo, Jayden."

Unaware of the predator in his midst, Jayden nodded. "Come with me." He headed toward the house.

Instead of following, Lucas turned full on to face me. He tilted his head in a silent question.

I shrugged. "He's just excited to see me."

His eyebrows lifted, but his tone stayed dry, neutral. "Who is he?"

"He's...no one."

Tension vibrated in every line of him, and his gaze traveled toward Jayden, studying him the way a cat would contemplate a mouse.

I reached for Lucas's hand, where tremors served as evidence of the stress still coursing through his body. "He was before you. He's not a threat."

"Everything is a threat," he murmured.

"Lucas?"

He shook his head—a tight, jerky movement. He was teetering at the breaking point, struggling to hold himself together the same way I'd nearly dissolved when he wanted to leave me to chase down Jack Miller.

One step closer, I pressed our joined hands to my heart. "Picture the trees, okay? They're tall. The rain is warm and smells of cypress."

His forehead dropped to mine. "Things are about to get so much worse, Sophia. Whatever happens, promise me you'll stay safe."

"Soph?" Jayden's worried voice hissed across the yard. "You coming?"

"Promise me," Lucas said, more urgent now.

"I promise." I squeezed Lucas's hand. "You ready?"

With the tiniest nod, he followed me toward the side entrance. Jayden knocked in the series of rhythmic raps required after curfew, and the door unlocked from the inside. We stepped into the main hall of Defiance headquarters.

Lucas snorted in disbelief. "Fucking hell. No wonder we could never find you. This is genius."

Inside, the place glowed with warm light. Several soldiers lounged around the common rooms on either side of the hall, snacking or chatting. Lucas glanced at the metal covering the windows.

"Don't let them see you," I whispered as people peered at us. He pulled his hood further over his face.

Luckily, none of my friends were nearby, or I'd have been inundated with questions.

"General's still working," Jayden said. "I'll let you head that way. I have to get back outside." He paused and placed his hand on my shoulder. "I'm glad you're safe."

Nodding his way, I dragged Lucas toward the staircase. My stomach twisted with nerves and questions. What would Theo do when I brought a Blood Colonel into his office? Was Lucas right? Would Theo really arrest him?

After a slight hesitation that Lucas clocked at once, shooting me a knowing look, I knocked on Theo's door.

"Remember what you promised," Lucas murmured.

I ignored him.

The familiar "Enter!" turned my hands clammy.

I poked my head in. "Theo?"

He stood at his desk, absently flicking a pen on the edge, but his body stilled. He closed his eyes while I opened the door.

"Theo, it's me."

A rough breath escaped him. "Soph?"

Neither of us moved once our eyes met. It took several seconds before his attention shifted to the person attached to me. Lucas had his hood raised, but he glared at Theo from the shadow underneath with undisguised hatred. Theo gripped his knife.

I hauled Lucas inside with me and closed the door. The lock turned with a loud click.

"Lucas Scott." Theo kept his voice assured and steady.

"Uncle Theo." Lucas matched the tone. Lips pressed in a flat line, vivid eyes locked on Theo, Lucas couldn't have exuded his hate any more clearly.

I rubbed my forehead, willing away the headache. "Put your knife down, Theo. He won't hurt you. He thinks you're going to kill him."

Theo's shoulders relaxed. "What's going on, Sophia? Are you okay? The quarantine house—"

"I'm okay," I said. "I'm…fine."

Theo's brow creased at my hesitation. "Why is he here?"

I bit my lip. "We had nowhere else to go."

"I've had people searching." His voice roughened. "Where were you?"

"When they— When—" I scowled at my own incoherency and straightened my shoulders. "I was captured. I ended up a prisoner."

Alarm sharpened Theo's dark eyes. His gaze whipped to Lucas. "*You're* in charge of the prisoners, are you not? What happened?"

Lucas launched into the story without hesitation or inflection, appearing unfazed—almost *bored*—but the claw of his fingers on my hand told me he'd nearly reached his limit of what he could tolerate tonight.

"He did *what*?" Theo's posture straightened when Lucas explained about my back.

Tears filled my eyes again, and I wondered when I'd run out.

Lucas bent toward me and murmured, "Will you show him?"

I turned, letting Lucas lift my shirt.

Theo cursed, his tone dripping with hatred. "What then? What did you do?"

"I killed them."

My shirt dropped, and silence followed. I leaned into Lucas's side.

"You killed…who?" Theo asked.

"The five other Blood Colonels currently in this territory. Though I didn't actually *see* Miller—"

"He was as good as dead, Luke," I said.

Scratching his eyebrow, Theo opened his mouth for several seconds before he said, "You—you did this—all this—for her?"

"Yes."

Theo's eyes sought mine. "And you brought him here, why?"

"He can't go back. You swore him exoneration if I continued to help you, and I did. I'm requesting asylum on his behalf."

Lucas turned, sending incredulity and outrage my way. "Please tell me that's not true."

I ignored him.

"Can he not ask for asylum himself?" Theo asked.

"He won't." I threw a scowl at Lucas. "He's a fool who doesn't think he deserves it."

Theo exhaled. "Maybe he's right."

"He saved my life, and you *swore*, Theo."

At Theo's clear displeasure, Lucas chuckled. "I'd be more than happy to disappear. You'd never have to see me again."

I whirled on him, pointing my finger at his face. "You shut up and let me do this!"

His undamaged arm lifted in a submissive gesture.

"You say *nothing* unless it's to help this situation," I said. "Do you understand?"

Theo's gaze ricocheted between us. "You just...listen to her?"

After a beat, Lucas said, "She gets what she wants no matter what I do. This tends to be the easiest course of action."

Theo had the gall to laugh. He dropped the knife back onto his desk. "Her stubbornness knows no bounds."

Lucas glanced at me, then raised a brow at Theo. "I've long suspected you sent her to me because you knew her tenacity would outlast mine. She thrives no matter what you throw at her."

I curbed the compulsion to kick them both in the knee.

"Yes, she does." Cogs turned behind Theo's eyes. "And you came here, even when you thought I'd kill you, simply because she asked you to?"

Lucas drew a breath, peering at the chandelier. Fractured light dappled his unshaven face. He merely shrugged, resigned to his fate.

"I'm trying to understand here," Theo said. "Give me something."

Lucas continued his perusal of the crystals. "She's safest here, and...I promised her I'd stay."

A troubled expression creased Theo's brow.

"I have a signed document hidden in my room that states you won't hurt him, Theo," I said.

"Yes, but that doesn't mean I have to harbor him as a fugitive. Williams will never go for this."

"But—" I took in his weathered desk, the riveted window. "This is the safest house we have."

An unattractive choke emerged from Theo's throat. "You think he'd be *safe* here? What do you think people will do to him once they recognize who he is?"

"Once they learn how he's helped..."

Lucas and Theo exchanged skeptical glances.

I glared hard at both of them. "We've all seen what he can do. They'd be stupid to come at him. He'll kill them without breaking a sweat."

Lucas snorted. "I'm not a magician."

Theo dragged a hand down his face.

Gaze distant, Lucas muttered, "I'd sweat a little."

Theo's hand paused over his nose and mouth, and he eyed Lucas as if he couldn't quite believe what he was dealing with. He shook his head and sat. I plopped into a chair when Theo motioned us to sit, but Lucas perched ramrod straight at the edge of his, hands resting on his knees.

"What do you want from me?" Theo asked.

Lucas shrugged one shoulder. "Ask her. I'm only throwing myself on your mercy because it's the best way to keep her safe."

Theo hummed. "Your motives, at least, speak well for you."

Lucas said nothing, but his potent desire to roll his eyes practically washed over me.

"I want to know the whole story. I've known this girl from the day she was born, and I've never seen her care about anything the way she cares about you." He paused. "You. A chauvinist with a penchant for killing anyone different than you."

My mouth fell open. "Theo!"

Unapologetic, Theo crossed his arms while Lucas set his faint smirk in place, reminding me of the killer I'd met on day one. He stared at Theo a moment, then turned to me with danger glinting in his eyes. "How much would you like me to tell him?"

"Tell him everything."

So he did. Lucas told the entire story—starting with what happened to his sister—from his point of view, and it was...eye-opening. He thought I'd lied about my name, that I used his sister's name to get in his head. He kept waiting for me to turn on him and analyzed every facet of our relationship until he fell in love. Then he stopped caring about my motives. Instead, he just wanted me to live.

His voice was atonal; his expression flat.

Hopeless and in love. That's what he was.

The story unfolded, and Theo's posture unwound. He had to snap his mouth shut when Lucas finished.

A needle of hope unknotted the icy fear in my chest. "I told you."

"I can't believe this." He leveled a stare at Lucas. "I'll have to discuss this with Williams. I don't know what she'll think."

"She'll think I'm a moron and he should die," I muttered.

Theo did not disagree. "I assume you're carrying weapons?"

"You assume correctly," Lucas said.

"You'll need to surrender them."

Lucas nodded.

"I'll have to place you under arrest."

I shot to my feet. "Theo—"

He raised a hand. "He is a colonel in the NSF, Sophia. He cannot roam free in Defiance headquarters. Not only is it against every rule and regulation within the *Articles of the Defiance*, but it's also for his safety. He wouldn't last the night, and that would put *you* in direct danger."

"I don't care—"

"I do!" both men snapped, and I wanted to growl at them.

Lucas stood and began removing the weapons from beneath his clothes. Theo's jaw clenched, but he came around the desk and took me into a gentle hug, putting no pressure on my back. "I'm so glad you're safe."

I hugged him back, burying my face in his chest. The faint scent of coffee clung to his shirt along with the familiarity of Theo, and I breathed in deep, relief squeezing out tears.

"Please don't hurt him," I whispered.

Theo sighed. After a moment, he murmured a soft, "Thank you."

I thought he was speaking to me until Lucas responded. "I didn't do it for you."

"Yes, well, you aren't the only one who loves her."

"You do a shitty job of showing it."

Theo released me, brown eyes boring into Lucas like knives. "Anything you want to say before I call in the guard?"

Lucas glanced between me and Theo, eventually deciding on the latter. "Don't let her be alone. She'll need someone, even if she says she doesn't. And a doctor needs to look at her back as soon as possible."

For the millionth time, tears flooded my eyes. He was about to be imprisoned, and still, all he cared about was me.

How had I earned this place in his life? This pedestal?

His gaze dropped to me. "No matter what happens, you're going to be okay. Do you hear me?"

Salt dripped down my face. "You said you'd stay with me."

"I will," he said, wiping my cheeks again. "Until I die."

I'd known this was coming, and yet I still hadn't believed it. When Theo called in the guards, panic took hold, but I tried to stave it off.

The two men froze in the threshold when they found Lucas. Their hands flew to their weapons.

"There's no need for that," Theo told them. "Colonel Scott is turning himself in. He will go peacefully."

Hesitantly, one man pulled out flex cuffs from his pocket. He approached Lucas as one would advance on a feral dog, but Lucas submitted to the zip ties without resistance. As soon as his hands were bound, my mind filled with images of him being marched to the gallows, and I lost it. I leapt at the guard. "No!" I screamed. "Take them off!"

Expecting it, Theo was quick to restrain me. "You can't!"

"Sophia," Lucas said, voice calm. "Look at me."

I met his steady gaze.

"Tall trees. Warm rain. Smell of cypress." His brows rose. "Picture it."

Wrestling from Theo's grasp, I threw my arms around Lucas's neck. I kissed him hard, in full view of all three men. The guards would probably spread this story through headquarters before I even fell asleep that night, but I didn't care.

Lucas's hands were bound in Defiance fetters, and I had no faith he'd ever be free of them.

"You promised," he whispered when I pulled back from the kiss. "You promised you'd let them take me. You promised you'd stay safe."

"I lied," I said with a sob.

"Sophia," Theo said with his stern general voice. "Let him go."

My hands obeyed even though I didn't want them to.

"Take him to the stockade," Theo said. "Back entrance. Private cell. Don't let anyone see you if you can help it. And his presence here is classified, soldiers. Do you understand?"

The soldiers nodded. "Yes, sir, General."

Tears flowed as I watched Lucas be taken from Theo's office, his gaze on mine until the last second. When he was gone, I crumpled to my knees.

"I'm going to call for Dr. Akbari," Theo said, though the words echoed from far away.

Lucas had been right all along. I was so sure that Theo would honor the exoneration, but did I really expect that Lucas would be allowed to walk freely amongst us?

"This is what is safest," Theo's voice murmured from somewhere above me. "Please trust me, Sophia."

But I trusted nothing.

Not even myself.

33
PUBLIC ANNOUNCEMENT

 *Loyalty isn't clean or moral. It's understanding the cost of the game and choosing to play it anyway.*

— THEODORE HARRISON

I hadn't risen from my kneeling position when Zara arrived in Theo's office, a puzzled frown on her face. When she saw me, her eyes widened, and she hurried to my side. "Sophia? I've been so worried." Her kind touch found my shoulder, but I couldn't gather the strength to look her in the eye.

"I'm fine," I said, voice dead.

"She needs an examination. She's been—ah—she's been in the company of Jack Miller for many days."

I squeezed my eyes shut against the thick silence that followed.

Zara's tone went careful. "Sophia, would you like to come down to the hospital wing? I can—"

"I just need you to look at my back," I said. "That's all I need."

She hesitated, but out of the corner of my eye, I noted her forced smile. "Alright. Let's go down and have a look."

Obediently, I stood and followed her to the door, but Theo stopped me before we left.

"I'll do my best, Sophia," he said.

I turned to meet his gaze.

"But I can't make guarantees. This isn't my decision."

Silent tears dripped, and I left with Zara at my side.

The hospital wing looked the same as always—cots lining the walls, some filled, some empty. Two of my fellow medics were on duty, and they jumped to attention when we entered, their wide eyes taking me in with disbelief.

"Reeves?" one of them said. "You're back?"

I turned to look at him, but I barely recognized his face. I was no longer close to any of the medics. Certain we'd inevitably die, I'd isolated myself from these people just like everyone else.

Clearly they recognized me, though.

"I'm back," I said. "Not sure when I'll return to duty."

He nodded, seeming to sense my skittishness. Both of them backed away, but their gazes followed Zara and me into the private examination area.

"So, your back?" Zara said, tone like velvet.

I slipped off my shirt, showing her the wound.

Her tender smile faltered as she took in the damage. She motioned me to lie on the bed, which I did with only a slight grimace.

Zara pulled a chair to the side of the bed. "It's—it's been well tended. I'm assuming Jack Miller is not the person who took care of it?"

"No."

She hummed. "How well did this person clean it? Do we need to worry about infection?"

"He's obsessive. He spent a lot of time cleaning and gluing."

Her fingers brushed my back. "Infection is still a risk. Are there... other injuries?"

I hesitated, thinking of the teeth marks and the bruises on my throat. "None that won't heal with time."

A few seconds passed, and she sighed. "I'm so sorry, Sophia."

The tears, which hadn't quite stopped, started anew. "You were there too. How'd you escape?"

"A few of us were on the third floor when the attack came. There were some hiding spaces they didn't check. I just... I got lucky. Only a handful of medics made it out. They were targeting the medical facility specifically. To weaken us."

"Aren't there laws against that?" I asked. "It's like...a war crime."

"I don't think they care, Sophia. We'll check on this every day, okay?" she said. "In the meantime, be careful with your movements and try not to put pressure on your back."

I nodded.

"Is there anything else you need from me?" she asked. "Would you like an internal examination?"

"It's not necessary," I said. "Nothing hurts but my back."

And my mind.

And my heart.

And my soul.

"Why don't you sleep in my quarters tonight?" Zara said. "It's no time to be alone, don't you think?"

I gave no argument and followed her to her small, private room in the sleeping wing, the bed big enough for two. She offered me pajamas, but I refused to remove Lucas's clothes.

Before I slipped into bed, Zara handed me a brown paper bag.

"You don't have to discuss it, but it's important you have this."

I peeked into the bag and froze.

Two white pills. Two labeled syringes. A pregnancy test.

My legs turned to jelly, and I sank to the bed. Why hadn't it occurred to me that this could happen? That there might be consequences?

The bag dropped to the ground, and I pitched forward, burying my face into my knees. The scent of Lucas filtered into my lungs—peppermint and incense.

Breathe.

In and out.

Zara kept quiet until the moment passed and I straightened. She retrieved the bag and handed it to me. "Would you like me to inject you?"

I nodded, standing so she could do just that. The medicine ached as it entered my muscle, and flashes of Jack Miller's hands around my throat were chased by the feel of his skin ripping open under my knife.

I hated him. Regret simmered that I hadn't done more to prolong his suffering.

With jerky movements, I accepted the water Zara offered and swallowed the pills.

Last, the pregnancy test. I held it between two fingers. "It wouldn't be positive this soon."

"When's your cycle due?"

Closing my eyes, I counted back. "A week or two? I'm not very regular."

She took the packet from my hand. "You can take it then, alright?"

"What if it's positive?"

There used to be medicines that could protect me. There used to be ways to keep me from bearing this burden. One by one, the NAO had destroyed them all...

Yet another thing they had taken.

Her hand landed on my shoulder, a gentle squeeze. "Don't think on that yet. Why don't you try to get some rest? It's late."

I slipped into bed, but my eyes wouldn't close. Behind each blink came memories I'd have rather purged from my mind.

My hands, cuffed to a bed.

Jack Miller's breath, hot on my skin.

Dozens of innocents, standing in a jail cell.

Lucas at a card table, gambling for my life.

With each one, my throat ached more, my heart beat harder, and I craved the embrace of the one person I couldn't have. I wanted Lucas the same way I wanted oxygen in my lungs. Only he could make this excruciating loneliness disappear. Only he could drive away the images stuck in my head.

But somehow, in some way, I fell asleep.

I woke with a jolt the next morning when Zara set a gentle hand on my shoulder. "Sophia, you need to wake up."

Blinking away the dark dream that submerged me, I sat up. "What's wrong?"

Her dark eyes skipped over my face, then dropped away. "Word has gotten out."

My movement slowed to a stop. "What do you mean?"

"There's a rumor we've captured one of the Blood Colonels," she said. "There's a lot of commotion, and they're saying you were seen… with him."

She asked no questions, but a tinge of dismay darkened her features.

"What do you mean by commotion?"

"They're… Well, they're calling for an execution."

I was calm—completely calm—but then terror attacked from all angles. It stole my breath, sharpened the pain in my back and deep in my soul.

I leapt out of bed and bolted for the stockade. Outside the hospital wing, the hallways were busier and louder than normal. Angry eyes followed my sprint down the corridor. My reckless hurry made the wounds spark to life as I charged down the stairs, pushing people out of the way.

"There she is!" voices shouted.

I ignored them.

The underground offices of the museum had been converted to holding cells for prisoners, all guarded by a single door now barricaded by five officers. To my surprise, I recognized one of them.

"Adam!" I shouted, and his gaze shot to mine.

I elbowed my way toward him, and the crowd's roar grew tenser by the second. I caught comments like *Let me have him* and *String him up*, and my heart thudded like it was pumping tar through my veins instead of blood.

Adam seized my arms as I tripped to the front of the crowd. "Jesus, Soph. Is what they're saying true? A Blood Colonel?"

"You have to let me see him," I said, breathless.

His eyes widened, and the surrounding officers glared at me like I was some sort of disgusting swamp creature.

Adam dragged me to the side and lowered his voice to a whisper. "What the fuck were you thinking, bringing Lucas Scott here?"

Once again, tears burned my eyes. "We had nowhere else to go."

He looked like he had a thousand questions, but his attention darted around the escalating mayhem. "They're going to crucify you for this."

"If they just knew—"

"I heard she's fucking him!" someone shouted, and the voices rocketed to full-on screams.

"Hunter whore!"

"Tie her up next to him!"

"Someone grab her!"

Hands clamped around my arms, pulling me away from Adam, and he morphed into the officer I rarely saw. In a deft maneuver, he flung himself between me and my attacker, and the soldier who'd grabbed me was immobilized with his hand wrenched behind his back.

"No one touches her!" he snapped. "She is one of us!"

"Not if she's fucking a Hunter, she's not," someone from the back bellowed.

Agreements tore through the small room.

"That is enough!" roared a voice from behind it all.

The horde went silent and leapt to attention, saluting their general as he made his presence known. Theo moved, and the crowd parted to allow him a path to the front. The officers guarding the stockade saluted him as he approached, including Adam, who blocked my view.

At the front of the crowd, Theo spun, his stiff arms behind his back as he addressed them in his military bark. "Everyone to the assembly room. *Now!*"

The soldiers fell back at once, all of them crowding the single staircase that led to the main level.

Once the room was empty, Theo turned to his officers. "You will not leave your station at this door. *No one* gets through. Do you understand?"

"Yes, sir!" they shouted as one.

Theo turned to look at me, still standing behind Adam.

"Lieutenant," Theo said. "Move aside."

After a beat, Adam dropped his guard. I met Theo's stern expression with a hard one of my own. "Let me see him."

Theo's jaw worked. "What were your orders, officers?"

"No one gets through!" they said as one.

"That includes you, Reeves," Theo said. "Get upstairs."

My teeth ached with how hard I clenched them, but I followed Theo like a scolded puppy, glancing back once to the door that led to Lucas. Adam's warm gaze latched onto me, and he winked.

Once I was alone with Theo, he side-eyed me. "Williams has been alerted to the situation. She'll be here as soon as she can. Scott will need to stay in lockup until she arrives."

"When can I see him?"

He sighed. "Let's get through this first, alright? I've called everyone for the announcement. I want you to wait out of sight."

We arrived at the stage entrance of the auditorium in short order. The low hum of voices vibrated beyond the closed door. Theo stationed me in the small antechamber to the side of the stage before heading inside. The crowd quieted at once, and Theo's heavy steps trod across the wood.

"Listen up, soldiers," he said, his voice carrying through the room easily. "You've heard the chatter, and I'm here this morning to make a few things clear. Today, I bring you news of a significant development. Last night, five Blood Colonels were killed in a high-risk rescue mission."

Three seconds of silence preceded a cacophony of shouts, gasps, and whoops of joy. The noise quickly died when Theo continued on: "It's an enormous victory. Monumental. And the assassin, the one who risked his life to rescue one of our own, was none other than Colonel Lucas Scott."

Hisses and boos followed this announcement, and I peeked around the corner to see Theo raising his arms to silence the room.

"I know what you're thinking," Theo said. "He's the worst of them all. Cold-blooded killer. Hunter. NAO supporter. What you don't know—what I'm telling you now—is that he's ours."

A stilted hush.

"For the past year, Lucas Scott has been working for the Defiance. Our advantage? It's due to him. Their armory? Him. Lily Wyatt? Him. The Ohio River? Him. The prisoner rescue? Him. Every trap they walked into and every convoy we intercepted were all thanks to him."

Dead silence.

"Half of you wouldn't be here if it weren't for him," Theo said. "That is a fact."

"So what?" a man said. "A few nuggets of information and he gets a full pardon?"

"Scott gave us more than a few nuggets. He fed us intel straight from the source. He and his contact took on more risk than any of you ever have. Yes, he killed. He wore their uniform. He bled for them. *But he made them bleed more.*" Theo paused, and his gaze flicked toward me, where I stood within the dark of the antechamber. Tension in the room drew taut as a piano wire. "When you're fighting evil like the NAO, the war won't be won with clean hands. It'll be won by people willing to do the unthinkable."

The crowd shifted with grumbles.

"His capture last night was not part of the plan," Theo said, now pacing the stage. "It happened fast, and now his cover is blown. His contact brought him here for asylum."

"He's an executioner!" someone shouted. "He shouldn't be sheltered! He should be six feet under!"

"We don't bury our knives while they're still cutting for us!" Theo barked. "Loyalty isn't clean or moral. It's understanding the cost of the game and choosing to play it anyway. Lucas Scott has been our most valuable player for months. It speaks to his skill that you didn't know it."

Whispers rippled through the room.

"I stand by Lucas Scott," Theo said, "and when the Prime Delegate arrives, I will tell her as much. He will be afforded his tribunal, just like the rest of the defectors. Until that time, he will be kept in a safe place."

The whispers ratcheted to low rumblings.

"Lucas Scott is now placed under my protection, as is the woman who served as his contact. They now exist within the bounds of a command sanctuary."

I almost gasped. The *Articles of the Defiance* weren't lengthy or even comprehensive, but the laws regarding those under the protection of the Defiance were absolute. Placing us under a command sanctuary meant no one could touch us. If they did, they faced dire consequences—likely execution.

"Reeves was his contact, right?" a voice spat, full of disgust. "No wonder she has handprints around her throat..."

Theo ignored him. "Anyone who chooses to engage against them will be charged with assault, failure to obey a direct command, interference with a high-level intelligence asset, and breach of a command sanctuary."

"That's bullshit!" someone yelled, and Theo's gaze cut his way.

"Stand, soldier."

I couldn't see into the crowd, but all sound fell away.

Theo shot a look at someone out of my view. "Sergeant, take this soldier into custody."

Shuffling and whispers provided a backdrop to the soldier's panicked apology.

"Insubordination will not be tolerated," Theo said, hard as stone while the soldier was taken away.

"But General, sir," someone said from the front row, and I recognized Isaac Johnson, Devon sitting just beside him. "He's a Blood Colonel. The man is dangerous."

"He is," Theo said, "but not to us. Not anymore. Should anyone care to test that theory, I'll warn you he's been given full permission to defend himself if attacked." He paused for a long moment. "Anyone who feels they can win in a knife fight against Lucas Scott is welcome to try."

34
SNAKE PIT

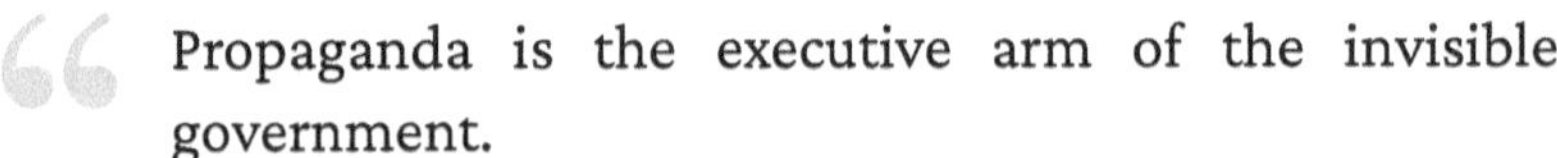

> Propaganda is the executive arm of the invisible government.
>
> — EDWARD BERNAYS

"Open up, Sophia!" a voice yelled, banging on the door to Zara's quarters.

Her wide eyes darted to mine. She'd just arrived back from Theo's announcement and hadn't even had a chance to ask questions. I'd beaten her here by only a minute or two.

"Sophia, it's me!" the voice said. "It's Dev."

My tense shoulders dropped an inch, and I cracked the door. Devon stood outside with Isaac, and I widened the opening to let them in. Crossing my arms, I prepared to be chastised. Instead, Dev caught me in a soft hug.

"Are you okay?" he asked. "I was so worried."

Sudden tears clogged the back of my throat, so I had to force the words out with a wobbly voice. "I'm—I'm fine."

Another knock, softer this time, pulled our attention to the door. "Soph?"

Zara opened the door for Adam. He slid inside, filling the room to the brim.

"Aren't you supposed to be guarding the stockade?" I asked.

"I switched shifts so I could come tell you congratulations," he said with a sly smile. "You've officially been outed as a Hunter lover."

My very soul sagged to the floor. "Not all of them. Just...him."

"*Lucas Scott,*" Adam said with a small laugh. "No wonder you wouldn't tell me who it was."

Isaac, who'd remained quiet in the corner, eyed me with barely disguised revulsion. "I've seen him kill people for an audience."

I sank to the bed. "He isn't what you think he is."

Isaac puffed out a breath of disbelief.

Devon shushed him, then turned back to me. "How long have you been his contact?"

"I've been meeting him weekly since March."

"Ah." Zara took a seat beside me. "That makes a lot of sense."

I bumped her shoulder with mine. "I knew you were curious. I couldn't tell anyone. It made everything hard. But every week I expected him to be a cold-blooded Hunter, and every week, he just...wasn't."

"Where have you been, Soph?" Adam asked, more serious now. "You've been gone for a week. The quarantine house... We thought you'd been captured."

I stared at my fidgeting hands in my lap and shoved the words through my mouth. "I was. Jack Miller tied me to his bed."

Silence fell, and one by one, they averted their pained gazes, all except Adam, whose compassion shone through those brown eyes. He opened his mouth.

"I don't want to discuss it," I said before he could speak. "*Ever.* Not ever. Do you all understand me?"

Each of them nodded.

"And Scott," Devon said. "He...saved you?"

"Yes. He came, and he killed them all." I paused, remembering a crucial detail. "Except Paul Kingston. I killed him. I killed him because I found out he killed Tekqua."

Adam's mouth went slack. "Tekqua's *dead?* I thought she was in the House."

I shook my head. "Lucas told me they killed her before he could get her there."

Hand to his chest, Adam fell back against the wall, his gaze distant. The others closed their eyes, grief washing over us all, but none of them had been as close to Tekqua as me and Adam.

"I wanted to tell you sooner," I said. "I'm sorry."

He shook his head, eyes bright. A long moment of silence passed before Zara asked, "Will you tell us about him? Help us understand."

Her face was earnest and open, and I glanced at the rest of them, each with similar expressions, even Isaac, skeptical as he was.

So I told them.

I started with our first meeting in March and glossed over all that had happened since then. It was such a relief to finally say it out loud, to unburden myself of these secrets I'd held so close. They remained quiet, though at times, one or another of them opened their mouth as if to ask a question, then closed it again.

By the end, my gaze was frozen on my knees. "I'd appreciate if none of you repeated that story."

Slowly, they nodded.

"So, it's...real?" Devon asked.

"Very real. And now he's imprisoned for saving me."

"You know *saving you* is not why he's in the stockade," Isaac said. Dev smacked his arm.

"We have a plan," Adam said. "Right, Johnson?"

Isaac cleared his throat. "Right. Ambrose and I are assigned the early morning shift to guard the stockade. We may be able to sneak you in to see the prisoner."

I gaped at him. "Really? Why would you do that for me?"

Isaac made a face like *I don't know*, but Adam laughed as if I were silly. "That's what friends do, Sophia."

"Are we friends?" I asked. "If so, I haven't been a good one."

Face a mask of sympathy, Devon dropped to his knees in front of me. "You lost your entire squad and both your parents, and you still found it in you to hold my hand every time this one—" he hooked a thumb at Isaac "—was sent on a mission."

"And you shared my cleaning detail even though you could have thrown me under the bus every time I tried to get out of it," Adam said with a laugh.

"And you saved my life," Isaac said, referring to the gunshot wound I'd treated months ago.

"That wouldn't have killed you," I argued.

"You've been grieving," Adam said. "We understand. That's all we're saying."

I couldn't hold his gaze. "We've all lost people. There's no place for grief in war."

"War is nothing but grief, Sophia," Zara said, covering my hand with hers.

My throat grew thick, but I looked her in the eye when I said, "I can't lose him too."

Her expression fractured.

"We can get you a few minutes with him," Adam said. "That will have to be enough for now."

I nodded, unable to speak, hoping my gratefulness was clear when I mouthed *Thank you*.

ACCORDING TO ADAM'S PLAN, I was to sneak away from the sleeping wing at four the next morning, but that was a more arduous task than I originally imagined. The night guards patrolled the hallways every few minutes, and unlike Lucas, I'd never been a quiet walker.

Dressed in head-to-toe black, I smiled at Zara as she sleepily wished me luck, then slipped from the room just as one guard turned the corner. I hugged the wall, tiptoeing as silently as possible. Another guard's flashlight bounced along the marble floor around the next corner, so I ducked into an alcove, hiding behind the statue of a naked woman. When he passed, I hurried to the next alcove, heart thudding.

One by one, I bypassed the guards with strategic sprints and stops, but when I reached the last stretch before the main stairs, I ran into two guards chatting in low voices.

I squeezed into a small space behind a column and waited for them to disband.

"Do you believe this shit about the Blood Colonel?" one of them asked. "Why aren't we just chopping the fucker's head off?"

"Right? We could send it to Haynes in a gift box."

The first guy laughed, then sobered. "Do you really think he helped rescue those prisoners?"

"I don't know, man."

"My mom was freed in that mission. She would have died."

His friend hissed. "She's lucky. He killed the ones we didn't save, you know."

"True. Fucking bastard."

Annoyed, I pulled my switchblade from my bra and hurled it down the opposite hallway. It landed with a bouncing series of clicks on the marble, and the soldiers leapt to attention.

"What was that?"

Both of them hurried to check it out, and I darted for the stairs, grateful they were carpeted to cushion my steps.

When I finally reached Adam standing guard at the stockade door, he tapped his imaginary watch. "You're late."

"I got held up. Can we still get in?"

Adam nodded. "Johnson's guarding his cell. You can have five minutes at most." He pulled out a ring of keys and slid one away from the rest. The door opened with an eerie squeak, and he motioned me inside. "Go straight to the end, then turn left. You'll see it."

My feet were moving before he'd even finished speaking. Every nerve ending sparked with anticipation, and I tripped over the worn carpet beneath my feet. The ghost of the offices this space used to be still existed—desks and unused computer equipment—but portions had been gutted, doors and walls replaced with prison bars. Crude track lighting had been installed at the edge of the walkway. The resultant blue gloom lent the place a spooky vibe, but at least none of the holding cells were occupied.

I ignored the bleakness, the memories of being thrown into a jail cell myself, and hurried down the corridor.

At the end, I turned left, pausing to take in the officer standing guard outside a lone cell, the furthest one from the entrance.

Isaac rapped his knuckles on the bars. "Scott. You've got company."

I stumbled toward the cell, the shadows obscuring the black shape moving within. I fell against the bars at the same time Lucas wrapped his hands around them.

"Sophia," he hissed. "What the fuck are you doing down here?"

The dim light gleamed over his face, underscoring the new bruise beneath his eye, the split in his lip, the blood dried under his nose. I reached through the bars, careful as I trailed my fingers over the damage. "What did they do?"

His head tilted just slightly into my touch, but when he spoke, he addressed Isaac. "Why did you let her in here?"

"I don't fucking know," Isaac muttered.

Lucas pressed my hand into his cheek, and days of stubble scraped my palm. "You're painting a target on your back being down here."

Rolling my eyes, I turned toward Isaac. "Open the door."

His eyes widened incredulously. "Absolutely not."

"Isaac!"

"It's *Lieutenant Johnson*, Reeves," he said, all exasperated, as if he knew I'd never call him that.

"Open the door, or lock me in there with him."

"Fuck, no. You're lucky I agreed to this at all. If my captain knew—"

I spun away from him, disregarding the rest of his diatribe. "Are you okay?" I whispered to Lucas.

"I'm more concerned about you at the moment."

"I'm fine." Pressing right against the bars, I sighed in relief when he dropped his forehead to mine. "Who did this to you?" I asked.

He shrugged. "Doesn't matter."

"Was it Theo?"

"No. But his visit hurt more than the black eye."

I pulled back to look into his eyes. "Why? He told everyone what you've done for us. He's trying to get people on your side."

Lucas's mouth lifted in a bitter smirk. "Yes, he was very clear on what he's done and how grateful I should be for it."

Huh? What did that mean? Was I missing something?

Lucas reached for me, his hand soft as it drifted over my cheek. "If I'd known what I was leading you into, I never would have agreed to come here."

I leaned closer. "What do you mean?"

"Harrison says your Prime Delegate wants me dead, Sophia. She never wanted anyone to know the Defiance deigned to work with me. Uncle Theo took a gigantic risk in outing me." His thumb stroked down my throat. "I suppose I should call you my savior. If he hadn't been so scared Williams would kill both of us to keep her secret, he would have handed me over to the wolves right away." He paused at the notch between my collarbones to write his name.

My hands curled around the bars. "What? What are you even saying, Lucas? Theo is trying to protect you."

"Yeah, for *you*. Williams didn't just want me dead, Sophia. Harrison suspects she planned to dispose of you, too. She was going to make it like the entire thing never happened, like the Defiance won without any help. Keep her hands nice and clean." He huffed out a humorless laugh. "We left a den of Blood Colonels just to walk hand-in-hand straight into a snake pit."

My breath whooshed out of me. "That can't be true. She—she wouldn't do that."

He pushed away from the bars, his bright eyes staring into mine with pity. "Come on, Sophia. You know better than anyone what the Defiance is willing to sacrifice to get what it wants. The NAO may be corrupt, but at least they're honest in their evil."

I glanced at Isaac, but he was looking away from us, his lips pursed.

"Harrison's trying to keep you alive," Lucas said. "Outing me as a good guy is his Hail Mary, but it won't work."

"It will! Once people understand—"

"No, Sophia. No one is ever going to look at me and see a good guy. And by aligning yourself with me, you've dragged yourself straight into the firing line."

"No, that's—that's not—"

Lucas reached through the bars with one arm—the arm without a bullet hole—and gripped my neck. "I didn't risk everything getting you out just to watch your own people slaughter you. You will go back upstairs and tell them I tricked you, that I'm just as evil as they think I am. Convince them you're not on my side. It's the only chance you have to keep from going down with me."

My mouth hung open as I took in his sincere request, spoken through lips bloodied by *my* people. "You want me to...forsake you?"

"I want you to protect yourself, Sophia, like you promised. *Please*."

"I'd rather die."

His hand fell away from me, and he sighed, defeated. "You will. If you keep on this path with me, they'll kill you for walking by my side. Why are you so determined to die with me?"

"I-I'm not," I said, hitching over tears I hadn't even realized had fallen. "I'm determined for you to live with me."

Silence descended, and we stared deep into each other's eyes. His bruised face was sliced by the shadows of the bars between us, the iron far stronger and more enduring than the promises he'd whispered in stolen moments under piles of blankets or scribbled in a note buried deep in my heart.

Grief is like snow...

That resolution on his face... He still fully planned to die. He'd walk gladly into his fate so long as I was safe when he did it.

My voice hitched. "Why don't you want to live?"

"I would live for you if I could," he whispered. "But this is what I deserve, sweetheart. Never forget that."

The tears came in earnest as that grief-snow drifted around me, icing me to something barely alive. "You can't die," I said with a sob. "I need you."

"The part of you that's me will never die, Sophia," he said, voice soft and coaxing as he caught the bars in his bruised fists.

Air snagged in my throat. "I won't do this without you, Lucas. What's the point of this without you?"

"*Living* is the point. We need to say goodbye."

"No, Lucas. You said you'd stay!"

"I said I'd stay *until I die*," he said. "The Defiance wants me executed. I am *dead*, Sophia, and you can't come with me."

"We can still—"

His hand darted out and gripped my shirt, dragging me right against the bars. His lips landed on mine, hard and possessive at first, but then softer...sweeter...slower.

Like a goodbye.

After a handful of heartbeats, he jerked away and retreated into his cell. "Take her," he said without looking at me. "And don't let her come back."

I tried to shove Isaac off when he took my arm, but the wounds on my back went electric with pain. "No, stop!"

"Patrol is coming soon, Soph. You have to get out of here."

"Lucas—"

The aquamarine flashed my way, haunted and torn. "I love you. Please take care of yourself."

Isaac's iron grip on my arm wouldn't relent, but I fought anyway, my gaze on Lucas's until Isaac dragged me around the corner.

"Please," I said, trying to pull him off me. "He doesn't know what he's talking about. Let me go."

"You can argue about it later. Get out of here before someone catches you."

The familiar panic piled lead right into my lung space.

I couldn't breathe.

By the time we reached the main door, Adam was pacing, and I was gasping for air.

"Shit!" Adam said. "What happened?"

"She's having a panic attack," Isaac hissed. "Help me calm her down."

Adam got right in my face. "Remember your forest, Sophia? What was in it again?"

"T-tall trees."

"That's right, and it's raining?" He looked at Isaac for help, but the other man only raised his hands.

"Hell if I know! This was Tekqua's realm."

"It smells like cedar, I think." Adam wrapped his arms around me, heedful of the injury on my back. "It doesn't matter. Just picture something peaceful."

As my breathing slowed, Isaac gave Adam a stilted version of what happened.

I wiped my eyes when Adam released me. "H-he's such an a-asshole."

Adam chuckled, but his gaze was wary, studying my face. "Get upstairs before you're caught, okay?"

Nodding, I turned toward the stairs with weighted feet. I made it back to Zara's quarters with only one sighting by a guard, easily explained away by pointing to my bladder.

She sat up from her place in bed when I entered. "How'd it go?"

"I—um—" I scrubbed my face. "I don't know. He needs medical attention, though. Would you be willing to see him later today?"

Her brow notched, and she swung her legs over the side of the bed. "Of course. What about you? Are you okay?"

My lips rolled inward as I fought the overwhelming urge to sink to the ground and cry. "I'm fine," I squeezed out. "I just need to sleep, I think."

She nodded and pulled back the covers for me. I slipped beside her, then stared at the ceiling until the sun came up, too afraid of what I'd see if I closed my eyes.

35

STAR-CROSSED

 A man who is good enough to shed his blood for the country is good enough to be given a square deal afterward.

— THEODORE ROOSEVELT

Days passed, and the only updates I received about Lucas were from Zara. Theo had permitted her clearance to treat his wounds, and she was the only one besides himself and his guards allowed entrance to the stockade. She spent half an hour with Lucas every day, but she never had much to report.

"He doesn't say a lot," Zara said after the third day. "But his gunshot wound is healing well."

A sigh of relief escaped me, and I relaxed into our shared bed. "Did you tell him what I said?"

Zara's mouth tensed, almost as if she was trying not to smile. "He said, *Tell her love isn't an excuse to act like an idiot.*"

I rolled my eyes. *That* was his response to me saying I wouldn't give up?

Zara perched on the bed beside me. "He's…"

"A dick?"

"A little irreverent."

"He wears cynicism like cologne."

With a smile, she moved toward a pile of medical books I'd been sorting through earlier, straightening them back into a line on the bookshelf.

I watched her for a time, wallowing in the jealousy that she'd just seen and spoken to the man I loved while I wasn't sure if I'd ever receive that privilege again.

"I'm so scared I'll lose him," I whispered.

She paused to look at me. "Don't give up hope, Sophia. If he truly is anything like the man you've described, then the two of you together are a formidable force. You may find a way through this yet."

I shoved the covers off my legs and stood, pacing the small space. I was so tired of hiding in this room, but every time I stepped out, I received death glares and catcalls. Theo had ordered a twenty-four-hour guard at my door, which meant even if Lucas was willing to see me, I'd be unable to sneak out.

I was no longer assigned shifts in the hospital wing. Dr. Grayson explained it was for my own safety, but really, soldiers didn't want to be treated by hands that had willingly touched a Blood Colonel. My only respite was my friends, who continued to visit Zara's quarters nightly. Even Isaac eased his discomfort after a few shifts guarding Lucas's cell.

"What changed your mind?" I asked him quietly while the others chatted about something else.

"I was thinking about what he said to you the other night," he said, attention focused on Dev. "He's sacrificing himself for you. When you told us the story, I thought he must have duped you, but… he's really planning to die to protect you."

My head fell back to rest against the wall. "He loves me."

He nodded in agreement. "It's something I understand. Something I respect."

I watched his profile, his gaze never straying from Dev, a desperate kind of fear in his eyes.

"It makes him human," he murmured.

I took his hand, and we spoke nothing more of it.

A FEW DAYS LATER, Adam escorted Zara and me to the hospital wing so Dr. Grayson could peel the glue from my back.

"Hello, Sophia," he said with his usual smile. "How are you feeling?"

"I'm fine," I said, but at his skeptical face, I added, "Just nervous."

He gestured toward the cot.

While I lay face down, Adam stood guard just past the curtain. None of my fellow medics had greeted me, but I hadn't made eye contact with anyone.

As Dr. Grayson worked, I clutched Zara's hand—more from fear than pain. Whatever the scars looked like under the glue, that's how they'd be forever.

I met Zara's eyes and whispered, "Distract me."

She forced a smile onto her pretty lips and told an inane story about a patient she'd had long before the war started who gave her one ripe banana every single day because he felt potassium was the key to eternal life. We then lamented for long minutes about how much we missed fresh fruit while I pretended the burning in my back didn't exist.

"If the war ever ends, the first thing I'll do is bake a banana cream pie," Zara said, and I giggled.

"I'm finished, Sophia," Dr. Grayson said. "Would you like to see it?"

Butterflies tickled my insides as I stood, and Dr. Grayson led me to a mirror hanging in his office. He gave me a hand mirror. Taking a deep breath, I angled it to see my back.

The lines glowed pink and shiny, thinner than I imagined, but standing out stark against my skin. Miller cut the emblem large enough to be seen from a distance. Crude and uneven, it spoke of pain and hatred.

After several minutes of staring at my back, I let my shirt drop. I forced down the memories crowding my mind. When I looked up, I met the sad gazes of all three. Adam was the first to speak. "One day, I'll pay for a massive tattoo to cover it, okay?"

I managed a weak smile.

"Sophia!" a voice shouted from the entrance to the hospital wing.

I poked my head outside Dr. Grayson's office to find Devon hurrying my way.

"What is it?"

"The Prime Delegate is here," he said, breathless. "They're interviewing him."

A fresh shot of adrenaline killed the residual sting in my back, and I darted for the door.

"Wait, Sophia!" Adam called, his heavier steps following me.

My shoes squeaked across the marble, drawing all eyes my way, but I didn't care. I skidded to the main stairs and pounded down them, only to stop short at the open door to the stockade.

The guard there rolled his eyes at me. "They took Limpdick upstairs an hour ago."

Adam caught up to me. "You're supposed to wait for me."

I ignored him to address the guard. "Did they go to Theo's office?"

"How the hell am I supposed to know? I'm just glad he's gone."

I spun, and Adam hustled with me back up the stairs.

"What are you going to do?" he asked. "You can't just barge in."

But that was exactly what I planned to do. We rounded the decorative stairs again and again until we reached the top floor, and I froze at the large guard unit blocking the hallway to Theo's office.

"Holy shit," Adam muttered.

I scowled. "Do they really need this many guards? He's just one man."

"One man who speaks knife as his native language," Adam muttered under his breath.

I approached the unfamiliar guards. They stood at attention, fully outfitted with ballistic helmets, tactical vests, and rifles that reminded me of scorpions—black and sharp and deadly.

They looked like the kind of soldiers who had opinions—unfriendly ones—like they didn't just expect to kill, but wanted to. Something in their eyes recalled unwanted memories of Jack Miller.

"I'm trying to see Harrison," I said, wishing my voice was stronger.

"No one in or out," a soldier said. "Prime Delegate's orders."

I looked past them to the abandoned hallway, wondering what was happening to Lucas beyond Theo's closed door.

Adam took my arm. "Come on, Sophia."

Despite the guards' menacing presence, I refused to go far. I strode to the opposite hall and paced, shooting far too many glances toward Theo's door.

"You're giving me a headache," Adam said after ten minutes.

"What do you think they're talking about?"

"The weather."

I glared at him.

He threw his hands up. "How am I supposed to know?"

"You know everything."

He sighed and lowered his voice. "I think Williams will want to bleed him dry of information. If he's smart, he'll bargain his life for anything he has."

Alarmed, I shot my gaze to Theo's door again. Lucas wouldn't bargain for his life, but he *would* bargain for mine. He'd give them everything if he could guarantee my safety, including a glamorized execution for the Defiance.

He'd waste his only shot protecting me.

As I fought the powerful urge to charge through the wall of soldiers to reach him, Theo's door cracked. My heart stuttered, and I craned my neck to see. It looked as if someone was speaking to the guard just outside. Then it closed again, and my spirits sank.

The guard marched down the hall. The line of soldiers parted to let him through, and he stopped not five feet from where I stood. He met my gaze, face expressionless. "Reeves. General wants to see you."

I snuck a glance at Adam. His mouth had turned down into a rare, worried frown, but he tried to screw it into a smile for me. "See? Your patience paid off. I'll wait right here, okay?"

Swallowing against a desert-dry throat, I followed the guard to Theo's office. I'd been there dozens of times, but this was the first time I'd faced such existential dread.

What would I find on the other side of that door?

The guard let me in, then shut the door behind me. Three pairs of eyes landed on me. The only ones I cared about looked away just as quickly. Lucas sat in the chair before Theo's desk, his hands cuffed behind his back. The bruise beneath his eye had faded to a morbid rainbow of pink and green.

It was the first time I'd really seen him in more than a week, and my heart went haywire. I tripped toward him, pulled by his magnet, and set gentle hands against his jaw so he'd be forced to look at me.

"I'm so mad at you," I said.

His ocean eyes darted back and forth between my own. "You're just mad I'm the first person who has battled your stubbornness and won."

"Miss Reeves," came a smooth feminine voice. "Please have a seat."

I obeyed at once, meeting Nia Williams' dark gaze with what I hoped was at least a measure of deference. Sitting at Theo's desk, she looked from me to Lucas and back. Seated behind her was Theo, his gaze downcast.

"This is interesting," she said.

Lucas's voice took a sharp edge. "Is it?"

Williams flashed her dazzling white teeth. "I thought the rumors would be exaggerated. Seems I was wrong."

Theo shifted in his seat, declining to grace any of us with his attention.

"Miss Reeves, we were just discussing Colonel Scott's future with us."

I chanced a quick look at Lucas. His mouth was set in a hard line.

"Does that mean he *has* a future with us?" I asked.

Williams tilted her head back and forth. "It depends."

"On what?"

"Many things," she said, "but we have some items to discuss."

I eased into my chair, sweaty palms gripping the armrests like I might fall.

"First, I'd love to hear your side of things," she said. "I've heard Harrison's, and now I've heard Scott's. Let's see if you have anything to add to the narrative."

Lucas's scorched-earth glare didn't bother Williams, but it had me chewing on my lip. "Me?"

"You."

In my silence, she set her clasped hands on her legs and waited. Afraid of what I might give away, I stuttered out the most basic form of the story I could, emphasizing the positive impact Lucas effected not just on the Defiance, but on me.

I went to him expecting horror. He proved me wrong at every turn. I fell in love. He saved my life. Several times.

When I finished, she nodded, digesting. "Fascinating."

"Um... why is it fascinating?" I couldn't help but ask.

"Have you ever read *Romeo and Juliet*, Miss Reeves?"

I blinked at her.

She crossed her legs. "The recklessness and drama, the forbidden love. It hits all the right notes."

"All the right notes for...what?"

Williams smiled, then abruptly changed the subject. "Scott here states he still has information to give us."

"Yes..." I glanced his way, though he ignored me.

Her brow perked. "He's offered it in exchange for your safe relocation to the refugee camp."

"What?" I snapped, glaring at Lucas. "No."

"I told him you'd say that," Theo said.

Williams's keen gaze intensified. "I declined his offer. I don't feel that is the best place for you."

I tried to reason through her strange tone, but couldn't figure it out.

"She wants you where she can use you to control me," Lucas said, sharper than a razor.

Williams smiled like his anger amused her. "He hinted he has a path across enemy lines. He has *also* hinted you are the only thing of any importance to him. Are you familiar with *quid pro quo*, Miss Reeves?"

Eyes wide, I reached blindly for Lucas's shoulder. I'd nearly forgotten this detail, the piece of information I'd withheld from the Defiance because it meant compromising Lucas's position. Lucas knew how to get us to DC, and now that he'd escaped the Hunters, yielding that information held no risk.

I'd concealed it to protect him, and now it might be the thing that saved his life.

"You can't have it," I said, tripping over the words in my eagerness. "Not unless you give us something in return."

"Ah. I see you *are* familiar with *quid pro quo*."

"I want his exoneration. Theo gave me a document promising him immunity, but I want you to sign it as well."

Lucas's incredulous stare burned across my face, but I ignored him in favor of Williams.

Her interest piqued. "Exoneration is a big ask for a Hunter with such bloody hands."

"He's on our side. He's one of us. He gave you information that turned things around for us. Why do you still want to kill him?"

"None of this is a matter of desire, Miss Reeves," she snapped. "A live execution of one of his infamous Colonels will send a message to Haynes that we are not weak. It shows our soldiers that we are making strides. It proves to the world that we will not tolerate the NAO's evil. That is a valuable display of power. If he can offer me something more than mere safe passage through Virginia..."

I wanted to strangle her. "What more do you want?"

Her expression, her body, her words... Everything sharpened. "What I want is an end to this war, Miss Reeves. I want my country back. If he gets me Haynes's head on a spike, *then* we can talk about a full pardon."

I jerked back from her ire, but didn't miss the hunger in her words. "Are you serious?"

"He will lead the mission to assassinate Richard Haynes."

Lucas's face scrunched into an incredulous mask.

Williams sliced her gaze his way. "You are an excellent strategist and a skilled killer. Don't you want to end the man who killed your father?"

Lucas merely stared, blank-faced.

"That's a suicide mission!" I said. "Absolutely not!"

Williams relaxed into her chair and addressed me. "I'm afraid it's non-negotiable. If he wants to live, he'll complete this mission."

"Assassinate the Commander," Lucas said, tone lifeless.

"You kill him, and not a single person would question your pardon."

He released a soft, embittered laugh, his gaze on his lap.

"You can pick your team from our most talented soldiers," Williams said. "You succeed, exoneration is yours."

He rolled his eyes. "That's all? Just a little murder before break-fast, and I'm free?"

Her smile twisted. "Well, there's one more thing, actually."

Chills slithered over my skin.

"I recently met with a Canadian reporter," she said.

My gaze darted to Theo, who grimaced.

"He's developing a story on the atrocities of the NAO, and he wants an exclusive," she continued, peering into my eyes, into my soul.

My mind whirred, trying to figure out what that had to do with me. "Okay?"

"You'll tell him your story."

"My...story?"

"Do you remember what I said about *Romeo and Juliet*, Miss Reeves? Everyone roots for the star-crossed lovers."

"Romeo and Juliet both die in the end."

"Do they?" she asked, unfazed. "Pity."

A headache blossomed. "I don't understand."

"You tell your story and show everyone the mutilation on your back, then explain how an enemy officer saved you from his own brutal regime because he fell in love with you. People will eat it up." Williams crossed her legs and set her clasped hands on her knee. "If we package your love story inside the truth of what the NAO is doing to its people, they will rally right when we're moving in on the Commander."

I snorted. "You're saying the world doesn't know what's happening here?"

Her lips pursed. "The NAO has a way of spinning their propaganda. It's artful, really, how they've painted us as criminals while their human rights violations go unheard."

I imagined trying to tell my story to a camera, and a wave of nausea washed over me. "And if I don't agree?"

Her joyless smile spread goosebumps down my spine. "It's my assumption that you don't enjoy seeing your colonel in pain?"

My blood turned to ice. "I won't let you hurt him."

Williams smiled calmly. "Then you agree to do this interview."

I said nothing. Lucas's glare grew savage, and his breathing deepened. The muscles of his arms bunched with the effort to break out of the plastic around his wrists.

Eyeing us both, Williams leaned forward, her expression darkening. "This is war, Miss Reeves, and we edge closer to extinction every day. If your love story hits the way I think it will, your matching scars will go viral. Imagine the outrage. They'll save us right as Scott delivers Haynes the killing blow, proving himself a hero. The country will need a new leader, and we will be right there—the champions of justice and love. It's perfect."

A hysterical laugh ripped through my throat imagining it all: the impossibility of Lucas succeeding in assassinating the most protected person on the planet, the unlikelihood of my broken, pitiful story making any difference at all, the sheer pipe dream of winning this thing…

We'd never succeed.

Still, she'd found the only weapon sharp enough to cut us both— each other. If we refused to help her, Lucas and I would be tortured, then marched to the gallows together. I'd stare into that aquamarine until our last moments.

This was a losing game.

Theo shifted again, his eyes pleading. "Sophia, please."

Swallowing down the roiling acid in my stomach, I nodded. "I'll do it."

There was no other choice.

Lucas's gaze cut to me. "Like hell you will."

"For you, I will."

"You're going to let them sit you in front of a camera to tell the entire world how you fucked a fascist murderer, and he let you be carved up by his own people? Could you even do it without having a panic attack?"

"A panic attack could garner sympathy," Williams said.

"Fuck off," Lucas snapped. "She's a human, not a story you can sell. You treat her like she's expendable."

"Because she *is*."

He paled. "You're supposed to be the good guys. This is how you treat your own?"

For the first time, Williams appeared a tad uncomfortable. "She volunteered for everything. She was never commanded or coerced."

"Then what is *this*? Is this not coercion?"

"The choice is still available to her." Her voice stayed calm, but tension radiated from it.

Lucas clenched his bound hands into fists behind his back. "You know this isn't a choice for her. If you continue to threaten her life—"

"I'd be very careful how you finish that sentence, Scott," Williams said. "I have soldiers outside with strict orders to end her life if you cross any lines."

My lungs constricted.

Lucas's stare went deadly, promising pain in a way I'd only seen when he looked at Jack Miller.

Theo turned wide eyes on Williams. "What?"

Williams ignored it all to focus on me, as if I were the linchpin holding this whole thing together. "If your story gets us aid, and Scott is successful in DC, we could win. That emblem on your back is a battle cry, Sophia. I need it."

Lucas spun toward me, his voice lower, quieter. "You're letting her use me as a blade against you."

He was the most dangerous one she could have found, poison-tipped and pointed straight at my heart.

"It's just a story," I whispered without looking at him.

"This will hurt you, Sophia. If they succeed in what they want, this will follow you for the rest of your life."

"It was always going to follow me, Lucas," I murmured. "The only difference is that now people will know why."

He exhaled and dropped his head, defeated.

I turned to Williams, her mouth stretched into a Cheshire cat smile. "I want one more thing."

Williams raised a brow.

"I want him out of the stockade."

"Oh?" Williams said, surprised.

"Yes, find somewhere safe to keep us both. Guarded at all times. I live, he is pardoned, then we'll help you."

Somehow, her smile widened even further. "I believe we have a deal."

36
NOT FINE

All citizens of childbearing capacity are obligated to fulfill their reproductive duties to ensure the survival and expansion of the State.

—NATIONAL STABILITY ACT, ARTICLE IV

After a long discussion, Theo agreed to let us stay in one of the abandoned rental cabins at the far edge of the property. The scary guards escorted us from the basement emergency exit and through the barren winter forest at gunpoint. Theo didn't remove the flex cuffs from Lucas's wrists until we were safely ensconced inside the cabin.

The three of us stood in a triangle.

The space was small and cold, with natural pine walls and cowhide furniture. A loft held a single bed at the top of a steep set of stairs.

Theo cleared his throat. "These facilities are used for covert teams to move on and off the property more quickly. I'll make sure the others remain empty while you're here. Protection detail will change every six hours. I'll assign the same soldiers who agreed to your guard duties. They're trustworthy men."

I nodded, but Lucas raised a skeptical brow.

"I'll do my best to keep the knowledge of your whereabouts hidden, but be careful. Sophia, you may leave *only* with an escort." He eyed Lucas. "You are not to leave for any reason. You are under house arrest."

"Yes, Uncle Theo," Lucas said, glib as ever.

Theo's eyes narrowed. "Williams and I will be in contact when we need to. Planning for the mission starts tomorrow. It will take place here. The reporter will arrive within a few days." He sighed, his gaze dropping to his feet.

"Thank you, Theo." I stepped closer, and he opened his arms for my hug. "I wish you would have told me the full story."

"I was looking for a solution, but I didn't want to get your hopes up. This was the best I could do." He lapsed into silence.

Releasing him, I took in the space again and shivered. "Is there heat?"

"It's on solar, but it can get chilly." A few more seconds passed, and he nodded stiffly. "Right. I'll leave you then."

My small smile went unnoticed by him as he retreated into the icy February air. As soon as the door shut, Lucas locked it. His attention wandered to the windows, and he looked as if he wanted to board them up. I drifted his way, distracting him.

His gaze hooked on mine, and his entire body stilled. He lifted his hand, knuckles brushing my throat. "What now, Juliet? These violent delights have violent ends."

"It's not the end yet," I whispered. "We found a small path."

"A treacherous path." He dropped his forehead to mine. We were both right at the edge of losing everything we had, and I wasn't certain how to move forward. Each step had too much gravity, too many ways to fall, and the Defiance had backed us into a narrow corner. There was no way left but forward—into the snake pit.

"At least I got you out of jail."

He set a soft kiss on my lips. "I won't sleep unless we cover the windows."

Without complaint, I assisted in scooting a bookshelf to cover one and a large painting to hide the other, then settled onto the couch while he slipped into the shower—his first in days. Not long after we finally relaxed into the space, a knock pounded at the door.

Like a wolf, Lucas lunged to protect me, knees straddling my hips on the couch, one arm holding a knife toward the door.

"Where the hell did you get a knife?"

"No one ever checked my boots," he said, predatory gaze fixed on the door.

"They *knocked*, Lucas. They aren't here to attack us."

He looked down at me, and a drip of water from his hair landed on my cheek. "Will you ever stop being naive?"

"Get off me! If you won't answer it, I will."

He unfolded himself from his crouched position, but didn't lower his weapon as he swung the door wide.

Devon stood there smiling, but his hands flew up once he spotted the knife. Isaac jerked Dev behind his body, and beside them, Adam grinned.

"Can we come in, Soph?" Devon asked, peeking out from behind Isaac.

"So much for our whereabouts remaining hidden," Lucas muttered, making a show of disarming himself, tossing the knife to a nearby table.

"We're your guards, asshole," Isaac said, pushing into the house. The others followed.

I locked the door behind them, and the five of us stood in strained silence.

Devon stared at Lucas without blinking. "You're Lucas Scott."

Lucas scraped a palm down his face while Adam broke into awkward laughter.

"Who are you people?" Lucas asked. Demanded, really.

"Think of us as the Sophia fan club," Adam said, and I rolled my eyes at him.

"They're my friends," I said. "That's Devon. And you know Isaac and Adam."

"We're just here to remind you that you have people in your corner," Adam said.

"*He's* in your corner." Isaac pointed at Dev. "I happen to love him."

Lucas chuckled, all bitterness and spite. "We have more in common than you think, Johnson."

Isaac's mouth twisted, but warmth bubbled in my chest, and I shot a smile Devon's way.

"So was I right?" Adam asked. "About what they wanted?"

I nodded. "Extortion."

He winced. "I wish I'd been wrong."

"See?" I said to Lucas. "He's on our side."

He threw me a pitying expression. "He's on *your* side, Juliet."

"Yours too. I'm officially Adam." He reached out a hand, and Lucas fixed his diamond-bright gaze on that invitation. His hesitation was likely only evident to me, but as he raised his hand to shake Adam's, Lucas's rolled sleeve revealed the Brotherhood Crosses branded into his arm, pink and shiny.

Adam missed a beat, but fell right back into character, pasting a friendly expression on his face. "I was there for the first attempts to cross the Ohio River. We hemorrhaged soldiers. Your intel was priceless. Saved a lot of lives."

"The prisoner rescue too," Isaac said, voice low and begrudging. "That was—"

"Game-changing," Devon said.

Lucas scratched his neck, then peered closer at Adam. "I think I recognize you. You show up on a lot of combat missions. You fight like a grizzly bear."

"Ha. Yeah. I've seen you too. I *avoid* you."

Lucas hummed and looked at me. "See? That's what sane people do. Avoid."

I glared at him.

Suppressing his laughter, Adam turned for the door. "We'll leave you alone. I know it's been a rough week. I'm taking the first guard shift."

Dev kissed my cheek while Isaac sped away without saying goodbye.

"Don't worry about him. He's on our side," Dev whispered. "He's just grumpy about it. Dr. Akbari said to tell you hi. She'd like to check on you both tomorrow and bring your stuff, if that's okay with you."

I nodded, and in a whirl, Lucas and I were alone again. Tension leaked from his body.

"This is going to be a long few days," he said.

Reaching for him, I slipped into his arms, right where I belonged, and set my head against his chest. "At least we're together."

He kissed my crown. "At least you're safe."

That night, I sank into the softness of the musty bed while Lucas lay beside me, reading a book he'd found in a bedside drawer. With him at my side once more, I was finally safe to explore the awful memories that had threatened to drown me for days. I examined them one by one, then purged them from my mind.

When I remembered the way Jack Miller's whiskers scratched my skin, I imprinted the image on photo paper in my mind and set fire to it, letting it curl and blacken. When I thought of the pain, I etched the memory into metal and melted it. I destroyed them all, hoping to permanently disrupt the neural pathways in my head. I had a headache by the time I finished and settled back into the pillows.

I turned onto my side. Lucas wasn't reading beside me like I thought. He regarded me with deep creases between his brows, his eyes bright with concern. "You've been staring at the wall without moving for twenty-seven minutes."

"I'm fine."

Dark, tousled waves fell into his eyes as he picked at the abandoned book in his lap. He started to say something, but stopped himself. He massaged the bridge of his nose. "Sophia…"

"Yes?"

"It's okay to not be fine. Especially with me."

I shrugged. "You're probably right. But it doesn't matter because I'm fine."

Shuttering his expression, he opened his arms. "Come here."

I crawled next to him and laid my head on his chest, letting him sign his name on my skin until I fell asleep.

As promised, Williams and Theo arrived the next morning with a posse of guards. To my ire, I was excused from the meeting and asked to keep myself busy for a few hours. Isaac escorted me back to the main building, and I offered my time to Dr. Grayson, who smiled.

"Of course, Sophia. We just got in some supplies that need stocking."

Isaac sat in a corner while I went to work. Two other medics were on shift, but the three of us stuck to stilted conversation that remained firmly within our shared duties—wishing for better supplies, dreading the deadly wounds, reminiscing over particular injuries.

Neither of them mentioned Lucas.

Neither of them even looked me in the eye.

At some point, Zara brought me a bag of my effects, mostly clothes, but a few books and Lucas's pager were stuffed in as well. She added some clothes for Lucas, and I thanked her through a throat thickened with grateful tears.

"You holding up?" she asked.

"I'm fine," I said, smiling.

She squeezed my shoulder. "Let me know if you need anything. I'm going to come by later to check on his injuries."

Isaac and I returned to the cabin a few hours later to find only

Lieutenant Salinas remaining at the door. Of all our guards, he was the one I knew the least.

"Lieutenant," Isaac said with a salute, relieving him of duty.

Inside the cabin, Lucas was brooding.

"What did they say?" I asked, throwing my bag onto the table.

He glanced up from his hands in his lap. "They want this mission done soon."

My stomach dropped, and I sank onto the couch beside him. "How soon?"

"Couple of weeks."

A couple of weeks.

Just a couple of weeks left.

At most.

I wanted to beg to go with him, but the ask was ridiculous. I was untrained, unskilled, loud and reckless. The mission would be harder and less successful if I accompanied him.

Still, I didn't want to say goodbye.

I also didn't want to discuss it.

I curled into his side, and we sat like that for a long time, holding on to each other as long as we could before they ripped us apart.

A few days later, I was searching through my bag for a pair of sweats when I came across the note I'd moved to my bedside drawer weeks ago.

Grief is like snow...

After Lucas had found it on my broken body the night I'd nearly bled out in his closet, I decided it was safer to keep where a Hunter couldn't find it if I was captured. Now that Lucas's cover was blown, it didn't matter if someone discovered it. I tucked it right back into my bra where it belonged and continued rifling through the bag.

I froze as my fingers brushed a familiar pink foil packet. Lucas sensed my stillness and was at my side in an instant.

The letters on the packet were so friendly and welcoming, as if taking a pregnancy test was some sort of joyous occasion.

Silence descended over us until he slid a finger over the edge of the packet. "You haven't taken one yet?"

I shook my head.

"Why not?"

I blew out a shaky breath. "What if it's positive?"

A beat passed before he murmured a soft, "It could be mine."

I thought back to that morning of hopelessness, when I'd been so desperate to keep any piece of him that I let him spill his seed right where I shouldn't.

If I was pregnant, yes, it could belong to him. But the timing was too close. I couldn't know for sure, and we had no way to stop this from happening to me.

No surgeries. No meds.

The NAO wanted women to fulfill their reproductive duties regardless of the circumstances. I was just another casualty of their blithe cruelty.

"I don't want to take it," I said, loathing the tremor in my voice.

His hand made gentle circles on my back. "Just pee in a cup, Sophia."

"No."

"I'll do the rest. All you have to do is pee."

I turned accusing eyes on him. "Don't make it easy."

He pulled me into his arms and trailed velvety kisses down my cheek. "You aren't alone," he said before he reached my mouth. "I'm with you. Until I die."

Irritated by their frequent appearances, I huffed at the tears that spilled. His mouth caught mine in a kiss deeper than any we'd shared since the incident. I dropped the packet to the floor in favor of throwing my arms around his neck.

The kiss was thorough, but careful. He made no advances. He asked for nothing more. He touched me like I was something precious, as if hurting me was sacrilege.

When he pulled away and handed me a cup, a full minute passed before I dredged up the courage to fill it. My bladder wouldn't cooperate.

It didn't want to know either.

But finally, I managed it.

After dropping the glass onto the counter beside the toilet, I fled the bathroom without a backward glance, taking the steep stairs two at a time. I dove under the covers of our bed, hiding in the dark. Several minutes later, his near-silent footsteps followed me. His weight sank into the mattress beside me. I squeezed my eyes shut, but my hand slid from beneath the covers and he took it.

"It's negative."

I sobbed.

Negative.

Absolute proof of my freedom.

The wounds on my back had closed and turned pink. The bruises had faded. My reproductive tract lived to see another day.

"Lucas?" I murmured from under the covers.

"Hmm?"

"I'm not fine."

"I know, sweetheart."

37

WATCH IT BURN

Any assault upon a person under the protection of a command sanctuary shall be treated as an attack against the Defiance itself, and punished without mercy.

—— THE ARTICLES OF THE DEFIANCE

Days passed, and Lucas fidgeted with nervous energy, pacing our cabin, reorganizing the scant decorative objects on the shelves, drumming his fingers across surfaces like the keys of his piano. Every morning, he took a private meeting with Theo and Williams while I was asked to piss off. Eventually, his meetings transitioned to the main building so he could run drills with his new squad. Adam and Isaac were selected for this covert mission, but none of them would tell me how much danger was involved.

"Obviously that means it's a lot," I said to Lucas one night while we ate dinner with Adam at our small table.

"You'll be fine," he replied, eyes on his plate.

"I'm not worried about me, Lucas. Clearly I'll be fine if I'm sitting at home waiting for you to come back."

Adam chuckled, but he declined to engage in the argument. Lucas said nothing.

"So there's a chance you'll come back, right?" I finally asked in a small voice.

Unsmiling as he met my gaze, Lucas tore off a piece of bread and chewed. "What do you think?"

I crossed my arms at his flippancy. Adam's smile died.

Lucas's bare smirk emerged. "Tragedies only hook an audience if there's suffering, sweetheart. There's a reason Williams is pushing the fearful passage of our death-mark'd love."

I hated that he was right. The crippling sensation of being used like this, our broken hearts manipulated to please an audience... It made me want to hit things.

"Please stop quoting that goddamn play, Lucas."

He leaned forward and touched his lips to mine. "Thus with a kiss I die."

As February plodded into March, the weather remained frigid and blue. My boots crunched in the dry grass as I trudged back and forth from the main building to our new home, cheeks red with the cold snap.

Around lunchtime a week into our cabin lockdown, I was heading back to Lucas with a paper sack full of food. My escort— Lieutenant Salinas today—hung back several steps. Deep in my own thoughts, I only noticed the other sets of footsteps when something squeezed my arm.

The powerful grip unleashed a vortex of fear. The sack in my hand dropped to the ground as a force slammed me back against a tree. Pain exploded across my barely healed back.

My scream tore through the air, sending winter birds fleeing.

A hand clamped over my mouth.

My lungs stalled as I took in the two men restraining me, hostility gleaming in their eyes. Behind them, a giant of a soldier had taken Salinas in hand, though it didn't escape me that my guard did nothing to break free or help me.

The man whose hand covered my mouth stared down at me with hate and revulsion, but also a tinge of thrill.

I whimpered behind his hand and squeezed my eyes shut.

I'd seen a look like that before.

On Jack Miller's face.

Images assaulted me.

The cuffs had been so tight. They'd burned my skin raw. The sandalwood invaded my senses. He held my mouth shut when I cried so I could smell every note of that cologne.

I thought of Lucas's voice. *Breathe, Sophia.*

A quick shot of air made it through my nose, but the panic wouldn't recede. I scratched at my captor's hand, but his compatriot snatched my arm and wrenched it against the tree.

Subdued.

Stuck.

Silent.

I can't breathe.

Trees.

"... brought him here ..."

I can't breathe.

Rain.

"... the kind of woman you are ..."

I can't breathe!

Cypress.

"... whore to a Hunter ... should put you out of your misery ..."

Something sharp pressed into my throat.

No sound. A bare flash of movement.

The hand ripped from my face, and I slid down the tree trunk to suck oxygen through my mouth. The man who'd silenced me pitched to his knees, clutching his neck. The knife he'd held to my throat dropped to the dry grass. Lucas stood behind him, bloody blade in hand.

His gaze touched my face for only a second before he turned on the others. Expression honed into that cold-blooded mask, he advanced on my attackers.

"Wait," I said, trying to stand, but my voice was weak and breathless.

Adam appeared in my peripheral vision, breathing hard as if he'd sprinted to us. Salinas struggled against the giant's hold.

Lucas canted his head like a cat, staring down the second man who'd held me against the tree.

"Sophia, get behind me," he said, his tone nothing but ice.

I scrambled to my feet, but instead of hiding, I leapt in front of Lucas. "If you kill him, it will only make things worse."

Lucas's predacious stare homed in on the man, who now had his own weapon raised. "No one touches you and lives. I don't need permission to protect you."

I glanced at the soldier at our feet, now dead in a pool of his own blood. He'd threatened to kill me, and now he was dead. Everyone had been warned, and he attacked anyway.

Stepping closer to Lucas, I wrapped my hands around his wrist, trying to lower his weapon. "I'm okay, Lucas. Let's just go back."

The giant holding Salinas snorted. "Only a pussy-ass bitch takes orders from his woman."

Adam moved closer to him, his combat knife at the ready.

Lucas flashed a glance the giant's way. "You sound like a Hunter."

The man's expression melted into rage.

"Lucas, please," I murmured. "Come on."

His gaze dropped to mine. His free hand cupped my cheek.

I leaned into it. "Please."

Without looking away, his arm jerked. The knife whipped through the air and buried in my attacker's upper thigh.

I cringed as the man screamed. While he wrenched Lucas's knife from his flesh, Lucas spun me behind him, raising another blade.

How many did he have?

"You can walk away with a flesh wound," Lucas said, "or you can join your friend. Your choice."

The soldier took in his fallen comrade, then the man restraining Salinas, still held off by Adam. "You'll die before this is all over, fuck-er," he spat at Lucas.

"I know," Lucas said evenly. "I forfeited my soul to the pits of hell, and I'm watching it burn." A few predatory steps had the man backing away. "I have no morals left, so if you come at her again, I will bleed you dry and enjoy every second. Do you understand?"

The man's wrath remained caged behind a hateful expression, but he nodded.

"You're alive right now by her grace," Lucas said. "You have ten seconds before I change my mind." He stayed motionless as both soldiers retreated, their watchful gazes on Lucas until they were far enough to run.

I tried to draw in air through an iron band wrapped around my chest. Fine tremors wracked my body, and a rapid pulse throbbed in my back.

I stumbled backward, hand to my chest, tears breaking through. Lucas appeared before me, face swimming through darkness. He was talking, but the words didn't make sense, echoing to me like he screamed them underwater.

"They attacked me," I whispered. "M-my own p-people."

"Breathe, Sophia," he said.

Trees.

My knees turned to jelly. He caught my weight.

Rain.

We sank to the ground.

Cypress.

"Take her," said a voice outside my bubble. "I'll deal with this."

Suddenly, I was weightless, my body swaying with Lucas's quiet steps as he carried me through the forest. I fisted his shirt and closed my eyes. "Stay with me."

"You know I will. Until I die."

When he set me down atop something soft, my body felt as if I'd run a marathon. I blinked around, recognizing our bed, the A-frame of the ceiling, the book he'd left on his pillow.

Sitting beside me, he brushed his hand across my cheek, fingers drifting down my throat. We remained that way for a long time, my heart rate slowing with each letter he drew on my pulse.

"He said he wanted to put me out of my misery," I whispered after minutes of silence.

"You don't have to worry about him, okay?" A seriousness crept into his eyes, bled into his expression. "You deserve so much better than this."

"You saved my life again."

"You save mine every day."

I slipped my hands up his chest, clenching slowly on his shirt. In an unhurried, even pull, I dragged him closer, and then my lips were against his.

The kiss was halting at first, careful, like neither of us was sure this was the right move. When he pulled back a touch, I cupped his face in my hands. "How did you know I was in trouble?"

His brows drew together. "You screamed my name."

"I—I did?" I remembered screaming, but not his name.

It tracked, though. Lucas equaled safety, and my subconscious knew it.

He nodded and kissed my temple, my cheek. "You call, I come. They hurt you, they die. They were warned."

They *were* warned, I thought. Theo told them Lucas and I had been placed within a command sanctuary. Adam would make sure the other two were charged as the Articles of the Defiance decreed. The soldier Lucas had left with a hole in his neck had intended to kill me. He deserved what he got.

I pulled Lucas back to my mouth. "I love you. Do you know that?"

"You've mentioned it," he said against my mouth.

When my hands wandered up his neck to tangle in his hair, he deepened the kiss. He'd been so vigilant with me since he'd rescued me from Miller, hesitant to do anything that might trigger bad thoughts, but now I sensed the bridle in him, the desire that pushed right to the edge of his control.

"Say you love me," I whispered.

His mouth trailed along my jaw. "Love is too soft. I'm obsessed with you."

Longing crashed with the force of an earthquake, and I clutched on to him the way he liked, as if nothing short of the world ending could tear him from my arms.

"Show me," I said when he dipped his mouth to the pulse in my neck.

His movements slowed, and his gaze met mine. "Are you sure?"

"Yes."

The blacks of his eyes expanded while he studied my face. The distance between us disappeared, and when his mouth finally touched mine again, I sighed in relief.

Worried I wouldn't be able to have this, that sex had been poisoned for me, I moved without hurry. What if certain touches brought it all back?

But his caress was tentative, mindful, and he undressed me with the kind of reverence one would use to unwrap a holy object. Soft lips wandered down my body, lingering first in my favorite places, and then his.

After long minutes of leisurely kisses, his hand drifted between my legs, and that first wash of sensation shimmered through my nerves, pulling a moan from my throat. I'd almost forgotten how good he felt, how perfectly we meshed. His chemistry reacted with mine to create something transcendental. When the pleasure hit, it extracted me from my body for endless seconds to set me in a place where pain didn't exist.

Afterward, I caught my breath while nuzzling into his throat, pressing open-mouth kisses across his stubbled jaw. He lay back as I pushed on his shoulder, then let me climb on top of him. Bracing my weight on his chest, I straddled him and sank down.

His fiery gaze flickered down my body, but mine riveted to his face. Flushed cheeks. Aquamarine thinned to a strip around his dilated pupils.

Even though he'd seen it dozens of times, my naked body still lit him on fire. A buzz shot through my stomach at the inherent power I held over him, all that danger and lethality lying docile beneath me.

"Lucas." His attention returned to my face, and I smirked.

He licked his lips. "I think you like watching me burn."

I did like that.

I liked it a lot.

His hands slid up my thighs, squeezing, but he let me go at my own pace. Taking my time, entranced by the adoring ocean in his eyes, I fell deeper into the bottomless sea between us.

In the end, I needn't have worried. Even when it was wild and unrestrained, sex with Lucas had never been just sex. A burning ribbon connected us. With his hands warm and sparkly against my skin, it was nothing like when I was abused and forced.

I kept my gaze on his until I came apart again, and afterward, I luxuriated in his touch while he kissed his way from my fingertips to my toes.

"Lucas, when did you realize that you loved me?" I asked, threading my fingers through his hair.

His kisses slowed to a stop, and he stretched out next to me. "That day you nearly killed me. You had your blade at my throat, and you were searching my face. Do you remember that?"

I did. The agony in his eyes that day had shredded holes in my hate for him. I'd known even then that this man had layers, but I had no idea how many.

Still, that hadn't been a good day for us. "You fell in love with me when I threatened to kill you?"

He flashed a smile, there and gone again. "You weren't searching for a reason to do it. You were searching for a reason not to. You were looking for my redemption."

I pushed to my elbow so I could see his face.

His thumb grazed my jaw. "You decided I was worth saving despite it all, and...that was it."

"You still tried so hard to convince me you were evil."

"I *am* evil." He smirked and rolled so my body was pinned beneath his, just as he liked it. His mouth brushed mine. "You're easy to love despite your stupidity."

I gasped when he kissed me and tried halfheartedly to buck him off, but soon, I gave in to the worship in his touch.

"You'll pay for that remark," I said when he let me breathe.

"Yeah? Show me how."

38

THE INTERVIEW

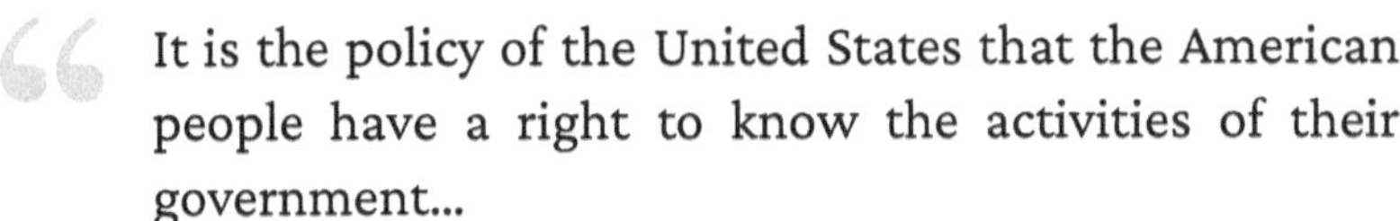

> It is the policy of the United States that the American people have a right to know the activities of their government...
>
> — FREEDOM OF INFORMATION ACT, 5 U.S.C. § 552

As I expected, the two soldiers who survived attacking me were charged as Theo had warned and locked in the stockade. Adam said the story of the man Lucas left dead in the forest had spread throughout headquarters, and he suspected we wouldn't have any more trouble.

"The dude must have been hit on the head a few too many times," Adam said with a timid laugh. "Only a fool would come at you knowing Lucas Scott had offed five Blood Colonels for you."

I considered telling him Lucas's total body count from protecting me was far higher than that, but the reminder of how many people had tried to kill me in the last year was hard to stomach.

I settled on a weak smile, and Adam had clapped me on the shoulder, commiserating.

Just one week before Lucas was meant to lead his covert ops team to assassinate Commander Haynes, the reporter arrived. The Prime Delegate sent me a summons to meet her at once, and my soul crumpled.

"You don't have to do this," Lucas whispered, sensing my dread.

"She'll find a way to punish us if I don't."

His mouth tensed into an angry line, and he didn't reply.

Adam escorted me through the forest, and I met Williams where she instructed—in a small room near Theo's office. Her smile when I arrived made my fist itch to find her nose, but I restrained myself.

I wasn't the only one giving an interview, apparently. Twelve others had volunteered, mostly escapees from imprisonment.

"Before we record anything, he wants to review each of your stories in private," Williams said. "You'll be last."

She extended an arm toward a bench, where a couple of others sat with fidgeting hands and pale faces. I perched in the corner and proceeded to ignore everyone and everything.

My forest served as my pastime.

One by one, the others were called back. They each spent a quarter hour with him, then went on their way, their faces tinged gray as they fled his presence. When it was my turn, I stepped into a small room with a decorative fireplace on one side and a large landscape oil painting on the other.

With a welcoming smile, Williams introduced me to the reporter.

Logan Bergeron, hailing from Toronto, looked like a college girl's wet dream. He had auburn hair parted roguishly off to one side, enough stubble to seem as if he'd just risen from a busy night in bed, and glasses he kept pushing up his nose when he'd toss a shy smile at the floor.

Charming. Coy. Obnoxiously trustworthy in his tweed jacket and plaid button-up.

I hated that I liked him.

"Sophia's the one we spoke about," Williams said.

Logan's eyes sparked with interest, and he looked at me with a new intensity.

A hunger.

"She'll tell you the whole thing," Williams continued, "and we'll decide which parts are best to share."

Logan offered me a seat. The three of us settled into chairs arranged in a triangle, and he rested his elbows on his knees. "My primary goal here is to get the truth out there. The NAO needs to be stopped, both here and abroad, and if we can strengthen the Defiance, we may just be able to do that. Human atrocities tend to rile people up."

My fingers plucked at the fabric of my pants. "Alright. What do you need from me?"

"The bald truth," he said.

Williams offered me another smile. "Sophia, why don't you start your story at the beginning?"

I took a deep breath and told them every tiny detail, unedited and without tact, and in far greater detail than what I told Williams.

How I'd gotten involved in the war in the first place—dragged along by my parents and their friendship with Theodore Harrison. My bond with Tekqua. The missions that resulted in the deaths of my friends and parents, and subsequently, the destruction of my humanity. How I'd considered death to escape the pain. I described the Lucas that didn't exist, the heartless Blood Colonel who killed at will. I detailed every reprehensible sin he'd committed, all the innocent lives he'd taken.

As my story evolved—shifting from fear and distrust to embraces and whispered promises of *until I die*—it became evident I fell in love with my mortal enemy, and a spark appeared in Logan's eyes.

After showing him the scars on my back, I resettled, and he stared at me for the longest time, chewing on his lip. "You're right. This is the exposé that will clinch it."

"Wait. You still think you can use that?" I asked with a laugh.

"Your story is a wartime fairytale, love. People will drool."

I gave him a hard stare. "The *edited* version."

"Well, yes."

For the next hour, Logan Bergeron and Nia Williams revised my life, removing the ugly bits. They erased my deep bouts of depression, my thoughts of suicide. They extracted Jayden entirely. My relationship with Theo was wholesome and intact.

They changed my entire affair with Lucas. Except for the kiss we'd shared to keep from being discovered, our physical relationship didn't start until after he'd saved me from that knife wound. He didn't execute anyone during our time together. The ring I wore symbolized his commitment to me more than his certainty that he'd die, like a wedding ring worn on the wrong finger.

I was never taken to Registration. They didn't like the idea of Lucas letting me be taken from him. Instead, he happened upon me at poker night. He didn't plan to kill them, but when he was caught helping me escape, we had to fight for our lives.

He was accepted as a Defiant without issue after that. We found safety with Theodore Harrison's forces.

They whitewashed my life, and I didn't care. Nia Williams held our safety in her hands, and I'd say whatever she wanted me to say. That evening, however, lying in Lucas's arms, I considered the irony. They wanted my story to bring us help, knowing if I told the truth, the world might not give it.

Political manipulation at its finest.

The next morning, I woke early. My only stipulation for filming was that Lucas would be nearby, so when the time came, Isaac escorted us to the main building.

People eyed Lucas, but his novelty appeared to have worn off. Or perhaps the story of my attack in the woods gave people pause because they stayed far away. We meandered toward the assigned place—a room in the southwest corner of the building, draped in sheets to hide the unique architecture. A table had been set up outside with beverages, and several of the interviewees dawdled around it.

Lucas eyed the meager spread with a raised brow. "How thoughtful," he said dryly.

Spotting me, one of the other interviewees volunteered a smile and handed me a cup of coffee, which I took despite a roiling stomach.

She held out a dish filled with white granules. "Sugar?"

Sugar.

The mug slid from my fingers, ceramic shattering and hot coffee splashing over my legs.

My lungs froze. Heart pounded.

The sandalwood. I could smell it.

You like the way that tastes, sugar?

No.

Just like that, sugar.

Stop!

"Breathe, Sophia!" The words echoed from far away.

Let's play a little game, sugar.

My hands shook as I touched Lucas's face, the only clear part of my vision.

"You have to breathe," he said. "In and out. Come on."

The room darkened, his face fading from view...

Something soft cushioned me. Voices nearby spoke in low tones, but my eyes stayed resolutely closed.

"...don't know what she'll do when we leave."

"She's strong. She'll be fine." This from Adam.

"Will she be fine if we don't come back?"

My stomach cramped, and I groaned, blinking my eyes open. Lucas had taken me to one of the common areas near the interview room, now empty. Isaac stood in the doorway, guarding us.

Adam smiled when my eyes opened. "Hey. There she is. You okay?"

"I'm fine," I rasped out.

Lucas sat on a table next to me, elbows on his knees, features harsh. "A single word took you back there. I could see it in your eyes, the terror and pain. You're going to let a stranger dig into that? Sell it to the world?"

"I can't even remember most of it."

"You remember enough."

I held a hand out. "Help me up."

He pressed his lips into a thin line and did as I asked.

I took his face in my hands. "I have to do this, just like you have to go on the...mission. We have one chance at both of us surviving, and this is it. Let's just get through it, okay?"

After a beat, he sighed, and the three of us went back to the interview area.

Just like before, I was the last to be interviewed, and by the time they called my name, the butterflies in my stomach had turned to clawed bats and my insides felt ravaged. Inside the room, two chairs sat facing each other beneath three blinding lights, and it occurred to me that thousands, maybe millions of people would see this interview, and I hadn't worn a drop of makeup in years. I hadn't even considered what I should wear for such an occasion.

What a stupid thing to care about. The camo pants and black tee would be fine.

Logan invited me to sit. I crossed my legs at the ankles and placed my clenched hands in my lap.

My breath caught in my throat.

His smile went soft.

And it went on for hours. Anytime I stumbled on one of my fabricated answers, Logan would help me until I got it right.

The questions increased in detail as we dove further into my time with Lucas. He teased out the broken elements and made them romantic. Luke's overprotectiveness became a product of love instead of fear. My attraction to him was less sexual and more fanciful, like a schoolgirl crush.

Logan began to ask specifics of our conversations. He focused on the poignant moments, like the conversation we had about psychological scars or Lucas's theories regarding the NAO's hatred. He liked me to quote Lucas's constant words of advice.

Never believe someone just because they're saying something you want to hear.

Play the player, not the game.

Never attack in anger. You will always lose.

Look for the details beside the obvious.

Grief is like snow.

Logan glossed over the injuries I'd obtained on that failed rescue mission, choosing to focus on what happened when I woke.

"We argued over my safety," I said. "He felt the Defiance was unnecessarily placing me in dangerous situations. He made me stay with him until I healed."

"Did he tell you then that he loved you?" Logan asked.

"No, he never said it. He thought he was going to die, and he didn't want it to haunt me."

"What did he say instead?"

I swallowed. "I would ask him to stay with me, and he'd..."

"Yes?"

"He'd say, *Until I die.*"

Logan smiled.

The interview continued, and I idealized the possessive, desperate months we spent together, lost in sex and eviscerating fear.

He asked about the ring on my finger, and I recited the story I'd been coached to tell.

"And before you left him that day, did you say anything?"

"I asked him to stay with me."

"What did he say?"

A beat.

"Until I die."

Logan's eyes glinted behind his glasses, and he continued on with his questions. They became harder to answer, especially as he asked about the fall of the quarantine house. He wanted me to describe how it felt to fear for my life, to know there was no hope of escape.

"Were you caught?" Logan asked.

"Yes."

"By who?"

"One of the Blood Colonels," I said. "Jack Miller."

"What did he do?"

"He—he hit me until I blacked out."

"And when you woke? What happened then?"

I blinked several times in silence as his face dissolved in my vision, giving way to things I'd suppressed far back in the nether regions of my mind.

"Don't worry. You'll like this."

"Doesn't that feel good?"

"Sophia?" came the faraway voice.

I couldn't breathe.

"What happened when you woke?"

Stars winked into view, and I lurched from the seat, upending the chair. "Where is he?"

I was already stumbling toward the door. I fumbled with the knob, trying and failing to draw air. When the door finally wrenched open, I called Lucas's name, begging for help from the only person I trusted to give it. He appeared at once, reverent, reminding me how to breathe. I locked into his aquamarine.

"That's it," he said. "Breathe."

I nodded. The world came back into focus by degrees, ebbing and flowing like a tide.

"You want to keep going?" he asked once my breathing calmed.

"No."

"You don't have to do this. I'll take you away right now. I'll take you anywhere."

I managed a small smile as the fantasy of us in some cozy cabin far away from here bloomed in my mind. But it was just that...

A fantasy.

"It's almost finished," I said.

He dipped closer. "I'm right outside, okay?"

My fist clenched on his shirt. "You'll stay with me?"

He pressed a kiss to my temple and whispered in my ear, "Until I die."

Nodding, I took a breath and turned back toward the interview room only to find Logan and the cameraman watching us. Blood rushed to my face, but their expressions were grim.

Logan's brow wrinkled. "Can you continue?" His curious eyes landed on Lucas, who hardened into the killer as their gazes clashed. Lucas said nothing, but the cold-blooded hatred went unmasked.

Logan paled.

"Let's just keep going," I said, pushing Lucas away.

Logan dipped his chin.

I left Lucas in the hallway and shut the door behind me. We re-situated ourselves so Logan could continue with his line of questioning.

"You ready?" he asked, straightening the cards in his hand.

I nodded.

"So what happened when you woke?"

I took a breath. "I don't remember a lot of it. I try not to think about it."

He nodded and teased out my answers while my gaze trailed the intricate patterns on the ceiling. I tripped on words like *teeth* and *rope* and *strangle*. Panic opened like a tap, pressure building higher with each question. Before it overflowed, he redirected me.

"How did it feel to be back with Lucas?"

"It felt like...coming home."

"Were there any particular words you said to each other?"

I hesitated. How many times would I have to say this? "He wanted me to leave him. To save myself. I reminded him that he promised he'd stay with me. That he wasn't dead yet."

"What did he say?"

"He still thought he wouldn't survive. He worried he was putting me in danger."

"And?"

"And I made him promise again. I couldn't stand the thought of abandoning him."

"How did he respond?"

I was silent, staring at Logan.

"What did he say, Sophia?"

"He said... 'I'll stay with you. Until I die.'"

His smile broke free, like I'd discovered the answer to a complicated riddle he'd pondered for ages. I prickled all over while conflicting feelings rose inside. Pride at having pleased him battled with an irresistible sense that I'd sold my soul to a devil waving a Defiance flag. An *American* flag.

But it would be worth it.

If we both lived, it would all be worth it.

39
CONSEQUENCES

A well-regulated Militia, being necessary to the security of a free State, the right of the people to keep and bear Arms, shall not be infringed.

—2ND AMENDMENT, U.S. CONSTITUTION

Logan Bergeron must have been desperate to get my interview out there because the edited version aired three days later, all by itself during prime time. The other interviews would be released at a later date, but mine was *special*.

Someone had to do some fancy tech work in order for us to watch them live, as Unified News certainly wouldn't be airing it. Theo invited Lucas and me to view privately with himself and Williams. We settled into chairs to watch on a small screen Theo had set up in his office.

Lucas gripped my sweaty hand when it started, and I grimaced at my pallid skin and dark circles. My curls at least had a bit of shine to them, but I swiftly forgot to care how I looked in favor of being horrified over my words.

In a generous sense, the story was true, but Lucas snorted at the removed details, the glossed-over ugly parts. His sarcastic voice kept a separate narration beside me. "Did it actually happen like this, or do I have memory loss? They painted me as a tragic antihero."

"Logan Bergeron should go into politics," I said.

Theo grunted in agreement.

All in all, it wasn't bad...until we reached the panic attack.

It couldn't have played out more dramatically if we were actors on a stage. My body froze at the question, the camera focusing on my face as blood drained from it. I lurched up, and the camera followed. The door slammed open, my hand clenching on the doorframe, holding myself upright. "Lucas?"

I took two steps into the hall. Lucas approached me, his cat-like paces quiet on the marble floor. That hungry expression on his face was familiar to me, but it surprised Williams.

"Oh, my," she muttered.

Lucas stared wide-eyed at the screen. "Do I always look at you like that?"

"Usually," I admitted.

Onscreen, Lucas reached me in a few steps, and his hands cupped my face. He murmured comforting words in a soft voice. The angle changed, and my face came into view as I stared at him, panicked and trusting.

"Damn!" I said. "Do I always look at *you* like that?"

"Why the fuck do you think I've been obsessed with your safety?" He pointed at the screen. "That is blind trust right there."

"It's not *blind*. I've obviously placed it appropriately."

The fear washed from my expression as Lucas coaxed me out of the panic, though the tears remained. Lucas's hand dropped to my waist and curved around my back, fisting my shirt with greedy fingers. My own hands did the same to him.

"You'll stay with me?" my voice hummed.

He kissed my temple, and his whisper answered, "Until I die."

The whole thing was an exercise in hopeless longing, like holding sand underwater, each grain slipping away no matter how tight the grasp. There was no heat or eroticism. Nothing remotely sexy. At least, not in my eyes. Just...desperation.

To me, we were two broken people clinging to the only thing they had left, but for the narrative, the story accentuated my brokenness and slapped a redeeming prince vibe on Lucas—exactly what Williams wanted. The story embodied the universal struggles of humanity—hope versus heartbreak, love versus duty. The stakes of life or death turned the tragedy of it all into something unforgettable.

People wanted to believe that love conquers all, and if the Defiance won, then Lucas and I could have our happy ending. With our story, Williams had given the world a concrete reason to fight for us. When she followed this up with the interviews of the NAO's prisoners, people of all walks would react.

I touched Lucas's hand. "Do you see what they did?"

"Yeah." He hadn't torn his gaze from the screen, but the dazed look morphed into one of horror. "Fuck!"

Williams startled at the volume of his voice. Theo whipped his head around.

"They filmed the hallway!" Lucas said, standing. "The interview room was covered, but they followed her into the hallway. The architecture..."

Williams and Theo also stood, their gazes on the screen. "They might not see—"

"They definitely fucking saw it," Lucas said. "You need to sound the alarm. They've been looking for your headquarters for years. They'll know exactly where you are now. They won't hesitate. You have minutes at most."

Theo leapt into action, marching from the room.

Lucas snatched my hand and dragged me after Theo. "Where are your weapons?"

"Cache is on the second floor." Theo stopped at a fire alarm on the wall and pulled the lever. A piercing bell squealed through the halls. He snapped a radio off his belt, but Lucas grabbed my arms, distracting me before I could hear his orders.

"Stay by my side," Lucas said. "We need to get weapons. Show me where the cache is."

Nodding, I tried to organize my scattered thoughts. We left Theo and sprinted toward the stairs. The hallways had come alive, soldiers darting to and fro, arming themselves, falling into line. No one paid us any attention.

The weapons cache was highly guarded, and with the alarm sounding, the soldiers on duty had their hands full. They issued weapons per protocol for every frazzled soldier. When Lucas arrived, both men's faces paled.

"You aren't cleared for weapons," one said while the other handed a rifle to an officer.

"Clear me," Lucas said calmly, "or I'll kill you."

"Give him a goddamn weapon," Theo yelled from the end of the hall. Behind him, a team of six escorted Nia Williams down the stairs.

Hands shaking, they hurried to issue Lucas a combat knife and a handgun. They did the same for me.

The building rumbled.

Beneath my feet, the floor vibrated.

"Shit," Lucas muttered. He grabbed my arm, dragging me back toward the stairs. "No playing hero, Sophia. No leaping into dangerous situations. No trying to save me. Your only priority is surviving this. You will do exactly as I say. Do you understand me?"

I nodded, wide-eyed.

"Promise me."

"I promise," I said.

"If something happens to me, go to our house on Evanston, okay?"

I hesitated, but nodded at his threatening glare.

Down the hall, the west wing of the building exploded. Lucas threw me against a wall, using his body as a shield.

As soon as the debris settled, he had a tight hold on my arm again, dragging me toward the main stairs. We made it to the landing of the first floor when the front doors of headquarters erupted in a shower of wood, glass, and fire, followed by a flood of Hunters.

With a curse, Lucas pushed me back upstairs. At the top, he darted left. Several Defiants trailed us. He pulled me behind a corner and waited, gun ready.

"You shouldn't waste bullets," I whispered.

"Bullets aren't wasted when they're inside Hunters."

Across from us, two Defiants mirrored Lucas.

The explosions downstairs shook the entire house. Gunshots roared an irregular tattoo of blasts through the air. Voices shouted from all directions.

When the first Hunter reached the landing, a shot fractured the air, ringing in my ears. Lucas's bullet whizzed through our enemy's body. The Defiant across from us did the same. Each explosion spiked my blood with more adrenaline. My heart tried to break my ribs with its pounding.

Four Hunters fell. The rest ducked behind a wall for cover.

Their counterfire flew. Lucas threw an arm around me even though I stood out of harm's way. Useless.

"Need help?" Adam approached from behind, armed to the nines. He grinned and yanked the safety pin from a grenade with a flourish, throwing it at the staircase.

Shouts of warning echoed down the hall before the explosion.

Wood and debris scattered across the floor as we retreated. We reached the rotunda. An iron banister encircled the balcony, and we stayed at the periphery, breathing fast. Hunters darted through the doorways below.

"What's the plan?" Adam asked.

"I have a safe house on Evanston Avenue. If we can make it out..."

"Got it," Adam said, and passed down a handful of grenades. Lucas waved two fingers, and he and Adam stepped forward, followed by a few other Defiants. He signaled to release, and six grenades sailed toward the lower level.

Metal clanked on stone as we ducked. Lucas jumped on top of me, his weight digging my bones into the carpeted floor. The doors shattered into shrapnel that rained over us.

Adam patted his pockets. "Grenades didn't last long."

"Come on." Lucas grabbed my elbow. "Get up."

I kept my pistol ready in my right hand, my knife in my left. We stayed low while bullets lodged themselves in the walls above us, plaster dusting my skin and hair.

On the opposite side, we slipped into the east wing of the building. The closest stairway was blocked by a door. Adam held a finger to his lips. We stilled.

Lucas crept closer, leaning his ear toward the wood. He listened for six of my erratic heartbeats before kicking the door inward. It broke off the hinges, taking down a Hunter on the other side.

Another Hunter jumped back. "Shit!" He pointed a gun.

Lucas lunged for it. Long fingers wrapped around the Hunter's wrist, shoving it away. The weapon discharged, and a bullet embedded in the ceiling.

Lucas slammed his elbow onto the man's forearm. The bone snapped with a nauseating *snick!* The gun dropped to the ground.

Another Hunter charged the stairs as several others closed in from behind. I zeroed in on the lone man coming for me.

"You're that bitch from the video." He raised his voice. "She's here!"

My gun rose as he sprang at me, and the kickback resonated in the bones of my hand. A single shot unloaded into his brain.

Heads spun in my direction.

One, two, three more Hunters fell from my bullets.

"Where is he?" one demanded.

Four.

I slammed against the wall as a couple of Hunters knocked into me. My bad leg spasmed.

Five. Six.

Blood sprayed with each slice and swipe of my comrades' knives. I leapt back at the sharp silver aimed toward me.

Seven.

Hunters swarmed like bees, and I squeezed the trigger until my magazine was empty. Heart slamming, sweat soaking the roots of my hair, I locked eyes with a large man in Hunter black.

His smile froze my blood to ice.

"If I make you scream, will he come running?"

He launched, and I raised my knife, prepared to collapse under his tremendous weight.

Lucas materialized between us. His knife sliced into the monster before giving it a violent twist. A kick to the chest, and the giant was gasping his last breaths on the floor.

Several Hunters turned to Lucas.

"...fucking traitor..."

"...slit your throat..."

I reloaded my magazine and handed him my gun.

The crowd of Hunters parted.

"Get down!" Adam shouted.

Lucas jerked me into the stairwell as I caught sight of a Hunter armed with something large.

"Come out, come out, Scott!"

Bullets came for Lucas through the wall. He shoved me away. Staggering, I tipped over the top stair, tumbling to the landing eight steps below, knife clattering away. My elbows and knees barked as they knocked into wood. Above me, plaster showered Lucas.

Left leg throbbing, I scooped up my knife and hustled back toward him. Lucas edged to the threshold, knife ready. He waited in silence as the gunman approached. The black metal of the barrel peeked through the doorway.

Lucas slid under the firing line. He swiped his knife, tearing a hole through the gunman's flank. The Hunter grunted, and I yanked the gun from his pliant hands. Trigger still warm on my finger, I blasted through his chest, then emptied the magazine on the nearby enemy.

Beyond the stairs, Adam and the other Defiants were locked in hand-to-hand combat in the hallway.

Lucas leapt at the swarming Hunters, flipping one and burying a knife in his chest.

"He's up here!" one screamed.

"Goddamn it." Lucas launched his only throwing knife at the man's throat. "Shut the fuck up!"

Breathing hard, bleeding, Lucas struggled to fight off the horde that closed in on him. Red stained his skin, and rage built in me like an inferno. I stabbed one of his attackers in the liver. Another, the kidney.

Defiants fought behind me. Beside me. Up and down the stairs. I staggered over debris and bodies, trying to keep up with the stronger fighters surrounding me.

Adam slammed into the wall next to me. A large grenade bounced off the wall near the stairs and landed beside us.

Shit!

Adam jerked my shoulder. My fingers barely clasped Lucas's shirt, pulling him with me as Adam shoved us through a door into a bathroom.

The room burst apart. Debris showered us at lethal speeds, embedding in my skin like razor blades. I lost my footing and crashed onto the tile floor. My leg spasmed and cramped. I clawed my fingers into the muscles to release them, eyes frozen on a dead Defiant beside me, impaled by pieces of wood.

Blue eyes, open and sightless.

As I struggled to stand, Adam snatched me behind a stall door. The world spun for several moments.

"What are you doing!" I hissed over my ringing ears.

He pointed through the crack left in the door. Lucas stabbed a knife into a Hunter's throat and used him as a human shield when another in the doorway unloaded a pistol.

"Traitor!"

Stinging pricks came to life across my body, and I extracted pieces of shrapnel from my hands without looking. Adam kept an arm around my waist.

Pistol empty, the Hunter raised a knife.

Lucas dropped the body and lifted his own weapon. "You really want to do this?"

The man spat and advanced. "I've got my orders."

Adam withdrew a pistol but found no clear shot. Lucas cornered his foe against a sink. He raised his knife. The man ducked, feinting to one side. His blade rammed into Luke's calf, and Lucas threw his knife, catching the man in the stomach, before falling to his hands and knees.

Adam dropped his gun to the floor and slid it to Lucas. It skittered to a stop next to Luke's hand.

The Hunter ripped out the knife and swung toward Lucas. Raising the gun, Luke shot once. A thump followed as the man dropped to the floor, a bullet in his head.

Adam released me, and I skidded to Lucas's side. "You okay?"

He fell to his side. "Give me a sec." He tossed the gun back to Adam, who kept cover.

Teeth gritted, Luke flinched as I unsheathed the knife from his leg. He had pieces of glass and metal buried everywhere.

"We've got to get out, guys," Adam said. "Smell that?"

I sniffed.

Fire.

Lucas stood and shook himself, exchanging a glance with Adam. The grenade had destroyed the stairs and landing. Bodies littered the area, and blood stained every surface. I lost my balance as I stepped out, slipping on the mess.

Lucas squeezed my elbow. "Come on."

We had to find another way downstairs. We tiptoed into the main hall. A shrieking explosion shook the ground beneath our feet. Fire burned far at the end of the hall.

Adam glanced up and down the empty space. "We need to get outside."

The three of us searched the dead bodies around us for firearms. I replaced my missing knife. Lucas found a single handgun with ammo left. He gave it to me.

I checked the magazine. Three rounds.

"Use them wisely." He coughed against the rising smoke.

Glass shattered several rooms away, and we hurried toward the main stairs. On the ground floor, the flames ate through the plaster and wood like hellfire. The cloistering heat suffocated me as we rounded the last flight. We ran for the French doors to the patio, all three blown wide open.

Vaulting into the nippy night air, we paused. Shadows shrouded the raging battle. Dozens of soldiers fought from the patio clear down the sloping, overgrown gardens to the gazebo at the far end of the museum. Sporadic bullets popped.

The fight swallowed us, and we lost Adam in the fray.

I treaded Lucas's heels as he flew down the cement stairs, ignoring the fighting soldiers around us. We wound up on a stone path near the wild gardens. We made it to the decorative pond when I caught sight of Devon battling for his life between two Hunters.

"No!" I slid over some rocks in my way and headed toward him.

"Sophia!" Lucas yelled.

Skidding underneath the swerve of a blade, I bypassed an enemy, burying my knife into one of Devon's attacker's legs. I stabbed over and over again, and he fell, twisting to thrash me. The tip of his blade sailed across my throat. Fire seared through the shallow cut. He swung again, but Lucas slid behind him. Grasping either side of his head, Lucas wrenched to one side. The man's neck snapped.

As Devon unsheathed his knife from the other Hunter's abdomen, he turned wide eyes on me, then Lucas. "How did they find us?"

"The interview," I said. "Listen. We have a safe house on Evanston. If we can get out, we can hide there."

"Alright—"

Isaac appeared, bleeding and limping. He grabbed Devon's hand and dragged him toward the gazebo.

"Come on." Lucas pulled me along the stone path.

Running with a limp, Lucas took us by the largest pond and branched off onto another dark path leading away from the fights, toward the parking lot. He guided us off the stone footpath and into the wooded area beside it, using the trees as camouflage.

Peering through the trunks toward the gazebo, I froze.

Lucas jerked on my hand, but my feet had turned to lead.

Because there, on a bench inside the gazebo, surrounded by at least six guards, sat Jack Miller.

40

ULTRAVIOLENT

 He wore our colors. He saluted our flag. All the while, he was sharpening his knife behind our backs. When we find this traitor, we will let him live long enough to watch everything he fought for burn. And then he will die like a coward—slow and in pieces.

—JACK MILLER

Acid dissolved my insides, eating through everything until it uncovered a core of hatred. My hands clenched into fists as I fantasized about sinking a knife into Jack Miller's throat. He sat with his legs crossed, lording over the chaos.

Lucas followed my gaze, and his body stiffened. His expression was one I'd never seen before. Animosity and resignation warred there, and he dropped his head. "I need to get you somewhere safe."

"I'm not leaving you. I'll do whatever else you say, but not that."

His eyes flashed in the darkness, then locked on something back toward the house. I analyzed the details of his face. A new plan was forming in his head, and I was ninety-five percent sure I wouldn't like it.

My nails dug into his skin. "You look like you're doing math problems."

"I'm trying to remove you from the equation."

"Good luck." I nodded toward Miller. "Why's he just sitting there?"

"I stabbed him in the chest last month. I doubt he's in any condition to fight."

A crash behind us turned our heads. The south side of headquarters caved in, cement crumbling and metal twisting. The earth shook as the building collapsed.

Lucas tugged me closer.

The soldiers fighting near the gazebo didn't pause. I monitored the fight—the bare remains of the people I loved, facing their deaths.

Faces slithered through my mind as the violence escalated... Theo's stern expression, Adam's wink, Devon's wry grin, Zara's smile, and then a host of others...Isaac, Dr. Grayson, Jayden.

How many of them would I lose tonight?

Lucas led me from the protection of the trees. "Miller's going to be hunting us. Getting out without being sighted just got a lot harder."

Anarchy reigned in the battle before us. Bodies hurtled at each other. Metal clanked. Small grenade blasts lit the night at irregular intervals.

Lucas skulked toward it. "You said you'd do what I say."

My gaze snared on his face.

He met my eyes as we skirted the outer edge of the fight. "Promise me again."

"I promise, Luke."

Adam's form emerged from the darkness, bringing down a Hunter. The man fell, and Adam jogged to us. We hid behind a large cement statue of an angel.

"Did you see who joined in the fun?" Adam asked, wiping sweat from his brow.

"Miller's nursing wounded pride," Lucas said, peeking out from behind the statue. "He's going to want to kill me himself."

Adam glanced at me. "What about her?"

Lucas met Adam's gaze, penetrating as if he was conveying a message I didn't understand. "If he gets her…"

"Yeah," Adam said, expression grim.

"And if she's with me, he'll use her."

Dread washed over me.

"Right."

"You were assigned guard duty today, weren't you?" Lucas asked, all innocence.

Adam nodded, a humorless smile lighting his face. "Got it."

"You got this?" Lucas said, harder now.

"Yeah, I got it." Adam leaned back, searching the crowd. "You see him?"

Lucas nodded.

I stomped my foot. "What's going on?"

Lucas took my face in his hands. "Stay with Adam. He'll protect you. Do not leave his side. Take him to the Evanston house."

"Lucas—"

"You hear me, Sophia? Don't leave his side under any circumstances."

"I'm not leaving you!"

"I'm not asking you to," he said. "But I'm leaving you. It's time."

What?

Adam grabbed my arms as Lucas took my chin in one hand and planted a hard kiss on my lips.

Wait, no!

"I'm trusting you," Lucas said to Adam. "If something happens to her, I'll come for you."

"Yeah, yeah," Adam said, and Lucas slipped away from us.

"No. Wait. Lucas!" I fought against Adam.

He held me tighter, pulling until his thick arm wrapped around my waist, and I struggled so hard my feet left the ground.

Lucas melted into the fight.

"Wait!"

"Let him hunt, Sophia," Adam said. "This is what he does best!"

"No—" My heart throbbed against a wave of panic.

"If Miller lives, he'll never stop chasing you. Let Lucas end this."

"Let me go!" I wasn't aware tears had fallen until the wind blew and the tear tracks grew cold. My struggles eased, and I coughed a few more sobs, then straightened. Fear and betrayal merged into a film of numbness.

He left me. He did the one thing he said he wouldn't do.

Until he died.

Did he think his time was finally up?

Something wrenched hard inside my chest. "I can't believe he left," I whispered.

"He's trying to save your life," Adam said and released me. "What weapons you got?"

Still numb, I showed him the knife and mentioned the three rounds in the pistol tucked into the waistband at my back.

"Don't use those unless you need them. And don't leave my side."

"Yeah, you've both been pretty clear about that part," I said, all bitterness. "Is your side immortal or something?"

"Yep, follow me."

He stepped out from behind the statue. Beyond the fight, the gazebo rose, and at the top of the steps stood Miller, searching the crowd like he knew we were in it. Revulsion boiled beneath my skin, and the cuts on my back zapped with electricity.

As if my hostility called to him, Miller's gaze sliced up, and his eyes locked on mine. The world fell away as we stared at each other. The melee between us ceased to be, and his evil face broke into a joyous smile.

He spoke to the guards without looking away from me, and three of them slipped from the gazebo, eyes on me.

"Adam." I tugged on his wrist.

He glanced at me.

"Adam, they're coming for me."

"Christ." He grabbed my hand. "Come on. We need to get off this property. What's the quickest route to the safe house?"

"This way." We circled the outskirts of the battleground. I glanced over my shoulder every few steps. The sensation of blood-hounds chasing me proved impossible to shake.

"If you get a shot, put a bullet in that fucker's brain," Adam said.

My cumulative injuries had begun to wear on my strength. My bad leg smarted like it had been wrapped in barbed wire, and I limped as I ran.

Isaac leapt into view. "Where's Scott?"

"Going after Miller," Adam said.

Isaac cursed a thanks under his breath, and Devon appeared at his side. "Wow. I can't believe he left her."

Adam laughed without humor. "Yeah, help me keep her unin-jured, will you? Otherwise, I'm dead."

Massaging my leg, I ignored them to take in the chaos of battle around us. A series of explosions erupted, and we ducked. Grass and dirt sprayed into the air as, one after another, small grenades burst through the crowd. Screams followed, and then a metallic thunk landed next to my feet.

The four of us glanced down. Wild fear swept through me. We scattered, and I pushed my aching legs to run. The blast rushed past me, lifting me into the air. Shrapnel embedded in my back. Some-thing hard knocked my head, and I crumpled as I fell, stunned, barely conscious.

Violent hands dragged me across the dry grass. A throb at the back of my head pulsed hard. Explosions continued to erupt behind me, but they drifted away. Bursts of agony snapped my eyes open as I was thrown to the ground, blinking at the slatted ceiling beams of another cabin near the edge of the property, identical to the one I'd shared with Lucas.

A face swam into my vision...sandy hair, mint-green eyes, straight crinkles across his forehead.

"Hello, sugar."

I whimpered, sliding away from him. The red scar I'd cut into his cheek pulled his mouth higher on one side when he smiled.

I crab-walked away from him until I hit an armchair. Four Hunters stood behind him.

I didn't have my blades anymore, but the pistol still pressed into my back, hidden beneath my shirt.

Miller strolled toward me. "I was hoping I'd find you here."

Heart in my throat, I said nothing. I was scared to blink, to breathe. Shivers racked my body. My gaze darted across all five men, trying to find a way to the single door behind them.

"You and me got some unfinished business." He withdrew a knife I recognized. The twisted blade sparked silver in the low light, same as it had before Lucas stabbed it into Miller's chest.

He ran a finger along it, smiling, and glanced over his shoulder at one of the men, who nodded and left the house.

"You went through all this trouble to kill me?" I asked.

Miller clicked his tongue. "You're just the bait, sugar. I came here to tear the heart out of that traitor's chest."

Eyes wild, Miller closed the distance between us and tugged me up by my arm. I considered reaching back for my gun, but didn't trust myself to be quick enough. Before I'd hashed out a plan, Miller sheathed his knife and extracted a length of rope from his belt.

The sight unlocked a vault of fear inside me. Heaving to get away, kicking at him, I yelled when he wrenched hard on my pinky, snapping a bone. I fell into the chair, tears falling, but he bound my hands, the ropes digging into the scars left from his handcuffs.

Where the hell was Lucas?

Miller withdrew the knife. "I just need a siren's call."

He jerked on the pinky he'd broken, forcing my bound hands

down on the armrest, and drove that wicked, twisted blade through both hands, pinning me to the chair.

I screamed—a harsh, inhuman noise that pierced the night.

I tried to yank, but the exquisite torture split my vision into black spots, and I swam at the edge of consciousness. Fury kept me tethered to the present.

Kill him.

Rip him apart like paper.

His voice dropped low, almost seductive. "That's it, sugar. Scream."

Claw that smile off his face.

I put all my hatred into my voice. "I can't wait to see what he does to you."

"I'm *so* scared."

The door slammed open, the guard Miller sent earlier blocking the threshold. He dropped, revealing a knife in his back, and Lucas Scott standing on the other side.

I tried to move, but every motion of my arms sent ribbons of fire through my hands. Lucas scanned the scene, lingering a beat on the knife in my hands.

Loathing unfurled in my gut at Miller's grin. "Look, gents! There's my traitor." He lowered his voice for me. "He took the bait."

Lucas's hair was windblown and sweat-drenched, his fair skin spattered in blood. He held his weapons ready for a fight, and Miller drew his own weapon. A loaded gun.

Leaping out of the way, Lucas dodged the first shot. One of the guards jumped at him, and Lucas's knife found purchase in his side. I screamed as the second bullet caught the man in the chest, and he choked.

Lucas backed against the wall, the dead soldier between him and Miller, who now stood behind me, hovering his gun above my left ear.

The remaining two soldiers sprang at Lucas, impeded by the arrival of Adam. He darted through the door, tackling one man while

Lucas threw a knife at the second. The man stumbled into a corner, knife buried in his throat.

I wrenched on my hands despite the pain, failing to free myself.

Miller's gun exploded again, a bullet burying itself in the wood behind Adam. With the guard now dead at his feet, Adam rose, aiming his own gun at Miller.

My heart tripped as I stared wide-eyed at his bluff. He had no bullets. He faced Miller's loaded weapon with nothing but a bullet-proof vest and an excellent poker face.

I yanked again, whimpering. The knife jiggled.

"You hurting, Jackie?" Lucas asked from behind his human shield.

I glanced at Miller. He had the gun in his left hand, his right being the one Luke had injured.

"I've had worse. Not sure how you got your reputation, Lucas. You couldn't manage to kill a wounded man."

Sweat beading on my brow, I rocked my hands back and forth, easing the knife from the armrest, swallowing whimpers of pain.

Arm steady, Adam's empty gun stayed trained on Miller.

"How'd you like cleaning my mess?" Lucas asked.

Miller spat.

Back and forth, back and forth.

The knife wiggled more. I kept my movements subtle. Adam hadn't shifted, penetrating cinnamon eyes locked on Miller.

In seconds, Miller would call his bluff. I had to do something.

Ignoring the searing torment, I wrenched my hands up, tearing the blade from the chair. I reached for Miller's wrist, knocking his aim off when his third round released. It burrowed through the wall and hit something outside that sent sparks flying into the night.

I stood, and the chair slammed into Miller as he reached for me. Lucas's familiar hands jerked me by the waist, tossing me out of the way.

Rounds discharged while I regained my bearings.

Adam and Miller struggled on the floor.

Bang! Adam grunted and rolled away.

My stomach dropped. "Adam!"

Lucas sailed over the furniture to kick Miller's hand before he could raise it again. The gun skittered away.

Useless with my hands tied and pinned together by the knife, I could only watch while Miller jumped to his feet. Lucas swung. Miller twisted away, his blade raised, and kicked hard, catching Lucas in the gut.

Miller grunted when Luke's knife swiped his ribs. He grabbed Lucas by the wrist, and together they stumbled toward the wall. Miller slammed Luke's arm over and over into the wood until he dropped his weapon.

Disarmed, Luke retreated, but Miller followed.

Smoke curled through the air, and my gaze darted to the open door, where the unmistakable orange glow of fire undulated in the night.

Urgency spiked. A moan ripped from my throat as my teeth gripped the handle of the blade, sliding it out. Blood dripped, but I sat, pinning the knife between my knees, blade up. I sawed at the rope binding my wrists.

Miller swiped, but Lucas dodged, maneuvering Miller's weapon into his hands. Miller withdrew another from a holster at his thigh.

The threads of rope frayed, and I sawed faster.

Adam moaned on the floor.

The lingering threads unraveled...

The fire outside licked at the pine walls.

The fight left paint strokes of blood across the wood. Miller arced a powerful strike that Lucas barely avoided, parrying with a hard hit to Miller's injured right arm. Miller kicked Lucas's trick knee.

The fire grew.

Saw faster.

Lucas dropped, and with a hard blow, Miller buried his knife in Lucas's chest.

I screamed.

Eyes wide, Lucas stared at the blade, blood pooling around the metal.

Saw faster!

Miller unsheathed one last knife. "You watching, sugar?"

The rope snapped, and I reached for the gun at my back.

Miller aimed his weapon at Lucas's throat.

As he thrust, Lucas struck. His hands gripped and twisted Miller's wrist. Miller couldn't avoid the momentum that drove the blade through the soft, fragile tissue beneath his chin and into his head.

And in case that didn't kill him, the three bullets I released into his back did. My hands screeched in agony.

Jack Miller fell, a wet, pathetic choke emerging from his throat as he slumped to the floor.

Lucas breathed hard, the knife still buried in his chest. His gaze met mine. The gun dropped from my hand with a loud clunk.

Behind him, the fire ate through the cabin.

A stuttered gasp and my name escaped his lips with his last breath. White as a ghost, his eyes fluttered shut, and he collapsed to the floor.

41

BREATHE

 This is the way the world ends / Not with a bang but a whimper.

—T.S. ELIOT

"Lucas!"

I flew to his side, my boot colliding with Miller's motionless face as I tripped over him. My knees hit the ground hard, and I rolled Lucas onto his back.

Black smoke choked me, but I searched his neck for a pulse. I felt nothing beyond the throbbing pain in my hands. The knife in his chest was an angry, hateful thing. I didn't dare touch it for fear of doing further damage. Instead, I leapt to my feet and took his wrists in my agonized hands. I tugged with all my might, dragging his six-foot-two frame of pure muscle toward the door.

The pain was unlike anything I'd ever felt, excruciating to the point of bursting black spots in my vision. Heat from the flames broke a sweat over my forehead that soon mixed with the tears.

I pulled, but he moved barely an inch, and I fell on my bottom.

Blood stained his skin and soaked his shirt. It may as well have been *my* blood. I was dying with him. That knife tore the life from my chest. My fingers dug into his carotid again.

Was that a pulse?

A moan caught my attention, and Adam stirred again, his hand clenching and unclenching.

"I'll get you next!" I said, then swatted Lucas's face. "Lucas!"

He didn't move. I dug my knuckles into his breastbone. Nothing.

I tried to shift him again, but I only dragged him another few inches before I was retching on the smoke.

A second, louder moan from Adam, and my frustration came to a head with a howl. I succumbed to a fit of hacking coughs. My vision swooped.

I pulled again, but this time, my bloody hands slipped off his wrists.

Another fit of coughs.

I'd have better luck with his feet.

I pushed myself to standing, then lifted his legs, hooking my elbows around his ankles. I walked, my vision murky, my head swimming.

The fire lapped at the ceiling.

I sank to my knees.

Tears fell.

The door was ten feet away.

Just ten feet.

I coughed.

Smoke swirled.

Then I didn't breathe at all.

42

GOODBYE

 The pain of loss is a reminder that we have loved deeply.

— BARACK OBAMA

Noise came first, low-pitched and rumbly, punctuated by a high beeping that made my head ache.

Pain came next. My hands felt as if someone had taken a sledgehammer to them. My lungs had clearly been scraped out of my body, mangled with a blender, then replaced. Every nerve ending was fire and torture. I moaned, but it emerged hoarse.

Light came last.

I blinked my dry eyes to find bright white walls. White ceiling. White curtains.

This... This was a hospital.

A real one.

Panic skewered my heart, and I tried to push myself to sitting. If I was in a hospital, that meant I'd been captured by the NAO. The Defiance had no hospitals. We had nothing.

"Well, hello," said a friendly voice. A woman with short blond hair and blue scrubs entered the room. "Good to see you're finally awake!"

"Where am I?" I asked, but the words barely emerged.

"Oh, try not to speak," the woman said, hurrying to my side. "You had some pretty hefty smoke inhalation. Throat's going to be sore."

I eased back onto the pillows, eyeing the logo on her hospital badge.

UNITY HEALTH TORONTO

"I'm in Canada?" I mouthed.

Her friendly expression fell. "Let me get your doctor."

She left the room, and I tried to calm the anxiety brewing in my blood. I'd been in a burning building, Lucas unconscious beside me, and now I was alone in a white bed.

Where was Lucas?

What about Adam?

How did I get here?

After a few minutes, an older woman in scrubs stepped into the room, wearing the same friendly smile. "Hello. We've been waiting for you to wake up. How are you feeling?"

I shrugged and looked at my bandaged, throbbing hands.

She followed my gaze. "Ah. Yes. Your surgeon will be in to explain the healing process, but he expects a full recovery."

Tears filled my eyes at the confusion. "Where am I?" I gasped.

Face strained, she lowered onto the stool beside my bed. "You're in Ontario. There was an attack, and the Prime Delegate of the Defiance called for emergent evacuation. There were mass casualties, and many of the wounded were airlifted out and brought to Toronto for treatment. You'd lost a lot of blood by the time you arrived, and your airway was swollen from smoke damage. We had to place a tube to help you breathe, so we kept you sedated."

"How long have I been here?"

"Five days."

My heart hammered against my ribs. Behind me, a monitor dinged, alerting everyone to my distress.

"There was a man," I rasped out. "I was trying to save him. Did he make it?"

Her brow creased. "There were hundreds of refugees brought in. I can check the list. What's his name?"

"Lucas Scott."

She blinked at me, then glanced at the band around my wrist, where my name was printed for all to see. They must have gotten it from my dog tags.

"Right. I'd forgotten who you are. Just a moment."

I almost smiled as the relief flooded me.

Settling back into my blankets, I closed my eyes. He'd be with me soon.

We'd *survived.*

Several minutes later, a soothing voice murmured my name. My eyes snapped open.

Zara sat at my bedside, dressed in a hospital gown, her arm in a sling and gauze taped along her neck and arms. A noose of fear strangled me.

"Is Lucas okay?" I asked.

She frowned. "Let's talk about you for a moment. Are you okay? Who did that to your hands?"

I looked down at my bandages. "Miller. He and Lucas fought, and Lucas was stabbed, and I was trying to drag him out of the burning cabin. And Adam..."

My sore throat thickened with tears.

"Adam's on a different floor," she said, her hand on my arm. "He took a gunshot to the chest, but his vest saved him. Broke several ribs. Punctured a lung."

A spike of relief was chased by a violent stab of debilitating fear. Why wasn't she telling me what I wanted to know? A hot tear splashed down my cheek. "And Lucas?"

Her eyes filled. "Sophia—"

The monitor behind me went haywire. "Where is Lucas, Zara?"

A beat passed, and her gaze dropped to the floor. "I'm sorry."

I stared.

She kept talking, but the words were just white noise. My brain stalled.

I'm sorry.

That couldn't mean...

No.

He was fine. He was recovering in another room. They'd repaired his knife wound. They'd replaced his blood.

After several moments, Zara's words finally made their way into my ears. "Lucas didn't make it out."

"No."

She paused. "No?"

"He's fine, right? He's... He's fine."

Zara hesitated, her hand squeezing my arm. "I've spoken with the general, Sophia. He calls here every day, checking on you. He found you in the cabin. You and Adam were still alive, but Lucas..."

Lucas what?

Lucas *what*?

"No. That can't be right," I whispered through my fried vocal cords. "That's not true."

"I'm so sorry, Sophia. He's gone."

Gone.

No...

That...

Amidst the rising chaos in my head, I tried to pull the memory of those last few moments from the haze.

Lucas had a pulse. I was pulling him to the door, but when I collapsed, he had a pulse.

... Right?

My mind tripped over the images of his bloodless lips, his lack of response to my slap.

Had his chest been moving?

A gasp caught in my sore throat as the truth crashed over me.

I never found a pulse. He never woke up. Had his heart stopped beating, and I didn't even notice?

No air.

There was no air anywhere.

The monitor behind me went berserk, and suddenly the room was full of people, all speaking.

To me. To each other.

Nothing made sense.

A curtain fell, and everything faded to black.

WHEN I WOKE AGAIN, I was already crying. I didn't want to be awake. I didn't want to exist in a body that hurt this much. I didn't want to be in possession of a heart in this many pieces.

Every beat of that broken heart hurt. Betrayal and sorrow floated down, coating me in a cold blanket.

Grief is like snow…

He *promised*.

He promised he'd stay.

Until I die.

But I never really believed he'd die. The thought of his last breath was so unimaginable that I hadn't believed it possible.

I tried to reason it out.

Maybe he'd woken after Theo pulled me out.

But Theo would know.

Maybe he'd been transferred here, registered as a John Doe.

They would have identified him by now.

Maybe his injuries were treated there.

With what resources?

Maybe he was really dead.

Agony sliced through my chest.

I forced my eyes open. The whiteness of the room had gone

shadowy and blue with nightfall, and the space was empty again. The door stood wide. I had a clear view of the nurses' desk. Men and women chatted around the computers, laughing.

It was like watching a movie, completely removed from my horrid reality. The beep of the monitor above me was surely a lie. I had no heart left, so what could possibly be beating in there? My chest was a dark cave I wanted to sink into.

What would my life be without him? Without all of them? Had anyone else survived?

Zara would know, but my room was empty and dark. I let my eyes fall shut again.

Memories flashed through my mind.

Are you the war whore?

If they waste you, they lose me.

Is your name really Sophia?

Are you brave or just stupid?

I wanted someone who wasn't on the front lines so she'd outlast me.

I hear voices begging me not to kill them.

You're mine.

Remember how scared of me you were in the beginning?

It's what I deserve.

You deserve better.

My soul ached for him. It had been ripped in half, and the shredded edges left every nerve exposed. Pain became my existence. I forced myself to turn over and go back to sleep.

THE SUN HAD RISEN the next time I woke. Zara visited again, but she only brought bad news. Neither Devon nor Isaac had made it to Canada either.

"What about Theo?" I asked. "Can I talk to him?"

"The general is on the move," she said. "He hasn't called in two days. I don't know much."

"And Dr. Grayson?" I asked.

Her eyes glistened with tears. "He was in the west wing when it was bombed. He didn't make it."

How it was possible that my heart collapsed even more, I wasn't sure, but it managed. I gave way to the sheer hollowness of this new existence.

Empty.

After that, we sat in lonely silence together, each of us wallowing in our own brand of pain. She left shortly after, returning to her own room with a promise to visit again tomorrow.

I should have gone to visit Adam, but I had no energy.

I had nothing.

I felt only pain.

I wished for the end.

Instead, I slept.

SEVERAL DAYS after I'd first woken in the hospital, I was picking at my dinner when the staff erupted into cheers, and a nurse ran into my room.

"It's happening!" He turned the TV to the news, where a reporter happily announced the end of the world war.

Unified States Surrenders screamed the headline, while footage played of a familiar city skyline in flames. The NAO had waved their white flag after a devastating battle in New York City. Thousands of lives were lost before Haynes finally capitulated. The terms of surrender were still under negotiation, but the feed cut to Commander Haynes orating at a podium clad in pristine white with a blazing black Brotherhood Cross.

I muted the TV, refusing to listen to anything that man said.

When the speech ended, the screen panned over vast Canadian cities, where tens of thousands of people flooded the streets in celebration.

"Freedom for Canada!" they screamed, tossing back their beers.

Canada's battle was over, but the Defiance still fought. My country was still ravaged by war.

I couldn't pretend to know what sort of political gymnastics the world had gone through in the past three years. I had no clue what manipulations and bargaining had happened while I lived under a totalitarian regime and a censored media.

All I knew was that it took the combined power of Canada, Europe and Russia to stop Haynes's army, which meant the Defiance had no chance. This was history repeating itself—an untrained guerrilla militia against the full might of King George III. It was a fluke the first time. To beat the giant again was impossible.

The world didn't turn upside down twice in a row.

We were going to lose, which meant Lucas had died in vain.

ADAM HAD a weak smile for me when I finally made it to his room the next morning.

"There she is," he rasped.

His face had thinned, and he had bandages all over, but he appeared otherwise well.

"How are you?" I asked, settling into a chair beside his bed.

"I've had worse," he said with an exaggerated grimace.

I laughed, but it sounded fake even to me.

"How are *you*?" he asked, brown eyes going soft. "Hands healing okay?"

I showed him the gauze around both palms. "So far, I think. Still hurts, though."

"Yeah." He let out a small cough. "Me too."

Silence blanketed us, punctuated only by the beep of his monitor.

After a moment, his low voice broke the stillness. "Soph, I heard about Lucas..."

My gaze dropped to the floor.

"I'm sorry, Sophia."

"He's gone," I said and added a few more tears to the millions I'd already shed.

Adam set a hand over mine. "At least he got his final wish. You're safe now."

Small consolation. I couldn't even acknowledge how much I hated being safe when Lucas was past saving. Instead, I changed the subject. "I wanted to thank you. I don't think either of us would have survived that if you hadn't shown up."

He chuckled. "I popped a lung for you. You owe me some KP duty."

A laughing sob burst from my mouth, but then I was crying in earnest. My head fell to the side of his mattress, and I bawled into his stiff white blankets. "I don't know how to go on now. Everyone's dead."

Another long silence followed until his soft, "I'm not," fluttered over my ears.

I peeked up at his solemn gaze.

"I know it's not the same," he added. "But you got me for life."

Managing a small smile, I moved to the edge of the bed and gave him a delicate hug, afraid to put any pressure on his shattered chest. "And you have me. We survived the trenches, didn't we?"

"Maybe the war will end someday and we can go home."

"Seems impossible," I muttered as I returned to my chair.

"Canada just won a world war, Sophia. Anything is possible." He punctuated this with a wink, and a genuine laugh bubbled in my chest.

Before I could explore it, the door to his room opened, and a nurse stepped in. "Time for meds."

I stood. "I'll go back to my room. Do you know when they're going to let you out of here?"

Adam shrugged, but something bleak passed through his eyes. "Come back sometime, will you? It gets boring in here."

"I will," I said. "I promise."

I LOST track of the time, but each day, I visited Adam, and my hands hurt less and less. I stared listlessly while the doctors explained my prognosis. My hands would heal over the next few weeks so long as I kept my activity light. My lungs had improved vastly, and eventually, the doctors saw no reason I needed to remain inpatient.

I'd fare better at the refugee base, they said, where I could heal with my own people.

People who understood.

But no one understood this crippling desire to never wake up. How often had I imagined death? It was almost like a fantasy, a recurring dream I wished to slip into.

Unsure how many sunsets had passed since I first woke in this hospital, I finally signed an X on my discharge paperwork. I dressed in donated clothes, and in a daze, I rose from my bed and settled into the wheelchair they brought. They gave me a plastic bag of my effects, and I gazed dully down at my bloody dog tags, Lucas's gold ring, and the note I always kept in my bra.

Grief is like snow...

I was surrounded by snow. Buried in it. I would never climb out from beneath it.

Still, I replaced the ring and stuffed the note against my heart where it belonged.

Inside the building, everything was quiet. The nurses smiled as I rolled past. The security guard at the front entrance waved a friendly goodbye.

Outside the hospital, my mouth slackened at the screaming crowd held back by steel barricades. They went wild when they laid eyes on me. Signs waved above them, and for a terrifying moment, I thought they were protesting the refugee presence at the hospital. We were foreigners using their resources, after all. Unwanted immigrants. Useless dependents.

But then three familiar words caught my eye, painted in red over a white background.

Until I die.

"What is this?" I asked the nurse transporting me.

He locked my chair before a black, nondescript vehicle. "NAO protesters. They support you, Miss Sophia."

My gaze darted over some of the other signs.

They chose love. You chose war.

We ship peace.

Team Lucas.

Let love end the war.

#reunitethem

Speechless, I took the nurse's hand as he helped me into the car. I was only aware my face was wet when the car had cleared the crowd.

"You okay, miss?" the driver asked.

Sniffling, I nodded. My hands ached to hold a person who wasn't there.

A person who no longer existed.

"It's just... They don't realize he's dead," I said.

The driver's sorrowful gaze met mine in the mirror. "I'm sorry, miss."

We drove for a long time, and finally, we entered a gated compound. A military base of sorts. He pulled onto a street of identical houses, then stopped at a grander one at the very end. When he opened the car door, I hesitated.

The pathway leading to the house's entrance was straight and even, no cracks in the cement. The March grass was still brown and crunchy, but no weeds punctured its immaculate surface. The place was clean and wholesome, inviting me to come inside, to turn my back on all the dirt and grit of my past and start anew.

But I *hesitated*.

Because I didn't know if I wanted to.

This was the moment.

It was the moment I had to decide whether I'd let all the tragedy crumble me to pieces or if I'd instead find the strength to go on.

I didn't want to be strong.

I wanted to disintegrate.

But my touch slid to the gold ring circling my finger, and in my mind, Lucas's voice appeared.

The part of you that's me will never die.

If I disintegrated, then his memory would go with me. He'd begged me again and again to protect myself. All he wanted was my safety, and he finally got it. Was I really going to sacrifice it for grief?

Grief was like snow. If I took it in my grasp, it would melt.

I set a foot on the asphalt. Then the second.

One step. Then another.

I stood tall against the gravity pulling me down and put one foot in front of the other all the way down the path. At the entrance of the two-story brick facade, I knocked.

Seconds later, the door swung inward, and, shocked, I stared into the dark eyes and catlike smile of Nia Williams.

"Miss Reeves." She stepped back to let me in. "I wondered if you'd make it in time."

Dressed in an ice-white pantsuit that gleamed against her brown skin, she was the very picture of political poise. Beyond her, a number of Defiance soldiers stood armed and ready to attack. She set her arm about my shoulders, guiding me deeper into the house. "I have fantastic news, Sophia."

"You do?" Confusion stayed my tongue, but I took in the generic, well-appointed home with increasing interest.

We stopped at the entrance to a den, one wall dominated by a large TV, its screen flashing with an all-caps headline.

COMMANDER RICHARD HAYNES, LEADER OF THE NEW
AMERICAN ORDER, ASSASSINATED

43
PRESS CONFERENCE

 ...these dead shall not have died in vain...

— ABRAHAM LINCOLN, GETTYSBURG ADDRESS

You'll stay by me for the press conference, do you understand?" Williams said in the seat beside me.

"Yes, you've only said it twenty times," I muttered.

The plane bumped over some rough air, and I gripped my armrests, only to wince as the healing wounds in my hands sparked with pain.

Williams patted my knee and smiled to herself. "How does it feel to be the face of our cause?"

"Like my life's greatest tragedy is being used for your political gain."

Her smile tightened. "Enjoy your reward, Sophia. You helped save our country from a dictator. You should be proud."

Pride was not how I'd classify my feelings.

Relief, maybe. Betrayed, definitely.

Mostly, I just felt empty.

A week had passed since news arrived of Commander Haynes's death, and Williams hadn't let me leave her side. Once New York City had been destroyed and Haynes repealed his Security Restoration Campaign, Williams capitalized on the human interest side of my interview. She'd wielded me and my heartbreaking tale as a rallying cry, then used the subsequent interviews to bolster it.

And it worked.

Backup from Canada and the European Union fortified the Defiance forces, and Theo carried through with Lucas's assassination plan without him. Leaderless, the NAO caved to the Defiance. Pockets of rebellion were swiftly throttled.

And just like that, it was over.

General Harrison won the war, and Nia Williams stood at the helm.

For the past several days, I hovered in corners while she became the de facto president of the reestablished United States. She gave interviews and speeches to cameras, always surrounded by a team of guards and aides. She discussed her plans to repeal the National Stability Act, to reinstate Congress and ratify a new and better Constitution. She met with the Canadian prime minister and secretary-general of the UN.

I was the pet she took everywhere, the rescue dog she'd groomed for everyone to see.

See how I saved her? I'm such a good person. Our new country will do right by people like her.

Strangers watched me with pity and kindness, their intrusive gazes catching on the gold band around my finger. A few braver souls offered their condolences.

"I'd been rooting for you," one elderly woman murmured to me. It was dinner the night before we were meant to leave for DC, and Williams was mingling with the Canadian and European bigwigs. "I was so sad to hear your fella was killed in action."

Killed in action.

Such a harmless phrase.

As far as I knew, he'd been stabbed in the chest and left to burn in a flaming building.

But sure. Killed in action was one way to put it.

"Do you mind if I ask," the woman continued in a low voice, "do you still have the note?"

Her clear blue eyes gazed upon me with nothing but kindness, and I found myself reaching into the neck of the gown Williams made me wear, pulling out the ragged note.

I unfolded it and showed her Lucas's words.

Grief is like snow.

She didn't reach for it, and I was glad for that, uncertain I could ever let anyone else touch this paper.

His handwriting. His words. His thoughts.

They were mine.

Her eyes grew bright as she read it, and once it was refolded and safely tucked away, she leaned close to me. "Would it be all right if I gave you a hug?"

Nodding, I melted into the woman's embrace. She smelled how I imagined a grandmother would, like talc and lavender, and she released me far too soon.

As I sat beside Nia Williams on the bumpy flight back home, I thought of that woman. For years, kindness had been so scarce, but like a hardy vine, it still seemed to take root and blossom, even in the bleakest of environments.

I dreaded what came next, but I wouldn't hide in the darkness. I belonged in the light.

THEO GREETED me with a tight hug as soon as I exited the car I shared with Williams. Behind him, the White House sat like a marble cake against the blue backdrop of spring sky.

I'd spoken to Theo only once while I was in the hospital—a brief conversation in which he'd confirmed I was still alive and that he wouldn't be able to speak to me for many days due to classified activities.

I wish I'd known his *activities* involved the assassination of a dictator. I might have been less mad at him.

"They tell me you had many injuries?" he asked now.

I showed him my bandaged hands. "It could have been worse." With a sigh, I added, "My heart is more broken than my hands."

His brows scrunched. "Sophia—"

I was shoved closer to him as armed guards surrounded us, safeguarding the Prime Delegate from potential assassination attempts. Theo put a protective arm around my shoulders and directed me toward the building. Our posse made it inside the West Wing, and I was shuffled to the side while a throng of people I didn't recognize surrounded Williams and volleyed for her attention.

After a moment, I realized they were her Cabinet.

These were the people who'd kept the Defiance alive, the ones who'd run our new government while we reestablished normal.

Theo carted me one way, and Williams and the crush of people moved the other.

"Where are they going?" I asked.

"The Cabinet room," he said. "They have a lot to discuss before the press conference."

I glanced back. "Is she really the president now?"

He directed me down a quieter hallway. "Not yet."

"Seems like it."

"It's complicated. Things are delicate right now. NAO loyalists are trying to convince the people that we're the bad guys. They have thousands of troops in Baltimore. We're barely holding them off."

My brows flew up, and the familiar panic tried to take hold. I hadn't realized things were still so precarious.

Theo glanced at my face and gave me his stern smile. "Don't worry. We're at the finish line now."

He pulled me into an empty room. A large table occupied the

center, and an unlit fireplace stood at one end. The walls were hung with gold-framed portraits of old white men.

Theo lowered his voice. "If we want to truly end this, Williams has to consolidate power fast. The NAO's brutality won them a lot of enemies, and they made themselves brittle by relying too heavily on their leader. To win the American people's full support, Williams needs to show them what our government will be. Strong *and* merciful. Resilient *and* compassionate."

I chewed my lip. "How is she going to do that?"

"I—"

"General?" A woman in a power suit hurried toward us. She handed Theo a small sheet of paper. "You're needed."

Theo's expression darkened. "Sophia, can you wait here?"

I nodded.

"Have a seat," he said, adding, "I'll be back," just as he rounded the door.

Out of place and alone, I wandered toward the table but decided not to sit. Instead, I paced the room, holding my elbows to keep from fidgeting. In one corner, several eagle-topped poles flew different flags.

My hand grazed over the familiar red, white and blue, but I froze at the one beside it.

A sea of white silk framed a black circle with a cross, the same emblem disfiguring my back.

The Brotherhood Cross.

I dropped the fabric like it burned me and backed away. Fetching up against the fireplace, I took in a slow breath.

Tall trees.

Warm rain.

Smell of cypress.

My hand clenched on the mantel, shooting pain up my arms, and I lifted my gaze to the painting above the fireplace. A man on a black horse with three white feet sported a dashing hat and a thick mustache. Drawing closer, I trailed my gaze over the intricate brushstrokes that somehow gave the impression of motion despite their stillness.

"One of my favorite quotes is from Teddy Roosevelt," a woman said behind me.

I startled, spinning to find a middle-aged brunette in a cherry-red boatneck dress.

"He said, *Americanism is a question of principle, of idealism, of character. It is not a matter of birthplace, or creed or line of descent.*"

Wary, I said nothing.

The woman smiled and held out a slim hand, scarlet nails matching her dress. "I'm Erica. The Prime Delegate has asked me to make sure you're prepared for the conference."

I managed to tell her my name, which only widened her smile.

"I know," she said. "Come with me."

She escorted me through a series of hallways, across an outdoor colonnade, and up the stairs into a more private area of the building. This portion of the building was empty of people, and prickles crept up my spine.

"Who did you say you were again?" I asked.

"I'm the press secretary." She opened a door for me, and I stepped into a bedroom, where three other women awaited me.

"Ah, there she is," an older one said, pushing horn-rimmed glasses up her nose. She took me by the arm and dragged me inside. "We only have an hour. Let's get to work."

"Get to...work?"

The woman didn't answer. Erica waved goodbye, and I was manhandled into an adjacent bathroom.

"Let's get that hair washed," the older woman said, then looked at me. "Do you want to take off your shirt? It'll get wet."

Hesitating only a moment, I opted to leave my shirt on. These women didn't need to see the scars on my body.

While the women chatted among themselves, I was subjected to a thorough shampoo. With their fancy products, they defined my curls into shiny spirals, soft but still wild, a sort of untamed neatness. I gazed at the gleaming black coils, and my thoughts drifted to Lucas…

… telling me I needed a hairbrush …

… poking fun of my mess …

… fisting my hair as he kissed me …

My throat ached.

The women took pencils and brushes to my face, using witchcraft to erase the bone-deep fatigue from beneath my eyes and give some pink color to my lips. Last, they held up a powder blue dress with a white lace overlay.

The thing was virtuous and feminine and everything I wasn't, but I didn't argue. What was the point?

Williams wanted me, the picture of marred innocence, at her side. No amount of dispute would release me from this prison.

Resigned to my fate, I stripped down to my underwear. To their credit, the women skipped barely a beat at the scars on my back and leg as they zipped me into the dress, then set a pair of matching heels on my feet.

Fully costumed, I was handed back to Erica, who eyed me with approval.

"We'll be using the Rose Garden," she said, as if I was supposed to know what that meant. "You are third from her right beside General Harrison, okay?"

"Got it."

She led me through another series of hallways, and then she was opening the door to a familiar oval room I'd seen dozens of times on TV screens. The room was filled with men and women in suits and professional dresses.

Before I could process it, Theo took my arm. "I told you to wait for me," he whispered.

I shrugged. "She said I needed to get ready."

"I was going to—"

"Alright, everyone," Erica called to the room, and the crowd quieted. "We present a united front. Positive faces. This is our first chance to show the world what the *United* States really stands for."

With a flurry of motion, she arranged us how she wanted, and then she was leading us outside single file, the spring air swirling around my bare arms and lifting the hairs there. Dozens of chairs had been set in rows on the lawn, all filled, and reporters spilled into the space behind them. Cameras clicked and questions volleyed our way. As instructed, I stood three down from the podium in the middle, right beside Theo, and once we were arranged, Williams took center stage.

The audience shushed to an eerie quiet.

"Good afternoon," she said into the mic. "Today, I can confirm to the world that the terrorist organization known as the New American Order has fallen. Several days ago, the Defiance conducted a covert operation that killed Richard Haynes, leader of the NAO, a terrorist who was responsible for the murder and torture of thousands of innocent people. It was nearly three years ago when American blood was shed on our own soil, in our nation's very capital. The Capitol Hill Massacre will live in our collective memory forever..."

She continued on, but I tuned her out while I wondered where I'd be taken after this show. Would I stay with Theo?

Could I run away?

Then Williams began to explain *how* she reached Haynes.

"A year ago, I was briefed on a possible route to Haynes. It was far from certain, and it took many months to fine-tune a plan to reach him, protected as he was by his zealots. I worked closely with a member of his own organization to perfect this strategy, and finally, last week, our plan came to fruition."

Unbeknownst to me, tears spilled from my eyes.

This was Lucas's plan. His contribution had outlived him, and it occurred to me that his story would never get told. He'd lived and fought and died, and no one would ever know the truth.

Not unless I told them.

"A small team of Defiants carried out the operation with

extraordinary courage," Williams said. "They killed Richard Haynes and those officials closest to him and took custody of his body. The death of Richard Haynes marks the most significant achievement in this country's effort to defeat the NAO. His death should be welcomed by all who believe in equality and human dignity.

"I have been in talks with Prime Minister Campari of Canada, and he agrees that this was a historic day for both our nations, and going forward, it is essential that we all continue to fight against the New American Order. As a people, we will not tolerate our security being threatened, and we will not stand idly by while our citizens are tortured and killed.

"Today, we will honor the men and women who carried out this extraordinary achievement, for they exemplify the patriotism and courage of those who serve their country: one nation, under God, indivisible, with liberty and justice for all.

"Please stand in their honor."

The crowd of reporters and journalists rose, and cameras clicked while a train of four individuals marched into the Rose Garden. Each of them wore identical Army Service Uniforms, so blue they were almost black.

My gaze dropped to the grass. I couldn't look upon the soldiers who had taken Lucas's spot, who had used his strategy. The men who were alive when he wasn't.

The crowd spurred into a frenzy of applause, but I was captured by a single word.

"Sophia?"

His voice sliced through me like a scalpel, fine-edged and precise. My head whipped up, heart storming in my chest, and there he was, first in the line of soldiers...

Staring at me with incredulous eyes.

He pushed the cap from his head, and it plopped to the grass just beginning to wake for spring. Orderly raven waves fell over his scarred forehead, and that ocean blue, a color so bright I couldn't understand how I'd already nearly forgotten it, gleamed in the sun.

A sob caught in my throat, and I took one step toward him. "Lucas?"

I had to be dreaming. Had I fainted? Was this a fantasy I'd manifested to avoid listening to any more of Williams's speech?

"You're alive?" I asked.

He started toward me. Williams made no move to stop us, so I lurched away from my place in her tidy line.

I crashed into him at the base of the stairs to the Rose Garden, wrapping my arms tight around his neck while he circled my waist, lifting me from the ground.

Our mouths collided with all the violence of a thunderstorm.

He smelled the same. Somehow, he still smelled the same. Peppermint and incense.

One heel slipped off my foot.

"How are you alive?" I asked at the same time he muttered, "How could they bring you here?"

Neither of us answered as we gave in to another devouring kiss.

In the background, the new president's voice said something about us, but I barely registered anything until she said, "...*like fire and powder, Which as they kiss consume...*"

I hated her.

I hated her so much.

But I couldn't think about that.

Lucas was in my arms, his heartbeat against mine, his breath in my lungs.

"I love you," I said over and over again, smothering him in kisses.

After several agonizing heartbeats, I became aware of the camera clicks. They inundated us, so numerous that they sounded like a horde of invading insects. Still, I couldn't release him.

"Please tell me you're real," I said when the kiss finally broke. "Tell me you're here."

He set me back on my feet, his forehead pressed to mine. "I'm here. God, you feel good."

"I thought you died."

"I almost did."

My fingers scraped hungrily through his hair, but it was Williams's voice that broke through my haze, spoken away from the mic so only those nearest her could hear.

"Enjoy your reward, you two. You fulfilled your end of the bargain."

I turned to her, brow raised.

"A full pardon," she said. "Exoneration is his."

Theo's voice floated back to me.

Williams needs to show them what our government will be.

Merciful...

Compassionate...

Loathing scalded every inch of my skin. She'd done this on purpose. She'd waited to reunite us until we could perform for a crowd of cameras.

She was still using us.

I gripped Lucas's face, my starving gaze roving over every feature, snagging on the rainbow blue in his eyes. "Tell me you'll stay."

"I'll stay," he whispered. "Forever."

EPILOGUE

 You don't fight because you think you'll survive. You fight because someone you love might.

—SOPHIA SCOTT, TO HER BROTHER

I refused to release Lucas for days. It was as if he'd risen from the dead, a miracle.

Between my unquenchable need for his body against mine and the necessary moments of rest, he explained the story. Theo had pulled us all from the burning building. He sent me and Adam with the medical evacuation teams, but Lucas had been transported to Max Aota's headquarters further east for treatment. Barely healed, he was forced back into action far too soon on Nia Williams's orders.

The strike team he'd trained for Haynes's assassination had mostly survived, and Williams wanted the deed done on the coattails of the NAO's destruction of our headquarters. She thought an attack when their guard was down would be most successful, and she was right. While I writhed in grief in a hospital in Canada, Lucas was sneaking Defiance soldiers right into Haynes's circle.

He'd been the one to put a bullet in Richard Haynes's head.

"I'm surprised you agreed to do it after everything they put you through," I said, my cheek resting against his bare chest in our new bed. The jagged scar where Jack Miller's knife had pierced his flesh was barely healed, and I trailed a soft touch over it.

His fingers threaded through my curls. "Williams made it clear your safety was dependent on my cooperation."

My hand clenched. "One day, I'm going to dance on that woman's grave."

Thanks to Williams's masterful manipulation of our entire lives, we couldn't leave our temporary housing without being devoured by cameras, but it didn't matter. I didn't want to leave. I preferred to stay in bed with him and bask in how lucky we were to be alive and together and safe.

As the news and internet returned, my voice spilled our fake story everywhere. Over the next several months, *Until I die* became a viral phenomenon, chanted in cult-like fashion across the country. Tattooed on skin, spray painted on buildings, decoratively splashed over wedding photos and love letters, the words bombarded Lucas and me until we cringed with each new example.

The worst was the kiss.

Our kiss at the press conference had been immortalized like the V-J Day kiss photo from World War II. The Lovers of the Revolution, they called us, and Lucas rolled his eyes every time he heard it.

"Would you have kissed me like that if you'd known the whole world would see it?" I asked one night.

"I kissed you like that *because* the whole world would see it," he said, caging me between his arms. "Now everyone knows exactly who you belong to."

I hummed as his mouth dipped to my throat. "I don't think it was ever in question."

In the weeks following the reestablishment of democracy, we had visits or calls from everyone. Once she was cleared to leave

Canada, Zara traveled to New York City to help the city recover, but promised to visit soon.

"I'm not sure how much longer we'll be here," I said over a late-night phone call.

"Oh?" she asked. "Where are you going?"

"I don't know," I said. "But I can't stay in this city where everyone knows my face."

She chuckled. "Well, let me know where you land, Juliet. I'll come visit."

Isaac survived the battle at headquarters and joined Lucas's assassination mission as planned. When he visited us a couple of days after the press conference, he'd given me a stiff hug.

"Where's Dev?" I asked.

Isaac swallowed. "He, uh... He didn't make it. That grenade got him."

The familiar darkness spilled into my heart, that ache of loss. My throat grew thick. "No."

Isaac's eyes went bright. "He was pushing me out of the way, and he just—"

I hugged him again, my chest tight. "He saved you."

He said little else, and when he left, Lucas held me while I cried.

"Do you really think it's over?" I asked once the tears dried up. "It's so hard for me to believe."

"It's over, Sophia," he said and kissed my temple. "Never again, okay?"

I nodded. "Even though it seems impossible, I'm choosing to believe you."

He chuckled. "It's about fucking time."

A few weeks after Isaac's visit, Adam had finally healed enough to fly from Canada. He stayed in the guest room of the apartment Williams had granted us in DC, but left after only a few weeks to help subdue the NAO riots in Baltimore.

"Stay safe," I said, gripping him tight before he shipped out.

"I always do."

When I released him, Adam turned to Lucas and offered a handshake. "It's been a wild ride with you, man."

Lucas gripped his hand, the hate brands freshly covered by a sleeve of ink. "Let's not do it again."

Adam's friendly smile creased the skin around his eyes. "Take care of yourselves. I'll see you soon."

He closed the door behind him, and another silly urge to cry washed over me. When would my emotions settle? It seemed they sat right at the surface, begging for release.

Lucas took one look at my face and pulled me into a hug. "He'll come back," he said.

Would the fear of loss ever truly leave me? Was this my new normal?

But it occurred to me as I settled into his familiar embrace that with the country in some state of normalcy, I didn't have to suffer in the dark anymore. I finally had options. Therapy. Counseling. Medications.

Those things had existed at one point, and they would again.

More than that, I had my autonomy back. I could choose how to address my mental health, when to see a doctor. Hell, I could choose to go outside in shorts and a tank top without worrying some soldier would lay eyes on me and think, *Mine.*

I was now an equal member of society again, and maybe, with some effort, with some *help*, I might have a chance at healing these deep wounds I'd thought were fatal.

WHILE WE WAITED for the clearance to move, Lucas and I debated where we'd go. Eventually, we settled on the wilds of the Pacific Northwest. We'd find something secluded. Something quiet.

Something safe.

After over six months of playing mascot to the Prime Delegate, she cleared us for travel. "But you can't leave the country," she said during an official visit to our borrowed apartment. "We may still need you."

Lucas's glare would have made most melt in fear, but not Williams.

"You can hate me as much as you want, Mister Scott," Williams replied, "but you are both civil servants, and if you're needed to help me keep the peace, you will do it with a smile." She turned for the door, leaving Theo to wince in apology.

"You have to forgive her," he said. "She did save all our lives."

Lucas clicked his tongue, mocking. "Oh, Uncle Theo. I thought that's what *I* did."

Theo's hard stare won him a smirk from Lucas, who left us to visit alone.

Theo eyed me. "You're going to keep him, aren't you? I have to deal with that for the rest of my life?"

I lifted one shoulder. "I love him."

"You have terrible taste in men."

Maybe he was right, but I still chose to become Sophia Scott as soon as Lucas was given signed confirmation of a full pardon for his crimes the following year. He'd refused to give me forever until he knew he could deliver.

On the night we took our vows, we held each other in our secluded cabin, dancing to soft music.

I gazed into those pretty eyes, grinning. "Now you *have* to stay with me."

He kissed me, his fingers on my back drawing his name again and again. "I should have known not to go to war with your stubbornness."

I buried my smile in his neck. "Can you believe we made it here, Lucas?"

"Despite all my warnings, you married the devil, and you're happy about it. I'm convinced all the blows to your head have caused brain damage."

I slapped the back of his head, ruffling his hair. "I could always annul."

Traces of the predator emerged, and he pressed a soft, possessive kiss right against my pulse. "No. You're mine forever now, sweetheart."

My smile would never leave me. I was sure of it. I thought of his face as he'd spoken his promise to be mine, that protective gleam in his eye.

Til death do us part.

The same vow. Different words.

Until I die.

"Forever," I agreed. "The people will be so happy you finally put the ring on the right finger."

He chuckled and took my hand from his neck to gaze down at the diamond on my ring finger, right beside the gold band I still wore. "The wolves really wanted a picture of this thing, didn't they?"

The number of paparazzi outside the courthouse was appalling, every single one of them shouting, *Show us the ring!*

"Do you think they'd still believe it was all so romantic if they knew the real story?" I asked.

He shrugged. "Who's going to tell them?"

I set my arms around his neck once more and peered into those eyes, thinking of the first moment I'd truly looked into them. I'd been so certain the beauty within was a mask hiding his infinite evil. Little did I know that the killer was the mask. In the beginning, his eyes had been the only truthful part of him. The part that told me his was a soul worth saving.

"Maybe I will," I said. "Maybe I'll tell them everything."

"Yeah?" he asked, now distracted by slipping the straps of my dress from my shoulders. "What would you call it? *That Time I Got Railed by a Psychopath*?"

The garment fell to the floor at my feet as I laughed.

"I think I'd call it, *Until I Die*."

FOR MORE

For bonus content, including character art and exclusive scenes from Lucas's point-of-view, please join my newsletter.

ALSO BY DEIDRA DUNCAN

Love Sick

Love and Other Side Effects

About the Author

Deidra Duncan spends her days (and some nights) living the dream as a board-certified OB/GYN, where every minute is either routine monotony or sheer terror. She lives in Florida with two human tornadoes and the wonderful man who helped make them. She's usually dressed in either scrubs or glitter, and would love for someone to magically combine them. She devotes every rare moment of free time to writing or reading. www.deidraduncan.com